Wakefield Libraries
& Information Services

2 2 JUN 2021

16-7-21.

3 -8-21

10-8-21

0 3 SEP 2021

0 7 MAR 2022

This book should be returned by the last date stamped above. You may renew the loan personally, by post or telephone for a further period if the book is not required by

TROUBLE IN BIG TIMBER

B.J. DANIELS

THE BAIT

CAROL ERICSON

MILLS & BOON

First Published in Great Britain 2021
by Mills & Boon, an imprint of HarperCollins*Publishers* Ltd
1 London Bridge Street, London, SE1 9GF

www.harpercollins.co.uk

HarperCollins*Publishers*
1st Floor, Watermarque Building,
Ringsend Road, Dublin 4, Ireland

Trouble in Big Timber © 2021 Barbara Heinlein
The Bait © 2021 Carol Ericson

ISBN: 978-0-263-28336-5

0521

Printed and bound in Spain
by CPI, Barcelona

TROUBLE IN BIG TIMBER

B.J. DANIELS

This book is dedicated to anyone still hung up on an old love. If you saw the person again, would it ignite those old sparks? Or would the fire have burned out? Or, would you realize that they were never quite as amazing as you remembered?

Chapter One

The narrow mountain road ended at the edge of a rock cliff. It wasn't as if Ford Cardwell had forgotten that. No, when he saw where he was, he knew it was why he'd taken this road and why he was going so fast as he approached the sheer vertical drop to the rocks far below. It would have been so easy to keep going, to put everything behind him, to no longer feel pain.

Pine trees blurred past as the pickup roared down the dirt road to the nothingness ahead. All he could see were sky and more mountains off in the distance. Welcome back to Montana. He'd thought coming home would help. He'd thought he could forget everything and go back to being the man he'd been.

His heart thundered as he saw the end of the road coming up quickly. Too quickly. It was now or never.

The words sounded in his ears, his own when he was young. He saw himself standing in the barn loft looking out at the long drop to the pile of hay below. Jump or not jump. It was now or never.

He was within yards of the cliff when his cell phone rang. He slammed on his brakes. An impulsive reaction to the ringing in his pocket? Or an instinctive desire to go on living?

The pickup slid to a dust-boiling stop, his front tires

just inches from the end of the road. Heart in his throat, he looked out at the plunging drop in front of him.

His heart pounded harder. Just a few more moments— a few more inches—and he wouldn't have been able to stop in time.

His phone rang again. A sign? Or just a coincidence? He put the pickup in Reverse a little too hard and hit the gas pedal. The front tires were so close to the edge that for a moment he thought the tires wouldn't have purchase. Fish-tailing backward, the truck spun away from the precipice.

Ford shifted into Park and, hands shaking, pulled out his still-ringing phone. As he did, he had a stray thought. How rare it used to be to get cell phone coverage here in the Gallatin Canyon, of all places. Only a few years ago the call wouldn't have gone through.

Without checking to see who was calling, he answered it, his hand shaking as he did. He'd come so close to going over the cliff. Until the call had saved him.

"Hello?" He could hear noises in the background. *"Hello?"* He let out a bitter chuckle. A robocall had saved him at the last moment? he thought.

But his laughter died as he heard a bloodcurdling scream coming from his phone. "Hello?" he yelled. "Who is this?" The scream was followed by a woman's desperate pleas.

"No, please, don't hurt me anymore." Another scream and the sound of breaking glass.

"Hello?" He was yelling, frantic, having no idea who was on the other end of the call—just that she was in trouble. Had the woman meant to call 911? Maybe it was a pocket dial and she hadn't meant to call anyone—let alone a stranger.

"Tell me where you are!" he yelled into the phone, but his voice was drowned out by another scream, this one filled with pure terror—and pain. He knew both too well.

The sound of something hard hitting soft flesh was followed by a choking sound. Choking on blood? The woman was being attacked. By an intruder? Or someone she knew? He'd never felt more helpless as he listened to more breaking glass and the woman's screams.

"No! Please, Humphrey, you're going to kill me! Please. Stay back. Don't make me…" The gunshot sounded deafening—even on the phone. Then there was no sound at all coming from his cell.

Ford stared down at the phone in his hand, shock shuddering through him. The woman on the other end of the line had called the man *Humphrey*. His already pounding heart thumped against his ribs, making his chest ache. It couldn't be. He stared at the name that had come up on his phone. No. He tried to call the number back. It went straight to voice mail. Someone must have found the phone and shut it off. Or declined the call.

His heart was pounding. For a moment, he was too stunned to move, almost to breathe, at what he'd just heard, what he'd been unable to stop. Rachel. The call was from his former college roommate's wife, Rachel Westlake— now Mrs. Humphrey Collinwood.

He'd only recently added her number to his contact list after she'd sent him a friend request on social media and they'd exchanged cell phone numbers.

His pulse pounded so loud that he couldn't hear himself think. Fumbling in his fear and panic, he hit 911. It couldn't be true. He knew Humphrey. They'd been roommates most of their time in college. His former friend wouldn't hurt anyone. Humphrey idolized Rachel. But from what he'd heard on the call…

Outside the pickup, the wind howled in the pines. A gust blew dirt over the cliff and into the abyss, reminding him how close he'd come to making that same descent. The only thing that had stopped him was the phone call. Or would he have hit the brakes on his own? He would never know.

The 911 operator came on the line. "What is the nature of your emergency?"

"I think I just heard someone being attacked and possibly killed on what I suspect was a pocket dial." His voice broke. "Her name is Rachel Westlake. Sorry, it's Collinwood now." He listened as the dispatcher asked him a question. "No, I don't know where she lives exactly. A ranch north of Big Timber. That's all I know. We only recently reconnected. That's how she had my number. Please, you have to find her. She might still be…alive."

Chapter Two

Dana Cardwell Savage looked out her kitchen window at the row of black clouds gathering over the mountains. She'd awakened this morning with one of her "bad" feelings. Her husband, Hud, used to joke about them. He still didn't necessarily believe in her foreboding "sixth sense." But over their many years together, he'd learned to acknowledge her premonitions with caution, if not take them seriously. Unfortunately, she never knew what was coming—just that something was.

At the sound of a vehicle pulling up in front of the main house on Cardwell Ranch, she squinted into the morning sun to see her cousin Jackson climb out. From the worry etched in his handsome face, she knew even before she opened her front door—someone was in trouble. She ushered him into the kitchen, a place where everyone knew they could get a mug of hot coffee and a kind word—if not advice. Good listener that she was, Dana dispensed it all—and usually with some warm homemade cookies fresh from the oven.

Jackson brushed a lock of hair back from his forehead as he took a seat at her kitchen table. It was large and marred like the floor under it from years of cowboys pulling up a chair and resting their boots under it and their arms on it.

She noticed her cousin's salt-and-pepper hair and felt a shock at how much they had all aged. She didn't feel her age most days. It was only when she looked in the mirror or thought about everything that had happened over the years, the good and the bad.

As she poured her cousin a mug of coffee, she could tell that something was bothering him. She hadn't seen him for a while, but knew that her cousin's barbecue restaurant with his brothers was doing well, so that wasn't the problem.

"Ford's back," Jackson said as he took the mug from her.

Dana brightened as she joined him at the table. She remembered the first time she'd seen the boy when he was about five and Jackson had brought him to the ranch. Such a sweet child. She said as much to his father.

"We'll have to have a party," she said, a part of her brain already making plans. She did love getting all the family together here on the ranch. When Jackson didn't respond, she looked at him closer.

He was holding the mug in his large hands, staring down at the steaming brew in a way that made her heart drop. "What's wrong?"

"Ford's not the same," Jackson said after a moment. "The war, losing his men in the plane crash…" He looked up and she saw fear in his eyes. "I'm worried about him."

She'd heard that Ford had gotten a Purple Heart for his bravery and that he'd saved most of his crew when his plane had crashed. "He wasn't injured, I heard."

"Not physically. But a lot of his crew died. He can't seem to get past it. Why did he survive and not so many others? It's his mental attitude that worries me. He seems…lost. He has a degree in engineering, but doesn't seem interested in pursuing anything. I told him we can find a place for him in the barbecue business…"

"You know he's welcome here on the ranch," Dana said quickly. "In fact, we could really use him. Please tell him that."

Jackson nodded. "As much as he loves the ranch and

working here in the past, I doubt even that would help right now."

"Is it PTSD?" she asked.

He shrugged. "Probably. He's been getting help. I just think being over there in that war took the life out of him. He saw too much death, too much pain, just too much." His voice broke and he took a sip of coffee. "I just got a call from him. He's on his way to Big Timber. Seems this woman he knew in college..." He looked up at her. "I shouldn't bother you with this."

"You know I'm here in any way I can help. Ford's family. Why are you worried about this woman?"

"Ford was in love with her. She married his best friend. It wasn't anything he told me, but I have a feeling that this woman did a number on him years ago," Jackson said. "Her coming back into his life right now..."

"She called him for help?"

Her cousin scoffed. "It's much worse than that. She was in a domestic dispute with her husband apparently. For all Ford knows, she might even be dead."

AFTER CALLING 911 and relating what he'd heard, Ford had called his father. He'd given him the abbreviated version of what had happened as he'd driven out of the mountains. He left out the dumbass thing he'd almost done. Just hearing his father's voice was a reminder of the pain he would have caused if he hadn't stopped. He felt embarrassed and guilty.

"I'm on my way to Big Timber now. All I know is that she lives north of town on a ranch. I'll call you when I know something more."

Now he concentrated on the highway in front of him. He was down the east side of the Bozeman Pass when he got a call from the Sweet Grass County sheriff, Charley Cortland.

"You the one who placed the 911 call?" the sheriff asked. His voice was gruff and he sounded like an older man.

Ford explained what had happened—and what he'd heard. "Did you find her? Is she…?" He couldn't bring himself to ask what had happened, fearing she may be dead.

"She's alive. Your call got us to her in time." The sheriff said he'd gone out to her ranch himself and gotten her to the hospital.

He breathed a sigh of relief. On the drive he'd kept remembering a young Rachel in a yellow sundress, her head tilted back, laughing at him and Humphrey. She'd been so beautiful. In his memory, she and Humphrey had looked so happy and so much in love. So what had happened over the past fifteen years to change that?

"How do you know Mrs. Collinwood?" the sheriff asked, pulling him out of his thoughts.

"We were friends back in college. Her husband was my roommate all four years. I was best man at their wedding."

"I see," the sheriff said. "You said you're on your way here? I'm going to need a statement from you. I'm at the scene, but will be returning to my office soon. One question. Why did she call you instead of 911?"

Ford explained what he suspected had been a pocket dial and how he'd only recently gotten her number and vice versa. "Can you tell me if Humphrey…? Is he…?"

"I'm afraid that's all the information I can give you now. We'll talk at my office. How soon did you say you would be arriving in town?" the sheriff asked.

Ford explained that he was driving from Big Sky, but was now only about an hour away, then disconnected.

Rachel was alive. But how badly injured? As far as he knew, there was only one hospital in Big Timber. Unless she'd been flown to Billings. But that would mean that her injuries were too critical to be taken care of at the local hospital. He knew he had to see for himself that she was all right—and that what he'd heard on the phone had really happened. It felt surreal. He knew Humphrey. They'd been like brothers. And Rachel… He shook his head, not wanting to admit even now the crush he'd had on his best friend's girl.

He passed Livingston, the Crazy Mountains growing closer and closer as he drove. With the speed limit being eighty, he was making good time. The thought of seeing Rachel had him both anxious and excited. He'd hated the way they'd left things for the past fifteen years.

The truth was, he'd never expected to hear from her again after her wedding to Humphrey. After what had happened, the three of them had gone their separate ways. Humphrey had reached out a few times, but Ford hadn't responded. Now he felt sick about that. If Humphrey was gone, he'd never get to make amends.

Then there was Rachel, the woman he'd compared other women to for all these years. Strange how fate worked, he thought now as a chill moved through him. If Rachel hadn't pocket dialed him when she did…she might not have gotten help in time. And Ford…well, he might be at the bottom of a cliff right now.

Chapter Three

"I know who you are," the sheriff said after the medical examiner introduced herself at the crime scene. He hoisted up his tan uniform pants over his protruding belly and rocked back on his boot heels. "I've heard stories about you. You go by Hitch, right? Well, we don't really need your help. George here can handle it just fine."

State medical examiner Henrietta "Hitch" Roberts smiled at the sheriff and the elderly man standing next to him in the entryway of the Collinwood home. "I'm sorry, Sheriff, but the governor himself asked me to handle this one personally. I believe if you check your emails, you'll find one from him."

"Is that so?" Sheriff Charley Cortland tucked his thumbs into the pockets of his pants and narrowed his blue gaze at her. A large fiftysomething man with a robust laugh and a belly to match, Charley had been the law for years. He liked to say to anyone who would listen that he'd seen it all. "George here is our local coroner and I've already assessed the situation. The wife was getting the hell beaten out of her. She grabbed a gun and shot her husband before he could kill her. It's cut-and-dried self-defense, the way I see it. Shot him right in the face."

"Does seem that way at a glance," Hitch said. She'd dealt with her share of rural law enforcement and already heard about Charley Cortland. As state medical examiner, she was brought into those areas that lacked access to more than a local coroner. On this one, she was lead investigator. "My job is to try to find out what really happened here, if at all possible."

She'd already called the Department of Criminal Investigation. By now they would have arrived at the Big Timber hospital and taken photos of the wife's injuries. They would have also collected the clothing she'd been wearing, checked under her fingernails and run gunpowder residue tests on her hands and wrists, as well as getting blood samples to see if she had been under the influence of alcohol or drugs at the time of the shooting—as Hitch had requested. They would have also gotten a video statement from her—if she was able—of what led up to the altercation and subsequent death of the husband.

"We already know what *really* happened," the sheriff snapped. "Got proof. She called someone during the fight and he heard the whole thing. I just got off the phone with him. He's on his way to give me a statement that will back up what I just told you." She listened to the sheriff describe what the caller had related to him. "So she definitely thought he was going to kill her if she hadn't shot him." He had a so-there smug look on his ruddy face.

She pulled out her notebook. "What is the name of the man she called?"

"Ford Cardwell. She married his best friend. He was in the wedding party."

Hitch looked up at him. "He told you that?"

"He did."

"I'll need to talk to him, as well as see the video statement you take from him," she said, pocketing her notebook and pen. "Also, did you document what you saw at the scene on your arrival?"

"I called an ambulance and got the poor woman to the hospital, if that's what you're asking," the sheriff snapped.

"No, I'm asking if you documented the scene." Law enforcement was trained to document everything, including the time of arrival, the location and condition of the body, and determining the identity of the person involved. "Did you observe any vehicles leaving the area?"

The sheriff looked put out. "No. There was just the two of them. Look here, young lady. You're trying to make more out of this than what it is."

"I'm trying to get to the truth," she corrected him. "And you can call me Hitch. Did you observe anything at the scene that seemed out of place?"

He laughed. "Practically anything breakable in the kitchen, I'd say." The coroner he called George laughed with him. "If you just look in the kitchen, you can *observe* for yourself that they had one hell of a fight, with her pleading for him not to kill her."

Hitch could see that she wasn't getting anywhere with the sheriff. He hadn't documented anything and had, in his mind, already solved the case. She glanced past the large living area to the kitchen. Even from here, she could see all the broken pottery and glass on the floor, along with blood and other matter from the body still lying in the middle of it.

"Someone was angry and took it out on the decor, that's for sure," she said. She'd seen this kind of fury before. It often ended in bloodshed.

"Looks like the damned fool had it coming to him," Charley said. "The wife's in the hospital. Beat the hell out of her." He shook his head. "Got to wonder what the two had to fight about, though. Look at this place. Can't even imagine living on a spread this large, let alone in a house like this."

"Guess it proves money can't buy happiness," Hitch said distractedly as she noticed where the sheriff and the coroner had walked through her crime scene. "DCI should be here soon to process the scene. We'll know more after that."

"Seems pretty obvious what happened here," the sheriff was saying. "Self-defense, plain and simple. Can't see why the state crime department had to get involved." He motioned to the body in the other room. "No judge would put her in prison for killing the bastard after what he did to her."

It certainly appeared to be a case of self-defense, but she preferred to wait until all the evidence was in. She said as much to the sheriff again. "So if you don't mind letting me do my job, Sheriff, I'd appreciate it if you would secure the crime scene and make sure no one else tromps through."

The sheriff said something under his breath that Hitch was glad she couldn't hear.

"Why don't we step outside, George, and leave the lady to her…work," the sheriff said.

"It's Hitch. Or Dr. Roberts. And, George, I won't need your coroner van to transport the body to the morgue. The DCI unit will take care of that for me," Hitch said.

Both men nodded sourly and left. She closed the door behind them and took in the scene before reaching into her satchel for her booties and gloves.

The victim lay on his back on the kitchen floor among broken glass and debris that had apparently originated from the couple's quarrel. The only heads-up she'd been given on the case was an urgent appeal for her to get to the Collinwood Ranch north of Big Timber as soon as possible and take charge of the case. Apparently, there'd been some concern of the crime scene being contaminated.

Fortunately, she'd just finished a case not far away. Otherwise, she was sure George, the local coroner, would have already removed the body. He and the sheriff had already walked into the kitchen. One of them had left a boot print in the blood and then used a paper towel to wipe off the sole.

Along with the urgency of the matter, she'd been told that she would be dealing with what was believed to have been a domestic dispute that had ended in gunplay—and that the wife had been taken to the local hospital with multiple injuries. She hadn't needed to be told that this was a sensitive case because of who was involved. None of that mattered to her. She treated all cases the same.

But she also knew that because the name Collinwood meant something to someone in power, this one would be under the media microscope, so she'd better make sure she left no stone unturned.

Carefully approaching the body through the broken glass, she could definitely tell there had been a violent argument. As she squatted next to the deceased, she could see that he had been shot in the face at close range. The single bullet had entered a half inch off center of his left eye and exited the back of the skull, taking a lot of brain matter and bone with it.

The husband had been so close... Had he been trying to take the gun away from her? Daring her to pull the trigger? Had he been that sure she wouldn't shoot?

Hitch rose to take her camera from the bag slung over her shoulder. She wanted to shoot photographs of the scene before even the state lab unit arrived. As she did, she considered the mess in the large, normally white kitchen. It was a cook's delight with its latest stainless-steel appliances, copper ranch house sink and white marble countertops. The tile floor was also white like the cabinets. It would make the crime scene investigators' jobs even easier, she thought. The perfect crime scene from a forensics standpoint.

At the sound of another vehicle, she looked out to see two DCI vans pull up. The sheriff and coroner had apparently managed to stretch some crime scene tape across the railing on the front deck and outside the door. The sheriff now leaned against his patrol SUV, watching the DCI team emerge from their rigs before he climbed behind the wheel and took off in a hail of dust and gravel.

SHERIFF CHARLEY CORTLAND swore as he roared out of the Collinwoods' ranch, the coroner eating his dust behind him. How dare that young woman treat him as if he didn't know how to do his job. He rubbed his neck with a free hand as he took a turn in the road. He was going too fast, but Hitch, or whatever she wanted to call herself, had gotten his temper up. Coming in like she had and finding fault right away with the way he did things.

Had he documented everything? she'd wanted to know. He thought about the notebook and pen he kept in his patrol SUV. He was sure they were still in his glove box. Glancing in that direction, he almost missed the next turn and finally forced himself to slow down.

What he hadn't realized, but was becoming abundantly clear now that he thought about it, was that this was going to be a big case. The kind of case that could make or break a career. He should have realized that. Hell, he knew the Collinwoods had money once he'd seen the spread—let alone that humongous house they'd had built for themselves.

But lots of rich people bought up the ranches in the area. What made these two so special that the governor would call in the state medical examiner and the DCI?

As he reached the main highway, he stopped and dug out his notebook and pen. From this point on, he would do this one by the book. He could remember well enough the scene when he had arrived, right? He'd put it all down.

The one thing he wouldn't do was let that woman make him look bad again.

Turning on his lights and siren, he raced back toward Big Timber. Just outside town, he called his office. "There a fella waiting to see me?" he barked into his phone. "Tell him I'm on my way."

He disconnected, smiling and nodding to himself. Ford Cardwell had heard the whole thing on his phone and was now cooling his heels in the office. Charley would get his story. If that didn't prove what he was saying about this case, then nothing would. All his years of experience had to account for something, he told himself. Even as he thought it, he found himself questioning his assessment of what had happened with this case.

It was a slam dunk, wasn't it? He couldn't be wrong about this one.

FORD HAD NO trouble finding the sheriff's department when he'd reached Big Timber. He'd been told to take a seat. Ten minutes later, the sheriff arrived in a flurry of movement. A large, heavyset man with a flushed face, the sheriff waved him back into his office. The room was small, unlike the rotund older man who took a chair behind the desk. He had a head of graying hair beneath his Stetson, which he removed and tossed in the direction of a hook on the wall as Ford entered the office.

"Sheriff Charley Cortland," the man said as he shifted his weight, making the chair groan under his considerable bulk. "You say you're Ford Cardwell, right? Let's get your statement while it's still fresh in your mind." He reached for his phone and called in a young man who set up a video recorder, turned it on and left.

"State your name, the time and the date for the record," the sheriff said, and Ford did.

Charley rocked in his chair and nodded. "So you heard the whole thing," he said, urging him on.

"I wouldn't say that. It actually felt as if I had come in toward the end. I heard what I believe was the last of the argument. At first, it was just background noise and then a scream."

"Can you describe from the start of the call everything you heard?"

He took a moment, reliving it, knowing now how it would end. He went through it, finishing with, "At the time,

I thought the call had just been random. I didn't know the woman was Rachel Westlake—I mean, Collinwood."

"Right. You knew her in college. So when was the last time you saw her?"

"It's been years—fifteen, actually. Like I told you on the phone, I only recently reconnected with her on social media and we exchanged phone numbers. I haven't seen her since college."

The sheriff nodded, studying him. "But you knew her husband?"

He caught the past tense. "Humphrey? Yes, we all knew each other at college. Wait—so he is…?"

"Deceased."

He had heard the booming report of the gunshot on his phone. "Humphrey's dead?" He felt an anxiety attack coming on and had to concentrate on his breathing for a few moments. His plane crash came back, filling his mind with horror just as it had when he'd realized they were going down and there was nothing he could do about it. Just as there was nothing he could do but save the few men he'd been able to drag from the wreckage before it exploded.

The sheriff's voice brought him out of the flashback with a shudder.

"He was killed this morning during the phone call you overheard. In fact, I believe you heard the shot that killed him."

Ford closed his eyes for a moment. Flashes of light radiated behind his lids. He opened them, chasing away the flames to face a different kind of horror. Rachel had shot and killed Humphrey.

"You said that he was your best friend."

"In college." He couldn't make sense of this. Humphrey and Rachel? This couldn't be happening. "Humphrey and I were roommates all four years. Look, if that's all, I'm anxious to find out how Rachel is doing." She must be devastated, he thought, not to even mention her physical injuries.

"Cardwell. Why does that name sound familiar?"

"My family owns a barbecue restaurant in Big Sky. My aunt owns a ranch there. Cardwell Ranch." When the sheriff's expression hadn't changed, he added, "Her husband is Marshal Hud Savage." Why was this man avoiding telling him Rachel's condition? "Sheriff, is Rachel all right?"

"I'm waiting to hear from the doctor, but she sustained multiple injuries from the beating she got." The sheriff picked up his phone and called to tell the young man who'd set up the video that they were finished. He said nothing until the man exited with the equipment. "Appears there were only the two of them home. We'll know more once she can tell us her side of the story. But at this point, it seems clear that it was a domestic dispute that turned tragic."

Ford's head reeled. He kept thinking of the call. Of Rachel's screams. Her pleas for Humphrey to stop. And the gunshot just before the line went dead. That had to be when she pulled the trigger and killed Humphrey. *Oh my God, Rachel, how did this happen?*

Chapter Four

Hitch did what investigating she could on the premises until she had the body on the examining table for the autopsy. She'd worked with this team of investigators before, so while they processed the scene, she did an inventory of the house. Putting on fresh gloves, she wandered around in fresh paper booties, trying to get a feel for the people who had lived here while she waited for the team to release the body.

All on one level, the house seemed to go on forever. She peeked in each room, not sure what she was looking for. Answers, always. Like the sheriff had said, this one seemed cut-and-dried. Mitigated homicide. So what was bothering her? She couldn't put her finger on it. Just that something always nagged at her when a case felt…wrong.

She found the master suite and stopped in the doorway to take in the breathtaking view before entering. A wall of windows looked out on rolling hills lush with grass and studded with pines. She tried to imagine the couple waking up to this each morning. Stepping to the bed, she checked the side tables, curious if the two were still sleeping together before everything went south.

There was a book lying facedown on one side of the bed. From the title, she guessed Rachel slept on the right. She pulled open the drawer. It seemed a little too empty, as if someone had gone through it, knowing that detectives would be doing the same thing soon.

Stepping to the other side of the bed, she found a notebook and pen. From the writing and what was written there, she guessed it was the husband's notes about a work appointment. She photographed the notes. There was much more in his drawers, though nothing that sent up any red flags. Except for the extra clip of cartridges for a .38 pistol. She photographed everything in both drawers, then hesitated.

If Humphrey Collinwood kept the gun in this drawer, how did it end up in the kitchen, where he died? Which one of them took the gun to the murder scene?

She thought of the .38-caliber weapon lying on the floor of the kitchen earlier. By now, the lab techs would have bagged and processed it. The question was, when did the wife take hold of the gun? Was it always loaded? Had she ever fired it before?

There were always more questions than answers at this point, Hitch thought. When the woman had gotten the gun could indicate premeditation, so it was important—and probably hard to prove since only one person knew the truth. The other one was dead.

So, she thought, studying the king-size bed, it appeared they had been sleeping together. But that didn't mean that things had been copacetic. The bed was huge. They wouldn't even have to touch each other if they didn't want to.

She checked out the his-and-hers walk-in closets, as well as looking in the chests of drawers. She found a lot of expensive clothing on both sides. She took more photographs, not sure which ones might prove important.

It was the small, seemingly trivial things that solved a case, she thought as she checked out the bathroom. She saw expensive beauty products and what appeared to be a container of birth control pills, most of the pills already taken, lying on the floor in the back corner, almost out of sight as if dropped there. Or thrown there? That was interesting. At least one of them wasn't interested in having a child.

As she started to leave the bedroom, she realized what she hadn't seen. The woman's purse. She checked the walk-in again. Lots of empty purses, but not one the woman had apparently been using. Nor had she seen one in the living room or the kitchen. As she wandered through the house, she kept looking. At the entry into the kitchen, she called to the techs.

"Have either of you seen her purse?" Hitch was curious if it was large enough to hold a handgun. Also, if it wasn't here, then where was it? The sheriff was so sure that no one else had been here. Would a ranch this size have some kind of hired help?

"Not in here," one of them called back.

She turned and headed down past the bedrooms again toward the garage. Living this far from civilization, maybe she'd left her purse in her vehicle. Just as Hitch had expected, none of the vehicles were locked. She opened the first one, a Range Rover that smelled of leather and men's aftershave. This would have been his car.

After searching it and not finding much of interest other than a few receipts, which she took photos of with her phone, she tried the next vehicle. It was a BMW convertible and smelled of the same perfume scent she'd picked up in the master bedroom. No purse, though. No receipts either.

The purse wasn't in the large SUV or the older-model pickup.

"You can have the body now," one of the techs called.

On her way back through the house, she had a thought and checked the powder room by the door to the garage. The moment she opened the door, she pulled up her camera and took a few shots of the room—and the large designer purse lying on the floor in front of the sink. The purse was made of soft leather and had more than enough room for the .38 now lying next to the body in the kitchen.

What had caught her eye was where it lay—on the floor as if it had been dropped there. Also, the large zippered compartment was open, the woman's wallet partially hanging out, as if Rachel Collinwood had been in a hurry and that was why it was open and lying on the floor like that.

Hitch stared at the purse, imagining the woman coming home from town. It was a fairly long drive. Had she come in, headed straight for the powder room and then heard a garage door open, signaling that she was no longer alone? She would have known it was her husband. Had she dug in the bag for the gun? And for her phone, or both, since both were found in the kitchen on the floor next to the body? She'd apparently picked up the phone after shooting her husband and called 911 for help. Hitch had already photographed the phone, covered with bloody fingerprints, lying next to the body.

Then hearing him enter the house, had she dropped the bag and followed him into the kitchen with the gun and phone? Or hurried into the kitchen to wait for him?

After picking up the purse, Hitch spread out a clean towel and dumped the contents onto the counter by the sink. A small box of handgun cartridges tumbled out. She inspected them. They were .38-caliber cartridges, the same caliber as those used in the handgun that had been on the kitchen floor not far from the body—and was assumed to be the murder weapon.

She put everything back into the purse and returned it to the spot where she'd found it, before going into the kitchen and telling the techs what she'd found. "Definitely want prints on that birth control container," she said.

The investigators put the deceased into a body bag and

loaded it into a van. One of them would follow her into town to the morgue and return to finish processing the scene.

"You know who he is, right?" Bradley Mar asked her. She'd worked with the young investigator before on other cases. He was smart, cute and definitely not her type, with his crooked grin and his bedroom brown eyes.

"Humphrey Collinwood," she said. "Is that name supposed to mean something to me?"

"The family is from back East. Old money. The father and grandfather are still powerful politically, and Humphrey was the heir apparent. There was talk that he might one day be president. This case will probably garner nationwide media coverage. Even if she had probable cause to shoot him, I wouldn't want to be in her shoes right now."

Hitch knew what Bradley was saying. Even if it was self-defense, the Collinwoods could probably want their pound of flesh. She was sure DCI had been warned to be especially careful with the evidence in this case. Any mistakes could cost them all their jobs. The DCI unit was always thorough, but with this one, they would make sure they dotted every *i* and crossed every *t*.

Closing the back of the van, she watched the other investigator return to the house. Lori Stevenson was about the same age as Bradley, but much more serious. Hitch hoped that Lori hadn't already fallen for Bradley's charm. The young man was a heartbreaker. Unfortunately, Hitch knew the type. It was one reason she hardly dated.

Climbing behind the wheel of her SUV, she started the engine and drove away from the huge house set against a backdrop of rolling hills and pasture with mountains off in the distance. As she did, she considered how isolated it was. The drive out was a good two miles to the paved highway. From there, it was another twenty miles into Big Timber. That kind of isolation could get to a person, she thought. Anything could have caused the altercation and subsequent shooting.

In her experience, money was usually the big issue in most marriages. After that it was infidelity. She thought about the rambling house, the two separate walk-in closets filled with expensive clothes and jewelry, the four-car garage with luxury vehicles, the ranch itself with its beautiful vistas.

For most people, this would be paradise, and yet one of the residents was dead and the other in the hospital facing possible homicide charges. So what had happened?

The purse on the floor in the powder room bothered her. It suggested that Rachel Collinwood had been somewhere and had just come in from the garage. Was the husband already home? Or had he just entered the house from the garage, not knowing she was in the powder room? Had the wife known her husband would come home angry? Had she felt she was in danger?

But if the gun had been in her purse along with the .38 cartridges, when had she taken it from her husband's bedside table? And why would she take the gun and her cell phone and go into the kitchen if she was afraid for her life? Why not get back in her car and get out of there?

The sheriff had said the man she'd accidentally dialed had heard it all—including the gunshot before the phone call ended. So had Rachel Collinwood attempted to call 911 for help in the middle of the altercation and accidentally dialed Ford Cardwell instead?

Hitch was anxious to talk to both Mrs. Collinwood and the man she'd called. Her cases often intrigued her, but none more than this one. She tried to put herself in the woman's shoes in that powder room, knowing it was all speculation at this point. But the wife had been in the powder room. The purse proved it. After returning from town? So where was the husband? Just driving in? Or waiting for her in the kitchen?

What had been her state of mind? Panic? Or cold-blooded calm? The purse could have been dropped in terror at the sound of the garage door opening. Rachel could have been in a hurry to reach the kitchen before her husband. Had the husband been looking for her as he moved through the house? Had the argument started somewhere else? Where had they been before the argument? A larger question was also more than relevant. Had there been prior abuse? Was that why she had the gun? Assuming it had been in the purse and not hidden somewhere else in the house.

All simple conjecture until she had more evidence. The real question for Hitch was, what had been going through the woman's mind when she'd taken the gun from her husband's bedside drawer in the first place—if she had? If Rachel Collinwood had been terrified of her husband, why hadn't she simply gone to the garage, gotten in her car and driven to safety?

In her mind's eye, Hitch could see her standing in the kitchen amid all the debris from the fight. What had she done with the gun? If she'd had it from the start of the argument, she hadn't used it. Had she threatened her husband with it? Or had she come in, dropped the purse in the powder room and hurried into the kitchen to hide the gun, hoping she wouldn't have to use it, until she'd felt she had no choice?

The moment the wife had armed herself, she had made up her mind that she was going to pull that trigger—whether she realized it or not.

AT THE HOSPITAL, Ford waited until the doctor received permission from the sheriff for him to see Rachel. He'd been warned that it would only be for a few minutes.

"She's going to be groggy," the doctor said. "Also, the sheriff has asked that she not be questioned about what happened."

Ford thanked him and headed down the hall to where a uniformed guard sat outside her door. Seeing the man sitting there gave him a shock. At first, he'd thought it was for Rachel's protection. But from whom? Then he realized with a start—the guard was there to keep Rachel here. Had she been arrested?

He felt sick to his stomach at the thought. But she'd killed a man. And not just any man. A man they had both loved. He couldn't imagine being pushed that far, and yet he'd heard enough of the fight on the phone to be terrified for her. That was why he had to see her and make sure she was all right. While he wouldn't ask anything about the incident as the sheriff had ordered him, he desperately needed to know at some point what had happened that the marriage had ended like this.

As he stopped at her hospital room door, he kept replaying what he'd heard on the phone over and over in his head. He still couldn't believe any of this was real. The scenes in his head kept overlapping with his own tragedy, blurring the lines.

He'd thought he'd known Humphrey. He never would have expected this of him. And Rachel… How long had the abuse been going on that she had to stop her husband with a bullet?

The guard at the door double-checked with the sheriff and then gave Ford a nod. Pushing open the hospital room door, Ford hesitated, not sure he was ready to see the beautiful woman he'd known and loved in whatever state Humphrey had left her.

After taking a breath, he let it out and stepped in. She lay in the bed, her eyes closed, her face as pale as the pillowcase beneath her head—except for the lacerations, stitches, bandages and bruising that made the woman he'd known almost indistinguishable. The extent of her injuries shocked him. He'd just assumed that the quarrel hadn't been going on long when he'd first gotten the call. But Humphrey couldn't have done this much damage in that short amount of time before the gunshot.

All Ford could figure was that at some point, Rachel had tried to call for help and either dropped the phone after accidentally hitting his number or Humphrey had knocked the phone from her hand.

The violence he saw mirrored in her injuries made his chest ache. He felt perspiration break out over his body. He grabbed the metal rail of the bed to steady himself as he felt another anxiety attack coming on.

THE RATTLE OF the bed rail awoke her with a start. Rachel let out a cry. She'd forgotten for a moment where she was. She shrank back from the dark figure beside her bed.

"I'm sorry. I didn't mean to frighten you," Ford said as he quickly took a step back.

She recognized his voice. It was low and soft and soothing, always had been. As her gaze focused on him, she tried to smile, but her cut and bruised mouth hurt too much. "Ford." His name came out a whisper. She felt tears rush to her eyes at just the sight of a friendly, familiar face in the middle of all her pain.

As she held out her hand, he moved closer and took it in his two large, warm palms. It had been years since she'd seen him, so she shouldn't have been shocked that he'd changed. His body had filled out from the lean college boy he'd been. If anything, he was more handsome. She'd heard what had happened to him during his time in the military and wondered how an experience like that would change a man like Ford. She could see now that there was a hardness to him that was only partially due to muscle and physical strength. There was also a darkness in his pale blue eyes.

"*Ford?* I'm so glad to see you, but what are you doing here?"

"I heard what happened to you," he said. "Are you all right?"

She shook her head, tears rushing to her eyes again. "Humphrey." The word came out choked on fresh tears.

He nodded and squeezed her hand. As he looked down at her fingers entwined with his, she thought about earlier when two state crime investigation officers had stopped by to take her fingerprints and take swabs of her skin around her hands and wrists. When she'd asked, they'd told her they were checking for gunpowder residue, and that brought it all back. The deafening sound of the gun. The damage the bullet made an instant later.

But more than anything, what she kept seeing was the shocked, disbelieving look on her husband's face. She would take that look to her grave.

Ford squeezed her hand gently. "I'm here for you." She looked at him, knowing he meant every word of it. She'd forgotten this side of Ford and felt her throat tighten.

"I can't believe any of this has happened," she said, wiping at the tears with her free hand as she focused on his face. To think she had actually thought about marrying this cowboy, she told herself, then pushed the thought away as her pain threatened to overwhelm her again.

"What about you? Are *you* all right?" she asked when she gained control again. "I heard about your accident… I'm so sorry."

"Don't worry about me," he said quickly. "I'm fine. It's you I'm concerned about. But I'm here for you. Whatever I can do. I'm not going anywhere."

At the sound of the hospital room door opening, she glanced toward it and saw a man in uniform and star enter.

She swallowed the lump in her throat at just the sight of the sheriff's grim expression. Only hours ago she'd been standing in her kitchen with the gun in her hand and her finger on the trigger. She closed her eyes but felt fresh tears on her cheeks as Ford let go of her.

She heard him step away from her bed as the sheriff said, "I need to talk to Mrs. Collinwood. Alone. But don't go far, Mr. Cardwell. I'll need a word with you, as well."

Rachel smelled peppermint on the sheriff's breath as she heard him pull up a chair beside her bed. She heard Ford's boots on the hospital room floor, the slow, deliberate gait of his walk and the swish of the door opening and closing.

"Mrs. Collinwood, you remember me? I'm Sheriff Charley Cortland. I'm the one who called for an ambulance for you. The doctor said you might be a little groggy, but I need you to answer a few questions if you feel up to it."

Rachel opened her eyes, turning her head to look at the man. What she saw made her relax a little. There was kindness in his weathered face rather than accusation. She wiped her eyes and said, "I'll tell you everything I can remember."

The hospital room door opened again. This time a young man came in with a video recorder. He set it up next to her bed. She touched the bandage on her cheekbone and realized she probably shouldn't be thinking about her appearance at a time like this.

"Don't worry—you look fine," the sheriff said. "We just need to get your statement while it's fresh in your mind so everyone knows what happened."

Chapter Five

Hitch looked up as a distinguished older man in a suit burst into the morgue. He had a head of salt-and-pepper hair and keen gray eyes with deep crinkles around them. His skin appeared ashen under his tan, and his hand shook as he clutched the doorknob and looked around the autopsy room.

"Where is the medical examiner? I want to see my son," he demanded.

She'd been expecting Bartholomew Collinwood. "I'm the medical examiner. Henrietta Roberts," she said. "If you give me a few minutes, you are welcome to make an identification for the record."

He stared at her in surprise and then what might have been slight embarrassment. He seemed to check his anger as she asked him to please wait outside the autopsy room. "I'll have someone show you where you can have a seat." She thought he would object. But then he looked past her to where the body bag was being unloaded from the state investigators' van.

The realization made him stagger a little before he caught himself and turned back into the hallway, letting the door close behind him.

She hurried to help roll the body into the morgue. Once she had it on the examination table, she went to find Mr. Collinwood. He was sitting on a bench outside, his head in his hands.

"If you'd like to come with me now," she said quietly. She never got used to the amount of grief she witnessed. She hoped she never did.

It took him a moment to rise from the bench. He was a man who clearly carried himself with unsparing confidence, and she saw that he was now struggling to maintain it. She often saw this kind of debilitating grief and felt it clear to her core. In these rural areas of the state, she was often alone in these duties of telling friends and family of their loss.

The hardest part was asking them to identify the bodies. Usually, that fell to the local coroner unless she'd been called in on a case.

If the dead man hadn't been Humphrey Collinwood, killed by his wife, Rachel Collinwood, then right now George would be doing this, she thought as she led Bart Collinwood into the morgue to identify his son.

FORD WONDERED WHY the sheriff wanted to see him again, but he stayed around the hospital. Down in the cafeteria, he got himself a cup of coffee. At the smell of the evening meal, he realized he hadn't eaten all day. No wonder he felt weaker than usual. But he suspected he wouldn't be able to get a bite down right now.

Back up on Rachel's floor, he parked himself in the waiting room and sipped his beverage. It was hot and bitter, which suited him just fine. He thought of Humphrey, but quickly pushed his image away. Instead, he tried to remember how it had all started and realized that would have been the moment he first saw Rachel. The moment Humphrey also saw her and Ford lost her.

It had been in the park near the university. He and Humphrey had been sitting on the grass under a large oak tree like they usually did after their chem class when a woman had caught Ford's eye. She was a vision in an orange-and-white polka-dot sundress that accented her slim, sun-kissed form. She was trying to feed a squirrel a scrap of bread from her lunch. He watched her for a few minutes, amused by her patience. Humphrey had been lying back on the grass, smoking and staring up at the blue sky overhead. Ford had been leaning back against a tree, watching the world go by.

He remembered that carefree feeling with his whole life ahead of him. It had felt as if anything was possible. That was when Rachel had caught his eye. She and the squirrel chattering at her from a nearby tree. What fascinated him was the way she could hold so perfectly still, kneeling on the grass, her arm extended, the scrap of bread pinched between two fingers. He'd been impressed by her perseverance, her naive belief that if she waited long enough the squirrel would come to her.

He hadn't been able to help himself. He'd pulled out the cell phone he'd gotten for Christmas and snapped a photo of her. The movement caught not just her eye, but also that of the squirrel, which took off up the tree.

Getting to her feet, she'd mugged a face at him as he'd gotten up and walked over to her. "I'd almost had him convinced to take the bread." It was a rebuke.

Ford had laughed. "That squirrel was never going to take that bread."

"How do you know that?" she'd demanded, glaring at him.

"I heard what he was saying to you." He'd grinned. "He doesn't eat white bread."

Her face had softened into a glorious smile, one that would haunt his dreams for years to come. "You understand squirrels?"

"Clearly better than you," he'd joked. "I'd be happy to teach you, though. I'm Ford Cardwell, squirrel whisperer."

Her smile had broadened as she said, "Rachel Westlake.

You do know that has to be the worst pickup line I've ever heard." Her gaze had shifted to Humphrey, who had spotted the two of them and gotten up to join them.

Ford had taken one look at his friend's face and known that he'd been as captivated by the woman as Ford had been. The difference was that Rachel had been looking at Humphrey with that same expression.

Rachel and Humphrey used to joke that it had been love at first sight. Ford knew it had been for him, not that he'd ever told anyone, especially the two of them. Rachel and Humphrey had started dating after that, the three of them often together. He thought of all the photos with Humphrey with one arm around Rachel and one around Ford. Humphrey always said that he couldn't live without either of them. It had been like that right up through graduation and their wedding.

Now in the waiting room, he felt that old guilt and pain. What hurt was how much he'd missed his best friend the past fifteen years and now Humphrey was gone.

As the waiting room door opened, Ford started. He'd expected it to be the sheriff. Instead, it was a man he'd only met a few times but recognized at once. Bartholomew "Bart" Collinwood walked in as if he owned the hospital. He certainly could have bought it if he wanted to, Ford knew. Humphrey and his father had had a tense relationship back in college. His friend always felt that he would never live up to his father's expectations. Ford wondered if that had changed over the years.

Bart stopped short in the middle of the room and frowned as he stared at him. "Ford, isn't it?"

"Ford Cardwell." He was a little surprised the man even remembered him.

"I recall you saying it was an old Texas family name, right? Or was it Montana?" The shock of his son's death wore heavily on the man. He seemed confused and unsure of himself for a moment. Then his gaze seemed to clear. "You know, you're the reason my son bought the ranch out here. All those stories you used to tell about ranch life."

He heard accusation in the man's tone. Did he believe that if his son hadn't bought a ranch in Montana he'd still be alive? Ford didn't know what to say, so he said nothing. The man was grieving. He was probably also looking for someone to blame.

"You two were good friends, roommates," Bart continued. "Had a falling-out at the end of your senior year at college, right?"

Was that how Humphrey had explained it? "I joined the military," Ford said.

"That's right." The man shook his head. "I'm surprised my son didn't follow you right into boot camp since he wanted to do whatever you did. Rachel knew how much he admired you. She must have stopped him. She wouldn't have allowed him to do anything but make more money for her to spend."

Ford shook his head, recalling that Bart had never been a fan of Rachel's. "Humphrey loved her."

The man let out a bitter laugh that almost sounded like a sob. "And look what it cost him."

Ford started to argue that Humphrey hadn't been the only victim in what had happened, but Bart cut him off.

"So you're here for his wife."

Was that an accusation or just Ford's guilt making him hear it that way? "It isn't like that."

"It sure looks like that."

The sheriff stuck his head into the door of the waiting room, drawing both of their attention. Bart moved swiftly to the lawman and grabbed his arm as he began demanding justice for his son.

The sheriff shook him off. "I thought you might be here wanting to know how his wife is doing after being severely beaten almost to death by your son," Charley Cortland said. "She's recovering nicely."

Bart huffed. "I want to see her."

"I don't think that's a good idea," the sheriff said. "You're just going to upset her and she's been through enough."

"*She's been through enough. She killed my son!* I was just at the morgue. She shot him in the *face!*" Bart's voice broke with emotion. "I *will* see her. She *will* look me in the eye and tell me the truth."

At the raised voices, a security guard pushed open the waiting room door.

The sheriff turned toward the uniformed man. "Hal, show this gentleman out of the hospital. If he comes back, let me know so I can arrest him."

"You have no idea who you are dealing with," Bart said angrily. "You'll be lucky to be the dogcatcher when I get through with you."

Chapter Six

Back at the morgue, dressed and ready for the autopsy, Hitch studied the corpse lying now on the metal table. After Mr. Collinwood had left, she'd gone online. It had been easy to find information about Humphrey Collinwood and his wife, Rachel. He'd been handsome, wealthy and a successful businessman. There were dozens of shots with him and his wife at gala affairs and fund-raisers before they'd moved from New York City to the ranch north of Big Timber, Montana. The two had been photographed at every party they attended as the VIPs they were.

That had been until about a year ago, when they'd bought the ranch and moved here, from what Hitch could tell. Was that the beginning of the end?

She'd also done research on Ford Cardwell. A cowboy turned hero flyboy who'd received a medal of honor after his plane had crashed because of a mechanical failure in war-torn Afghanistan. Miraculously surviving the crash, he'd fought to save his crew, rescuing some but losing others when the plane exploded. He'd only left the military a few months ago. Interesting, she'd thought. Before that, it had appeared he was making the military his career.

But what intrigued her more was how he'd gotten involved in Humphrey Collinwood's death.

Pulling up her mask, she turned on her video recorder and began the autopsy.

Cause of death: a single gunshot wound. She went through the steps, documenting each into the camera.

She frowned as she noticed the deceased's hands. If he had been beating his wife, there would have been bruises, abrasions, some sign of trauma.

Carefully, she removed first his wedding ring and bagged it. Then the ring on his other hand. His right hand. It was large, gold and heavy with a diamond at its center. She noted the blood and skin that had been caught in the design before taking a sample and bagging the ring. If he'd been right-handed, then this was the hand he would have used to hit his wife.

Still, the lack of abrasions or bruising on his hands bothered her. She took photographs of each hand. But until Hitch saw the extent of her injuries, she wouldn't know if he had used something other than his fists.

The sheriff had already decided it had been a case of self-defense. But she knew most were never as simple as that. Had Rachel Collinwood feared for her life? Had she used the proper amount of force based on that fear? Had she shot to stop the man or kill him? Hitch recalled one case where the location of the gun had been a deciding factor in whether or not the woman had planned to kill her husband—and whether she was exonerated.

Rachel had a witness of sorts already waiting in the wings. Hitch couldn't wait to meet Ford Cardwell and hear how it was that his old friend from college just happened to call him at one of the most tragic times of her life.

"HOW LONG ARE you going to be in town?" the sheriff asked Ford after the security guard left with Bart in tow.

"I'm not sure yet," Ford told him. "I'm not leaving right away. I want to be sure that Rachel's all right. Truthfully, I also would like some answers. I still can't believe any of this. Humphrey was like a brother to me. This just doesn't make any sense."

"People change," the sheriff said. "Either that or he was always like that and just hid it well."

After being told that Mrs. Collinwood was down in X-ray and he wouldn't be able to see her again until tomorrow, Ford left. He'd just walked out the front of the hospital when he saw a woman etched against the last of the sunset. She stood off the sidewalk, at the edge of the deep shadows that had settled in around the hospital. It had been a long day, so no wonder he thought he was seeing things. The woman resembled someone he used to know. He was about to turn toward his pickup when the woman spotted him and called his name.

"That is you, isn't it?" she said as she stubbed out her cigarette and moved from the shadows so he got a good look at her.

"Shyla?" He couldn't help his surprise. Like with Rachel, it had been years since he'd seen her best friend from college. He frowned. How had she known about what had happened and gotten here this quickly? "What are you doing here?"

"The same thing you are, I would imagine," she said. "Have you seen Rach? Is she okay? The guard wouldn't let me in to see her."

"I mean, how did you get to Montana so quickly? Did you fly in with Bart?"

"Bart? Good Lord, no! I live here now. I guess you haven't heard. My last name's Birch now. I married a cowboy." She laughed. It was high-pitched and loud—just like it had been in college. Like Humphrey, Shyla had come from old money. It was no surprise that she'd said at college that her family considered her the black sheep. "I know. It was my dream, right?"

"How long have you lived here?" he asked.

"I was out here visiting Rach a year ago and…" She waved a hand through the air. "It just kind of happened. Listen, if you aren't doing anything right now, I could really use a drink. Think we can find a bar close by?"

Ford had to smile. Shyla Earhart hadn't changed in the least. Brash, abrasive, loud and completely without filters. He didn't want or need a drink, but he needed to know about Rachel and what had led up to today's tragedy.

"I'm betting that you already have a bar in mind," he said.

She laughed again and looped her arm through his. "You know me so well. So how have you been, Ford?"

"Just dandy," he lied as they walked to his pickup.

The bar Shyla chose was small and dark and surprisingly quiet. It definitely wasn't a cowboy bar. He wondered idly about her husband and how they'd met, but after getting them two drinks from the bar, he asked about Rachel.

"So what happened with Rachel and Humphrey?" he asked.

Shyla mugged a face. "He turned out to be a real bastard." She quickly raised a hand as if she thought he would argue and rushed on. "I know he was your friend, but he'd changed." She grimaced. "You have no idea how bad it got once they moved out here. Rach didn't want to move here, you know. She hated living out in the sticks. Like he cared. He was often gone to the big city on business, so she was out there, terrified in that big house, all alone. That's why I came out to stay with her for a while and ended up meeting my cowboy and getting married. My family had multiple heart attacks over it." She laughed and picked up her drink.

"Did you know he was abusive to her?" Ford asked as Shyla drained her glass and signaled the bartender for another. He hadn't even touched his yet.

"Sure, I knew. I mean, I'd seen the bruises a couple of times. She always had a story. Walked into a wall. Got hit by a tree branch. Fell off her horse. The usual." Shyla rolled her eyes. "I knew something was wrong."

"Why didn't she leave him?" He took a sip of his drink.

"Why do you think? His father forced her to sign a pre-nup before they got married. Divorce was out of the question unless she wanted to live like a pauper."

"She could have gotten a job."

Shyla laughed. "Rachel? She majored in psychology at college and hasn't worked all these years. You want fries with that?"

"But if he was abusing her—"

"He traveled a lot and it didn't happen all the time, but I had suspected it was getting worse when he returned to the ranch. When they first married, she'd wanted kids. He didn't. You knew about the miscarriage, right? Then they moved out here and he decides he wants kids. She reminds him that she can't get pregnant. Something about that miscarriage after their wedding. He wants to adopt. At thirty-two, she felt like that ship had sailed."

"A lot of women are having babies later in life," he said.

"Not with a husband who is abusive," Shyla said, leaning toward him. He could smell cigarette smoke and her cloying perfume mixing with the booze she'd drunk. "He was a spoiled rich kid and he wasn't happy, so he took it out on her."

He didn't remember that about Humphrey. Sure, his friend came from wealth, but he'd seemed almost embarrassed by it. Ford reminded himself that he was getting only one side of the story: Rachel's, as told to Shyla. But then again, that might be the only side he was ever going to get now.

"She might go to prison," he said.

Shyla's eyes widened. "How is that possible? For killing the bastard when he was trying to kill her?"

"I heard a lot of it while it was happening," he said.

She froze. "You *what*?"

"Rachel called me. I heard her screaming and pleading with him not to hurt her—"

"Wait. You two have been talking?"

"No. She contacted me on social media recently. We exchanged phone numbers. That's all it was. I never planned to call her…"

"She called you for help?"

He shook his head. "It wasn't like that. I think she pocket dialed me by accident. Anyway, I heard all of it right up to the gunshot before the call ended."

"You told the sheriff this?" He nodded. "Then there is no way she's going to prison, Ford. Clearly, it was self-defense, right?"

"It sure sounded that way," he said as he finished his drink and she downed her second one.

Her cell phone rang. He could hear only one side of the conversation but it seemed pretty clear. Her husband was reminding her that she was supposed to be cooking dinner and she needed to get home.

"We should go," he said, although Shyla had told her husband that she'd be home when she was good and ready and it was high time he learned to cook.

She smiled almost sheepishly. "He really is a good guy. Just a little too much sometimes."

He took her back to the hospital where she'd left her car. "Are you going to try to see Rachel again?"

"Tomorrow," Shyla said as he walked her to her car. It had gotten dark while they were in the bar. She opened her car door and turned to look at him. "Is it bad? What he did to her?" Ford nodded. "She was lucky he didn't kill her. You asked what happened between them. She thought he was having an affair. And get this—it was with a local woman who works as a waitress at the Corner Café in town. Emily Sutton."

"You know her?" he asked.

She shook her head. "Rachel only told me a couple of days ago. She'd just found out. I went by the café after that, but Emily wasn't working, and the next thing I knew, I heard about what had happened out at the ranch earlier today. Thanks for the drinks." She climbed into her car and drove away.

Ford watched her go. Shyla was out here in Montana married to a cowboy. He couldn't believe that any more than he could that Humphrey was having an affair, had beaten Rachel and she'd felt forced to kill him. But as the sheriff said, people changed. Ford wondered if the alleged affair was what the two had argued about. Or was it about adopting children?

His cell phone rang. He pulled it out, saw that it was his father and realized he wasn't in the mood to explain everything that had happened today. Or how he found himself involved again in Rachel's life. He knew his father wouldn't have thought it was a good idea. Jackson had met Rachel and Humphrey back in college. And while his father had been taken with Humphrey, he hadn't been a fan of Rachel's. Or maybe what his father hadn't liked was Ford's obvious infatuation with the woman who was clearly more infatuated with Humphrey than his son.

Ford wasn't getting involved with Rachel. But he didn't want to argue the point, so he texted back, saying he was fine and would be away for a few days. Not to worry. Then he went looking for a place to stay.

HITCH WAS JUST finishing up the autopsy when the sheriff stuck his head in the door.

"About done?" he asked, sounding impatient and out of sorts.

She looked at the clock on the wall in surprise. She hadn't realized how late it was. Behind the sheriff, she could see through a far window that it was dark outside. She'd lost track of time—as she often did. But she had needed to get on this one right away.

"I should have the report to you by tomorrow afternoon," she said. "Do you have a minute?"

He had started to leave. She could tell he wanted nothing to do with the autopsy room. After shrugging out of her garb, she washed her hands and stepped out into the hallway with him.

"Tell me it's a slam dunk," he said. "Gunshot to the face, I don't really need to ask the cause of death."

"I was wondering about the woman's injuries. You were the first one on the scene, right?"

"Like I told you, I found her in the kitchen, sitting on the floor, leaning against a cabinet, looking terrified. She was still holding the gun in one hand and the phone in the other. She dropped both when she saw me and tried to get to her feet. The floor was slick with her blood and his. I had to help her up." He grimaced as if recalling the scene. "I could see that she was in bad shape and that he was dead. I could see what happened. What more is there to say?"

"There is no doubt that she fired the fatal kill shot," Hitch said as she pulled out her phone to consult the report DCI had sent her. "The techs found gunpowder residue on her hands and wrists along with the clothing she was wearing at the time." Slacks, blouse, heels. Dressed like a woman spending the day on the ranch? Or one who'd been to town?

"That seems pretty obvious since there was just the two of them in the house," the sheriff said sarcastically. "She fired the gun and killed him. It wasn't like he shot himself in the face."

"Did she say anything to you about what had happened?"

"Like confess? She was hysterical, in pain, bleeding. I handed her my handkerchief."

"The lab will want that if you still have it," she said, making him roll his eyes.

"You're just going to beat this one like a dead horse, aren't you?" He shook his head. "Let the state get involved and they'll blow this up for no good reason… Fine." He pulled out the soiled handkerchief from his pocket. She could see only a few spots of blood and something dark. Gunpowder residue? As he tried to hand it to her, she made him wait until she grabbed an evidence bag, getting her another eye roll.

"So she didn't say anything about shooting her husband?" Hitch asked again as she sealed the bag.

"No. She just cried. Clearly, she was in a lot of pain." His jaw muscles clenched and unclenched. "I interviewed her at the hospital. Before you ask, I videotaped her statement."

"Thank you, Sheriff. Oh," she said as she started to turn away and pretended to change her mind. "I'll need to see any statements you've taken, including the ones from Ford Cardwell and Rachel Collinwood."

"I'll call my office and tell them to send you both video interviews." He didn't move for a moment and she could tell he was chewing on something. "I'm damned good at my job, I'll have you know. It's why I've been in this office as long as I have." With that, he turned and left.

She felt the weight of the day. Often she worked late rather than eat alone at some restaurant before going back to an empty motel room. If she didn't love her work so much…

Turning out the light, she started to leave when she looked out to see a pickup parked outside. The lights were on and the engine was running, but she couldn't make out who was behind the wheel.

As if the driver had seen her staring out the window, he sped off. Was it a male driver? She'd just assumed so. She watched until the taillights disappeared around a corner, surprised by the anxious feeling she'd gotten. The driver had just been sitting out there as if watching her. She didn't spook easily, but being alone this late here at the morgue and seeing the driver of the pickup just sitting there...

She shook it off, telling herself it had been nothing. Just a long day and the violent case she'd found herself embroiled in. Tomorrow she would be getting a call from the governor wanting answers. She hoped she had some by then.

Chapter Seven

After a rough night filled with nightmares, Ford showered and drove down to the Corner Café Shyla had mentioned for breakfast. He was curious about the kind of woman his old friend would jeopardize his marriage over. If true. His head ached from the images that had played in his mind and kept him from sleep.

He kept seeing Rachel's bruised and battered face. But it was Humphrey, once his best friend, who haunted his nightmares the worst. In them, the man had been pleading with Ford to forgive him, as if it had been Ford who'd pulled the trigger on that gun.

He took a seat in an empty booth and waited. The café was busy. He saw there were several waitresses scurrying around. One had short dark hair. The other, long blond hair tied back. Humphrey had always preferred blondes. He figured this one had to be Emily Sutton. When the woman came to his table with a menu tucked under her arm, a glass of water and pot of coffee, he got his first good look at her and felt a start.

She could have been a young Rachel with her big blue eyes and bee-stung mouth. "Coffee?" she asked, smiling. He could only nod, still taken aback. She righted the cup in the saucer that was already on the table and poured, commenting on the beautiful summer day outside, then said, "I'm Emily. I'll give you a minute to look over the menu.

But don't worry—I'll be back." Her smile was devastating in its beauty and innocence—just as Rachel's had been all those years ago.

Humphrey would have seen the similarities between the waitress and his wife. Would it have been like falling for Rachel all over again?

Ford opened his menu, surprised at the impact the realization had made on him. What had happened between Rachel and Humphrey? Had he just been looking for a newer model? How deep had the rift between them gotten that it had led to such a catastrophic ending?

He tried to concentrate on his menu. He hadn't been hungry for a very long time. Loss of appetite was only one symptom, he'd been told. As if he didn't know the rest of them. He was apparently the poster boy for post-traumatic stress disorder. He had it all, from the flashbacks, memory loss and nightmares, to the severe anxiety, the emotional numbness and feelings of hopelessness—right down to the despondent suicidal thoughts.

He started to close the menu, thinking he should go back to Big Sky. Rachel didn't need him. Anyway, there was nothing he could do to help her. Other than what he'd already done. His cell phone rang. He saw that it was from the hospital and quickly picked up. His heart rate did a little bump as he heard Rachel's voice on the other end of the line.

"Are you all right?" he asked as he hurried to take the call outside.

"I'm much better, thank you. I was hoping you were still around."

"I am."

"I'm so glad to hear that. I need to see you." The café door opened as several people exited. The clatter of dishes and laughter followed them out, along with the smell of bacon. "You're having breakfast. Please, finish eating.

They're taking me down to X-ray again, but then I should be back in my room in the next hour. Come see me?"

"I will." To his surprise, when he disconnected he felt like going back inside the café. The smell of food that had nauseated him earlier now made his stomach rumble. He sat down and the waitress hurried right over.

"Have you decided?" Emily asked. On closer inspection, she wasn't as pretty as Rachel.

He nodded and ordered the special, flapjacks and bacon.

"Good choice," she said and hurried off.

Ford picked up his coffee cup and took a sip. Rachel wanted to see him. What was it he'd heard in her voice? Fear and something else, something he remembered from a very long time ago. He heard her words from fifteen years ago at the wedding. "It should have been you, Ford." And then her mouth and hands were on him and he was kissing her—the woman who'd just married his best friend.

That memory had always come with guilt like a weight around his neck. This morning it didn't feel so heavy. Maybe even just hours after the wedding, Rachel had realized the mistake she'd made.

He felt lighter. He'd been wrong. Rachel *did* need him. He hadn't realized how much he'd needed her right now, he thought. She'd saved his life on the mountain. Not that he would know if he would have gone through with it. But he felt as if she had literally pulled him back from the brink. Maybe he could do the same for her. At least for the moment it would give his life meaning.

BACK FROM X-RAY, Rachel itched to get her bandages off, head home and soak in a hot bathtub. She had a slight concussion. Her ribs were cracked, not broken. Same with her cheekbone. She felt dirty, grimacing when she saw the dried blood still under her fingernails. Emotions, hot and fierce, bubbled to the surface. Was it her blood? Or was it Humphrey's? The thought of his blood made her wince.

She closed her eyes, wishing for sleep. Last night she'd lain awake, haunted by the memory of her husband's face—and what she'd seen in those blue eyes—that instant before she'd pulled the trigger. Where once there had been such love, such admiration, such gratitude, she'd seen—She couldn't bear to think about it or what their lives had come to.

At college, Humphrey had been the shy, wealthy young man who studied hard, partied little and dated even less. She'd expected him to be cocky the first time she met him after finding out who he was. Instead, he'd been sweet. It didn't surprise her that Humphrey and Ford were good friends. They'd been a lot alike. Ford hadn't even seemed to notice how wealthy his friend's family was. But that was Ford. Money had never mattered to him.

Ford. Of course, he'd been there when she'd needed him. If only she had married him, she thought, then remembered what he'd said when she'd asked him what he planned to do after graduation.

"Maybe work in the barbecue business with the family. Although I think I'd like to work on Cardwell Ranch with my dad's cousin Dana first. I've spent a lot of time there growing up over the years. It holds special memories for me."

Rachel had been shocked at how little he'd wanted. "You must have another dream. Aren't you majoring in engineering?"

He'd actually laughed and said he didn't need to set the world on fire. He just wanted to have a simple life and give his kids what he'd gotten growing up, an appreciation for Montana living and family. "What I've learned would come in handy on the ranch."

"But didn't I hear Humphrey say that he could get you a job with his dad?" she'd said.

Ford had looked shocked. "That was nice of him, but that's not the life I want."

Was that when she'd been glad that she hadn't set her sights so low? Ford was nice, but she needed more. She needed his roommate because she'd dreamed of the nicer things in life.

She cringed at the memory. Humphrey was dead, while it had been Ford who'd come to her rescue. She had a flash of memory of her lovely kitchen covered in shattered glass and pottery, with Humphrey lying in the middle of it. That vision now served as a nightmare snapshot of her shattered dreams. She closed her eyes tightly, trying to wipe it all away.

At the sound of someone coming into her hospital room, she opened her eyes and braced herself. This waking nightmare wasn't over any more than the ones that ruined her sleep. In fact, she feared the horror was just beginning.

FORD HAD STARTED down the hallway toward Rachel's room when a female voice called after him. Turning, he saw an attractive brunette woman wearing jeans, boots and a Western shirt headed toward him.

"Mr. Cardwell?" she asked when she reached him.

The title felt wrong. "I'm Ford Cardwell."

She held out her hand. She had pale green eyes under dark lashes. "Henrietta Roberts, state medical examiner. Most people just call me Hitch. I'd like to ask you a few questions, if you don't mind. The doctor said we could use his office down the hall, if you'll please follow me." She didn't wait for an answer. Everything about her said she had authority, from the steel in her spine, to the tone of her voice and the no-nonsense look in those eyes. He gathered that she was a woman used to giving orders and having them followed.

He hesitated, though, anxious to see Rachel. She should be back from X-ray. She would be waiting for him. "I was just going to see—"

The medical examiner stopped to look back at him, seeming almost amused. "She isn't going anywhere. I promise you. This way."

In the doctor's office, she closed the door behind them and told him to take a seat. To his surprise, she didn't go behind the desk and take the doctor's chair. Instead, she pulled up the second one in front of the physician's desk. Their knees were only a few inches apart.

Taking out her phone and notebook and pen, she said, "I'd like to record this, if it's all right with you."

"You know that I already did this at the sheriff's office, right?"

"Yes, but if you don't mind, I'd like to hear it directly from you." She set up her phone to record on the edge of the desk so it was facing him. "I understand you know those involved. Can you please explain?"

He did, going over his relationships with Humphrey and Rachel and then the phone call and what he'd heard.

"So you never heard the victim say anything."

"Is that what you're calling him?" Ford asked. "What does that make Rachel?"

"At this point, they're both victims. I'm trying to find out what happened so I can sort this out. So voices. You heard…"

"The only person I heard was Rachel. I thought at the time that she was being attacked by an intruder. I could hear glass breaking and her screaming…"

"Humphrey never spoke before she called him by name?"

"No."

"Did you hear anything else in the background other than breaking glass?"

"Not that I can remember."

"When you knew Rachel in college, do you know if she owned a gun?"

"No. I mean, no, she didn't. She hated guns."

"Did she learn how to shoot one, that you were aware of?"

"I have no idea. I hadn't seen her for fifteen years until yesterday." He remembered telling her goodbye the day he'd left. More memories hit him like typhoon winds, making a rushing sound in his ears.

"It's clear to me that you care a great deal about her."

Was he that transparent? He started to deny it, but decided to save his breath. "I was half in love with her way back when. I was young. We all were young, that is. But like I said, that was years ago."

"Humphrey Collinwood was your roommate and your best friend, you said. Did the friendship survive the years?"

He didn't know how to answer that. He could feel her studying him with those sea green eyes that seemed to notice everything. "We drifted apart."

She nodded. "You said the last time you saw her was at her wedding to Humphrey?"

He realized he must have told the sheriff that and now she was making too much out of this. He nodded, wishing he'd denied having feelings for Rachel.

"Did Humphrey know how you felt about her?" Those eyes widened. "Did you ever consider getting back at him?"

The accusation caught him flat-footed. He glanced at her phone. Was it still recording? "What are you suggesting? Yes, I had a crush on Rachel years ago, but I wasn't… jealous, not like that."

"I find it interesting that it was your phone number that she called during the altercation with her husband."

"I explained that—"

"So just a few weeks ago, she contacts you out of the blue on social media. Whose idea was it to exchange phone numbers?"

He shook his head. "I don't remember." But when he thought about it, he did. It had been Rachel's.

"Also, you drove right here, making really good time apparently, after the call."

"I was worried after what I'd heard. I knew the sheriff would want to talk to me." He couldn't believe what she was insinuating. "Wouldn't you have done the same thing after hearing something like that involving old friends?"

She didn't answer. "You don't find it a little odd she just happened to call *you*?"

"I explained that. It must have been—"

"A pocket dial, right. Making you a defense witness. Was Rachel surprised when you showed up here?" She didn't give him a chance to answer. "I didn't think so. She knew you would come to her rescue after the call since you were old friends. She had to have known how you felt about her. Even though you'd lost touch for fifteen years, she'd known you'd come when called."

Ford didn't like where this was going. "You'd have to ask her. Look, if we're about finished here..." He stood.

The medical examiner turned off the video on her phone. "I'm assuming you're planning to stay around for a while?" She again didn't give him a chance to answer. "Good. But I can always find you back in Big Sky. If I need to."

He felt a chill run the length of his spine. All those days of feeling nothing but an emotional numbness were gone. Like a bucket of ice water poured over his head, he was now wide-awake as he realized what this woman was accusing him of—and Rachel, as well. She thought he was somehow involved in Humphrey's death? Because of a phone call?

With a silent groan, he thought about what had happened between him and Rachel at the wedding all those years ago. He hated to think of what the medical examiner would make of that.

Chapter Eight

Ford felt so shaken after his encounter with the medical examiner that he didn't go right to Rachel's room. Instead, he went outside and walked around town for a little while to clear his head. Big Timber was a small Western ranch town set in the middle of several impressive mountain ranges along the Yellowstone River.

The views would have taken his breath away if he wasn't already short of breath from what the medical examiner had accused him of doing. That he'd always wanted Rachel and had helped her kill her husband out of jealousy and was now her...defense? That was insane. How could she think such a thing?

By the time he returned to the hospital, he was still shaken but more in control. He'd come here to help Rachel. That Hitch—as she called herself—thought Rachel might have planned the whole thing so she could kill her husband was even crazier. Had the woman seen Rachel's face? The doctor had just taken her down to X-ray. Clearly, she'd been beaten.

If the medical examiner believed that was what had happened, then Rachel needed him even more than he'd thought. He had to see her again and he'd kept her waiting long enough. But he felt off balance as he found the doctor and got permission. The guard at the door let him in. As he stuck his head around the corner into her room, he did his best not to let her see how upset he was. He wondered how much of it was guilt over what had happened all those years ago.

"The doctor said you can have some company for a few minutes."

She waved him in. "I must look awful," Rachel said and touched the bandage at her cheek.

"You couldn't possibly look awful and you know it," Ford said as he pulled up the chair next to her bed. "Since you're fishing for compliments, you must be feeling better."

She chuckled even though it seemed to cause her pain. "That's what I always loved about you, Ford. You tell it to me straight." Her expression softened and he felt a slight electrical charge in the room. It was dated and weak, but still he felt it. "I'm so sorry." She began to cry. "The sheriff told me that I called you and that you…heard. I can hardly face you. Now I've involved you in all this."

"Rachel, really, it's all right."

"No, it's not. I never wanted anyone to know and now…"

He reached for her hand, thinking they all had things that they never wanted anyone to know. "When I got your call, it caught me at a really low point. The truth is, Rachel, your call saved my life."

She wiped her eyes. "Ford, you don't have to say that."

"I'm not." He hesitated, but only for a moment. "When you called, I was driving toward the edge of a cliff. I'd planned to end it."

Her blue eyes widened. "No," she said, looking horrified.

He nodded. "But then you called. So I'm the one who should be thanking you."

She studied him for a long moment and then laughed. "Look at us. Who would have ever thought this is where we would end up." He squeezed her hand.

For so long he hadn't felt anything and thought he never would again. Yet when he'd gotten her phone call yesterday and realized who it was, he'd felt as if his numbed emotions had been touched with a cattle prod. He'd known he had to come to Big Timber. Her wrong number had brought him back into her life. If that wasn't fate, he didn't know what was.

After his interview with the medical examiner, it was clear that Rachel needed him—even if she didn't know it yet. "How are you doing?" he asked.

"You've been through something like it, so I suspect you know."

He did know. Their situations were nothing alike except for the feeling of horror at where life had landed them. He hated to think what she must be going through. Seeing her again, it felt as if no time had passed since they last saw each other. He wanted to ask if she'd been happy at least some of those years with Humphrey, but didn't want to remind her about her marriage. She must have loved her husband. At least until the abuse began.

"Do you want to talk about it?" he asked.

She shook her head. "He just wasn't the man I thought he was. I really thought when we married that we would live happily ever after. Silly, huh?"

"I think that's the way most people go into a marriage."

Rachel picked at the edge of the sheet, her eyes downcast. "He was so sweet, so caring, so generous. At first." She looked up. "You know, he bought the ranch because of you."

"That's what his father told me." Ford remembered what Shyla had told him about how miserable Rachel had been at the ranch. Bart had even wanted to blame Ford for Humphrey's buying the ranch and dying here.

"Bart's here?" she said, her voice breaking. "You know, he hates me. Always has. He'll do everything in his power to get me sent to prison for life."

"We won't let that happen."

Eyes shiny and bright, she smiled up at him, taking him back to that day in college—those few precious moments in the park before she saw Humphrey.

HITCH HAD WATCHED Ford Cardwell from the hospital window as he'd left earlier. He'd had his hands in the pockets of his jeans, his head down. She'd obviously upset him. Because it hadn't been true? Or because it had?

She had seen how anxious he'd been earlier to see Rachel Collinwood. At the window, she'd decided to wait him out, knowing he would be back once he'd calmed down. The fact that he'd been so upset told her how deep his feelings apparently went for the woman in question. Sure enough, he'd come back and gone straight to Rachel's room.

From down the hall, she now watched him exit the woman's room. It was time to take this to the next step. Hitch put in a call to the sheriff, then headed down the hall toward Rachel Collinwood's room. As she walked, she mentally processed what she'd learned from Ford Cardwell. If Rachel needed someone she could depend on, well, then she'd certainly made the right call—so to speak—when she'd hit Ford Cardwell's number.

Hitch pushed open the hospital room door, already knowing what she was going to find. Still, she stepped in and stood for a moment studying Rachel, who lay in her bed, eyes closed. Hitch was curious what kind of woman inspired the kind of loyalty the flyboy hero had for her.

Rachel Westlake Collinwood even in her current condition radiated that kind of beauty that few women possessed. Though bruised, lacerated and swollen, her face still had the heart shape so popular on magazine covers. The woman's eyes, she knew from her online search, were big and deep blue. Those eyes now opened in surprise to find Hitch studying her with speculation. Hitch saw the woman's guard come up. Had the sheriff warned her about the female medical examiner?

"Rachel Collinwood?" she said, stepping to the bed. "I'm state medical examiner Henrietta 'Hitch' Roberts." She pulled up a chair beside the bed. "I need to ask you a few questions about what happened yesterday. You don't mind if I video this." She set up her phone so it was aimed directly at the woman, not waiting for her approval. "So, Mrs. Collinwood, why don't you tell me in your own words exactly how this all happened. I know the sheriff already took your statement. You don't mind going through it for me, though, do you, just for the record?"

Rachel glanced at the phone, then at Hitch. Her eyes instantly filled with tears. "He's dead, isn't he?"

Hitch met her watery gaze. "He is. Why don't we start with what happened before you got home." She caught that moment of surprise, just a flash in the woman's eyes. Rachel hadn't mentioned that she'd just gotten home from town when she'd been questioned by the sheriff.

"Or do you want to start with the argument that began before the two of you returned to the ranch?" Hitch asked.

Rachel Collinwood swallowed and seemed to be buying time. "This is very hard to talk about. I've suspected for some time that my husband's been having an affair. When he said he had to go into town to pick up some part or another, I followed him. I caught up with him outside the woman's house and we argued. I went home, upset, and he followed me."

From there, Hitch noticed that this was the same story she'd told the sheriff on video, almost verbatim. She'd learned that interrupting the speaker often changed their account because they were so used to telling it in order, they would forget where they were. She didn't intend to get the same exact story from Rachel Collinwood if she could help it.

"That two-lane highway into town doesn't get much traffic," Hitch said, stopping the flow of the woman's words. "It must have been difficult to follow him into town since he would know your vehicle."

"I took the pickup. I figured he'd expect me to take my car."

"Your car being…"

"The BMW. Anyway…" She picked up her water glass next to the bed, adjusted the straw and took a sip. "When I got home, I heard him coming. He'd been angry in town. I was suddenly afraid for my life."

"Why would you go back to the house if he'd physically abused you before?"

"He had, but never like…that day," she said, dropping her gaze to her hands lying on the sheet as she toyed with the space where her wedding bands had been. The hospital staff normally removed jewelry for safekeeping. But in this case, the DCI investigators had taken all of her jewelry as evidence.

"But you had to be expecting trouble, right? Otherwise, why carry the gun in your purse? Unless you planned to kill him."

The woman's gaze shot up to hers in surprise. "I… I want a lawyer. And turn that thing off." She made a swipe at the phone, but Hitch got hold of it before Rachel could knock it to the floor. "I have nothing more to say to you. You're trying to twist my words. After everything I've been through, I can't believe…" She glared at Hitch. "I would think another woman would understand. He could have killed me! He would have, too, if I hadn't…" She clamped her lips shut and looked away. "Please go. I have nothing more to say to you."

"I need to inform you that you are under arrest pending the results of this investigation and a possible trial," Hitch said. "Once you are able to leave the hospital, you will be taken into custody until a hearing before a judge, in which case you will either be allowed bail or put behind bars."

"You can't be serious!" the woman cried. "He would have *killed* me. He told me he was going to kill me!"

"In the meantime, you will be fitted for an ankle bracelet that requires you to stay on this floor of the hospital." Hitch pocketed her phone as she heard the sheriff talking to the guard outside the room. "If you'll excuse me for a moment," she said and stepped out.

The sheriff lumbered toward her looking angry and upset.

"Sheriff, I need you to inform Mrs. Collinwood of her rights and make sure she understands she is under arrest for the death of her husband."

"That's why you got me down here?" he demanded angrily. "You got me away from my lunch for this?" He shook his head. "You are one heartless woman."

"I'm just doing my job. Isn't that proper procedure in a domestic homicide? I see no reason to let this run the full seventy-two hours. Mrs. Collinwood has admitted to shooting her husband with the intent to kill. Sheriff, if you prefer, I can call——"

The man growled. "I don't need you calling anyone," he snapped.

Minutes later, after the sheriff had read Mrs. Collinwood her rights, she was fitted with an ankle bracelet. Hitch stood at the door and watched. Rachel Collinwood lay in the bed, her face turned to the wall, quietly crying.

Hitch's cell phone rang. She took it on the way out of the hospital.

"I thought you'd want to know. Two shots were fired from the weapon that killed Humphrey Collinwood," Bradley from DCI told her.

She stopped just short of her SUV. "How many casings did you find?"

"Only one in the kitchen on the floor."

"Were there any slugs found in the wall?" she asked, frowning as she tried to understand when and where the other shot might have been fired.

"Negative. But both shots had been fired close to the same time."

Hitch swore under her breath. "We have to find that other slug and casing."

"Have you seen the size of that ranch?" he asked.

"Let me see what I can do. That casing is somewhere out there, and I have a theory that the first shot was a practice one."

Chapter Nine

Hitch couldn't get the news off her mind as she drove out to the Collinwood Ranch. Pulling up to the house, she thought she saw movement inside but realized it was only the reflection of the crime scene tape flickering in the breeze.

After getting out of her SUV, she stepped under that tape and entered the house with the code the sheriff had given her. The first thing that struck her was the absolute silence, followed almost instantly by the smell of cleaning supplies.

The kitchen shone white—all signs of the violence gone. She stepped in and looked around. The DCI unit had been thorough; she didn't doubt that. Which meant the second casing hadn't been in this room. Just as the slug wasn't embedded in any of the walls. Glancing around, though, she knew that the other shot hadn't been fired in here.

Her gaze went to the sliding glass door from the kitchen out onto the deck. She carefully opened the door. The breeze brought the sweet scent of pine and summer as she stepped out. Had Rachel stood here, with the gun in her hand? Rachel Collinwood wasn't the kind of woman who left things to chance, right?

Because of that, she would fire the gun to make sure it worked. To know how it felt, how much it kicked in her hand, what it would do when the time came.

Hitch walked to the edge of the deck and leaned her elbow on the railing to take aim. She spotted the closest pine tree and pretended to fire. Then she glanced down at the thick shrubbery below. The weapon would have ejected the casing.

But before Hitch went digging in the shrubs, she wanted a look at that pine.

A dozen yards from the deck, she stopped in front of the tree. She didn't see it at first. The bullet hadn't skinned much of the bark. Instead, it had lodged in the soft wood and was nearly covered by a piece of bark. She walked back to her vehicle for her satchel, took a few photographs, then pulled on latex gloves and went to work with her pocket-knife.

As the slug came out, she dropped it into an evidence bag. Hitch told herself that anyone could have fired the weapon from the deck. But Bradley had said the two shots had been fired close together.

Holding the slug up in the sunlight, she knew it didn't prove that Rachel had orchestrated the murder of her husband. But then again, it did add to growing evidence that she had.

Putting down her satchel, she bent at the edge of the deck. If she found the empty casing… She had been looking in the shrubbery directly off the deck railing when something farther back under the deck, closer to the house, caught her eye. The casing lay next to the house and the door out to the deck.

Goose bumps rippled over her skin. She'd thought that Rachel had taken the first shot as target practice so she knew how the gun would react when she pulled the trigger. She would have put her elbows on the railing to take aim because she wasn't used to firing this weapon.

But Hitch knew now that it didn't happen that way. Rachel Collinwood had fired the shot that hit the tree standing at the open kitchen doorway. She had practiced with the gun long before the day of the shooting.

It explained why Humphrey Collinwood's voice was never heard on the phone call to Ford. Because he was already dead from the first shot fired—before Rachel had "accidentally" made that alleged pocket dial.

While Humphrey Collinwood lay in a pool of his own blood, his wife had taken the phone, made the call, acted out the attack and then stepped to the open glass doors and fired the shot that Ford heard before she'd disconnected and called 911.

That would explain why Ford Cardwell hadn't heard Humphrey Collinwood say a word.

After taking a photo of where the casing had landed in relation to the house, Hitch put her camera away to leave. But as she did, she felt an icy chill and turned quickly, unable to shake the feeling that someone was watching her. Her gaze took in the sliding glass door into the kitchen. For a moment, she'd expected to see someone standing there.

But the doorway was empty. So was the yard. So was the land that ran from the house to the rolling hills to the mountains in the distance. Behind her, the breeze stirred the boughs of the pine tree, making an eerie moaning sound.

Hitch laughed at her foolishness, but it sounded hollow. She didn't spook easily, but this wasn't the first time she'd felt…something that raised goose bumps across her skin. She doubted it would be the last, given her job. And yet, as she climbed back into her SUV to leave, she found herself staring at the house, unable to shake what felt like a warning.

WHEN FORD VISITED Rachel again later that afternoon at the hospital, he was glad to see that she seemed in better spirits. Her face was badly bruised, but several of the bandages had come off. Also, she seemed glad to see him.

"You look as if you're feeling better," he said, going to her bedside.

"Looks can be deceiving," she said, meeting his gaze. "I'm scared, Ford. I'm under arrest."

"My uncle's a marshal in Big Sky. I talked to him earlier. He said that it's police procedure. What does your lawyer say?"

"That we'll fight it. The problem, he says, is that self-defense claims are fairly common. Because of the amount of force I used…well, it could complicate things. If I hadn't killed him, only wounded him…" She met his gaze. "He was so close. I knew that if he got his hands on me again…" She looked down at her own hands knotted together on top of the sheet. "I was holding the gun. You heard me tell him not to come any closer or I would shoot him." She closed her eyes. "He wouldn't listen. I had no choice. I pulled the trigger."

He placed his hand over hers, surprised someone had told her not only that she'd accidentally called him, but also what he'd heard her say before the gunshot. "What can I do to help you?"

Rachel opened her eyes and wiped them before she turned that high-wattage smile on him. And he'd been so certain just forty-eight hours ago that he'd never be able to feel again. There was a time that her smile would have filled him with so much joy. He told himself the reason he didn't feel that joy now, couldn't because of everything that had happened to them both. He realized Rachel was still talking.

"I don't know what I would have done if you hadn't been here," she was saying. "It's crazy, it's like fate, but I'm so thankful that somehow I hit your number. What are the odds?"

What were the odds? he thought.

"So just your being here is enough," Rachel said. "I can't tell you what it means to me."

"I'm sure your lawyer will get you bail and fight this," he assured her.

"I don't know. He says we have to prove that I was defending myself and believed I was in imminent danger."

"Your injuries should prove that."

She nodded. "It's just hard to prove when there was only the two of us there." She brightened. "But I guess it wasn't just me and Humphrey. You were there." She looked away. "I can't believe any of this is happening."

He knew the feeling. "How is your head?"

She grimaced. "It hurts. The pain pills help. I can't believe what he did to me." She began to cry. "The doctor is releasing me tomorrow, and if I don't make bail, I'm going to jail."

"Do you have money for bail?"

She nodded. "I was afraid all our assets might have been frozen until the outcome of the investigation. But thankfully, they weren't. The thing is, Humphrey always handled the money. I have no idea how much I will be able to raise."

"I'll help what I can," he said.

"I know." She flashed him that smile again. "I knew I could count on you. Oh, Ford." She took his hand in her two. "I'll never be able to thank you enough."

"I should have known you would be here," said a female voice behind him. He turned to see Shyla come into the hospital room. She moved to the bed to give Rachel an awkward hug and a kiss on the cheek. "How's our girl?"

Ford looked to Rachel and smiled. "She's doing okay, under the circumstances." A silence fell over the room. "I'll leave you two alone so you can visit."

"Don't run off on my account," Shyla said, even though he got the feeling that she was anxious to talk to Rachel alone. Because she would be more honest with her than she'd been with him?

He realized that he was letting Hitch get to him, her and

her suspicions. "I've got to go anyway," he said, as if there was anywhere he needed to be. But maybe he should see how much money he could raise on Rachel's behalf if she needed more bail money. "But I'll be back."

Rachel grabbed his wrist as he started to turn away. "Thank you," she whispered.

Ford stepped out into the hall, closing the hospital room door behind him. He stood in the hallway for a moment. Why had this visit with Rachel left him feeling…not so sure of her? The medical examiner had him questioning everything Rachel said, and he hated her for doing that to him. He shook his head and reached into his pocket for his pickup keys. Empty.

He swore under his breath and turned back to Rachel's room, remembering putting them down on the side table when she spilled her water.

But as he pushed open the door, he froze as he overheard Rachel's words. "I should have married Ford." He started to ease the door closed and stopped.

Shyla laughed. "Oh, please. He wasn't even in the running and you know it. His father owns a barbecue joint with his brothers."

"They have a dozen barbecue joints, as you call them, and were worth a bunch even back in college."

"You ran a financial on him?"

Rachel's laugh was like a fingernail down a blackboard. "Why does that surprise you?"

"Actually, nothing you do surprises me," Shyla said. "I know you, Rach. Ford told me how you two met. A squirrel? Really. You just happened to be there feeding a squirrel? You went after Humphrey and you used Ford to do it."

Silence, then Rachel's voice, stronger than it had been when she was talking to him earlier. "I wanted to marry someone who could take care of me in the way I wanted to become accustomed. What's wrong with that?"

"*Really?* Have you noticed how that turned out? You're on your way to jail when you get out of here."

"Maybe. We'll see. I'll make bail. Ford's going to help me."

"Of course he is."

Ford saw his chance and said "I forgot my keys!" as he pushed the door all the way open. Both women turned in surprise as he hurried in, grabbed his keys and waved an apologetic goodbye as he left again.

He reached the door and stopped just out of their sight around the corner at the edge of the hallway. The deputy was no longer outside her door since she'd been fitted with an ankle bracelet. Ford didn't let the door quite close.

"Do you think he heard us?"

Shyla laughed. "Even if he did hear, Ford's still so in love with you he'd forgive you anything. Oh, don't give me that look. This comes as no surprise to you. So tell me. How is it that you just happened to call his number?"

"I have no idea. But he saved my life."

Ford closed the door softly behind him. He stood in the hall trying to catch his breath. His stomach roiled with what he'd heard. He tried to still it, assuring himself that he hadn't heard anything he hadn't already known. He'd seen how Rachel felt about money even back in college. She'd been at the university on loans and small scholarships. She'd hated being poor and had made no bones about it.

Yet he couldn't help but think about the medical examiner's suspicions. He felt sick to his stomach. Worse, Hitch thought he and Rachel had planned this whole thing to get rid of her husband. He'd come running to save her—even though he hadn't forgotten what had happened at her wedding.

What had she gotten him involved in this time? Murder?

Chapter Ten

Hitch decided since she was already at the ranch that she would see if she could find the hired hands. If Rachel Collinwood was being abused by her husband, then someone must have noticed.

According to the sheriff, the Collinwoods employed only two young men who lived in the old ranch house several miles from their employers' home.

As she approached, she could see horses in a pasture and a corral and several outbuildings next to a large barn. The house was a modest two-story farmhouse with a wide porch complete with a swing. Hitch wondered about the former owners of the ranch. Had they moved to Arizona? One of them died? Why had they sold to the Collinwoods? Often it was because there was no one who wanted to keep the place and work it. But in this case, maybe they'd been made an offer they just couldn't refuse.

Hitch parked in front of the house, and before she could get out, two young men headed toward her from the direction of the barn.

Both men appeared to be in their early twenties, tall and gangly and green behind the ears. She introduced herself. The more handsome of the pair was Pete Baxter. He was also the more cocky of the two. Clayton Mandeville was the more talkative of the two.

"So what does a state medical examiner do?" Clayton asked, grinning. "Cut up dead bodies?"

"That and investigate for the state," she said. In this case, she had been given carte blanche from the governor. Which was flattering, but she could feel the weight of it on her shoulders. The message had been clear: don't screw this up. "Can we step inside and talk for a few minutes?"

The house was homey, though dated. Once seated in the living room, she asked, "So the two of you live here?" They nodded. "What is it you do here on the ranch?"

Pete laughed. "We look after things."

"Does the ranch run cattle?"

"It's not a real ranch, if that's what you're asking," Clayton said. "The only animals are the horses."

"I saw a tractor out there," Hitch said. "Does the ranch grow anything?"

They shook their heads. "So you basically take care of how many horses?"

"Six. When the boss wants to ride, we saddle one of them up for him," Clayton said. "We muck out stalls and exercise the horses."

She nodded, looking from one man to the other. Clearly, they had a pretty good setup here. "What about Mrs. Collinwood? Does she ride?" They both shook their heads. "So you don't see her often?" More head shakes. "Where were the two of you yesterday?"

"We had the day off," Clayton said without hesitation.

"Was it your usual day off?"

She asked the question of Clayton, who scratched his neck before saying, "I had some extra time coming. The missus told me to go ahead and take it off."

She looked to Pete, who added, "It was my regular day off."

"So you were both here at the house?"

Clayton shook his head. "I went into town for a while. We were out of a few things."

"He went to see his girlfriend," Pete said with a chuckle.

"And you?" she asked Pete.

"I was here all day. I took one of the horses out for a while and then did chores since someone has to muck out the stalls." He elbowed Clayton.

"So you usually both don't have the same day off. Why yesterday?"

Pete shrugged. "Clayton wanted to see his girlfriend. I didn't mind filling in for him. It isn't like we have a lot to do around here."

"So the Collinwoods don't really know what the two of you do here," she said and hesitated since she wasn't sure how to ask the next question. "Have either of you seen any trouble between Mr. and Mrs. Collinwood?"

Clayton started to speak, but Pete cut him off. "We shouldn't be talking about our employers," Pete said.

"One of them is dead and the other arrested," Hitch pointed out. "I'm not sure how long you're going to be employed. What I need to know is if you had reason to see the two of them together since she didn't ride any of the horses."

"We'd get called up to the house sometimes to do a chore for the missus," Clayton said.

"Did you hear them fighting? Ever see him hit her?"

"Never," Clayton said quickly. "They argued. You know, like old married couples do. Like my parents. He got annoyed with her, but I could tell he loved her. Can't see him raising his hand to her, though."

She looked to Pete, who was studying his boots. "You disagree?"

"I don't like telling tales out of school, but I'd seen her a few times in tears and noticed some bruises on her. I also saw him looking at her a few times like he wanted to kill her."

She studied the ranch hand, curious why his story was so different from Clayton's. "*Like he wanted to kill her? What kind of look is that?*"

Pete shrugged. "You'd know it if you saw it."

"So what happened yesterday doesn't surprise you?" she asked, sure they both had heard all about it.

Pete shook his head. "Not everyone can take living out here in the middle of nowhere. She wasn't raised for this kind of living. Like her husband cared."

Hitch could hear the sympathy in his words. It was clear which side he was on. "She ever talk to you about how she felt?" He looked at his boots again, confirming it. Rachel had complained to the older of the hired hands, the one closer to her own age. There was nothing illegal about that—unless she needed his sympathy for when she killed her husband. Or worse, had been hoping to get him to help her.

"Well, it shocked *me* what happened," Clayton was saying. "I can't imagine what might have set that off, but I never thought he'd do something like that, let alone her ever shoot him. I would have doubted that she even knew how to fire a gun."

Pete merely stared at his boots and said nothing more.

As Hitch drove away from the ranch, she considered the differences between their opinions. Rachel had gone to Pete with her complaints about living on the ranch—and about Humphrey. But Pete didn't seem like the type she would trust as her accomplice. He seemed to Hitch like the kind of man who would have bled her dry for the rest of her life.

That was what had been bothering her, Hitch realized. Rachel couldn't have pulled this off without help. But who had she turned to? She needed a man who was more than sympathetic. She needed one who'd get involved with murder.

She thought about the man who'd allegedly come running the moment he heard the gunshot, Ford Cardwell. After pulling onto the two-lane paved highway, she hadn't gone far when she looked back and saw a pickup behind her. It had one of those large cattle guard grilles on the front. With the sun glinting off the windshield, she couldn't see the driver at this distance. Had the pickup come from the Collinwood Ranch? She didn't think so. Wouldn't she have noticed if either Pete or Clayton had followed her?

The pickup appeared to be the same color as the one that had been sitting outside the morgue last night. She sped up. The pickup driver did the same. She slowed down. The pickup driver did the same.

She told herself that it didn't mean anything, but she was glad when she neared the outskirts of Big Timber and looked back to see the truck gone. It wasn't like her to feel this jumpy. But she couldn't remember ever having a case like this one. Since the first day on this case, she'd had a bad feeling she couldn't shake that things would get worse before they got better.

At the back of her mind was always that one big question. What if she was wrong? What if Humphrey Collinwood's death was exactly like what it appeared to be and Rachel Collinwood was innocent?

Her cell phone rang. She quickly picked up when she saw it was coming from the DCI lab.

"We found something interesting when we began checking the broken shards of glass and pottery found on the floor of the kitchen at the crime scene," Bradley told her. "Fingerprints."

She frowned. "*Fingerprints?* Of course there would be fingerprints."

"Yep, of the lady of the house. But what's missing are the fingerprints of the deceased. If he had broken up the kitchen—"

"You'd have found his fingerprints on the shards," she

said and felt that light-headed feeling she always did when a case began to come together.

FORD HADN'T WANTED to go back to the hotel right away. He kept replaying what he'd heard Rachel and Shyla talking about. Rachel had planned the whole meeting with him—and Humphrey. She'd already staked out the man she planned to marry. That day with the squirrel... She must have known that he and Humphrey often came to that spot in the park after chem class. The woman had done her homework.

There was something so cold and calculating about that. He knew Rachel had been driven, but clearly there were things about her that he'd missed. He shook his head, feeling off balance. Was it possible she'd set this whole domestic homicide up for the money?

He refused to believe she would do something like that even though he knew what money meant to her. Once at a party, the two of them had struck up a conversation outside. That was back when she'd smoked. He'd found her standing at the deck railing. When he'd joined her, he could see that she'd consumed more than she usually drank.

She'd opened up to him about growing up living hand to mouth and her fear of being poor. "My father used to call it the snake pit, saying it was hard for people like us to climb out. That we could never feel like we belonged, even if we made a whole lot of money. No one like us gets out of the snake pit, he used to say."

"Rachel," he'd said that night on the deck. "Look at you. You're going to an Ivy League university. Your father was wrong."

She'd looked at him with tears in her eyes. "Are you sure about that?" She'd scoffed. "What if we have to be born into a family like Humphrey's with real old wealth to ever be one of them?"

He'd forgotten about that conversation until now. Rachel had married into money, but had she still not felt as if she belonged or ever could?

"Ford?"

He turned to see Shyla come out of the hospital.

"Are you all right?" she asked, smiling oddly at him. "You were just standing here on the sidewalk as if you didn't know which way to go."

She was joking, but she had no idea how true that was.

"Just enjoying this beautiful day," he said.

Shyla lit up a cigarette. As she let out a cloud of smoke, a sheriff's department car pulled up. The deputy on the passenger side put down his window. "Hey, baby," the officer behind the wheel called. Ford couldn't see him without stooping down. He didn't. The officer on the passenger side was studying Ford openly and making him nervous. "We were just going to the drive-in for lunch. You wanna come?"

"Sure. I'll catch up to you." Shyla turned to Ford. "You want to join us?"

He declined and her husband took off, making the tires squeal on the cruiser. "You go on ahead. I have some things I need to do. I thought you said you were married to a cowboy?"

"Don't let the uniform fool you," she said with a laugh. "He's all cowboy. You should see his Wild West fast draw. He could be a movie star," she said as she stubbed out her cigarette on the sidewalk and headed toward her car.

Ford watched her go, wondering at how people changed. The lawless young woman who Rachel had bailed out of jail back in college had married a cop cowboy with a fast draw? He shook his head. Wasn't it possible that if Shyla could change, Humphrey could have turned into a man who'd tried to beat his wife to death?

Chapter Eleven

Hitch got the call from Lori Stevenson from DCI on the way back into town. "Those phone records you asked about? I'm emailing them to you. We're still checking out the numbers. Only one call jumped out at us. Didn't you tell us that Rachel Collinwood believed her husband was having an affair with a woman named Emily Sutton? Well, Mrs. Collinwood called her cell phone number at ten the morning of the shooting."

"She called before she went into town?" Hitch said, frowning. "How long was the call?"

"Four minutes."

"*Four minutes?* She wasn't simply checking to see if the woman was working. She'd actually talked to her that long?" Hitch had two quick thoughts. How had she gotten Emily's cell phone number? And why had Rachel left that part out of her statement? "Okay, thanks. Anything else?"

"Bart Collinwood wants his son's body so he can have him flown home and buried. He's called everyone, from what I can tell, including the governor."

Hitch was surprised the governor hadn't called her. Yet. "Great. I need to run a few more tests," she said. It wasn't quite true, but she wasn't ready to turn over the body. She had a feeling that she'd missed something. "I'll let Mr. Bart Collinwood know." She disconnected and drove to the morgue.

Once in the autopsy room, she pulled Humphrey Collinwood's body out of the cooler, that niggling feeling growing. She was certain the reason the deceased hadn't said a word during the fight was because he was already dead. But what if he was unable to speak for another reason? She began to search the body for injection marks.

THE SHERIFF STOOD at the foot of Rachel Collinwood's hospital bed, Stetson in hand. She was so pretty and sweet and looked so shattered and afraid. "I have some good news for you." At least he hoped she'd see it as that. "A bail hearing has been scheduled for tomorrow, the day of your hospital release. That means, if you can make bail, you won't have to even spend one night in my jail behind bars."

Her smile was weak, but it still warmed his heart. "Thank you so much, Sheriff. You've been so kind. I can't tell you how much I appreciate it. I know this is just standard procedure, that you aren't responsible for me being arrested."

"No," Charley quickly assured her. "I don't understand why a woman like yourself has to be put through this. It makes no sense to me. Anyone can see that you feared for your life. Justifiable use of force. That's what it was."

"Unfortunately, not everyone feels like you do. That woman, the medical examiner, for one."

"Hitch Roberts. I know," he said with a shake of his head. "You'd think as a woman, she would be more understanding."

"My father-in-law is even worse. Not that I blame him. His son is dead, but he *raised* him. That's why Bart doesn't want to believe what really happened. It would reflect on him and the Collinwood name."

All the sheriff could do was nod for a few moments. "You got yourself a good lawyer?"

"I hope so. If I do get out on bail, will I be able to go back out to the ranch?"

"I don't see why not," Charley said. "They're through with your house. I had someone go out there and clean things up for you. I hope you don't mind."

"Sheriff, that is so sweet." Tears filled her eyes. "Thank you so much. That is so thoughtful. But I doubt I can ever go into that kitchen again."

"She never went in there much anyway," Bart Collinwood said behind the sheriff as he came into the room. "It wasn't like she was much of a wife to my son."

The sheriff turned on him. "I told you, you aren't allowed in here. I won't have you badgering this woman."

"You told me a lot of things, Sheriff, but I just talked to the governor and he said I have every right to face the woman who killed my son."

"In court. In the meantime…" Charley pulled out his phone to call Security as Collinwood took a step toward the bed.

"You will pay for what you did," Bart declared, pointing a finger at her. "If I have my way, you'll rot in prison."

"Security is on the way," the sheriff said. "Unless you want me to arrest you—"

"On what charge?" Bart demanded. "Anyway, I'm leaving. I've had my say." He looked again at his daughter-in-law. "You might have fooled this local yokel with your crocodile tears, Rachel, but you have never fooled me. You married my son for the Collinwood money. I'll kill you myself before I'll let you spend a dime more of it."

With that, the man stormed out, pushing past the hospital security guard on his way through the door.

"I hope you heard that, Sheriff," Rachel said, her voice breaking. "He just threatened to kill me. Father like son." Then she burst into tears.

EMILY SUTTON SQUIRMED in the chair as the video recorder was turned on. She looked so young in her jeans and T-shirt. Hitch had asked to sit in on the interview with the waitress who was allegedly having an affair with Humphrey Collinwood.

The sheriff grumbled and complained but agreed. After introducing herself to Emily, Hitch had taken a seat and pulled out her notebook and pen.

"State your name and occupation," the sheriff said after giving the date and adding that the state medical examiner was also here.

As soon as Emily finished, he asked, "Were you having an affair with Humphrey Collinwood?"

Her eyes widened in alarm. "No." She shook her head adamantly. "We were just friends."

"Friends?" the sheriff asked mockingly.

Hitch shot him a warning look. "Would you please describe your friendship, Miss Sutton?"

"He came into the café a lot of mornings."

"Without his wife?" the sheriff said.

"He said she wasn't an early riser." Emily smiled. "He said he liked to watch the sun rise and that he loved the café's waffles. He always ordered the same thing. He said his wife didn't cook."

"What else did he say about his wife?" Hitch asked.

Emily shook her head and looked away for a moment. "Nothing bad. He just seemed…lonely. I got the impression he needed someone to talk to." She smiled. "I'm a good listener."

"You aren't going to tell me that he didn't talk about his wife, are you?" the sheriff said, ignoring Hitch's look.

"It wasn't like he complained about her. He didn't. I just got the feeling that they didn't have a lot in common. He'd been looking for a horse for her birthday. She loved pintos and paints. My cousin up in Malta raises them, so I put him in touch with Tom."

"We'll need your cousin's contact information," Hitch said.

"I can give it to you. He'll tell you."

"Did Mr. Collinwood buy a horse for his wife's birthday?" Hitch asked. "I understand she didn't ride much."

"He did," Emily said. "He showed me a photograph. It's a beautiful horse. He was hoping that his wife would love it and that they could ride together. He'd hoped it would encourage her to ride more."

"Humphrey ever come over to your house?" the sheriff said, drawing her attention to him again.

"Just to drop off a thank-you present, that's all. It was my day off and he said he had to fly out the next day for a board meeting. He wouldn't even come inside."

"What did he give you?" Hitch asked.

She beamed, clearly pleased with the gift. "It was a miniature carousel. I'd mentioned once that one of my happiest memories was riding a paint horse on a carousel." She blushed, her joy in the gift from Humphrey reddening her cheeks.

Hitch studied her for a moment, seeing her embarrassment and so much more. "You liked him."

She nodded. "He was nice. He reminded me of my father." She looked to the sheriff. "My father died in Afghanistan. He was a marine."

"You more than liked Humphrey Collinwood," the sheriff said.

Her head came up, eyes widening. "No. He was just nice to me. He was married. He would never have..." She shook her head and lowered it again. "He told me how much he loved his wife. That's why he wanted to surprise her with the horse. He said he was trying to find a way to make her happy in Montana."

"Tell me about the phone call you got from his wife, Rachel Collinwood," Hitch said, surprising both Emily and the sheriff. "She called you the morning of the shooting."

Emily nodded, tears in her eyes. "She thought we were having an affair. I told her we weren't, but she wouldn't listen. She was upset and wouldn't believe me." She paused for a moment. Then said, "Tell me that isn't what they argued about, what…got him killed."

"It wasn't," Hitch said before the sheriff could speak. "You aren't to blame." She stood. "I think we've heard enough."

"Maybe he didn't have an affair with the waitress, but he wanted to," the sheriff argued after Emily Sutton left and Hitch had returned from making a call out in the hallway.

Hitch shook her head at him. "You heard her. Humphrey Collinwood loved his wife. He was buying her a horse for her birthday. I called Emily's cousin. Humphrey Collinwood paid for the horse. It was going to be delivered on his wife's birthday next week. Does that sound like a man who's having an affair?"

The sheriff clearly refused to give an inch. "Sounds like a guilty conscience to me."

Hitch sighed and left before she said something she'd regret.

Back in her hotel room, she watched the videos the sheriff had sent her again of both Ford Cardwell's statement and then Rachel Collinwood's. She was even more suspicious of why Humphrey Collinwood hadn't said a word during the altercation. Ford had heard only Rachel's voice. It was almost as if the husband hadn't been there. And yet she hadn't found any needle marks on the body.

"What are we looking for?" the lab tech asked when Hitch called to request more tests to be run on the samples.

"Run the whole drug spectrum," she told her. There had to be a reason Humphrey Collinwood hadn't spoken at all during the time Ford had been listening in on the alleged pocket-dialed phone call. If he wasn't already dead, then he had to have been drugged or incapacitated in some way.

"Can you put a rush on it?" Hitch asked. "I'm worried that my suspect will make bail tomorrow and that might be the last time we ever see her."

"You're that sure she's a flight risk?"

"If she thinks she might be doing time, she'll run."

The lab tech asked, "Anything in particular you're thinking you're going to find?"

"Something that would debilitate a two-hundred-pound male. Or possibly enrage one. I'm betting it's the first—if there was a drug in his system at the time of his death. Look for something…unusual." Rachel wouldn't have used anything she thought would show up in a normal drug sample taken during the autopsy.

"That is the whole spectrum," the lab tech said with a laugh. "I'll see what I can do."

Hitch disconnected and sighed. She doubted she was going to be able to sleep. She'd talked to the doctor earlier. Rachel Collinwood would be released from the hospital and arraigned tomorrow. If the judge gave her bail, then the woman would be free. Rich, as well. The judge would confiscate her passport, but any fool knew how easy it would be for a woman with her resources to get one in another name and slip the loop.

Except Hitch was determined that wasn't going to happen if she had anything to do with it.

The question was, where did Ford Cardwell fit into all this once Rachel was free?

She'd seen the haunted look in his eyes. After what he'd been through, what was it doing to him being this involved with an old flame suspected of murder?

Hitch guessed she would know tomorrow. What would Ford do once Rachel was out on bail? Go back to Big Sky?

He was Rachel's defense, her proof that she feared for her life. Would she want to keep him around? Now that he'd given his statement to law enforcement, she really didn't need him anymore.

All Hitch's instincts told her that the woman was through with Ford. He'd played his part and now he needed to walk away. But would he? It would depend on how deep he was in all this.

Either way, if Hitch was right, Ford was in a very dangerous place. She wondered if he was beginning to realize it. Pulling out her phone, she called his cell phone number.

"It's state medical examiner Henrietta Roberts. Hitch? Where are you?"

It seemed to take him a moment, as if he had to place her name. "At the hospital."

Of course he was, she thought. "I need to talk to you again."

"It's late. Can't this—"

"No, it can't wait," she said. "I'm on my way. How about we meet in the waiting room on Mrs. Collinwood's floor?"

It took her longer to get there than she'd planned. When Hitch pushed open the door to the waiting room, she stopped cold with the realization that she'd caught Ford in an unguarded moment. He looked so miserable that she knew instinctively that it had more than something to do with this case. She couldn't imagine the trauma he'd gone through when he was overseas with the military. She knew a little about survivor's remorse and wondered if that wasn't playing a part in this.

Did she still believe that he'd been in on this with Rachel? The woman had needed an accomplice to pull it off. She hadn't beaten herself and neither had Humphrey Collinwood. Whoever had helped her kill her husband had to be as cold-blooded as she was. Or he'd gotten himself into something he now regretted. As miserable as Ford looked, she feared he might be that man.

Right now, sitting there in this room alone, he looked like what she realized he was. A broken man. Her heart hurt for him. She wanted to go to him, take him in her arms, mend every broken part of him. The emotions surprised her, especially with him so deeply involved in this case.

But she pushed those emotions down. She had to come at him again. It felt cruel, but she had to do her job. He was involved one way or another. Maybe it had only been when Rachel had "accidentally" called him in the middle of her life-and-death situation. Or maybe long before that.

Either way, Hitch had to get to the truth.

She cleared her voice and Ford looked up, a shield coming back up as he quickly rose to his feet. "Why don't we step into the doctor's office again? It will be more private."

He looked as if he'd rather have a root canal, but he came with her.

Again, she turned on her phone to record their interview. After she'd entered the date, time and who was in the room, she said, "I'll tell you what's bothering me. It must be bothering you, too. Why didn't Humphrey speak during the phone call?"

"I have no idea, like I told you. The call wasn't that long."

"It was actually longer than you think. During that time, the only voice you heard was Rachel's. Where were you again when you got the call?"

"I was up in the mountains." He glanced away. He was definitely hiding something.

"What were you doing in the mountains? Hiking, fishing—"

"Just driving around. It's been a long time since I've been back in Montana. I just needed some time to myself."

"So you were alone." A nod. "What was your first thought when you heard—" she checked her notes "—a scream?"

He seemed to think about it. "I realized it was a woman in trouble, but I had no idea who it was. I hadn't checked to see who the call was from. I tried to get her to answer me."

"But she never did?"

"That's when I realized it must have been a pocket dial."

Hitch gave it a minute. "You didn't recognize her voice?" He shook his head. "Once you heard her say her husband's name, you must have been shocked."

"More than you can know," he said. "I couldn't believe it was Rachel and that the man she was begging not to hurt her was Humphrey. I still can't believe it."

"Neither can I," Hitch agreed. "What would you say is your relationship to Mrs. Collinwood?"

"I don't have a relationship with her."

"Because you hadn't seen or talked to either of them for fifteen years, since their wedding, right?"

"No. Not until we reconnected through social media a few weeks ago." He looked as if he wanted to say more but had stopped himself.

She raised a brow. "I believe you said in your statement that he was your best friend, and yet the three of you went fifteen years without talking or seeing each other. Something must have happened. Did he realize you were in love with his wife?"

He opened his mouth, closed it and opened it again. "Are we back to this?"

"You dropped everything to come running when she needed you. This sounds like your feelings run deeper than that of an old friend from college whom you hadn't even been in contact with for fifteen years."

His laugh was edged with bitterness. "I didn't have a lot going on when I got the call."

"You still care about her."

"That's not a crime. Look, she called *me*. Check her phone records. I was miles from here."

"Can you prove that?"

He started to say something but stopped and shook his head. "I told you. I was up in the mountains outside Big Sky."

"Did anyone see you?" she asked.

"Not that I know of."

"Then you raced here to save a woman who you hadn't seen in fifteen years."

"If you must know, she saved me." He looked away, then met her gaze. She saw his jaw muscles bunch. "I was about to drive off a cliff." He must have seen her shock. "I'm apparently suffering with PTSD—at least I have all of the symptoms. It was stupid and I regret even considering what I almost did. But I was only yards from the edge of the cliff, driving too fast in my pickup, when I got the call." He exhaled gruffly. "Happy?"

For a moment, she didn't know what to say. "You think she saved your life."

"That's what I thought at the time." He shook his head. "I don't know if I would have hit the brakes or not if my phone hadn't rung." He looked away again.

"I'm sorry." She realized this explained so much. If he thought she'd saved his life that day… "Do you still feel that she saved your life?"

"I don't know how I feel. All of this…" He raked a hand through his hair.

"Do you deny you have feelings for Rachel Collinwood?"

He chuckled. "I care what happens to her. But none of that has anything to do with what happened. I told you.

I only recently reconnected with Rachel. That's how she had my number."

"When was the last time you reconnected with Mr. Collinwood?"

He looked down at his feet. "Years ago, just like I told you."

"At their wedding?"

He nodded, a muscle in his jaw tightening.

There was something there she couldn't put her finger on. Whatever had happened at the wedding, though, was the key. "When you and Mrs. Collinwood reconnected recently, did she mention any conflict in her marriage?"

"It wasn't that kind of *reconnection*," he said. "We didn't share anything more personal than phone numbers."

"She was the one who contacted you? So you're on social media."

"One of my nieces insisted on signing me up. I hardly pay any attention to it."

"Until you saw a friend request from Rachel. But after you shared your number, you didn't call her?"

"No. I doubt I would have. She was married and a lot of water had flowed under that bridge."

Hitch nodded, confirming her suspicions about whatever had happened at the wedding. But did it pertain to the murder? It could be simply because Ford Cardwell had never gotten over the woman and had to distance himself from the two of them. Had Rachel known about his crush on her? Of course, Hitch thought. That was why she'd called him. "But here you are, coming to her defense."

"I came here to tell the sheriff what I heard during the phone call, that's all."

"You also said you came to Big Timber to make sure Rachel was all right."

When he didn't answer, she stared him down until he

said, "Why are you trying to make something more out of this than it is?"

"Because Humphrey Collinwood is dead and I want to know why." She studied him openly for a moment.

He sighed, sounding worn out. "I want to know, as well. Maybe I want to know more than even you do. But other than the phone call, that's my only involvement in all this."

She wondered if he actually believed that. "Have you ever heard of a case of domestic homicide involving a husband's shooting where the wife put the gun outside the house because she was afraid he would use it on her?"

"I'm not familiar with any domestic homicide cases," he said impatiently.

"The wife got off because it appeared she hadn't planned to kill him. And yet she ran outside, knowing the gun was there."

Ford shook his head. "You really do think that Rachel took a beating so she could kill her husband. That would mean that she set this all up."

She heard something in his voice. The idea wasn't a new one for him. He was wondering the same thing, but afraid to admit it. "Humphrey Collinwood is a very wealthy man, but I think you know that. Did you also know that Rachel signed a prenuptial agreement that she couldn't benefit from that wealth if they divorced?"

"I didn't know anything about their…marriage arrangements."

"Dead, she walks away with everything the two have accumulated since the marriage, which is no small amount. Had she divorced him, she could have gotten half of whatever their high-priced lawyers didn't take. In other words, a whole lot less, and it could have been years before she got her share if there was a long legal battle, since his business is tied up with his father's."

She watched him grind his teeth but he said nothing.

"Here's what bothers me. Other than the huge coincidence of her pocket dialing you in particular, you didn't hear him threatening her on the phone. Normally in an argument like the one you thought you overheard, the husband would have been saying something as he attacked his wife. Also, why did she have the gun with her in the kitchen? If she was really afraid for her life, why not leave? Why not call 911? Because she needed him dead to get the money."

He shook his head. "What if it was exactly what it seems and Humphrey was beating her?"

"Do you really believe that?"

"I don't know what to believe, but I'm starting to wonder if Bart got to you. He wants his brand of justice and he has the money to buy it. And if I know him, which I do, he wants Rachel to pay for shooting his son. Did she really believe that Humphrey was going to beat her to death? I don't know. You're the one with all the answers. Not me." He got to his feet. "This interview is over." With that, Ford Cardwell stomped out.

Chapter Twelve

Ford walked away from his interrogation by the medical examiner feeling angry, scared and confused again. As if he hadn't been all of those since he'd answered his phone and heard a woman screaming. All of this felt…complicated. Complicated like Rachel herself.

Since the phone call, seeing her, overhearing her and Shyla talking earlier, one thing had become clear to him. Love was often blind. His certainly had been. This had made him see Rachel more clearly than he ever had before. The thought almost made him laugh. The shine had definitely come off those old feelings he'd had for her back in college.

Did he have his doubts about her story? Hell, yes. He kept remembering how completely awestruck Humphrey had been with her. Even though Humphrey had known that she'd married him for his money, he'd still loved her passionately, blindly, unconditionally. So what had happened? Whatever it was, it had destroyed not just their marriage, but their lives.

He'd come to the hospital to see Rachel. But after his interview with Hitch, he didn't feel up to it. As he started out of the hospital, though, he received a text from her. Need your help. Rachel. XOXO. Hugs and kisses, followed by a smiley face.

As he pushed open her door, he heard her on the phone.

She sounded…happy. The moment she saw him, she quickly disconnected.

"You're in a good mood," he said to her, hating that the medical examiner's suspicions had only made him aware of his own. Her injuries aside, her cheeks were flushed and she was the old Rachel, the one who turned heads when she walked past. It was as if she'd forgotten what had happened not all that long ago, ending with her killing her husband.

"That was my attorney on the phone," she said, smiling. "He said I will be booked tomorrow, but once I'm arraigned, he thinks he can get me bail so I won't have to spend any time in jail. That is such a relief."

"I'm so glad to hear it," Ford said. If her attorney really thought he could get her bail, then he must think the evidence to support her case was sufficient. Did that mean she was innocent? Would a jury see it that way?

"What can I do to help?" Ford asked, noticing that the bruising on her face was more pronounced even though her cuts and abrasions appeared to be healing.

"The sheriff took my clothing as evidence," Rachel said. "I can't show up in court in a hospital gown. I need something to wear."

Ford hadn't thought of that. Of course she would need clothes. He'd been feeling so helpless since he'd arrived here. Now there was actually something he could do to help. "I can buy you whatever you need."

"No, that's really sweet, but I prefer my own clothes since you can't get anything decent to wear in this town. Would you mind going out to the house?"

This was definitely the old Rachel, he thought, feeling more of the shine come off his infatuation with her. He didn't want to see her house, where she and Humphrey had lived until…it ended.

She gave him a pouty look he remembered so well when

she'd wanted something. "It's a terrible inconvenience, I know."

"I don't mind." It felt like the least he could do.

Brightening, she smiled a wide smile, even though it seemed to hurt her to do so. How many times had she turned that smile on him back in college? The medical examiner had asked if Rachel had known how he'd felt about her all those years ago. He looked into her blue eyes. This time when his heart ached, it had nothing to do with an old crush. Of course she knew. Wasn't that why the medical examiner questioned why she'd called him even accidentally?

"I just want to look my best tomorrow in court." The smile instantly disappeared, replaced with tears. "I look awful enough after what Humphrey did to me."

It was so like Rachel to worry about her looks at a time like this. He wanted to laugh at how he'd romanticized coming to her rescue. Had he really thought that her call had been fate? That she'd saved his life? That if anyone could bring him back to life, it would be this woman he'd fantasized about for so long?

"Ford, I don't know what I would have done without you," she was saying. She held his gaze for a long moment before she reached for the pad and pen on the nightstand next to her bed. He wondered why she hadn't asked Shyla to do it for her. Then he felt guilty for even questioning it. Hadn't he told her he would do anything for her?

"I've made a list of what I need from my closet. I put the passcode on there so you can get in."

"That won't be necessary." He turned to see Hitch had come into the room. "I'd be happy to take Ford out to the house to get what you need. They've finished cleaning for your return and I have the passcode to get inside."

"I don't need you to come along," he said quickly. "I can handle it."

"I want to check something out there anyway," the medical examiner said. "We can go now. Unless you have some-thing else you have to do," she said to him.

She knew he had nothing he had to do. "No. Now's fine." He shifted his gaze back to Rachel in time to see dislike written all over her face. Her jaw was tight. Ice glittered in her blue eyes. She quickly changed her expression.

"Perfect," she said and handed him the list before grab-bing his hand. Her hand was as cold as her eyes as she smiled up at him and said, "I owe you. Thank you again."

"I'll wait for you in the hallway," Hitch said and left.

Rachel let go of his hand as she stared after the medi-cal examiner. "That woman." She shook her head. "She scares me."

Ford nodded. "She scares everyone."

"No, she has it in for me. I can tell. She's questioned me repeatedly. Is that her job?"

"I think in this instance it is." He wasn't sure if he should tell her Hitch's suspicions. But didn't she have a right to know what she was up against? "From what I hear, she has free rein. The governor apparently asked her to look into your case. At least that's what I overheard when I was down at the sheriff's office."

"Bart's doing, no doubt." Rachel's jaw tightened again, muscles bunching before she unclenched it. "If he gets his way, I'll go to the electric chair."

He could have told her that Montana didn't have an elec-tric chair, but the state still had lethal injection—though it hadn't been used for a while, as far as he knew.

"It's so unfair." She touched the small new bandage on her cheekbone and winced. "It doesn't matter what his son did to me, not just that night but others." She looked away as if embarrassed.

"Why didn't you leave him?" Ford asked impulsively. "If he was hurting you…"

When her blue eyes met his again, they were swimming

in tears. "Because I loved him and I thought…" She shook her head. "He was always so sorry afterward and so sweet for a while until…he wasn't." She covered her face with her hands for a moment. "I still can't believe he's dead. All of it just seems like a bad nightmare. I keep waiting to wake up."

"I know." He felt the same way. "I better go. I'll get everything on the list," he said, carefully folding the paper and putting it into his shirt pocket. "I'll bring the clothes back tonight so you'll be ready in the morning."

"I'll never be ready for what I'm going to have to face tomorrow. Why do I have to prove anything? Can't they look at me and see…?" She shook her head. "How could this be happening? I'm the real victim here. Our judicial system is so messed up that a woman can't defend herself against a husband who's trying to kill her?"

He didn't know what to say. "You rest. I'll see you later."

Out in the hallway, Hitch was leaning against the wall, waiting for him.

On the drive out to the Collinwood Ranch, Hitch could tell that Ford was still wary of her as if she was the enemy. She'd seen enough from the doorway of Rachel Collinwood's hospital room, though, to see how the woman manipulated him. The question was, how long had she been playing him?

As the huge rambling house came into view, Hitch saw that all the lights in the entire house must be on. She suspected a person could see it from space. The cleaners must have left the lights on. Hitch knew that she hadn't turned them on.

The crime scene tape had been removed since the last time she was out here. The sheriff had told her that he'd hired cleaners with Rachel's permission. Hitch parked and glanced over at Ford. He was staring at the house, looking a little dumbstruck. "Nice digs, huh."

He said nothing as he opened the passenger-side door and stepped out. She followed, curious what he was going to think of this house and the way Rachel and Humphrey had been living.

Once inside the house, she asked, "Would you like to see where it happened?"

"No," he said, glancing toward the kitchen and then looking away as he removed his Stetson.

She saw that he had the list Rachel had given him in his other hand. He seemed to be in a hurry to get this task finished. "You've never been here before?"

His gaze shot back to her. "No. I already told you—"

"It was just a question."

He shook his head. "No question is just a question with you, State Medical Examiner Roberts, and we both know it."

"Please, call me Hitch."

"Are you always so suspicious of people's motives, Hitch?" he asked.

"It comes with the job. Getting to the truth isn't always easy."

"Whom are you kidding?" he said. "You've already made up your mind about this case."

"What makes you think that? Just because I'm suspicious?"

"No," he said with a laugh. "You were suspicious of Rachel right from the very beginning. Admit it."

"Not right from the very beginning."

"Then when?" he demanded.

"If you must know, it was the phone call. I have trouble with coincidences."

"They happen."

She smiled and nodded. "But did it happen this time? The fact that it wasn't just any number she happened to call has to make a person wonder. Calling a man who she knows is still in love with her—"

"I'm not still in love with her."

He sounded adamant about that. "No?" she asked in surprise.

"Can we please get this over with?" he asked, his voice cracking with anger. "You're wrong about me. Humphrey was my friend. If I thought for a minute that she'd somehow set the whole thing up so she could murder him…"

"What would you do, Ford?" Hitch asked. "Walk away?"

"Yes," he said. "And not look back—after I was sure that justice had been done."

She studied him for a long moment. She thought of what she knew about his military career, the man who'd risked his life to save the men on his plane. She believed him. "I suppose we'd better get to that list of yours," she said, turning to lead the way down the hall to Rachel's massive walk-in closet. "I figured you'd need my help to find whatever she's planning to wear tomorrow."

"I think I can manage, thank you."

She laughed. "You haven't seen her closet yet."

As they reached the master bedroom, Hitch walked in and stopped to look back so she didn't miss Ford's reaction. He tried to hide it, but she could tell from his expression that he was taken aback at the size and splendor of the place.

"The closet is this way. They also had separate bathrooms." She walked into the closet with its sitting area. The walls around it were full of clothes, shoes, purses, coats. It looked more like an upscale department store. Hitch wondered if a person could wear all of this apparel even in a year.

"Some people would kill to keep this kind of lifestyle,"

she said, baiting him in the hopes of getting an honest re-action out of him.

"So Rachel's guilty because she married well?" Ford said.

Hitch turned to look at him, pleased that she'd ruffled his feathers. "She's guilty if she orchestrated what happened here in order to kill her husband for his money. I'm suspicious for the same reasons you are."

"I didn't say I was suspicious." He raked a hand through his thick dark hair. He wore it longer than usual and wasn't used to it, she thought, because this wasn't the first time she'd seen his long fingers raking through it. It certainly wasn't the military cut she'd seen in the photos she'd found of him during his distinguished career.

"You didn't have to say you were suspicious," Hitch said.

He sighed. "What about proof? Don't you need that?"

She met his gaze. "Of course. Proof goes both ways. She could still surprise me. The call could be a coincidence and she could have killed her husband in self-defense." She saw that he hadn't expected that. What she didn't say was that from experience, she knew that Rachel wouldn't surprise her. All her instincts told her that the woman was guilty as hell.

But she could use Ford's help, so she didn't share that detail with him. Rachel trusted him because she believed she could control him. It was Hitch's hope that the woman would lower her guard and make a mistake. Ford was an honorable man. He'd proved that. What would he do if he found out that Rachel had murdered her husband in cold blood? Walk away like he had fifteen years ago? Not until he'd seen justice done, he'd said.

Which was why Hitch was more worried about what Rachel would do if Ford suddenly became more than dispensable. If he became a liability... The thought made her shudder. If Ford found out the truth about Rachel, it could get him killed.

Rachel had no intention of going to prison for the rest of her life. And if Hitch was right, the woman had already killed once. To save herself…? Hitch had no doubt that Rachel would kill again.

"So let me help you with the list." Hitch held out her hand and waited until he handed the note to her. Rachel's handwriting was neat, the list organized right down to the smiley face on the bottom that was for Ford. Just like the small heart the woman had drawn on the smiley face's cheek. And the kisses and hugs. She handed the note back. "Why don't you read it to me and I'll find the clothes?" He seemed relieved to let her. "Let's see, first on the list. Was that a white suit with navy piping?" She moved to the suit area. "Nice that she has everything color coordinated. That will make it easier."

"I'll find the pumps she wants," he said behind her as she thumbed through a variety of white suit sets.

It took them a while, but they found everything on the list. As they loaded the items into the largest piece of luggage from the closet, as per Rachel's instructions on the list, Hitch said, "Tell me about Humphrey. You roomed with him for four years at college, were his best friend. Did you ever see any indication that he would do something like this?"

At first, she didn't think he would answer. But as they carried the luggage out to the car—a large suitcase and Rachel's makeup case—he said, "No, I never did. But that doesn't mean—"

"Did he know how you felt about Rachel?" She sensed the heat of his gaze.

"No. Maybe." He shook his head. "Apparently, I'm pretty transparent—at least according to *you*."

She slid behind the wheel and waited for him to climb

into the passenger side. "Why do you think Rachel reached out to you on social media after all this time?"

"She'd heard I was back in Montana. She wanted me to know she was in Montana, too." He looked out his side window for a moment as she started the SUV's engine. Was that when the idea had come to Rachel, the beginning of a plan to kill her husband? "Maybe there was trouble in her marriage and she needed someone she could trust to talk to."

"She doesn't have a friend she could confide in?" Hitch started up the road that would lead them off the ranch. In her rearview mirror, the Collinwood house was dark again—just like the night around them.

"Look, I don't know why she contacted me. Maybe out of nostalgia. Anyway, she has a best friend here. Shyla. Shyla Birch. She's probably the one you should be talking to. She's a friend of Rachel's from college. Shyla should know more about Rachel and Humphrey's marriage than I do."

"Another friend from college?" Hitch said, glancing over at him in surprise. "Did they also only recently reconnect?"

"You make me wish I hadn't said anything."

"You told me because you're worried about Rachel. Like me, you want to know the truth. You're also worried that I might be right."

He shook his head again. "Don't be telling me what I'm thinking, all right?"

"I'm not psychic, but I have good eyesight. Rachel knew about your accident and discharge from the service, didn't she? She caught you when you were…vulnerable, knowing she could count on you."

His expression said she'd hit the nail on the head.

He glanced away quickly and swore. "I understand you digging into Humphrey's and Rachel's lives, but I really wish you would stay out of mine." His voice was rough with emotion.

"I wish I could, but once you got that phone call? Rachel pulled you right into her mess."

"I don't know how many times I have to say this. She didn't mean to call me. She was probably trying to call 911."

"Glad you brought that up. She botched calling 911, but didn't have any trouble doing it after she killed her husband," she said as she drove away from the Collinwood Ranch.

"He was attacking her during the first call," Ford pointed out.

She glanced over at him. His eyes were dark with anger. Or was it worry? "You're right. It could have been just one of those strange coincidences. Then again, some might even call it fate."

"Not you, though," he said, an edge to his voice. "You only believe what you can prove."

She smiled. "Exactly."

FORD WAS GLAD when the ride out to the Collinwood Ranch was over. After seeing the place, he couldn't help but remember what Shyla had told him about how unhappy Rachel had been living there. It was isolated, but so grand. Rachel had once told him that she wanted one day to live in a palace and have so many clothes to wear that it would be hard to pick out something to wear. And yet she'd been miserable.

He couldn't understand it. Now Rachel was in more trouble than he felt she realized. If Hitch and Bart had their way, Rachel would be going to prison for life or worse. Hitch had done her best to make him doubt what he'd heard. Like her, he had his questions. And maybe, if he was being truthful, his suspicions.

Hitch had dropped him off at the hospital. She'd offered to help him with the luggage but he'd declined. "I can handle it, Ms. Roberts."

"Hitch. I'm sure you can," she'd said before pulling away in her patrol SUV.

"Did you have any trouble finding everything?" Rachel asked anxiously when he brought in her large suitcase and cosmetic bag.

"No. Hitch helped."

"Hitch? You're on a first-name basis with that woman?"

He looked at her, unable to miss the razor-blade sharpness of her tone, and saw that she was visibly upset. "What is it you're asking?"

"She wants to put me in prison. She'll do whatever she can to do that—especially if she thinks she can use you against me," Rachel snapped.

"Because I'm your defense?"

She started to say something, but apparently changed her mind, closing her mouth. Her blue eyes flashed with anger. He watched her try to gain control again. She hadn't expected him to stand up to her.

"I'm sorry," Rachel said quietly. "I know none of this is your fault. It's just that she keeps trying to dig up something against me."

"There's nothing she can dig up, right?" he asked.

"No. But she said she had to go back out to the house. What was that about?"

"I don't know."

"She didn't search the place or act like she was looking for something?"

"No, not that I saw," he said and felt himself frowning. "What would she be looking for?"

"I don't know," Rachel cried and busied herself smoothing the sheets over her. "All of this is so terrifying."

He said nothing, studying her. Even with the years that had passed, he realized with a start that he still knew this woman. While he'd definitely put her up on his own pedestal all those years ago, he didn't think she'd ever truly hidden her flaws from him. He'd just forgotten how she'd used her smile to always keep him on her side when she and Humphrey had an argument.

Ford thought of what Hitch had said, insinuating that he'd put all the blame on Humphrey—rather than Rachel—for forcing him to walk away from the two of them after the wedding.

"I didn't mean to snap at you," Rachel said into the heavy silence that had fallen between them.

"You're under a lot of stress."

"I am," she said, sounding close to tears. "I never thought my life would turn out like this."

"I'm sure Humphrey didn't either." He hadn't meant it the way she'd taken it. Her shocked look, the color that shot to her cheeks, the horrified widening of her eyes, made him regret it.

"You blame me, too?" she said, her voice breaking.

"No, no. That isn't what I meant. I don't know what happened that day. But I do know that Humphrey would never have wanted it to go so wrong."

She turned her head away, clearly dismissing him.

"I should go," he said and started to move toward the door. "I'll see you in court tomorrow."

As he stepped out of the room, he felt that familiar melancholy take hold of him. He fought to pull himself out of it. He had to see this through. But that thought didn't lift him back up—not the way it had at first.

He considered the woman he'd left in the hospital room as he left. Hitch thought he was a fool. She didn't think he saw through Rachel's helpless act. Rachel was scared, no doubt about that. But the woman had never been helpless. Was that why she'd had a loaded gun? When had she learned to fire it? Or had she just gotten lucky with that one shot?

Ford swore under his breath. Hitch and her suspicions

had him doubting everything. Rachel had always used her feminine wiles to get what she wanted. But not all women did. The thought made him think of Hitch.

So what if Rachel loved the finer things in life. That didn't make her a murderer. And Humphrey? Ford couldn't help but remember when they'd been best friends. Like brothers. Had Humphrey turned into a violent man who'd done so much damage to his wife's face and taken a bullet for it?

With a start, Ford realized that if he were a juror at Rachel's trial, he might find her guilty of setting this whole thing up to kill her husband for his money. Never in his life would he have thought Rachel—the woman he'd once adored—could be a cold-blooded killer. Until now. And he hated himself for even considering it.

Chapter Thirteen

The courtroom had a chill to it this morning, Ford thought as he took a seat on the hard wooden bench a few rows back. Bart was already seated in the row behind the prosecutor. Ford watched the two talking quietly. They separated quickly when Rachel was brought in to take her seat alongside her attorney.

Attorney Denton Drake was an elderly man with a pleasant smile and a fatherly attitude toward Rachel, Ford noted. He wondered if the lawyer was good at his job. Rachel needed all the help she could get, if the medical examiner and Bart Collinwood had anything to do with it.

But Rachel was a worthy opponent. In her expensive, beautifully cut white suit, she looked beautiful. Her blond hair was up, gold gleamed at her earlobes and her bandage had been removed. He noted that she hadn't used the makeup he'd brought to the hospital. Her attorney's idea to let the judge see the damage Humphrey had allegedly done? Or had it been Rachel's idea?

Ford saw Hitch drop off some papers for the prosecutor before she spotted him and, to his irritation, slid in beside him.

"Good morning," she said quietly.

"Is it?" He caught her scent, clean and understated, just like the woman herself. He scrutinized her more closely. All the other times he'd seen her, she'd been dressed in either canvas overalls and jacket with *Medical Examiner* stenciled on the back or jeans and a T-shirt with a jean jacket. Her auburn hair was usually pulled up in a knot at the back of her neck. But this morning she wore a nice-fitting gray suit with a white blouse that was opened at the neck. Her hair fell below her shoulders in a cascade of burnished curls. The woman was striking. He wondered how he hadn't noticed it before.

She turned those tropical green eyes on him and seemed to be taking him in with the same kind of scrutiny. He'd had to go shopping for clothes since he'd left in what he'd been wearing, so his jeans and Western shirt were new. His boots were old ones he'd left at his father's place years ago.

"Didn't get much sleep, huh," she said, studying him with that observant look of hers.

Before he could comment, she shifted her gaze to Rachel, who was talking animatedly to her lawyer. "Looks like she got more sleep than either of us."

"The sleep of the innocent," he said.

Hitch chuckled, but then turned serious. "Does that mean you aren't innocent? Or maybe you have more of a conscience?"

Ford shook his head. He wasn't up for another word battle with this woman. He was relieved when the bailiff called out "All rise!" and the judge came into the room. Her Honor signaled for everyone to sit. "Let's make this quick. I have a lot on the docket today."

Ford listened as the charges against Rachel were read. Deliberate homicide? The judge asked how she pleaded and Rachel said, "Not guilty, Your Honor."

Her attorney asked that she be given bail since this was a justifiable use of force. "She has already surrendered her passport and isn't a flight risk, Your Honor. She has agreed not to leave the state, but simply return to her home north of town."

The prosecutor rose from his chair. "Mrs. Collinwood has sufficient assets to get herself another passport in another name and disappear. I don't think the lack of her passport would stop her."

Rachel's attorney argued that she had no priors, had been a model citizen and that most of the assets were in her husband's name and not accessible to her due to a prenuptial agreement she'd signed. "Mrs. Collinwood is the victim here, Your Honor."

The judge banged her gavel. "Bail is set at five million."

Rachel gasped loudly. In the stunned silence that followed, she turned to look back at Ford, tears in her eyes. He felt that old familiar pull at his heart in spite of everything. But it was accompanied by nausea. He honestly didn't know the truth about her and feared he might never know.

"WHAT WILL HAPPEN to her now?" Ford asked Hitch as Rachel was being led to a jail cell until she could post her bail bond. The courtroom began to fill again. They walked out into the deserted hallway.

"If she can raise enough liquid assets, she'll be released until her trial," Hitch said. "Otherwise, she can post a property bail equivalent to five million dollars."

"If she can't?"

"Then she'll stay in jail until her trial."

"You're that sure this will go to trial?" he asked.

"She killed a man."

"Yes, but—"

"The law doesn't recognize…yes, but."

"What will happen to her if…she's found guilty?"

"During the trial it will be decided if she used justifiable force to stop her husband. If so, she could be charged with mitigated homicide and serve anywhere from two to forty years."

"Forty years!"

"But if the jury finds that she used extreme force that wasn't justifiable, then she could be convicted of deliberate homicide and could be sentenced to life, which is a minimum of thirty years."

He looked sick.

"Or, depending on the judge, she could get ten to a hundred years. We do still have the death penalty in Montana. Lethal injection, though there hasn't been an execution in years."

He clearly couldn't stand the thought. "How is that possible if she was fighting for her life?" Ford said angrily.

"It will be up to a jury and what evidence there is to the contrary."

"Evidence you're gathering against her."

"Only if the evidence is there."

He raked a hand through his hair, looking miserable. "No one is stupid enough to gamble their life for money." She raised an eyebrow, making him furious. "Rachel might be materialistic, but she isn't stupid." He got a smirk at that. "You're wrong. She would have had to know that she might not get away with it."

"Not if she covered all her bets, including making sure you heard enough of the argument that you are now a very large part of her defense. I have to admit, the phone call was pretty brilliant. A medaled war hero just back home? You make a good witness because any jury would see that you're also an honest, honorable man."

He swore under his breath. "You're making Rachel out to be a mastermind criminal and me a saint."

"Most criminals think they're smarter than law enforcement." Her eyes twinkled mischievously. "And I don't think you're a saint. I just think you're a nice guy who fell in love with the wrong woman and has never let himself get over it or the guilt."

"I'm glad you have me all figured out," he said.

She could tell that he was having trouble getting his mind around all this because he didn't think like a criminal. In her job, she'd learned to do just that.

"You still believe she would do this knowing she might go to prison for years?" he said, sounding even more incredulous because he couldn't imagine doing anything like it.

"I'm still on the fence. But it isn't up to me to decide. Once I finish my investigation and provide what evidence I've found to the prosecutor, then it will be up to a jury to make the final decision." She didn't tell him that she'd talked the governor into letting her tap Rachel's phone now that she would be getting out on bail. Hitch couldn't wait to see whom the woman called over the next few days.

"Admit it—you want her to be guilty," Ford said.

"The way you want her to be innocent? No. I just want the truth."

"What makes you think I don't?"

She smiled. "You don't want to believe that she's capable of cold-blooded murder because even if you aren't still in love with her, Humphrey was once your best friend." Hitch started to step away. "Maybe sometime you'll tell me what happened at the wedding. In the meantime, be careful. We have your testimony about the phone call. Your job is done until the trial. Rachel won't be needing you anymore. I don't think you want to stay beyond your welcome or you're going to make her regret calling you."

He shook his head. "You think she used me." Hitch said nothing. "I'm not as blind when it comes to her as you think."

"I hope for your sake that's true, Ford. By the way, someone slid a note under my hotel room door this morning right before I left to come here. You wouldn't know anything about that, would you?"

BACK IN HER ROOM, Hitch considered the note she'd found and bagged as evidence. It was short and to the point: *You need to leave town while you still can.* It had been typewritten, probably on a computer, on plain white paper. She would have it checked for prints, but she wasn't hopeful.

She had ruffled someone's feathers—nothing new there. She didn't think the note was from Rachel, but from someone close to her. Now, who would that be? Not Ford. She'd seen his surprise when she'd asked him about the note.

Spreading out all the evidence she'd collected on her bed back in her hotel room, she went through it again. She was missing something. She could feel it. But she had someone worried. That gave her hope that she was getting close.

Picking up the photos of Rachel Collinwood's injuries that DCI had sent her, she studied them, wondering what it was that was bothering her besides Ford Cardwell.

He was a principled man who believed in right and wrong. Yet he still had feelings for Rachel Collinwood, no matter what he said. Hitch liked him, which made this case even harder. She hated that he was involved and might get in even deeper before it was over. Would he help Rachel cover up her crime, if she asked? Rachel wouldn't ask unless she was desperate, and that was what worried Hitch maybe the most. What would Rachel do if Ford turned her down?

Hitch tried to concentrate on the cuts, bruises and abrasions on Rachel Collinwood's face in the photos. Frowning, she noticed a distinct mark on the young woman's cheek that she hadn't before. Pulling out her magnifying glass, she took a closer look. It appeared to be an odd-shaped bruise, the kind an unusual ring might make. It definitely wasn't Rachel's husband's ring with the traces of her blood and skin on it.

Pulling out the photos she'd taken during the autopsy,

she studied Humphrey Collinwood's ring again. Nothing about it would have made that distinctive bruise. Was there anything in the kitchen that could have made that kind of mark? She studied the photos of the items lying on the kitchen floor and counter. She was becoming more convinced by the moment that the bruise had been made by a ring—just not one worn by the woman's husband.

All along, she'd known that if the murder scene had been staged, Rachel Collinwood hadn't acted alone. The evidence seemed to be piling up. That was what she loved about criminals. They usually made at least one mistake—often more—even with the best-laid plans. If Hitch could find the person who had been wearing this unusual ring…

Her cell phone rang and she saw that it was the lab on the toxicology samples taken from Humphrey Collinwood. "Tell me you found a drug in his system that would have made him immobile," she said into the phone, knowing it would be the last piece she needed to prove her suspicions were true.

Chapter Fourteen

Ford wasn't sure that Rachel would want to see him. When he'd heard she'd made bail and had been released to return home, he'd called her.

"Ford, I thought you'd gone back to Big Sky," she said, sounding surprised he was still in town and annoyingly reminding him of what Hitch had said. "I appreciate everything you've done for me, but there really isn't anything anyone can do now until the trial. Not that you have to come back for that. I wouldn't want to put you through all of this again. It's bad enough I'm going to have to go through it."

She was dismissing him. Both the sheriff and the medical examiner had his statement. It was all Rachel had needed from him, just as Hitch had said.

"What will you do now?" he asked, hating these gnawing doubts that were haunting him. He knew he'd been listening to Hitch and had bought into her suspicions that he'd been a pawn in Rachel's plan to kill her husband. It wasn't a comfortable place for him—questioning whether the woman he'd once loved hadn't just used him, but instead had set him up so she could get away with the killing of his once best friend.

"There is nothing I can do but hope that all charges will be dropped and that it won't even go to a trial," Rachel was saying. "The sheriff seems to think I might have a chance of avoiding any more pain." The sheriff might feel that way. But not Hitch. She would keep digging. "Thanks for calling, though," she said, clearly trying to get off the line.

"You'll let me know what happens?"

"Oh, I'm sure you'll read about it in the newspapers."

And just like that, she disconnected. He knew he couldn't leave town feeling like this. He didn't think he could live with these doubts about her. She couldn't have involved him, setting this all up, knowing how he'd felt about her. He wanted to be wrong in the worst way. He had to see her again.

As he topped the rise, he spotted the ranch house sprawled below him in the evening light. He passed a side road that went back into a stand of pines. A stray thought hit him. What a perfect observation point. A person could park in those trees and see all the comings and goings at the main house.

He hated that he'd even thought such a thing as he drove down to the house. Given the way she'd been on the phone, he doubted she'd be happy to see him, but he couldn't leave until he put his mind to rest. This felt unfinished. Not that he knew what kind of closure he expected to get. Certainly not a confession.

A shadow passed quickly before a large plate-glass window as he pulled up in the front yard. Getting out, he walked up the steps to the massive deck that spanned across the front and side of the house. The views from here were incredible—all rolling hills and green pines and pasture all the way to the mountains. He hadn't noticed when he'd come out here with Hitch. He'd been too uncomfortable in her presence knowing that she was watching him every second.

He paused now, taking it all in, wondering if she appreciated how breathtakingly beautiful it was out here. After ringing the doorbell, he turned again to stare out at the expanse.

Where he lived in Big Sky was different but equally as beautiful. He just hadn't noticed it either since he'd gotten back to Montana. He'd been too much in his own head, too consumed with what had happened when the plane he was piloting went down. Coming here had forced him to feel again, he thought, telling himself he shouldn't have any regrets no matter how this ended.

It took Rachel a while to answer the door. He'd had to ring the bell several more times even though he'd seen her shadow pass that window when he'd driven up. He knew she was home. He'd almost think that she didn't want to see him. Too bad. He wanted to see *her*.

"Ford? What are you doing here?" she said when she opened the door only partway.

"I couldn't leave without telling you goodbye in person."

"Well, isn't that sweet. But you needn't have driven all the way out here." She was standing in the doorway, blocking him as if she didn't want him inside. It made him sad and all the more determined to see what she was hiding.

"I wanted to see for myself how you were doing. I don't like how we left things at the hospital yesterday." She started to say she was fine when he cut her off. "Why don't you invite me in? I promise not to take up too much of your time."

Rachel flushed as if just realizing how rude she was being since he was her alibi—her defense. A fluke, just as he'd thought? Or all part of a murderous plan?

"Of course. I'm sorry," she said, stepping back. "You had sounded on the phone like you were anxious to return home. Come in." She said it loud enough that he felt she was warning someone that they had company. It made him sick inside.

"Are you alone?" he asked, wanting to watch her lie to him.

"Why would you ask that? Of course I am."

He met her gaze, his disappointment in her making him feel even more nauseous. It was true. Over the past fifteen years and probably longer, she'd been the perfect woman in his memory. He'd always imagined her in that dress trying to feed that squirrel. The vision used to make him smile. But apparently the squirrel scene had been a well-planned scheme only to meet Humphrey. Rachel, it seemed, had a talent for staged plots.

"Why don't you come in here?" She motioned toward the kitchen—the same kitchen where she'd shot her husband. "I'll get us something to drink and we can take it out on the deck. It's such a lovely evening." As he followed her into the very white open room, he felt himself cringe. This was where it had happened. Right here. He found himself staring at the floor, imagining Humphrey lying dead there.

"You still like a cold beer, don't you?" she asked, her back to him as she grabbed up some dirty drink glasses and put them in the sink. He'd stopped in the middle of the room and was still staring at the floor, trying not to imagine the gruesome scene.

When she turned, she must have seen his expression. "Are you all right?"

He realized she was standing in front of him holding out a bottle of beer.

"You do still drink beer, don't you?"

He nodded and took it from her. "Rachel, isn't this where—"

Belatedly, she seemed to realize what was wrong with him. She flushed, cheeks hot with anger. "I can't think about that anymore. I have to live here. I can't leave the state. I have to make the best of it," she said, taking her glass of wine and heading for the glass doors. There were two chairs facing the east and a small table between them on the deck. He watched her pick up an ashtray from the table and empty it over the side of the deck railing.

"Are you smoking again?" he asked, feeling shaken by how insensitive she was about all of this.

She shook her head, her back to him. "One of the hired hands stopped by earlier. Nasty habit. Let me get rid of this." She moved past him to return to the kitchen. When she came back out, she had the wine bottle in her hand—a hand she seemed to be fighting to keep from shaking.

He sat down in one of the chairs and watched her slide into the one next to him, exposing a lot of thigh. She wore shorts and a sleeveless top, both in a pale yellow that accented her fresh spray-on tan. There were bruises on her arms that looked like dark fingertips pressed into her flesh. Were they from Humphrey?

"What happened, Rachel?" She looked startled for a moment before he added, "What happened with you and me?"

With a relieved look, she leaned back in her chair and took a sip of her wine.

"Nothing. We've always been good friends. It's my fault I let you walk out of Humphrey's and my life."

"You know I wanted to be more than friends."

She smiled over at him. It wasn't one of her smoldering sunshine smiles.

It held a note of pity that made his heart ache even more. "It was always Humphrey, wasn't it," he said. "From that first day with the squirrel."

"He said it was love at first sight."

"Was that what it was for you?" he asked, suddenly aware of the sweating beer bottle in his hand. He took a drink. It was cold and bubbled all the way down his throat. It was the first sip of alcohol he'd had in a long time.

"I suppose it was love at first sight," she said, not looking at him.

"When did Humphrey…change?"

"Change?" She sounded puzzled by the question as she looked at him and frowned.

Ford met her gaze. "Surely he didn't hurt you at first."

"No, you're right. It started when he was having trouble with his father, the business, you know. He would come home from New York in a bad mood and any little thing would set him off. He knew I wasn't happy here and that upset him. Things just kept getting worse."

"Why weren't you happy here?" he had to ask as he looked out at this beautiful country.

"Are you kidding? After New York City?" She shook her head. "It's duller than dirt out here. He brought me here to punish me."

"For what?"

She shook her head again and sipped her wine.

He looked away, trying to imagine this Humphrey Collinwood compared to the one he'd lived with most of their time at university. There had never been an easier-going man. "I thought I knew him, so it is so hard for me to understand how this could have happened."

"Why are you questioning me about this? Humphrey had a dark side that he hid from everyone else," she snapped. "It's typical of abusers. I suspect his father abused his mother. That's usually how it works."

"You've researched the subject, have you?"

She didn't answer, but he saw her stiffen in anger. Nor did she look at him. He dragged his gaze away, unable to look at her either.

After a few moments, he relented. "I guess most people hide their…dark sides," he said and finally glanced over at her again. "You're different than I remember."

Rachel flipped her hair back, her blue eyes sparking. "You're angry with me because I had to shoot him." She bit her lip. Tears welled in her eyes. "I'll never forgive myself. Is that what you need to hear? I should never have grabbed that gun. I thought that if he saw it, he wouldn't…"

She looked away, wiping at her tears before taking a gulp of her wine.

At that moment, she made him doubt himself. Maybe Humphrey *did* have a dark side. Maybe she *had been* afraid he would kill her. Maybe she *was* here alone. The house was so huge, it probably did take her a while to get to the front door. And the glasses she'd put in the sink? Hadn't she said one of the hired hands had stopped by? It would explain the cigarettes in the ashtray on the deck, as well.

He hated mistrusting her, questioning everything about the young woman she'd been in college, comparing her to the one sitting out here with him right now. The beautiful warm summer Montana evening was like a caress. He realized that, if anything, Rachel had gotten more beautiful. Maybe she was the same young woman he'd known in college. Maybe he was the one who'd changed. Maybe Humphrey had, too. Ford reminded himself that he was a big enough mess without rewriting what had once been the sweetest part of his life, his friendship with Humphrey and Rachel.

And yet he couldn't seem to help himself. "You knew I was half in love with you," he said and met her gaze.

Her expression softened. "I know." She reached for his hand and squeezed it. "I always cared about you, Ford. I wanted the best for you. Humphrey and I never knew why you'd exited our lives like you had right after our wedding. Did you know he tried to reach you numerous times?"

He knew. "You know why I left like I did."

Her light laugh didn't quite come off the way she must have meant it. "You and I should never drink that much together." She turned back to him, something almost coquettish in those blue eyes.

"Neither of us were drunk, Rachel. You dragged me into one of the spare rooms and told me you wanted me to make love to you," he said.

Her lips quirked up on one side. "I believe you kissed me back, and as I remember, that was your hand on my—"

"If someone hadn't tried the door, would you have actually gone through with it?" Would he have? It was something he'd always wondered about even in his guilt over the incident. The memory of it filled him with shame. He'd kissed his best friend's girlfriend and he'd wanted to make love with her. If he could have, he would have stolen her away in a heartbeat. Knowing that, he knew he was no longer Humphrey's best friend and couldn't stand being around the two of them after that.

"We'll never know, will we?" Rachel took a sip of her wine and gazed out at the rolling hills of the ranch.

He put his nearly full beer bottle down on the small table. A breeze blew her long hair into her eyes, and for a moment, she looked like the girl he'd known. "I should go." Getting to his feet, he walked toward the end of the deck that led to where he'd left his SUV. He had no desire to go back through that kitchen.

"Ford!" she called after him.

He turned to look back at her. For a moment, in that soft pale twilight, she looked just as he'd remembered her.

"Thank you."

"I didn't do anything."

"You were here for me when I needed you most. I'll never forget that."

He nodded and started to say it was nice seeing her again. But that would have been a lie. All the pain he'd felt before that phone call seemed like nothing compared to this.

Behind him, he heard Rachel's cell phone ring. Once, twice... She picked up. "Shyla, hi. I'm glad you called." She rose, the chair scraping as she headed back inside the house.

As he passed the front window, out of the corner of his eye, he saw movement. Rachel had lied. She wasn't alone. He wasn't even sure that had been Shyla on the phone.

Chapter Fifteen

"Tell me you found something," Hitch repeated into the phone. If there was a drug in Humphrey Collinwood's system, one that would have made him a walking zombie—

"We ran the entire spectrum of possible drugs," the lab tech said. "I'm sorry. We found nothing."

Nothing? Her mind whirled as she got up to pace her hotel room. She'd been so sure that in order to shoot her husband in the face the way she had, Rachel would have had to subdue him somehow. Otherwise, the reaction of a man who was beating his wife wouldn't have been to just stand there while she pulled a gun. Had he charged her and Rachel got lucky, getting a shot off before he reached her? The marks on his back showed that he'd fallen backward, landing on the broken pottery and glass on the floor.

"Thanks for trying," Hitch said into the phone, hating that she'd wasted the lab's time and her own.

"Wait a minute. Lori's here. She wants to talk to you." She handed over the phone.

"Hitch, I heard about the lab tests you asked to be done. Bradley and I both looked on her computer for anything that might need to be red flagged."

"I'm guessing she was too smart to look up How to Kill Your Husband and Make It Look Like Domestic Abuse."

"No, but something came up that you might find interesting. Mrs. Collinwood did research a common drug used on horses called ketamine."

Hitch sat up, feeling her pulse take off. Bingo. Hitch almost let out a *whoop*, before she caught herself. "But you didn't find it in the drug tests you ran."

"That's because it leaves the system quickly. It works as an anesthesia and is often used on horses. The drug would have been readily available on the ranch. Mrs. Collinwood would have had access to it." Hitch thanked her and quickly got off the phone.

She knew a little about the drug, but quickly looked up the symptoms, especially for large doses. The words leaped out at her.

Blocks sensory perception.

Distortion of environment.

Diminished reflexes.

Muscle rigidity.

Available in a clear liquid or powder form.

"I think I know how she did it," Hitch said to the empty room, unable to hold back her excitement. Unfortunately, it wasn't enough to convict Rachel Collinwood of murder. It was just another piece of a larger puzzle.

Her excitement waned. She had enough to confirm her suspicions—including that odd bruise on Rachel's face. But she didn't have enough for a conviction. Had there been a drug in Humphrey's bloodstream, she could have wrapped up this case. There had to be a way to prove deliberate homicide because all her instincts told her that Rachel Collinwood was lying. She couldn't bear the thought that she hadn't done a good enough job and the woman might get away with murder.

At a sudden pounding at her hotel room door, Hitch quickly opened it. Her mind was already wondering, what now?

"Are you going to let Rachel get away with murdering

my son?" Bart Collinwood demanded as he pushed his way into her room.

"I'm still gathering evidence," she said and hurried to gather up the papers and photographs she had strewn across her bed. She finished and turned to look at him. His face was flushed with anger and grief. Her heart went out to him because she felt his frustration only too well.

"I know my son." He shook his head angrily, looking close to tears. "He would never have laid a hand on her unless…"

She felt her pulse jump. "Unless?"

Bart looked away. "He just wouldn't have."

She knew even before she asked the question. "He'd hit her before?"

"No, no," he said at once. "Not my son."

She saw him swallow and knew.

"My wife and I…." He couldn't meet her gaze.

"Your son saw abuse at home is what you're saying."

His head rocked up. "Not like you're thinking. I lost my temper and slapped my wife in front of him once. Humphrey was horrified. He never forgave me or believed it had never happened before or since."

She wasn't sure she believed him. "You're worried he might have done this," she said.

Bart looked ready to deny it with a vengeance. "You don't know what Rachel is like," he said instead, biting off each word. "She antagonized him, belittled him, did everything in her power to provoke him."

"You're saying she asked for it?" She couldn't keep the edge out of her voice.

"No, that's not what I'm saying," he snapped, looking like a man who wished he'd kept his mouth shut.

"Mr. Collinwood, domestic abuse is often generational."

He let out a curse. "I only lost my temper that one time. I've regretted it ever since."

"It's that attitude—"

"Oh, please. You're just looking for an excuse to let her off. She murdered my son. Humphrey never raised his hand to her. He didn't do this. I'm telling you. I don't know how she pulled it off, but that woman set this whole thing up."

"What if you're wrong and he lost his temper? What if he did do this?"

Bart Collinwood met her gaze and she saw the doubt that she knew had been lurking in there, the fear and guilt. What if he was more like his father than even Bart had realized?

FORD DIDN'T FEEL better as he left the ranch after seeing Rachel. He thought about driving home to Big Sky, but it was dark and late enough that he knew he should wait until morning. Even as he thought it, a part of him wanted to see this all the way through. But rationally, how long was that going to take?

Hitch had her suspicions, but that was about all, from what he could tell. This could go on for weeks or even months before finally going to trial. He got the impression, though, that Hitch wouldn't be on the case that long if she didn't find something fairly soon.

Ford couldn't believe how naive he'd been. He'd thought that by seeing Rachel one last time, he could find some kind of closure. If anything, his visit had made him even more suspicious and upset about the part he'd inadvertently played in all this. Worse, he kept asking himself, "What if Humphrey wasn't an abuser? What if Rachel had lied about everything? Or what if Rachel is telling the truth but goes to prison for thirty years or more for only trying to save herself?"

He honestly didn't know what to believe, except that Rachel had lied to him. His faith in her had been more than tarnished. He'd come here to save her—and had, since his statement about the phone call was on record now. His work here was over. He could get up in the morning and go back to Big Sky. Back to… That was just it. He didn't know what he was going back to.

When he thought about what he'd almost done before her phone call, he felt foolish and embarrassed that he'd let himself fall that low. Maybe it was Humphrey's senseless death and its repercussions, but he knew he'd never try anything that stupid again.

Tonight, though, just the thought of going back to the hotel and packing what little he'd bought since being here was too depressing. He kept thinking about Rachel and the shadow he'd seen at the window. He'd tried to tell himself it had been his imagination. But he knew better. Rachel hadn't been alone. Who was in there with her that she hadn't wanted him to see? The accomplice Hitch suspected had helped Rachel stage the killing?

A set of bright headlights suddenly filled his rearview mirror. He flinched as his gaze went to his side mirror. Only minutes before, there hadn't been another vehicle on this stretch of black two-lane. Not only did the driver have his high beams on, but he was coming up behind him way too fast. The damned fool acted as if he didn't see him. Was the driver drunk?

Ford touched his brakes, but the act seemed to have little effect. He felt his initial alarm grow into fear. The driver wasn't slowing down. He looked to the road ahead. There was no place to turn off the shoulder-less highway. Worse, the highway took a tight turn ahead as it dropped down through the hills and creek bottom.

He didn't realize he'd been holding his breath until the vehicle behind him went flying around him and kept going. His breath came out in a whoosh. He realized that his hands were shaking. He'd been so sure that the driver was going to hit him. Slowing down, he tried to make sense out of the panic he'd felt only moments before. Was this another flashback? No, the driver had wanted him to think he was going to hit him and force him off the road—if not kill them both.

Ford stared after the red taillights. It had been a pickup, but that was all he could be sure of. He hadn't even tried to get the license plate number. Pickups in this part of Montana outnumbered cars and even SUVs. It was probably some ranch hand anxious to get into town to see his girl.

But he knew that wasn't what was bothering him. Had he, for that split second, thought Rachel's accomplice was driving that truck? He had. Because of Hitch's suspicions or his own? He thought about the threatening note she said someone had slipped under her door.

Well, it hadn't been Rachel's accomplice—if there was such a person, he thought with relief.

Until he came around a corner and saw the headlights coming right at him.

Instinctively, he turned the wheel hard to the right and hit his brakes as he went off the road an instant before the other vehicle swept past, only inches from hitting him. He left the pavement, flying off the road and down into the shallow borrow pit.

Something slammed hard against the undercarriage and then he was back up onto the highway before he got his pickup stopped in the darkness. His thundering heart lodged in his throat. He had a death grip on the wheel and was shaking inside.

His gaze quickly went to his rearview mirror, expecting to see the other driver and vehicle crashed in the ditch. But all he saw were taillights before they disappeared over the next rise.

Ford sat for a moment, fighting to catch his breath. The near miss had a tight grip on him, but to his surprise, it didn't call up a flashback. He stared at the empty highway for a moment. His first instinct was to chase down the vehicle. Fortunately, he was thinking clear enough that he didn't. It was long gone. Or maybe it had only gone back to the Collinwood Ranch.

Whoever had come flying around him had been the same pickup that had run him off the road. But did that mean that the person was involved with Rachel? There was only one way to find out.

He did a highway patrol turn in the middle of the empty two-lane and headed back toward the ranch.

Chapter Sixteen

It was getting late. Hitch had been parked in the pines on the mountainside overlooking Rachel Collinwood's house long enough that she'd seen Ford arrive and leave. Soon after that, she'd spotted a pickup kicking up dust on one of the back roads on the other side of the house. Had it come from the ranch house and she'd just missed it? Or had whoever had been driving it parked at a distance and walked up through one of the ravines to the house?

The pickup was so far away and moving at a speed that she doubted she could catch up to it. Had whoever was driving the rig been at Rachel's? If so, the driver had gone to a lot of trouble not to be seen. The accomplice? If so, there probably wouldn't be any more visitors tonight.

She was thinking about leaving her hiding place and going back into town for something to eat when she heard a vehicle approaching. She glanced toward the road into the ranch. No headlights. She watched the dark shape as it headed slowly in her direction. She reached for her weapon.

Setting the loaded Glock next to her right thigh, she waited, curious who was joining her on the side of the mountain. One of the hired hands? Was this secluded spot with the great view a make-out spot? She recognized the pickup even before she recognized the broad shoulders behind the wheel. Ford made several attempts to get his driver's-side door open and had to put one of those broad shoulders into it. What was wrong with his door? she wondered. It was the lawman in her that she noticed such things.

The bigger question was what he was doing here.

As he reached for her passenger-side door, she unlocked it and watched him climb in. "Couldn't sleep?" she asked.

"Probably for the same reason you couldn't," he said. She saw that he'd brought his own binoculars. Had he also brought his own gun? He glanced at hers lying against her thigh, then turned to look through the binoculars, glassing the house below them.

"Seems we both had the same idea," she said.

Without looking at her, he said, "Been here long?"

"Long enough," she said and studied him. "How was your visit with Rachel?" He looked pale even in the dim starlight and she realized there had to be a reason he'd come back after leaving. "Are you all right?"

"I had a close call on the way into town."

"How close?" she asked, feeling her heart do a little bump.

"Close enough to make me question what's going on." He sounded as if that was hard to admit.

"What happened?" She thought she might have to drag it out of him, but he continued after a moment.

"Rachel was acting…oddly. She said she was alone, but I don't think that was true. After I left, a pickup came roaring up behind me and then passed me and kept going over a hundred. I thought it was just some reckless kid until I realized that the driver had gone up the road and turned around and was coming right at me. If I hadn't taken the gully…"

Hitch couldn't speak for a moment. Hadn't she feared something like this might happen? "That's when you sprung your driver's-side door."

"Apparently, since it was fine before that," he said.

"Was it something you said to Rachel?" she asked. "Or something she said?"

He still had the binoculars up, watching the ranch house. "I might have asked too much about Humphrey and the past. Then I saw someone in the house even though she swore she was alone. As I was leaving, she got a phone call. Supposedly it was Shyla, but I'm not sure she was truthful about that either, especially since not too many miles down the road, someone driving a pickup ran me off the road. I know you don't believe in coincidence—"

"That's a lot of coincidences," she said. They were quiet for a long moment. "If Rachel thinks you suspect her and might do anything to recant what you'd heard on the phone…"

"I won't change my story, because it was the truth."

She nodded. "Still, if she thinks you aren't on her side anymore, it could get dangerous." Picking up her binoculars, she studied the house for a moment. Wasn't this what she'd feared might happen? "You need to go back to Big Sky."

He seemed to ignore that. "Is there another way into the ranch besides the main road?"

She lowered the binoculars for a moment to study his face. His binoculars were trained on the house. "Isn't there always, if you know the ranch well?" she said. "You think he came back here?"

"I didn't pass him on the highway."

"About the truck—I'm assuming you didn't get the license plate number."

He shook his head. "Just a set of bright headlights. But as it went flying by, I caught a glimpse of it. Dark colored. Large pickup. Probably a king cab. That's about it. Except it had a large guard grille on the front of it."

It sounded like the pickup that had been parked outside the morgue. "You didn't see the driver?" He shook his head. She could tell the entire episode—from his visit to Rachel, to him coming up here—had shaken him. He had wanted so desperately to believe in the woman he'd loved. Maybe still loved.

"We're probably wasting our time tonight," Ford said. "If you're right, Rachel planned all this too well. She'll know she's being watched. She's too smart to mess up now."

"Maybe," Hitch said. "But if we're right, her accomplice has already gone off script. Him and his recklessness is her Achilles' heel. I suspect it was his stupid idea to scare you earlier. She won't like it. All he's done is make you more suspicious. She can't have any mistakes at this point. She doesn't need a hothead trying to protect her—but then, that's how he would have gotten involved in the first place. He had to think he was saving her by helping her get rid of her husband. Why not get rid of you, as well?"

He lowered his binoculars to glance at her. "Which means the accomplice isn't as smart or as patient and composed as Rachel," he said.

"He's already made one mistake by running you off the road. I doubt it will be his last. Let's just hope that you're smart enough to get out of town before the next mistake the man makes kills you."

He chuckled at that. "I'm assuming that's the way you dispense advice? Did anyone ever tell you that you're a scary woman?"

She laughed. It felt good to laugh. She'd been worried about Ford because he was so dang trusting and because of how he felt about Rachel. After tonight, maybe his eyes were finally open. Hopefully now he would take her advice and go back to Big Sky, where he should be safe. He was a nice guy. She didn't want to see him hurt any more than he had been.

The dark night, the closeness inside her SUV, the slight summer breeze coming in her cracked open window all made her feel strangely vulnerable, as if she had more in common with this man than she could have ever thought.

"You're not the first person to think I'm scary. My ex mentioned it on his way out the door," she said and laughed again. It didn't come off as light as she'd meant it. She could feel his gaze on her.

"I'm sorry."

"Don't be. It was for the best." She glanced at him. "What are you really doing here?"

"Same thing as you. I want to know the truth. I *need* to know the truth since Rachel dragged me into it. Now she wants me gone. I think it's because she's afraid I'm suspicious, and if I think she used me, I might be determined to discover the truth."

"Is she wrong?"

"No," he said.

She stared at Ford. She'd been so sure he was a sheep and Rachel was a wolf leading him to slaughter. She realized she was going to have to reassess what she thought of him. Love could make you blind and stupid, she knew well. But the smart ones paid attention to the red flags. There were always red flags when a relationship wasn't right.

"So the driver of the pickup," he said, looking through his binoculars again. "I figure he's the boyfriend."

"What makes you think her accomplice is a boyfriend?" she asked, pretending that wasn't exactly her thought.

Ford chuckled. "For the same reason you do. If she orchestrated all of this, then she had to have someone she trusted to pull it off. It had to be someone she had wrapped around her little finger. That usually involves money or sex, in my experience. Sex is the cheapest."

She laughed. "You surprise me," Hitch said, leveling her gaze on him.

"I must look dumber than I am."

She shook her head. "Rachel thinks you're still in love with her and will do anything for her."

He chuckled. "Not after my visit this evening," he said

with a grimace. "If she deliberately set Humphrey up to kill him…" Ford looked away for a moment, and she knew he was thinking of the consequences of Rachel's actions if true.

"You know what they say about secrets," Hitch said. "Two people can keep them, as long as one of them is dead. Her accomplice made a mistake tonight by trying to run you off the road. He best watch his back, because I'm betting his days are numbered."

FORD LOWERED THE binoculars and looked at Hitch in the dim light. She had raised her binoculars and was watching the ranch house again. The lights were still on even though it was after midnight. There was a sweet innocence about her face that was at odds with her career choice, he thought, and that determined strength that made her indomitable. "I'm curious. How did you get into this line of work?"

"My dad was a cop. My mother was an attorney. They argued all the time because of their jobs, especially at the dinner table in the evening after work. My brother became a psychologist, my sister a schoolteacher, and I studied to become a medical examiner." She shrugged. "I always liked dissecting frogs in school."

Ford couldn't help but smile. "How does your family feel about it?"

"It makes for interesting discussions on Thanksgiving," she said with a laugh. "What about you?"

"Me?" He shook his head. "Nothing interesting. During my parents' divorce, Dad moved us to Montana. I was just a kid when he and his brothers opened a barbecue restaurant in Big Sky. My uncles, all of them, ended up moving to Montana. My dad's cousin Dana Cardwell Savage lives on a ranch, so I spent a lot of time there growing up."

"You went into the military after college?"

He nodded. "I'd majored in engineering. What I really wanted was to fly."

"And now?"

"Not so much." He picked up his binoculars and scanned the darkness around the house below them on the mountain, desperately wanting to change the subject.

"Have you thought about ranching?" she asked. "It sounds like you enjoyed that."

He hadn't thought about anything. For so long after the crash, the rehabilitation, the end of his military career, he had felt as if he was in a black hole. Rachel had yanked him out of it. He'd always be thankful for that even though he now suspected that she'd had her own reasons for reaching out to him.

Ford thought of Cardwell Ranch and the position his aunt Dana had offered him. He'd thought he'd lost all his enthusiasm for life. He'd been so down, so depressed, so despondent. The doctor's visits didn't seem to be helping the PTSD. But maybe they'd been doing more good than he'd thought.

Because he was beginning to realize that it had been more than Rachel's phone call that had brought him back from the brink. He'd had to hit bottom before he could climb back out. Now here he was.

"I might ranch." Even as he said the words, they surprised him. But he realized they just happened to be true.

HITCH FELL SILENT, aware that something intimate had passed between them. She stared out into the darkness at the house down the mountainside for a few moments.

"You know what bothers me?" Ford asked. "Rachel doesn't seem that heartbroken about Humphrey being dead."

Hitch glanced over at him. "She wouldn't be if she was telling the truth and her husband beat her until she feared for her life and had to protect herself. She also seems to believe that he was having an affair—which he wasn't, according to the woman in question. But the alleged girlfriend did say that Humphrey seemed lonely. He was getting Rachel a horse for her birthday this coming week." She waited for his reaction.

"Doesn't sound like a man who would beat his wife."

Hitch laughed. "The sheriff thinks it made Humphrey look guilty."

Ford lowered the binoculars and looked at her. "He could have been trying to assuage his guilt and make it up to her if he really was abusing her."

"All possible," she agreed as she caught movement out of the corner of her eye and picked up her binoculars again. "Well, how about that? It appears someone is finally making a move."

Hitch pulled out her camera with the telephoto lens and aimed it at the man coming out of the house. Unfortunately, it was too dark to see his face. He'd walked out of the house and was now going around to the back.

She lowered the camera and started the SUV. "I want to see what he's driving." She punched the gas before Ford could move, forcing him to hang on.

"Do you always drive like this?"

"Usually. Am I scaring you?"

"I don't scare that easily," he said, and she sped up.

As they came around the last curve, she spotted the lights of a vehicle racing up the ranch road. "I think I can cut him off down at the highway," she said as she took a side dirt road and increased her speed. He'd asked earlier if there was a back road into the ranch. She'd already checked them all out online, so she had a pretty good idea where the pickup was heading.

They were flying along, bouncing over ruts and bumps. She glanced over at Ford from the corner of her eye. He looked a little green around the gills. "If you're going to throw up, please do it out the window."

"Throw up?" He scoffed. "I can take whatever you dish out."

She grinned at that. "I do love a challenge."

Not far down the road, she hung a right and came roaring up onto the paved highway before hitting her brakes. Looking both to her right and left, she saw no sign of vehicle lights.

"He could have gone the other way," Ford said just an instant before a set of headlights topped a rise and shot toward them.

"Let's see if we can get a make and model of this car," she said as she pulled to the edge of the road and cut her engine and lights. "A license plate would be even better."

A dark-colored pickup sped past at the same time Hitch restarted the SUV and gunned the engine. Her vehicle jumped up onto the highway again, tires squealing as she went after the truck.

FORD FOUGHT BACK the nausea. He would rather die than prove Hitch right by vomiting. His stomach roiled, though. The wild ride was giving him flashbacks of his plane crash—as well as his recent race to the end of a cliff. He felt disoriented and out of control. Sweat broke out on his back as he struggled to separate the events and fight off the anxiety attack.

Taking deep breaths, he stared straight ahead at the two red taillights. The lights grew larger and larger as Hitch closed the distance. He saw that the back of the pickup was covered in mud, making it almost impossible to read the license plate.

"It's a Chevy half-ton pickup. Newer model. Dark blue or gray. Hard to tell with all the dust on it," Ford said, concentrating on the truck rather than the flashbacks that flickered like an old-timey movie in his head. He could smell the smoke, feel the flames licking at him as he fought to get his men out before the plane's gas tank blew.

"Can you read the plates?" Hitch asked.

"Starts with 40."

"Big Timber."

"I think it's 19 after that, but I can't read the rest," he said.

She turned on her blinker and passed the truck, getting the SUV up to over a hundred. "You might want to duck down. If he sees you and recognizes you—"

"I'll take my chances, thanks." His head hurt and he still felt sick to his stomach. Given the vibration of the SUV, he estimated that she had to be pushing the SUV to over a hundred and thirty. They zoomed past the pickup.

"Well?" she asked as she whipped back into the right lane and kept going.

"He was wearing a cowboy hat, so I couldn't see much of his face." She shot him a look, making him more nervous. "The road," he said. "Also, aren't there deer out here at night?"

"Was the man behind the wheel the one who had tried to run you off the road earlier?"

He shook his head. Wrong pickup, he was pretty sure. His head ached. He could hardly think. But he was sure this wasn't the same driver or the same pickup.

"Well?" she asked.

He rubbed his temples. "I don't think so, but honestly, I don't know." He felt as if he had disappointed her.

"We should go back and get your rig," Hitch said, hitting her brakes and doing a highway patrol turn in the middle of the road. Once they were headed in the opposite direction again and slowed down, she said, "Tell me you can do better than that on a description of the man since you're about to get another look at him."

He looked out the windshield as the pickup sped past. "Strong jaw, straight nose. Dark designer stubble. Nice looking. Are we assuming this is the boyfriend? The age looks about right. Maybe a little young for her."

She chuckled at that. "I guess I'll find out once I know who he is."

Chapter Seventeen

It didn't take long for Hitch to match the make and model of the vehicle the man had been driving last night to the partial plate number.

"Who is Lloyd Townsend?" she asked the sheriff when she walked into his office first thing the next morning.

Charley didn't look happy to see her. "Why are you asking about Lloyd?" She waited him out until he finally sighed and said, "He's one of our most respected businessmen in town. You don't want to go messing with Lloyd. Everyone in this town loves him. He's always the first to donate to any cause. Salt of the earth."

"Got it," Hitch said and turned to walk out.

"Hold up there a minute," the sheriff said. "Mr. Collinwood is on my back about his boy's body being released."

"He can take him today," Hitch said and saw Charley's surprise. "I think I have everything I need."

"To convict that poor woman?" the sheriff demanded, an angry edge to his voice.

"If she's guilty, then hopefully yes," Hitch said and left the sheriff's department. As she headed out the front door, she spotted Ford leaning against his pickup as if waiting for someone. She smiled, realizing she was that someone.

"HAVE YOU HAD BREAKFAST?" Ford asked as he pushed off the side of the vehicle and stepped toward her.

"As a matter of fact, I haven't."

"Well, I'm hungry and I don't like to eat alone. Hop in. I'll drive."

He drove the few blocks to the café, neither of them saying anything. Once inside, they sat across from each other in a booth.

"Why do I suspect you have something on your mind besides breakfast?"

He nodded. "I had a lot of time to think last night. I'm not as convinced that Rachel had something to do with me being run off the road." Hitch nodded as if she wasn't surprised. "Did you find the man we saw last night coming out of her house?"

"Might have." She pulled out her phone, tapped in the name and came up with a photo of an elderly man with a thick head of gray hair. "How old would you guess the man was who you saw driving the pickup?"

"Forties maybe. He could have been younger. As you know, I didn't get a good look at him either time."

She turned her phone screen so he could see it. "Could he have been sixty-seven with gray hair and glasses?"

Ford chuckled. "My eyesight is better than that. Who's the man?"

"Lloyd Townsend," she said, putting her phone away. "Clearly not the one driving last night. But it was his truck." The waitress brought them coffee, water and menus, and they both ordered quickly without hardly glancing at their menus.

Ford's mind was on the woman across the table and their surveillance adventure last night. He'd seen another side of Henrietta Roberts, one he rather liked. "I don't think that pickup and driver was the same one that ran me off the road. The more I've thought about it, I think it was just a drunk driver and I was being paranoid."

"That it was a coincidence that this driver showed up

shortly after you left Rachel Collinwood's house? Like the coincidence of her pocket dialing you just before she killed her husband?"

He met her gaze. "What if you're wrong about her? What if we both are?"

Hitch leaned her elbows on the table, giving his question some thought. "Then the lack of evidence will allow her to either walk or get a lighter sentence. She did kill a man. If she truly was an abused wife, she needed to leave him—or in this instance do what she could to get away from him. If she'd hit him with a frying pan, well, she would have had a better chance of getting off. Having the gun makes it look as if she was laying for him."

"What if she was afraid to leave Humphrey?" he asked. "I've looked into this a little, and from what I've read, the highest risk time for a homicide is not when she's *in* the relationship but when she's trying to leave it."

"In order to prove self-defense, she has to prove that she was or at least believed that she was in imminent danger. The problem is that she had the gun. Did she have other alternatives other than to use what could be seen as unreasonable force? That will be up to a jury to decide. Why did she have the loaded gun handy? If she feared they were going to have a knock-down, drag-out fight, why wouldn't she get out of there?"

"Because she felt safe. She had the gun if things got out of control," Ford said. "If he'd beaten her up before, then this time she planned to stop him."

"We can't know what was going through her mind at the moment she pulled the trigger. We might never know."

The waitress brought their breakfast orders and they ate in a companionable silence, until Hitch pushed her plate away and asked, "What do you know about Humphrey's parents? Did he ever mention that they didn't get along?"

"You're asking if Bart was abusive." He frowned. "You

found out something about Humphrey." He could tell that she didn't want to share the information with him.

"Bart let it slip that his son had seen him hit his wife. A slap. Bart swore it was the only time and that Humphrey had been horrified and never forgave him."

Ford groaned as he raked a hand through his hair. "You're thinking father like son."

"It could be that Humphrey mentioned what he'd seen to Rachel. It could have given her the idea. Or he could have been so angry with her…"

"This makes you have doubts," he said, shaking his head. "So your mind isn't completely made up after all." He smiled at her, liking her even more. Not that he wanted it to be true of Humphrey.

She looked at the time on her phone. "I have to go. Thanks for breakfast."

"My pleasure." He watched her leave, wondering how Lloyd Townsend's pickup played into all this.

LLOYD TOWNSEND OWNED a hobby ranch on the Yellowstone River just a few miles from town. As Hitch drove up into the ranch yard, she spotted the pickup she'd seen last night and parked beside it.

Getting out, she walked over to the truck and looked inside, seeing nothing of interest.

"Can I help you?" asked a male voice from the front porch of the house. She hadn't heard anyone come out.

Turning, she considered the elderly man for a moment, before she stepped to the house, stopping at the bottom of the stairs. "I'm Hitch Roberts, state medical examiner." He seemed to be waiting for more. "I'm currently working on a local case. Were you driving this pickup last night sometime after midnight?" She waited, wondering what his answer would be. If he lied, he might be involved. If he didn't—

"No," he said, frowning. "You're sure it was my truck? After midnight?"

She nodded. "It was this truck. Who else might have been driving it?"

Lloyd Townsend rubbed his jaw for a moment before he said, "I suppose one of my sons could have taken it. What's this about?"

"I was hoping the driver of your pickup last night might be able to help me with the case I'm working on. Are your sons around?"

"I believe they're out by the corral behind the house working with one of the horses. You're welcome to go back there. It's just around the side of the house." He made a motion with his right hand and started to turn back inside.

The light caught on his hand from the movement.

"Excuse me—I just noticed your ring," she said as she climbed a couple of steps to take a closer look. Lloyd looked down at his ring and smiled as he held out his hand so she could admire it. "It's quite unusual."

"It's our family crest," he said with no small amount of pride. "Both of my sons wear one. Rather a family tradition. Are you familiar with the history of the coat of arms?"

"I can't say I am," she said, her pulse having jumped when he'd told her that both of his sons also wore the same design of ring.

"Coats of arms were used for centuries to identify a certain family. They were created for the battlefield," he said, clearly warming to the subject. "Other knights couldn't tell who was inside of a suit of armor, so they created symbols to attach to the armor. Not to be confused with the crest, which is only a portion of the coat of arms that was worn above the helmet."

"Fascinating," she said, taking the steps back down the stairs. "Thank you for the information. Oh, by the way, what are your sons' names…?" As she went around the side of the house, she called the sheriff on her phone. "Meet me at Lloyd Townsend's ranch as quickly as you can." She hung up before he could argue. She figured he'd come racing out here, hoping she hadn't upset a town favorite.

As she reached the corner of the outside of the house, she spotted the corral. One of the sons was leaning on the corral fence, while the other was inside it with a large bay he was apparently trying to break.

As she joined the one outside the corral, she climbed up on the fence to watch. It was a beautiful bay being green broke by what appeared to be the youngest son, Paul. Out of the corner of her eye, she saw the cowboy next to her look over.

"You must be John," she said, turning toward him. His father had described him as the oldest and bigger of the two. "I'm Hitch. Hitch Roberts, state medical examiner." She held out her hand, he shook it and she went back to watching what was going on in the corral, even though her mind was on the ring on his right hand. "He seems to know what he's doing."

She was wondering if she could get any of Rachel Collinwood's DNA off it after all this time. The lab wouldn't need much, and with the deep grooves of the ring...

"Paul *should* know what he's doing. He's been at this most of his life. Not that he won't hit the dirt before the day is out," John said with a laugh.

What their father hadn't told her was that Paul was the more handsome of the two. In fact, he was gorgeous, from his muscled lean body to his chisel-cut jawline and the styled stubble covering it. With his hat on, he definitely appeared to be the man behind the wheel of the pickup last night. She could also see how he might turn the head of a married woman—and vice versa.

"You here about a horse?" John Townsend asked.

"Actually, I'm looking for whoever was driving your

father's pickup last night north of town sometime after midnight," she said.

"Don't look at me," John said. "I was in bed by then."

She noticed the wedding band on his left hand. Married. So he'd have an alibi—if he were telling the truth. "Anyone else drive the truck besides you, your father and your brother, Paul?"

"Not that I know of."

"Well, that narrows it down, doesn't it," she said and watched as Paul finished putting the saddle on the bay. He led the horse around the corral a few times before he swung up into the saddle. His behind hadn't touched leather but for a moment before the bay began to buck.

Hitch and John jumped back as the horse tried to knock Paul off by putting him into the corral fence. To his credit, the cowboy hung on longer than she suspected most would have before he and the horse parted ways.

Paul was getting up from the ground and dusting himself off when the sheriff arrived. Hitch went to meet him away from the corral and the two Townsend sons. She could tell Charley was already upset from her call. He was about to get even more upset, she thought. "I need the rings both of the Townsend sons are wearing."

"What the hell?"

"One of them—I suspect the youngest, Paul—paid a visit to Mrs. Collinwood late last night."

The sheriff looked both surprised and confused. "Maybe he was just—"

"Giving her his condolences?" she asked.

Charley spurted for a moment before he demanded, "Why in the hell do you want their rings?"

"For evidence."

"Evidence of *what*?"

"Murder. You do realize, Sheriff, that this is what the

case is about, don't you? Finding out what really happened at the Collinwood Ranch and why Humphrey is dead."

He stared at her, openmouthed. "What are you talking about? You think one of the Townsends—"

"I want to bring Paul in for questioning. The governor has given me the authority to do whatever I have to. But you know them, so I'd prefer you do the honors."

The sheriff let out an angry sigh and stared at his boots for a moment. "If you're wrong about this—"

"I'll take full responsibility."

RACHEL STOOD IN the middle of the kitchen trying to catch her breath. She'd never had an anxiety attack, but she thought this must be what one felt like as she tried to calm herself.

She hadn't recognized the number when she'd gotten the call. For a moment, she'd almost not taken it. "Hello?"

The moment she'd heard the voice, she'd snapped, "Shyla, why are you calling me from some number I don't recognize? I almost didn't pick up."

"I borrowed a phone. I'm at the sheriff's department. I just heard the craziest thing. That medical examiner? She and the sheriff just went out to the Townsend place and confiscated both Paul's and John's rings. Supposedly it has something to do with Humphrey's death."

That was when all the air in the kitchen felt as if it had been sucked out. She'd had to grab the counter to steady herself. "Why would she care about their rings?"

"Beats me. Apparently," she said, lowering her voice, "they're evidence. But evidence of what? Not only that the medical examiner knows that one of the Townsends came out to your place last night. You aren't still—"

"Of course not." She tried to catch her breath. "I thought I heard someone. I was in the tub. Why would he come out here?"

"Why do you think? What if he tells them about the two of you…?"

She groaned inwardly, still fighting the lack of oxygen. She felt as if a ton of bricks had fallen on her chest.

"Well, I thought I'd warn you," Shyla said. "Listen, it sounds like the medical examiner is building a case against you."

"I know. But she's wasting her time. There isn't anything to find."

"Are you sure about that? Rick thinks it isn't just the medical examiner but Ford who's the problem. Did you and Ford have an argument?"

Rachel had to sit down and put her head between her knees. "Tell Rick that everything is fine and for him not to worry about me. You either. I have to go."

Chapter Eighteen

Paul Townsend looked more amused than anything as he lounged in one of the chairs across from the sheriff's desk.

"The medical examiner wants to ask you a few questions," Charley said, sounding apologetic as he leaned back in his chair and made it perfectly clear that none of this was his idea. "I'm sure it won't take long."

Hitch tried not to grind her teeth. She'd worked with enough small-town sheriffs that this shouldn't come as a surprise. "I happened to see your pickup on the road north last night after midnight. Want to tell me where you were coming from?"

The cowboy seemed to lose some of his cockiness for a moment. "Just went for a ride."

"A ride? No place in particular?"

"Nope."

"Paul, I should advise you that I witnessed you leaving Rachel Collinwood's house not long after midnight. I took photos of you and then later of the pickup you were driving."

He sat up a little and shot an uncomfortable glance at the sheriff as if he expected Charley to bail him out. Hitch gave the sheriff a warning look, daring him to do so. "So what? I wanted to see how she was doing."

"At midnight? That's when you decided to stop by?"

Paul looked around the office for a moment. "What's this about?" He wasn't as cocky as he'd been earlier.

"How did you get the scrapes on your knuckles?" Hitch asked.

He glanced down at his hands as if surprised to see them. "I don't know. Working on the ranch. You saw me working today. I get beat up." He sounded proud of that.

"What is your relationship with Mrs. Collinwood?" Hitch asked.

His eyes widened. "We don't have a relationship exactly."

Hitch leaned toward him. "I know you didn't pull the trigger, but how were you involved in Humphrey Collinwood's murder? If you tell the truth—"

"Wait! What? I don't know what you're talking about," he said, shooting to his feet.

"I'm talking about you doing less time in prison by telling us what really happened out at the ranch the day Humphrey Collinwood died. Otherwise, you will go down with her."

"No, you got it all wrong. Yes, I went out there last night. I don't know what I was thinking. I just wanted to see if she was all right." Hitch cocked her head at him and waited. He hung his head. "I'd had something to drink, okay? Maybe too much. I got to thinking about her."

"How long have the two of you been having an affair?" she asked.

He wagged his head. "It isn't like that," he said as he sat back down looking deflated. "It was just a few times."

"When was this?" Hitch asked.

"A year or so ago. I tried to see her again, but she…"

"Was married."

"Yeah," Paul said, lifting his head. "Look, my father doesn't know." He glanced at the sheriff. "Does he have to find out?"

"When was the last time you saw her before last night?" Hitch asked.

"A year ago. I called a few times, and when she quit taking my calls, I gave up. But I swear, I just went out there to make sure she was all right, but she didn't answer the door, so I left."

"I saw you coming out of the house," Hitch said.

He nodded. "I know the passcode. Like I said, I was worried about her, so I went inside, but her bedroom door was closed. I knocked on it, thought I heard water running. I got to thinking that she might shoot me, too—you know, thinking I was a burglar or something—so I left."

"When you were involved with Rachel Collinwood a year ago, did you notice any bruises on her that might have indicated she was being abused?"

He shook his head. "But I could tell she was afraid he would find out, you know?"

Hitch thought she did. "Would you please remove your ring, Mr. Townsend?"

He closed his hand into a fist. "Why?"

"I'd like to take it for evidence," Hitch said.

Paul looked at the sheriff, then back at her. "You can't take my stuff without a warrant, right?" he asked, his gaze back on the sheriff.

"If you are unwilling to relinquish it and allow me to take it as possible evidence, then I will have to ask the sheriff here to arrest you for conspiracy to commit murder, at which time your possessions, including your ring, will be taken and used as possible evidence in the case."

"But I just told you—" The cowboy looked like a trapped animal. "I want a lawyer."

She looked to the sheriff. "Would you please arrest Mr. Townsend for me, Sheriff?" Her look said, *Don't make me call the governor.*

"I'm sorry as hell about this, Paul," Charley said, lumbering to his feet. "Why don't you just give her the damned ring?" The cowboy covered the ring with his other hand and shook his head. "She's going to get it, one way or another," Charley continued. "You want to spend time behind bars over a stupid ring? Don't make me have to arrest you."

Paul angrily jerked off the ring, rose and threw it down on the sheriff's desk. As Charley reached for it, Hitch beat him to it, using her shirtsleeve to pick it up before bagging it.

"I want that ring back," Paul said angrily. "And a public apology."

The sheriff sighed deeply before saying, "You're free to go now and we'll make sure at some point that you get your ring back."

"But let me know if you decide to leave town," Hitch called after him as the cowboy stormed out and got on his cell phone. "I wonder who he's calling. Rachel Collinwood to warn her?"

"He's probably just callin' for a ride back to the ranch," Charley said, picking up his keys. "You might recall that he rode with me." The sheriff shot her an incredulous look as he walked out after Paul.

"I'm going to need his phone records," Hitch said to his retreating back.

She was anxious to check the ring against the photographs of Rachel's bruises before sending it to the lab. Back in her hotel room, she pulled out her magnifying glass. She studied first the bruise, then the surface of the ring. Tilting the ring this way and that, she imagined slipping it on her finger.

"If I were to punch someone..." She made the motion with the ring still in the evidence bag and then checked the position of the ring against that of the bruise. The resemblance was there. But would a jury see it? Maybe.

Her real hope, she knew, was what the lab would find.

The grooves in the ring's design were so deep… She had to believe that the evidence would still be there. Unless Paul Townsend was telling the truth.

"I KNOW. I UNDERSTAND. No, I—" The sheriff pulled the phone away from his ear for a moment. "Lloyd, I totally agree with you. But it's out of my hands. This came all the way down from the governor. I can't do anything with that woman." He listened to the man rant and rave and threaten to sue. "I don't know why she wanted your sons' rings. I know they're valuable. Nothing's going to happen to them. But at least Paul's not behind bars. Be happy about that. If she'd had her way…" He pulled the phone away again and looked up to find Ford Cardwell standing in his doorway. "Lloyd, I have to go. Do whatever it is you have to do." He hung up. "What do you want?" he snapped and then quickly apologized. "Sorry, it's been one of those days."

"I didn't mean to interrupt," Ford said.

"No, actually, I should thank you. What can I do for you?"

"I was looking for Hitch," Ford said.

Charley made a rude sound that went with the face he pulled. "Well, she isn't here. She was. I have no idea where she is. Probably starting trouble somewhere else. She won't rest until she has this whole town up in arms." He realized Ford was still standing there. "Try the morgue. I know it's late, but that's where she's been hanging out. You know where that is?" He didn't wait for an answer and quickly gave him directions. Big Timber was small enough that it was pretty easy to get around.

As Ford started to leave, the sheriff took his first good look at the man since he'd appeared in the doorway. "You don't look good," Charley said and frowned. "You look like someone punched you in the gut. You all right?"

"I've been better."

"You sticking around?"

"I'm not sure."

Charley nodded. "But you'll be back for the trial—if it comes to that. Rachel's going to need your testimony, so you'd best take care of yourself. Without you…"

Yes, without him, Rachel wouldn't have as strong a case. "Thanks again for the directions." As he left, the sheriff's phone rang. He heard him curse and say, "Who wants to chew off my ear now? On top of everything, I'm missing my supper, damn it."

SO MUCH HAD happened in the past seventy-two hours. Hitch had gone through all her notes again. She'd stuck her neck out bringing Paul Townsend in. There was pressure on the governor from both Bart Collinwood and Lloyd Townsend now. She had to wind things up and soon.

After pacing her hotel room floor, she knew there was only one way she could unwind. Drive. As she walked out of the hotel, she noticed something flapping in the breeze on her windshield. A piece of folded paper under the wiper of her SUV. She pulled on the extra pair of latex gloves she always kept in a pocket when on a case and carefully removed the typed note.

The message was much like the other one that had been slipped under her hotel room door.

You messed with the wrong people bitch.

Leave town or wish you had.

She bagged the note—just as she had the first one—shaking her head in wonder. It wasn't the first time she'd received threatening notes in her career. Nor did she suspect it would be the last. Such notes never made her want to leave town. On the contrary, it assured her that she was on the right track—and getting too close to the truth for someone's comfort.

Like the first note, this one had been written probably

on a computer on plain white paper. She doubted it would have any fingerprints on it either, but she would have the lab check.

She'd been planning to go for a drive. It helped her to think. But the note had changed her mind. She decided that the walk to the morgue might be a better choice. Her assumption was that the note had been from Rachel's accomplice. But it could have just as easily been from someone in the Townsend family. Or even someone who believed Rachel was being treated unfairly. Her friend from college?

The walk to the morgue wasn't far, but it was off the main drag. The streets here lacked sidewalks, pavement and lighting. She walked along the edge of the packed dirt road, thinking about Paul Townsend. He was young and handsome and naive enough that he could have fallen for not just Rachel Collinwood but her alleged need to protect herself from her abusive husband. Paul could have thought he was saving her, being her hero, seeing the killing of Humphrey Collinwood as ridding the world of a monster.

Lost in thought, she didn't hear the vehicle coming up behind her until the sound of the engine roared. Hitch only had enough time to glance over her shoulder to confirm what she already knew. The driver was bearing down on her.

Chapter Nineteen

Hitch wasn't at the morgue. Nor was she in her room when he called the hotel. Ford thought about what the sheriff had said about him taking care of himself. He couldn't remember the last time he'd eaten more than a few bites of anything.

As he drove through Big Timber, he looked for a place to eat. There weren't that many options this time of the night. He'd gone down a side street when he spotted red taillights disappearing in the distance. Closer, a person came stumbling out of a hedge along the road directly in front of him. He threw on his brakes. With a shock of recognition, he saw that it was Hitch and that she was injured.

BLINDED BY THE HEADLIGHTS, Hitch jerked away from the man who ran toward her, thinking it was the same one who'd tried to run her down.

"Hitch, it's me." She felt a wave of relief as she recognized Ford's voice. She let him take her in his arms, because right now she wasn't steady on her feet. The pickup that had tried to run her down had come too close. She'd felt the brush of the bumper against the side of her thigh. She didn't think anything was broken from the contact or her dive into the hedge, but she hurt all over and was definitely shaken.

Whoever had been driving that truck hadn't just been

trying to scare her. If she hadn't thrown herself into the hedge, the impact would have killed her.

"What happened?" He sounded scared. "That pickup that just went past? Did it hit you?"

"No. I'm all right." But her legs seemed to give out under her because of the shock that came with the realization of how close a call it had been. "I just need to sit down for a minute."

He caught her, scooping her up, her trembling in his arms as he carried her over to his truck. Reaching behind her, he opened the door and set her down on the seat. "I'll take you to the hospital."

"No hospital," she said quickly. "I'm not hurt. Just shaken up."

"Your cheek is bleeding."

She leaned back, eyes closed, until the dizziness passed as she tried to catch her breath and calm down. When she opened her eyes, she saw that he'd already dug out a first-aid kit. She smiled up into his handsome face, wondering where he'd been her whole life.

"This is going to hurt," he said as he wiped away the blood with an alcohol swab. She winced more from the cold liquid than the pain. "Sorry," he said, his fingers so gentle that she felt her eyes smart. She wasn't used to a man treating her as if she were made of glass. She was too independent, too strong, too determined. At least that was what most men she'd dated had said.

But not this man, she thought as she watched him open a sterile bandage and apply it to her cheek. "Thank you." Her voice came out a hoarse whisper, almost choked with an emotion that surprised her. She told herself it was just her brush with death and his gentle kindness. But as he finished bandaging her cut and looked down into her eyes, she felt a jolt clear to her core. Then his fingers were cupping her uninjured cheek. His rough thumb pad slipped under her chin to lift it as he leaned down and kissed her. The impulsiveness of the kiss, the surprise of it, the tenderness of it all caught her completely off guard.

His lips brushed hers, urging them open. They didn't put up much of a fight. As her lips parted, he cupped the back of her head, deepening the kiss. She grabbed a handful of his shirt, drawing him even closer as she lost herself in the startling passion of their combined kiss.

A groan rose from deep in his chest as he drew back a little to look into her eyes again. "I'm sorry. Here you are injured, and I…" His warm, strong fingers still holding the back of her head were buried in her hair. He seemed as shocked by the powerful kiss as she was.

Still bunching his shirt in her fists, she pulled him down for another kiss. He dropped his mouth to hers and deepened the kiss, this one even hotter than the first.

She loosened her hold on his shirt. His look mirrored hers. Wow. Everything about the kisses had been unexpected in so many ways.

"I've been wanting to do that for a very long time," he said, his voice sounding rough with emotion as he drew his hand from behind her head and straightened. "The timing, however—"

"Was perfect. I hadn't realized how much I needed that." She smiled at him and he smiled almost shyly back. "You don't find me too scary, then?"

"Oh, I wouldn't say that." He chuckled as he tucked her into the seat and closed the passenger-side door. She watched him walk around to the driver's side and slide behind the wheel.

"Any chance the truck driver just didn't see you?" he asked.

"No. Whoever was driving that truck wanted me dead," she said, leaning her head back against the seat and looking out into the darkness, thinking not about her near-death experience, but Ford and that kiss.

For a moment, he simply sat behind the wheel before he glanced over at her, drawing her attention back. "You feel better?" She could only nod. "You're probably not hungry."

"Starved," she said. Her stomach rumbled at the thought, reminding her she hadn't eaten all day.

He chuckled and started the engine. "Any chance you got the license plate on the rig that almost hit you?" he asked as he drove them to the local burger shop.

She thought of that glimpse she'd gotten before the headlights had blinded her. She could almost hear the roar of the engine as the driver bore down on her. "It happened too fast. Too dark to even make out a model of the pickup. All I really saw was the metal guard on the front. I think I would recognize it, if I saw it again."

"I think I know that grille guard," Ford said. "I didn't mention it because most trucks around here have the guards on them because of all the deer on the highway at night. But the truck that ran me off the road had a huge shiny metal guard on the front, as well. I think we're looking for the same man."

"If I were a betting woman, I'd say he's the same man Rachel Collinwood talked into helping her kill her husband."

It felt ironic, Ford thought as he and Hitch finished their cheeseburgers, fries and chocolate milkshakes and he drove her back to the hotel where they were both staying. He'd come here for Rachel. He would leave here missing Hitch. In a few days' time, he'd come to admire this strong, capable woman.

He scoffed, knowing it was more than that or he wouldn't have kissed her. He felt a fire again in his belly that he'd thought had been extinguished. Desire. He'd actually forgotten what that felt like. But Hitch had fanned the flames and now he burned inside for her and the passion he'd felt kissing her.

All during the meal, Hitch had seemed her old self—except for the bandage on her cheek and a few scratches and probably bruises from her dive into the bushes. They'd talked about growing up in Montana—skirting away from the investigation. It had been one of the most pleasant meals he'd had in a long time.

When he'd walked her to her door at the hotel, there'd been a moment when they'd both seemed to hesitate.

"Good night," he said and took a step back. As badly as he would have loved to be invited into her hotel room, he knew it was too soon. "I'm right down the hall, if you need me."

She'd nodded and smiled. "I'll keep that in mind."

His cell phone rang right after he'd stepped inside his hotel room. For a moment, he was hoping it was Hitch. She'd been just as surprised by what they'd shared. He'd seen it in her eyes, in the trembling of her lips. She wasn't one to leap blindly. At least not when it came to men. He wasn't sure how he knew that, just that he did.

Still, he tried to hide his disappointment. "Dad, I was going to call you. I'm coming home tomorrow."

"Good. You sound…good."

Ford had to smile. He and his father were both short on words in uncharted territory. He knew Jackson had been worried about him. Hell, Ford had been worried about himself.

"Coming over here has been good for me," he told his father.

"Did you resolve anything with Rachel?" Jackson asked.

He chuckled. "Did I get closure? Yeah, I did. I feel better about a lot of things." He envisioned Hitch for a moment.

"I can't tell you how glad I am to hear that," his father said. "It will be great to have you back."

As he disconnected, he saw movement on the street below the window and looked out. Hitch? It was just like her to go back out to the Collinwood Ranch tonight to see if she could catch the man she suspected of being the accomplice visiting Rachel again.

He'd been so sure that her brush with death would keep her safe and in her room—at least for tonight. He should have known better. As he saw her climb into her SUV, he reached for his coat. She had no business going out there alone—especially after what had happened to her tonight.

But at the same time, he wasn't at all surprised. She was one determined woman and he admired the hell out of her for that. Not that he was about to let her go alone.

As Hitch started to pull away, someone pounded on her window, startling her for a moment—until she saw Ford's handsome face. "Couldn't sleep again?" she asked.

"Felt like going for a ride. Looks like you had the same idea."

She studied him for a moment before she smiled. "All right. Get in."

He grinned as she unlocked the door and he climbed in.

"How are you feeling?" he asked.

"Fine."

"I thought you might have decided, after what happened to you, to stay in tonight," Ford said.

She glanced over at him as she pulled out and headed down the street toward the highway that would take them north. "No, you didn't or you wouldn't be here."

"Maybe I'd hoped you'd had enough for one day."

Hitch kept her attention on the road as they fell into a companionable silence until she turned off into the Collinwood Ranch. On the side of the mountain in the pines where they'd sat before, she cut the lights, pulled to the edge so there were no trees blocking their view and cut the engine.

"He wouldn't be fool enough to come back out here tonight," Ford said.

She chuckled. "Wanna bet?"

"I have a new twenty that says if he's the lover, he'll stay away."

Even in the dim starlight coming through the SUV's windows, she could see his smile. She liked that smile. "My twenty says the lover will visit tonight."

"Guess we'll see." He reached into his jacket pocket for his binoculars.

They sat quietly for a while. The pines stood in dark shadow next to the vehicle while the landscape beyond the mountaintop was cast in a silver glow from the magnitude of the stars out here so far from town. She heard an owl hoot from a nearby tree, and somewhere farther off a hawk answered.

She turned the key to let down her side window, needing the cool summer night's air. Earlier at the hotel, she'd been so close to asking Ford into her hotel room. If she had, they wouldn't be here now. They'd be wrapped up in each other's arms. The thought sent a ball of heat straight to her center. And she knew the real reason she hadn't invited him into her room earlier.

Most men she could take or leave. Ford wasn't like that. She told herself she wasn't ready for the kind of commitment even one night with him might take. She had to keep her mind on this case, but it was hard to do that with Ford just inches away and this spark between them like a live wire.

"Does it worry you that just a few days ago I was ready to drive over a cliff?" Ford said inside the dark SUV. He thought that would give any woman pause, even one like

Hitch. He had to know because he didn't want any secrets between them if they were going to become lovers. And he was pretty sure that they were.

"No, because you wouldn't have done it," she whispered, not looking at him.

He chuckled. "How can you be so sure?" he asked, turning toward her, studying the outline of her face in the darkness.

She turned to meet his gaze. "Because you didn't want to go over that cliff."

"I wish I believed that."

"Doesn't matter now anyway," Hitch said. "You're not in that state of mind anymore. You're not that man."

He smiled at her. "You know that how?"

She held his gaze. "I see it in your eyes. I also felt it in your kisses." She turned back to her surveillance. "You want to live."

Ford realized that she was right. He tried not to stare at her, even though he loved looking at her face, staring into her eyes. She had mesmerized him in a way that he thought could never happen to him again.

The pain of what he'd been through was still there and always would be. But Hitch had made him realize that he could go on. He might even be able to find happiness in this world he'd only seen as too broken to repair.

He cleared his throat, changing the subject. "Other than you losing twenty dollars, what if he doesn't show tonight?"

"I haven't lost yet. He can't stay away from her and they both know that a phone call will show up on their bills."

"You think it will go to trial?"

Hitch continued to study the ranch house for a long moment before she lowered her binoculars and answered. "If she suspects that could happen, she'll run before she's locked up."

The answer surprised him. "But the bond she put up—"

"I suspect she already planned to lose that and the ranch. It isn't the only money she has—you can bet on that. If she was smart, and she is, she would have planned this for some time and taken into account all possible outcomes. This wasn't an impulsive act. Who knows how long she's been hiding money for the day when she might need it? She could have been planning this for years. She thought of *almost* everything. What worries me now is what she plans to do with her accomplice."

Ford shot her a look. "You think she'll kill him."

"She doesn't have much choice. He keeps going off script. She can't trust him. He's too much of a liability. She's already killed her husband. What's one or two more murders," Hitch said as the garage door at the ranch house suddenly rolled up and Rachel's SUV rolled out.

"One or two more?" Ford said.

Hitch met his gaze. "If she thought you might change your story about what you heard on the phone call, well, you'd be in the same boat. That's why the sooner you go back to Big Sky, the better off you'll be."

She started the patrol SUV's motor and took off down the mountain without headlights to follow Rachel—wherever she was headed at this time of the night.

"And you owe me twenty dollars," Hitch said as she raced after the disappearing taillights in the distance.

Chapter Twenty

Hitch had expected Rachel to turn toward town as soon as she drove off the dirt ranch road. To her surprise, the SUV turned right at the highway and headed in the direction of Harlowton.

"Where is she going?" Ford said, sounding as surprised as Hitch was.

"Wherever it is, she's going there in a hurry." By the time Hitch reached the end of the ranch road and turned onto the highway headed north, she could barely see Rachel's taillights in the distance. "I think she's trying to lose us."

Turning on her headlights and tromping on the gas, she raced after her. While it had been Rachel's SUV that had come out of the garage, Hitch hadn't been able to see the driver. What if it wasn't Rachel behind the wheel?

Clouds had moved in, cloaking the night. Ahead, she could make out the dim taillights. Rachel, or whoever, was driving fast as if she knew she was being followed. Hitch didn't want to lose her, but she also didn't want to come running up on her in the growing fog and careen into the back of her vehicle either. As the terrain became more hilly, she only got glimpses of the blurry red taillights ahead of her through the fog.

Hitch was going eighty-five when she came up a hill and saw brake lights off to the side of the road. She recognized the SUV. The driver had pulled off onto a wide spot.

As Hitch sped past, she glanced at the driver of the SUV. Rachel was behind the wheel. She caught a glimpse of the woman's face and the smug smile plastered on it. As Hitch kept going, she watched in her rearview mirror as Rachel turned back toward the ranch.

Over the next hill, Hitch hit her brakes and did a highway patrol turn in the empty road before heading back to Big Timber. Ahead, she could see that Rachel was no longer speeding. Hitch followed her until she turned into her own ranch road.

"Was that what I think it was?" Ford said.

"She tricked me. Got me to follow her while whoever was visiting her got away," Hitch said. She had to hand it to the woman. Rachel had been one step ahead of her from the beginning. The subterfuge only made Hitch more convinced that the woman was guilty of cold-blooded murder.

Hitch just had to prove it, and that was the problem.

It was late by the time they reached the hotel.

"I don't know about you, but I could use a drink," Ford said and glanced at his phone. "Bar closes in less than an hour."

She smiled. "I thought you didn't drink."

"Only on special occasions."

"And you think this is one of them?" she asked with a chuckle.

"It just might be." His look said he wasn't ready to go to his hotel room alone. She knew the feeling. Maybe tonight they needed each other. She realized with a start that she more than needed him. She wanted him, which was entirely different. This kind of want made her ache inside.

The bar was empty except for a few regulars watching TV at the other end of the room. She ordered herself a screwdriver. Ford raised a brow and laughed and said he'd take the same. Taking a sip of her drink, she slid off the stool, went to the jukebox and punched in a few of her favorite songs.

The bartender saw her and turned down the volume on the TV as she took her stool again and the first song came on.

"Seriously, why are you involved in such a dangerous job?"

"Someone has to do it. I would think you'd know better than anyone why I do this."

"That was war. This is…"

"Its own kind of war," she said and ran a finger down the sweating fog on her glass. "I'm sorry I suspected you."

"Thanks, since I take that to mean you no longer do," he said.

"Do you still love her?" She hadn't meant to ask the question, but once it was out of her mouth, she was anxious to hear his answer. She hated that she was hanging on his answer, knowing he would be truthful with her.

He took a sip of his drink and chuckled to himself. "No. I've realized that I've never been in love with Rachel. Not the real kind. I was in love with the idea of her." He met her gaze. "But I'm not even in love with that anymore."

"Good," she said as a new song began on the jukebox.

Ford stepped off his stool. "Dance with me." He reached for her hand. His large one was warm and dry. A strong hand. It wrapped around hers as he gently led her out onto the small dance floor. A strong man, she thought as he took her in his arms.

They began to move to the slow country song. She breathed in the distinct male scent of him and was tired enough that she was almost tempted to rest her head on his shoulder.

She drew back a little to look into his face. "I'm serious about you leaving town."

He grinned. "Otherwise you won't be able to resist me?"

"Something like that. Ford, I'm serious. It's too dangerous. She saw us together tonight." She leaned back a little to meet his gaze. "Promise me that you'll leave in the morning."

"If that's what you want." He pulled her closer. This time she didn't resist. She rested her head on his shoulder, relishing being wrapped in his protective strength. What was it about this man that brought out such powerful feelings in her? It had happened so quickly that it had caught her off guard.

The song ended. When she raised her head from his shoulder, she met his gaze. Heat speed-raced through her veins, reminding her how long it had been since she'd even dated.

"Ford?"

"I know," he said. "Maybe when this case is over, if you—"

"I thought I'd find you here," said a deep male voice behind them.

Hitch turned to see the sheriff, thumbs hooked in the pockets of his jeans, his chest puffed out. "That lab of yours is trying to find you."

Chapter Twenty-One

When Hitch pulled out her phone, she saw that she had several messages from the DCI lab—and the governor. "I'm sorry. I have to go take care of this," she told Ford. Their gazes locked. "Thank you for the dance."

"We'll have to do it again sometime," he said with a slight bow of his head.

The look in his eye made her cheeks actually flush. "I hope so."

She rushed upstairs to the quiet of her room to listen to her messages. She desperately needed a break in this case and soon. She wanted this one over for more reasons than ever before.

After closing her door to the quiet of her room, she listened to the governor's first message. Bart Collinwood had been kicking up a lot of dust and so had Lloyd Townsend. If Hitch didn't find something solid on the case soon…

She listened to the DCI investigator's message and held her breath. Maybe this was the break she needed. "I have news, just not the news I think you were hoping to hear. We found no blood or tissue evidence on the ring to suggest it had been used in a violent attack. Nothing on the ring matched Rachel Collinwood's DNA either."

Hitch let out the breath she'd been holding and told herself it had been a long shot. Still, when she'd seen the Townsends' rings, she'd thought she'd found a clue. Those grooves were so deep in that design that something would have been found. And Rachel and Paul had been lovers. She'd thought she'd found the key to breaking this case wide open.

"As for the design and the bruise left on Rachel Collinwood's face, we ran both the ring and photo through a variety of tests. Our conclusion? It doesn't match. There are parts of it that are close… Sorry. We have a unit coming out your way tomorrow. I'll have them return the ring to you."

Hitch tossed her phone on the bedside table. She couldn't help but feel even more deflated. She'd been so sure that she'd found the accomplice. The ring that had made the bruise wasn't Paul Townsend's ring—nor was it the husband's. All Hitch had to do was find the ring that matched that bruise. Talk about looking for a needle in a haystack.

Another dead end. All her instincts told her that her suspicions weren't wrong. But unless she found evidence… Worse, when she thought about it, Paul Townsend was too young and too undisciplined to be the accomplice. Wasn't that why a year ago Rachel had cut him loose? Rachel had realized that she couldn't count on him. So who had she turned to?

As she got ready for bed, her thoughts kept straying to Ford. She'd met few men who could occupy her thoughts as much. She thought about what he'd confessed to her about the day he'd gotten the call from Rachel. It hadn't been easy for him to admit. She could tell that he was embarrassed by even the foiled attempt to end his life. She couldn't imagine how low he'd been at that moment to even consider it. Ford Cardwell wasn't the impulsive type. If suicide had been his intention, then Rachel really could have saved his life.

If so, then Hitch now believed in fate.

She realized that she had no solid proof that Rachel had planned the killing of her husband. That was what frustrated her the most. She had the lack of fingerprints on the glass and pottery. She had the lack of the husband's voice on the call to Ford. She had the bruise. She had the cartridge casing by the kitchen door. She had the lack of bruises and abrasions on the husband's hands. But even with all of that, it still might not be enough to hold up in court.

Had she lost her perspective? Had she wanted Rachel to be guilty? "What if your instincts are wrong?" she asked herself in the empty hotel room.

"I'm not wrong." Whatever Rachel had been hit with, it also hadn't been with her husband's ring. So whose had it been?

Whoever had hit her had forgotten to take off his ring. But Rachel would have realized it at some point and had him put Humphrey's ring on. Which meant Humphrey was already dead.

But without that ring… This was the part of a case that she hated the most. Being so close she could feel it, but not being able to find that one crucial piece of evidence that would complete her investigation. She'd been here before. Usually, it was something small that she'd overlooked. Or a mistake the criminal had made or was going to make.

She needed the accomplice—and that ring.

She climbed into bed, telling herself she'd never get to sleep, not with her roiling emotions—and her growing feelings for Ford Cardwell.

A few hours later, she was startled awake by the ringing of her phone. She picked up. "Good morning, Governor."

"Is it? What have we got on this investigation?"

"Nothing definite yet, but—"

"The sheriff seems to think that you're on some kind of crusade against this woman."

Hitch groaned inwardly. "I'm just trying to get at the truth like I always do."

"You have a great record at doing just that. But this case is…"

"Complicated."

"That's one way of putting it," the governor said. "I can't give you much more time on this. I have another case you're needed on. Not to mention the fact that you seem to have stirred up a hornet's nest."

"Give me forty-eight hours. If I don't have evidence by then, I'll leave it to the sheriff." Hitch knew what that would mean. Rachel Collinwood would get away with murder.

"Forty-eight hours."

The clock was ticking.

FORD WAS WAITING for Hitch when she came out of the hotel. He pulled her aside behind a pillar at the edge of the building. "You okay?" he asked, his hand still on her arm. She nodded, but he could tell something was wrong. "It wasn't the ring, was it," he said.

She groaned. "You know about the ring?" Shaking her head, she said, "These small towns. No. It wasn't the ring I was looking for. I'd hoped it matched a bruise on Rachel's face." She described the bruise. "It didn't match close enough. So I'm back to square one, since I'm almost positive the bruise was made by a man's ring—just not her husband's."

Ford had heard about Paul Townsend being brought in. It had been his pickup that they'd seen leaving the Collinwood Ranch. But not his ring.

"I have an idea," he said, having given this some thought last night after they'd parted. He couldn't leave town. Not now. "Rachel trusts me. Put a wire on me and let me try to get the truth out of her."

Hitch was shaking her head before he could even finish speaking. "Not happening. I need to wind this investigation up in the next forty-eight hours, and quite frankly, you've become a distraction I can't afford."

"Is that what I am to you?" he said, grinning.

"I'm serious. Please go home so I know you're safe."

"I can't do that." He held her gaze. "I came here to save Rachel if I could. Instead, I find myself getting involved with you."

"I wouldn't say we're involved."

"Wouldn't you?" He cupped her cheek, drawing her face up to his own. "Tell me there is nothing between us and I'll walk away right now."

She parted her lips, but no words came out. He pulled her into his arms. He could feel her heart pounding in her pulse. "Last chance," he said.

Chapter Twenty-Two

Hitch had flat-out refused to even think about his plan. She was determined that he leave and go back to Big Sky. Did she really believe that Rachel would harm him? Kill him? Even if she'd murdered Humphrey, Ford didn't believe that she would kill him.

But he could also be wrong about that. Wrong about a lot of things when it came to Rachel. He knew it was risky. The thought made him laugh. It wasn't that long ago that he was racing toward a cliff with only one thought in mind—ending his life as he knew it.

Now, though, his life felt precious. He didn't want it to end. He wanted to live—even if Hitch Roberts wasn't part of it. Not that he was ready to give up on the two of them. She needed this investigation over and so did he. He could tell that she'd hit a wall in the investigation. If he could move it along, he would do whatever he had to.

As he drove out to Rachel's ranch, he told himself that maybe Rachel didn't trust him as much as she used to. But she didn't see him as a real threat. She saw him as naive and weak because of his feelings for her, which he'd more than demonstrated at her wedding. If anything, she found him dispensable, just as she had fifteen years ago. Now that he'd already given his statement to the sheriff, she wanted him gone.

But would she trust him enough to tell him the truth?

He had to pretend he was still blindly in love with her. That wouldn't be easy. Rachel had been his fantasy woman for years. Unfortunately, that woman had never existed, and it had taken her to show him that. Had Humphrey come to that same conclusion those last few seconds before she'd killed him?

Ford realized now that he'd used the fantasy of Rachel so other women never quite measured up and he didn't get hurt. As a boy, he'd seen the hell his father had gone through during the divorce. Ford's own mother had deserted them. No wonder he had commitment issues.

Until now. He'd never met anyone like Hitch before. She'd made him realize what he wanted in a woman— knocking Rachel off that pedestal he'd put her on.

As he pulled up in front of the ranch house, he knew this was going to have to be the acting job of his life. Rachel was smart. She was also leery of him after his last visit. If she spotted the lie… He pushed the thought away. He would just have to make sure she didn't.

As Rachel opened the door, he caught a whiff of familiar perfume. Her hair was pulled up, a gold necklace twinkling at her slim throat. She was wearing a slinky jumpsuit in a turquoise blue that brought out the blue in her eyes and hugged her curves. The woman was drop-dead gorgeous and she knew it.

"Ford, I was glad when you called. Come in."

She let him into the living room. "I hate the way we left things the last time you were here." Soft music played in the background. The lights had been dimmed. "Have a seat. Let me get us something to drink."

Still standing, he watched her walk into the kitchen, taken aback by this warm reception. Earlier when he'd called, he'd said the same thing. He didn't like the way they'd left things. She'd sounded wary at best on the phone but had said of course she wanted to see him before he left.

Now he felt a sliver of concern work its way under his skin. This could be a huge mistake. But he was already here, he told himself as he looked around. He spotted Rachel's phone on the table next to the couch. Hadn't the sheriff taken her phone? This must be a new one. He realized that she must have been looking at it when he knocked and put it down and forgotten it.

Ford quickly picked it up. She hadn't signed off. He wasn't sure what he was even looking for. Certainly not a confession.

After glancing at her emails, he opened her photos. He went to the most recent ones. He was scanning through them when one caught his eye. All the breath rushed from him. It was of Rachel. She was tied to an iron bed, wearing nothing but what appeared to be a fireman's jacket that barely covered her private parts. He zoomed in to make the logo larger. Sweet Grass County volunteer fireman's jacket.

Had Humphrey been a local volunteer fireman? Ford knew it would be easy enough to find out, but he doubted it. In the photo, Rachel was laughing and saying something to the person taking the shot. It was the gleam in her eyes that told him the photographer wasn't Humphrey. That and the fact that this photo had been taken on her new phone, so it had been shot recently.

He quickly switched to open Rachel's contact list, curious about whose number he'd find, when she called from the kitchen.

"I hope you still like dark beer."

"You know me," he called back and quickly looked around for a place to put the phone. He stuffed it between two of the large, heavy fashion magazines on the coffee table as he heard her coming back and sat down next to it.

"I was so glad I had a beer for you," Rachel said, returning to the living room with a bottle of dark beer and a frosted glass, which she put down on the table at the far end of the couch next to him. She sat down at the opposite end of the couch, picked up her glass of red wine and turned toward him. Her smile looked glued on and slightly crooked. He figured it wasn't her first glass of wine tonight.

"I'm so sorry we had to reconnect after all these years in such a tragic way," she said. "It appears that all of Humphrey's and my dirty secrets are now local gossip. I'm so embarrassed."

"You shouldn't be embarrassed," he said. "I'm sure you never expected to find yourself in such a situation."

"Exactly," she agreed. "People like Humphrey and I... Well, I never expected something like this to happen. Not to us. I know you were shocked," she said, leaning toward him a little.

He got another wave of her perfume. It made him nauseous. He reached for his beer and poured some into the glass. The cold made him shiver a little. "I *was* shocked," he admitted. "I had no idea."

"No one did. Shyla said I should have told someone. Called the police on him. Done something more before things got totally out of hand." She shook her head and took a sip of her wine. Cupping the glass in her hands, she looked at him. "I was so ashamed. I didn't want anyone to know. I especially didn't want you to find out. What you must think of me."

"You can't believe that I would think less of you because of this."

Tears welled in all that blue. She licked her lips and gave him a sad smile. "You were Humphrey's best friend, but I always felt you and I... I don't know. That we had a special connection."

There would have been a time when those words would have warmed him to his toes. Instead, he found himself comparing this visit to the last one, when she'd been trying to get rid of him. Apparently, she wasn't hiding her boyfriend in the back bedroom this time.

"Ford, there's something I have to ask you." She put down her wineglass and turned all of her attention on him. "There's a rumor going around. I'm sure it's not true. Some people saw you dancing with that woman, the medical examiner, and the other night I went for a drive and…" Her gaze locked with his. "I thought I saw you in her patrol car."

"It's true," he said and picked up his beer as he broke eye contact with her. This part had to be the most convincing, so he took his time. "That's another reason I wanted to see you before I left." He took a drink and set down his glass to turn to her. "Rachel, I don't know how to tell you this." He could see that she was nervous and trying very hard not to show it. "Hitch, well… I suspect you already know that she doesn't believe your story."

"It wasn't a story," Rachel said automatically and looked as if this wasn't news. She seemed to remember something. He saw her look around and frown. She was looking for her phone. He saw her glance toward the kitchen.

"Hitch says she has solid proof," he said, drawing her attention again. "That's why I wanted to see you, because I want you to know. I would do anything for you. I don't think it's a secret how I've always felt about you." He looked down as if embarrassed by his confession. "I always thought you and I…" He heard her move before he felt her hand on his arm.

"Ford. I've been so stupid from the very beginning. You were one of the few people who knew about my background, how poor I was, how scared I was of not having anything to call my own. I can't tell you how many times I've wished it had been you instead of Humphrey."

He looked into her eyes. The woman was amazing. So beautiful with her lips trembling like that and her eyes shimmering in tears. He'd always been so taken with her, never looking too deeply below the surface. Otherwise, he might have realized what an astonishing liar she was, he thought as he pulled her into his arms.

HITCH CAUGHT HERSELF pacing the floor as she read over the list of phone numbers she'd received from DCI of Rachel's calls to and from her cell phone as well as Humphrey's in the days that led up to the shooting.

No surprise, there were mostly calls to Humphrey's number and vice versa. Also, a lot of calls to her friend Shyla, who Ford had told Hitch about. She couldn't concentrate after Ford's message saying he was going out to the ranch. He would try to get Rachel to confess on his phone. Did he have any idea how dangerous that could be if he got caught? She'd called him the moment she'd gotten the text, but his phone had gone straight to voice mail.

She kept thinking of the danger he was putting himself in. She should have stopped him. Or at least tried harder to talk him out of what he was doing.

Rationally, she knew she couldn't have done either.

But she also couldn't sit around waiting to hear from him. After seeing all the calls to the same number, she'd realized that she should talk to Shyla Birch, allegedly Rachel's best friend. Not that she expected to get anything from the woman. But she had to do something.

Birch, who'd married a local deputy in town, lived in a small house just outside of Big Timber. As Hitch crossed the Yellowstone River, she caught sight of the house and a flock of geese etched against the evening sky. She hadn't called to see if Shyla was home, deciding to take a chance. She had, however, called to see if the woman's husband was working tonight. He was. She doubted Shyla would be forthcoming if there was a deputy in the room.

Parking, she got out and headed for the front door. She could smell the river. The night air had a wonderful summer-is-coming feel to it. In Montana, summer usually arrived somewhere before the Fourth of July and ended shortly thereafter.

The woman who opened the door wasn't what Hitch had been expecting. She was wearing a too-large T-shirt and shorts. Her red curly hair formed a halo around her head, accentuating large brown eyes. Her feet were bare and she was holding a bowl of what smelled like buttered popcorn.

"Shyla Birch? I'm state medical examiner Hitch—"

"I know who you are," the woman said, tucking the large bowl of popcorn against her hip.

"Ford suggested I talk to you."

Surprisingly, those words seemed to do the trick. Hitch saw the woman hesitate and then sigh before she said, "Come on in, then."

The house smelled of stale cigarettes and popcorn. Shyla motioned to a chair by the couch as she grabbed the remote and muted the television before curling back under the blanket lying on the couch, with the bowl of popcorn in her lap. "Ford tell you that I'm Rachel's friend?"

"He said you were her *best* friend." That seemed to please her, Hitch saw, as she took the chair. "That's why I wanted to speak with you."

"I wondered when you'd get around to me." She shoved a handful of popcorn into her mouth.

"You probably know, then, what I'm going to ask you," Hitch said.

"Did I know he was abusing her? Did I see bruises? Did she ever talk to me about it?"

"And?" She waited for the young woman to answer.

Shyla pulled a face and put down the bowl of popcorn on the couch next to her as she picked up her cigarettes from the end table next to her. Hitch watched her light one and take a long drag before tilting her head back to let out a stream of smoke.

"She didn't tell me, but I saw bruises once or twice. She always had a story for how she'd gotten them. Looking back, though, oftentimes Humphrey would be there when she told me, so she was clearly covering for him and he was letting her."

"So you weren't surprised when you heard what had happened."

"Actually…" Shyla stared down at her cigarette for a moment. "I was shocked. I thought they were happy—in their own way. Did Ford tell you that I met my husband through Rachel?"

"No, he didn't. How did that come about?" she asked, trying hard not to sound like a medical examiner on a case. She must have succeeded, because Shyla seemed to relax a little, loosening up.

"Rick had gone out to the ranch after Rachel had called about a possible break-in. She'd come home and the front door was standing open. Humphrey was in New York on business and she was scared out of her wits. She called me to come out while she was waiting locked in her car." Shyla chuckled. "And the rest is history, as they say. Although I never thought I'd fall for a lawman." She rolled her eyes. "No offense."

"None taken. So had the house been broken into?"

"That's what's so weird. The door must have not been locked properly and had simply blown open. Rick had been going off shift when he got the call, so he stayed around to keep us company. Rachel made us some drinks. Humphrey came home and it kind of turned into a party. By the end, I was in love."

"Sounds like it was meant to be."

Shyla nodded, finished her cigarette and stubbed it out. "I heard that you think Rachel planned the whole thing."

There was something in the way she said it that made Hitch wonder if she also had thought the same thing. "I suspect she might have." She waited for a few moments before she added, "What do you think?"

Reaching for the popcorn bowl, Shyla took her time picking out a few kernels before she finally answered— instead of instantly defending her best friend.

"Rach is amazing. She really is. Did you know that she came from nothing? I mean, we were poor. Well, maybe not *poor* poor, but my parents both worked. They paid for my college, though, not like Rachel, who was on loans and scholarships. I don't blame her for wanting more than she got out of life, you know?" Hitch nodded. "But…" She looked down at the piece of popcorn in her fingers and tossed it back into the bowl, wiping her hand on the hem of her T-shirt, her thoughts clearly elsewhere. "I never thought she really loved Humphrey. Oh, she wanted him, but if you've ever been in love…"

Hitch remembered being in Ford's arms. It was an unexplainable feeling, an amazing, scary-as-hell feeling.

"But that doesn't mean she planned the whole thing," Shyla said, looking uncomfortable.

"No, possibly not," Hitch agreed. "I suppose you know about the prenuptial agreement she signed?"

"That was Humphrey's father's doing. Bart never liked Rachel. He thought she was a gold digger."

"Still, the agreement aside, Rachel could have divorced her husband and walked away with a lot of money."

Shyla let out a bark of a laugh. "Not near enough for that woman's tastes." She seemed to bite her tongue. "I shouldn't have said that."

"It's okay. I've seen her closet." An uneasy silence filled the room. "I have just one other question. I really appreciate your candor, and nothing you've said will go beyond this room. Is Rachel capable of putting together a plan to get rid of her husband and make it look like he was trying to kill her?"

Hitch knew she was putting the woman on the spot. Shyla's first instinct would be to protect her friend. And yet there was something refreshingly honest about the young woman.

"I'm not saying that's what happened," Shyla said carefully. "But Rachel... Well, she's always gone after what she wanted and not let anything stand in her way. She's definitely capable of doing anything she sets her mind to. She's got that kind of personality. But would she purposely kill her husband?" She gave a shake of her head. "Who does that?"

Someone cold-blooded enough that she wanted out but refused to give up the money, Hitch thought as she thanked Shyla and got to her feet. As she started toward the door, she heard a vehicle pull up. The front door flew open before she reached it and a handsome, broad-shouldered man in uniform came in and stopped dead at the sight of her.

"Rick, this is the medical examiner. She's looking into Rachel's case," Shyla said as she came off the couch. She sounded embarrassed and a little too anxious. "She was just leaving."

Rick Birch's brow furrowed. "Did you tell her that we're good friends with Rachel? With her husband, too, before all this?"

"Of course," his wife said quickly.

"Nice to meet you, Deputy Birch," Hitch said and started to step past him. He didn't move for a moment, blocking the doorway out. She continued toward him until he had to make a choice. He moved aside, but he didn't look happy about it.

On her way out the door, she heard him say, "What did you say to her?" before the door closed behind her.

Hitch walked to her car, thinking about everything she'd heard—and felt—from Rachel's best friend. Shyla had her doubts. Hitch wasn't the only one who suspected

Rachel of far more than shooting her husband during a domestic dispute.

Climbing into her SUV, she started the engine and checked her phone, anxious to hear from Ford. She was getting even more worried after her talk with Shyla. She was about to pull out when her headlights glinted off something in the garage. She hit the brakes and stared at the small single-car garage attached to the Birch house. The garage door had a chunk missing where it appeared someone had driven into it. Through the opening, she saw what looked like the chrome of a cattle guard on the front of a pickup.

Putting the SUV into Park, she got out and walked to the garage door to look inside through the large hole. A pickup was parked inside. The large grille-guard bumper on the front was what had caught her eye. She stared at it, recognizing the design. It was exactly like the one that had nearly hit her the other night.

Chapter Twenty-Three

Rachel hugged him, pressing her breasts against him. He felt her hand move across his chest around to his side, down to his hip. He realized with a start that she had checked him for a wire. Then her hand slipped into his pocket of his jacket. It came back out with his phone.

She drew back, looked down at it in her hand and touched the screen. "Oh, I'm sorry. This is yours. I thought my phone must have slipped down between the couch cushions." She didn't hand the phone back as she moved to the middle of the couch and reached for her wineglass with her free hand. She took a sip before she set his phone down between them.

She looked around again. "I thought I left my phone in here."

"Your phone?" He pretended to look around for it, and as he sat up, he kicked the leg of the coffee table. "Oh, there it is." He'd sent one of her fashion magazines sliding to the edge of the table, exposing the phone he'd put there. "Is that it?"

She stared at the phone. He could see her trying to remember where she'd laid it down and if it could have gotten covered by a magazine.

He took advantage of her momentary confusion to continue what he was saying. "Hitch has discovered incriminating evidence against you. I tried to find out what it is, but she wouldn't tell me. I'm just afraid it's going to get you sent to prison for the rest of your life."

She picked up her phone, pocketing it before taking another sip of her wine. She grimaced as if it tasted bitter on her tongue and put down her glass. "Has she taken this evidence to the prosecutor?"

"I don't know. Rachel, you know how I feel about you. Is there anything I can do?"

"Having you here, it's meant so much to me. I'm surprised you've stayed this long." She studied him for a moment. "I need more wine," she said, getting to her feet. She picked up his empty beer bottle. "Can I get you another beer?"

"Sure," he said as she headed into the kitchen. He realized that from here he could see her in the mirrored cabinets across from the sink. He watched her lean against the granite counter as if she needed it for strength. With a shaking hand, she refilled her glass and got another beer for him out of the refrigerator.

It was what she did next that stopped his heart cold. She opened the beer, poured some into a new frosted glass from the refrigerator's freezer, and then she took a small vial from her pocket.

He watched in horror as she poured something into his beer, holding up the glass to the light to make sure it had dissolved. Calling from the kitchen, she said, "You know me so well. That's why I'm glad you're here. I can tell you the truth."

She smiled as she picked up his beer and her wineglass. He watched her take a breath and then head into the living room.

IN THE LIVING ROOM, Ford quickly picked up his phone and hit Record. He put the phone back down where she'd left it and tried to still his breathing. His heart pounded so loudly, he feared she would be able to hear it. Of course Rachel was suspicious of his motives. But then again, he'd come running at the first sign that she was in trouble, reinforcing her belief that he adored her, that he'd always adored her, that he would always wish it had been him instead of Humphrey she'd fallen in love with. Did she think he was hoping for another chance with her, now that Humphrey was gone? Probably, knowing Rachel.

"Here," she said as she came back into the room and handed him the glass of beer.

He set the frosted glass with the doctored beer on the coffee table. Rachel quickly reached to put a coaster under it. "Thank you," he said but didn't touch the beer.

She returned to the kitchen to snag a full opened bottle of wine, then returned to her place at the end of the couch, facing him. "Humphrey loved a chilled glass for his beer, but I guess I don't need to tell you that. You probably remember."

He nodded. "I'm so sorry things turned out the way they did." She took a sip of her wine and didn't look at him. "I mean it, Rachel. If there is anything I can do... You know I'm here for you."

She looked up then, and their eyes locked for a few seconds before she said, "I wish there was, Ford. Having you here, it's meant so much to me. How will I ever be able to repay you?"

He thought about what he'd seen her put into his beer glass. Was it something that would kill him? Or just make him deathly ill? Gut-wrenching poison or truth serum? With Rachel, he had no idea.

One thing was clear. She hadn't bought his act.

"Remember the first time we met?" she was saying, a cheerfulness in her voice that didn't quite ring true. "I wish I could go back to that day. If you had left me alone, that squirrel would have eaten out of my hand."

He smiled in spite of himself. "Because you wouldn't have given up until it did. You were always like that. When you wanted something, you hung in until you got it."

"Like with Humphrey," she said, the cheerfulness gone. "You know he had second thoughts about marrying me, don't you? Of course you did. You were his best man, his best friend. He would have told you. He wouldn't have married me if it wasn't for the pregnancy. You probably thought that I got pregnant on purpose so he didn't get away. That's what his father thought. After we got married, when I lost the baby, Humphrey was devastated. He wanted that child so badly." She looked away as she took a sip of her wine. "I don't know why I'm bringing all of this back up. Bad memories."

"He loved you."

She met his gaze again. "Yes, he did. But he never forgave me." She let out a bitter laugh. "He would have left me, except that it would have proved his father right."

He frowned. "Forgave you for what?"

"I didn't lose the baby, because there never was one. His father hired a private investigator. I lied about the pregnancy. Humphrey didn't find out until we'd been married almost a year."

"What was the fight about the day he died?" Ford asked.

She looked away for a moment. "He found my birth control pills." She laughed. "Stupid me. I never kept them in my purse."

He stared at her in shock. "Why wouldn't you want his child? Wouldn't Bart have changed his mind about you if you'd given him a grandchild?"

"I wasn't anyone's broodmare," she snapped. "I wasn't ruining my figure, let alone having a child to take care of. That wasn't the life I wanted."

He didn't know what to say. His shock must have shown.

"Didn't I have the right? It's my body."

Ford couldn't help but wonder what his old friend would have done when he found out that his wife had been lying to him for years. "You could have adopted."

She let out a bitter bark of a laugh. "That's exactly what he said, telling me that we could adopt children no one else wanted because we had this amazing place to raise them." She looked horrified. "Children no one else wanted? Over my dead body."

Could her lies have led Humphrey to attack her? Maybe Rachel was telling the truth.

"Also, some money had gone missing from this foundation Humphrey had started. I was involved in it and he had the gall to ask me if I'd stolen it." She took another sip of her wine, anger pinching her classic features.

Ford let out the breath he'd been holding. Now he realized how little he'd known about their relationship or the lengths Rachel would go to get what she wanted. "Did he threaten divorce?"

Rachel laughed. "He said he needed time to think. That he still loved me. But that he couldn't look at me right then. He took off into town to see his girlfriend at the café. It doesn't matter if they were actually sleeping together," she snapped before Ford could correct her. "The girl was all doe-eyed around him. Just the kind of woman he'd thought he'd married."

"That sounds like Humphrey," Ford said. "The part about still loving you. He told me at the wedding that he suspected you were lying about the pregnancy and even why you wanted to marry him so badly, but he said he didn't care. He loved you."

Tears filled her eyes. "I never knew that." She looked away again and downed more of the wine. "I hate to imagine what you must think of me." Her gaze went to his beer glass sweating on the coaster on the coffee table. "You haven't touched your beer."

"Did you do it, Rachel? Did you stage the whole thing to get rid of him so you didn't lose the money?"

Her head jerked around so she was facing him again. Color rushed to her cheeks, anger glinting in her eyes. "That's what you think, isn't it? You and the medical examiner."

He couldn't deny it. "Is it true? It's just you and me here, Rachel. Tell me so I can help you."

She glared at him for a long moment before she put down her wineglass and rose to her feet. "I think you should leave."

He nodded. "Just one more question." He motioned to the room, taking her in with it. "What did you hope to accomplish tonight with the dim lighting, the perfume, that silky outfit you're wearing and the chilled beer glass? Were you worried that you'd lost my undying admiration and love?"

She shook back a lock of her blond hair that had come loose and fallen around her face. Her blue eyes were hard as ice chips and just as cold. "You have always underestimated me, Ford. If I wanted to seduce you, we'd be in my king-size bed right now."

He smiled. "No, Rachel, this time, you overestimated yourself." He picked up his phone. Turning off the recording, he looked up at her. "I came out here hoping you would tell me the truth. After all, you pulled me into this." He glanced at his beer glass. "I can't even imagine what you put into my beer, but I know now that you used me—just like you did Humphrey until you got tired of him. Was he going to divorce you? Is that why you killed him?" Her answer was that icy glare. "I wasn't kidding about the medical examiner being on to you. You thought your old life was bad? Wait until you get to prison."

With that, he turned to walk out. The wineglass hit the wall next to him and shattered, red wine droplets splattering against the white wall like blood.

He turned to look back at her seething angry face. Was this the last thing Humphrey saw before she pulled the trigger?

HITCH WAS SO relieved when she opened her hotel room to find Ford standing there that she threw herself into his arms. He smiled as if touched by her concern and kissed her. They stayed like that for long minutes.

"She didn't buy it," he said as they moved deeper into her room. "But she did try to drug me."

"What?"

"I saw her put a powder substance in my second beer. But I did get something. She left her new phone in the room with me when she went into the kitchen. There was a recent photo taken of her tied to an iron bed. The only thing she was wearing was a Sweet Grass County Volunteer Fire Department jacket. It's her new phone, so the photographer wasn't Humphrey. She did it," he said quietly. "I know she did it. I saw it in her face." He sat down on the foot of her bed. "She killed him. She planned the whole thing right from the beginning fifteen years ago. I just don't know why she waited so long."

Hitch sat down next to him as he told her everything that had happened. Then he let her listen to the recording on his phone. When they'd finished, Hitch actually felt shocked. As long as she'd been in this business, she'd believed that she could no longer be shocked. "That woman is cold."

She got up and went over to the bed where the case notes were spread across the top. It took her only a moment to find what she was looking for. "The fingerprints found on the birth control pill package on the floor were Humphrey's."

He turned to her. "She admitted that's what they fought about. So maybe he didn't threaten her with divorce and she saw only one way to have it all. You have to stop her. No matter what it takes. She can't get away with this."

She smiled at him. "Don't worry. I'm working on it." She told him about her visit to Shyla Birch's house and meeting her unfriendly husband, the deputy, along with what she'd found in the garage.

Ford's eyes widened in alarm. "Are you telling me the pickup that almost killed you was driven by a deputy?"

"Or his wife. *Possibly.* The problem is the grille guard on the front of the pickup. When I got back, I found the manufacturer. The company sold nine in this area. *Nine.* But I can tell you one thing. Rick Birch and his wife are both with the Sweet Grass County Volunteer Fire Department. I saw one of their jackets hanging by the door as I left—not that it narrows it down. A lot of locals are also volunteer firemen. So tell me what you know about Shyla."

He raked a hand through his hair. "She was impulsive and a little wild, but I can't imagine her trying to run you down."

"I agree. Between the two? I would pick the husband."

Ford let out a curse. "You think he's Rachel's accomplice?"

"I think it's possible." She told him the story Shyla had related to her about how they'd met and fallen in love. "She credits Rachel for getting them together."

"You think Rachel knew him before then?"

Hitch shrugged. "I suspect he's protective of Rachel. He wasn't happy to see me with his wife. As I was leaving, I heard him demand to know what she said to me. He seems like the kind who went into law enforcement to bust heads. If he bought into Rachel's story about her husband, he might have seen helping her as a way to right a wrong. Or he could just be sleeping with her and agreed to do whatever she asked him to."

"He's *married* to Shyla."

Hitch rolled her eyes. "Right, Rachel's so-called best friend. You really think that would stop him?"

Ford shook his head. "How are you going to prove it one way or the other?"

"I wish I knew. The fact that he's a deputy makes it harder."

"But if you told the sheriff about the truck that tried to run you down…"

She saw realization sink in before he could finish. "Exactly. My word against his deputy. In the first place, I can't prove it was even him, let alone that he was trying to kill me. Nor did I get a license plate number. Just a metal guard like at least eight others like it around… So even if I could put his pickup on that street that night definitively, he could say that he never saw me. It is a very dark street."

"What are you going to do?" he asked, his voice softening as he looked at her.

She shook her head. "I'm just glad that you're all right."

"I'm sorry it didn't work. Rachel's too smart for me."

Hitch laughed. "She's not too smart for either of us and she's going to prove it. She has to be rattled right now. I would think she'll be contacting her accomplice."

"Another night on the mountain?"

"Not this time," Hitch said. "I have her phone tapped. We should be hearing something soon."

He tucked a lock of her hair behind her ear. "What should we do in the meantime?"

RACHEL HAD STORMED around her house after Ford left. Who did he think he was? That he'd come out to her house to try to get her to admit to something she hadn't done? What kind of friend was that?

She stopped to stare at the wall, still red from her wine, the broken glass twinkling on the carpet, and she felt all the anger rush from her. Stumbling back to the couch, she looked for her phone until she realized she'd put it in her pocket earlier. Frowning, she glanced at the coffee table. The magazines were no longer neatly displayed, but they had been before Ford arrived. So how could her phone have gotten under one of them?

It couldn't have.

She felt an icy chill run like spider legs down her spine and shuddered. He'd had her phone. She opened it. A photo came up of her on the bed and she dropped to the edge of the couch. With trembling fingers, she placed the call.

"Rachel, what's wrong?" Shyla said when she answered and heard her crying. "Do you want me to come out there?"

"No," Rachel said quickly. "It's… Ford was here earlier. He said some awful things to me."

"Like what? Rachel? Did I lose you? Are you still there?"

"It's my new cell phone. I don't know what's wrong with it. The battery keeps running down. I'm plugging it in. Just a minute."

"Rach," Shyla said when she came back on. "Rick is standing here. He wants to talk to you."

"Did I hear you're having trouble with your new cell phone?"

"I can't seem to keep it charged."

Rick let out a curse. "Rachel, they've got your phone tapped. The taps run down the batteries. Have you seen any apps that have suddenly appeared that aren't yours?"

She gritted her teeth and tried not to snarl. "I've had a little too much on my mind to be checking my *apps*."

"What about any weird text messages?"

Rachel opened her mouth to snap at him but closed it. "I got something about winning a prize that I had to redeem."

He swore. "Is your phone warmer than your old one? They often overheat if someone is using GPS to track your phone." She said it was. "Which means they're not just tapping into your calls—they're tracking you."

Rachel felt her skin grow clammy and cold. "What can I do?"

"Get rid of any apps you don't recognize, then update your phone and don't use it."

"And how am I supposed to hear from you?" she cried.

"I'll get you a burner. I'll have Shyla bring it out. But you have to quit running scared and acting like you're guilty. Remember, you're the victim here. Humphrey would have killed you."

She nodded as she looked at the wine staining her wall. "Rick, I'm scared."

"Don't be. You did what you had to do. They're just try-ing to rattle you. Shyla wants to talk to you."

"Are you sure you don't want me to come out there?" her friend asked.

"No," Rachel said, looking at her phone where she'd plugged it in. "I'm fine. I'm going straight to bed. I think I just need a good night's sleep." She disconnected, and picking up Ford's beer where he'd left it, she walked into the kitchen and poured it down the drain.

For a moment, she stood at the sink staring out into the darkness before she walked down to her bedroom and began to pull out her luggage.

Chapter Twenty-Four

"So you're really going," Hitch said the next morning when she woke up next to Ford. She'd been encouraging him to go for days. She'd seen the change in him, though, last night. He was finally free of Rachel Westlake Collinwood. She wished she was.

Last night after their lovemaking, Ford opened up to her. They'd shared stories, confided hopes and dreams and fears. Then they'd made love again and held each other like two lost souls caught in a storm.

"I need to go back and figure out what I'm going to do for a living," he said. "But I'm only a phone call away." He smiled at her and she felt the heat of it race through her veins. Last night had been amazing. Ford was a tender, thoughtful lover who took it slow—the first time. She smiled to herself, remembering the passion of the second time. Her cheeks heated at the memory.

"I'll miss you," she said, snuggling against him.

"No, you won't. You'll be too busy getting to the truth."

"I wish, but the forty-eight hours the governor gave me is almost up. On top of that, the sheriff told the governor about us. Not that I care," she was quick to add. "It just…"

"Complicates things. Another reason I need to leave."

Unfortunately, she had to agree, especially after what Ford had told her about Rachel trying to drug him. "This investigation has to break soon."

He laughed. "You'd know better than me, but I sure hope so."

"I have just a little more time before I have to put this one behind me. But just the thought of turning it over to the sheriff... As if he's going to continue gathering evidence between now and the trial. If there even is a trial." She shook her head. "So basically, nothing will be done, and Rachel will either get off entirely or receive a light sentence. There's nothing I can do about it."

Ford pulled her closer. "You still have a little time."

She chuckled. "At this point, I could have a month and I'm not sure I'd know exactly what happened on that ranch that day. And the worst part is that if I'm right that is exactly what Rachel is counting on."

He kissed her passionately before he let her go. "I'll call when I get back to Big Sky. Once you wrap it up—"

"The governor said there's another case waiting for me. But don't worry. I'll find a way to see you." Because she couldn't bear the thought of being away from him very long.

He pulled her closer. "I can't wait for you to meet my family."

She felt at a loss for words, wanting to tell him how she felt, but knowing that the timing was wrong. "We'll talk soon."

FORD KNEW IT was time to go home. He could tell during his father's last call that he was getting worried. It was Rachel. Jackson worried that he was too involved in this case—if not involved with Rachel herself.

Mostly, Ford knew he had to let Hitch do what she did so well and quit distracting her. She couldn't do her job if she was worried about him. He'd played amateur detective, and if he hadn't seen whatever Rachel had put in his beer, he would be buried now in the garden on the ranch.

He was on the edge of Big Timber leaving town when

his cell phone rang. He saw it was Rachel calling and almost didn't take it. "Rachel?" For a moment, he didn't hear anything but crying. Then he heard the words that had him hitting his brakes and pulling to the side of the road.

"You're right about me. I don't deserve to live," Rachel said, her words slurred as if she were drunk. Drunk? Or drugged?

"What's going on?" he asked, his pulse jumping at her words.

"I can't do this anymore," she said. "I should have told you everything last night. I should have… I can't live with myself…" She began to sob again.

"Have you taken something, Rachel?" He heard her drop the phone, the rest of her words inaudible.

Swearing, he quickly turned around and headed toward the ranch. He debated calling 911 for an ambulance, but he was already on his way and would be there in a matter of minutes at this speed. Maybe she was just drunk. But if she'd taken something… He thought of that time in college when she and Humphrey had a fight and she'd taken a bottle of pills. Ford and Humphrey had walked her for hours until she came out of it.

He was just north of town near the creek when he caught lights in his rearview mirror. A highway patrol cruiser came racing up behind him, siren blaring, lights flashing. Ford swore but pulled over, planning to tell the officer why he'd been speeding and ask for his help. Rachel would hate that he brought the cops into it, but he had no choice now. He reminded himself that this was the woman who'd planned to drug him just last night. Still, he didn't want her overdose death on his conscience. Nor did he want Hitch's case to end like this.

When he started to pull over, the cruiser drew up beside him. The officer behind the wheel motioned for him to pull off the road onto a side road. He did as ordered, anxious to talk to the cop. He could feel the clock ticking and thought about calling 911 but knew it would take too much explanation. Pulling out his phone, he quickly called Hitch, but before he could speak, the officer tapped on his window.

Ford whirred down his window. "Officer, I know I was speeding," he said to the sandy-haired young cop. He saw that he was a deputy sheriff—not highway patrol as he'd first thought. "I just got a call—"

"Please get out of your vehicle."

"What? No, you don't understand." His pulse jumped. Something was wrong. His gaze went to the man's hands resting on the edge of the open window. A large ring on the officer's right hand caught his eye. Something about the design... He heard Hitch's voice far away and realized that she was still on the phone. "Officer, Rachel Collinwood called. I was on my way there before you pulled me over here by the creek—"

"I said get out of your vehicle now!"

"Okay, but this is highly unusual. Kind of like your ring..." He spotted the man's name on his shirt. "Officer Birch." His heart was now a hammer in his chest. Shyla's husband. The ring. The grille guard on the pickup that tried to run Hitch down. "I feel as if I've seen that ring before," he said, praying that Hitch was still on the line, that she was hearing this.

Movement in his side mirror. "Rachel? No wonder you weren't worried about her. She just climbed out of your patrol car."

"What the hell?" Birch said and spotted the phone lying on the seat next to Ford. The cop leaned in, snatched the keys from the ignition and, shoving Ford back, scooped up the phone. He swore and quickly ended the call, but hopefully Hitch had heard it all.

HITCH HAD BEEN going through the evidence on the Collinwood case when she'd gotten Ford's call. "Hello? Hello?" She could hear Ford talking and realized he wasn't talking to her but to someone else. As his words registered and the call ended, she threw down the photos she'd been studying, grabbed her gun and her purse, and raced out to her patrol SUV, her heart in her throat.

Her mind whirred as she played what she'd heard over and over again. He'd been headed for Big Sky. But Rachel had called. Whatever she'd said had him headed for her ranch, where he was pulled over by Officer Rick Birch. Why had Birch pulled him over by the creek? And why was the deputy demanding Ford get out of the car? As Ford said, very unusual. And the ring...

She felt her pulse thundering through her veins. If she was right, Ford was in serious trouble. He'd passed as much of a message as he'd been able to before the call had been disconnected.

With her siren blaring and lights flashing, she sped out of town, across the bridge over the Yellowstone River, headed north. She had a pretty good idea of where Ford had been pulled over. He'd said by the creek. It was the turnoff to the Crazy Mountains. She zipped past several cars that had pulled over at the sound of her siren. She took a few curves and hit the brakes as she saw the turnoff ahead.

But she couldn't see if Ford's pickup and the deputy's cruiser were still parked down by the creek yet. It had taken her only minutes to get here, but what if she was too late?

"LET ME HANDLE THIS," Rachel said as she walked up to the driver's-side window and pushed the deputy aside.

"I see that you're feeling better," Ford said, wondering what these two thought they were going to do as he opened his glove box to take out his gun. With a sinking feeling, he saw that it was gone.

As he turned to look at her, Ford foolishly still believed that they weren't going to kill him. He heard the deputy come around to the passenger side of the pickup and open the door. They wouldn't kill him—not right here beside the main highway north. He turned back to Rachel, since she was clearly in charge, saw the expression on her face and knew that he was a dead man.

He had only a second to react. Way too little time to see the syringe in her hand before she stabbed the needle into the back of his shoulder. He tried to grab for it, but the deputy was on him, restraining him until she pulled the needle from Ford's flesh. By then, it was too late. He already felt the drug rushing through him.

"What the hell, Rachel?" he managed to say.

"Drag him over to the passenger side," Rachel said, reaching in to unsnap his seat belt. The deputy grabbed him. Ford tried to fight him off, but he could feel his muscles already going slack. "Now give me the keys and wait for me in your car for a moment."

Birch looked as if he didn't like taking orders from a woman, but with a grunt, he snapped Ford's seat belt in place, climbed out, slammed the passenger-side door and returned to his patrol car, parked behind Ford's pickup.

"Rachel?" He felt dizzy, his vision beginning to blur. Whatever she'd injected him with, it was fast acting. His fingers felt like they were no longer his own as he tried unsuccessfully to unhook his seat belt. He heard Rachel lock his door with the child safety lock system.

"Sit tight for a moment," she said and closed the driver's-side door. He could see her walking back to the cruiser in his side mirror.

Ford knew he had to do something, but with his coordination getting worse as the drug took hold, he realized even if he could get out of the pickup, he probably couldn't stand, let alone run.

At the sound of a gunshot, he flinched.

The driver's-side door of his pickup opened a moment later and Rachel climbed in.

"What did you do?" he asked, his words slurred. He tried to get his arms to move, thinking he would go for her throat, but both arms hung useless at his sides.

"*I* didn't do anything," she said as she wiped the pistol in her hand clean with a handkerchief. He recognized it as his own gun. "*You* did." Then, taking his right hand, she pressed his palm, then trigger finger into the cold steel. Using the handkerchief, she tossed his gun behind the pickup seat.

When had she gotten it out of his glove box? Or had it been Birch who'd taken it on one of the occasions Ford had stopped by the ranch to see Rachel? Had she been planning this the whole time?

She started the pickup and headed down the dirt road toward the Crazy Mountains. He didn't bother to try to ask what she planned to do with him. His tongue felt too large and useless in his dry mouth to waste speech on a question when he already knew the answer. She planned to kill him—just as she had her accomplice.

Hitch raced up to the turnoff. It wasn't until she dropped off the highway into the creek bottom that she could see the sheriff's deputy's patrol cruiser still parked there. But there was no sign of Ford's pickup. She could, however, see that Deputy Birch was sitting behind the wheel.

She quickly pulled up behind the cruiser and, gun drawn, stepped out to cautiously approach. The deputy was wearing his Western hat. He appeared to be looking down at something in his lap. He didn't move as she inched along the driver's side of his vehicle.

As she drew nearer, she could see that his window was down. The summer breeze coming up off the creek was warm. It made a slight whistling sound through the patrol cruiser's antenna. Hitch came alongside, the weapon pointed at the man's head, and grabbed the door handle and pulled. It took her a moment before she realized that she wouldn't be needing her gun. Officer Rick Birch had already been shot in the side of the head.

Slamming the door, she looked up the road and spotted dust boiling up some distance away between her and the Crazies. She glanced around to see if there were fresh tracks where someone had turned around. There weren't.

Her nerves were taut as she rushed back to her rig, jumped in and took off. As she did, she called DCI and gave them the information as to where they would find sheriff's deputy Rick Birch. Disconnecting, she drove, following the dust trail, praying she was right about the vehicle kicking up the dust being Ford's pickup. If she was, then Rachel was with him. Which meant that if Ford was still alive, it wouldn't be for long.

Chapter Twenty-Five

"You wanted so badly to hear the truth?" She glanced at him before going back to her driving.

Ford saw the gleam in her blue eyes. She wanted to tell him. She wanted someone to know how clever she was.

Rachel suddenly hit the brakes so hard that even with his seat belt on, he flew forward. She caught him before his head hit the dash. "You're not wearing a wire, are you? Surely there wasn't time after my call." She tore open his shirt, checked under the waist of his jeans and then behind him before she sighed. "Of course you're not. And I have your phone. Even if I didn't, you wouldn't be able to record me." She laughed as she got the truck going again.

"You want my confession? You got it. I killed him. I set the whole thing up. It wasn't that hard," she said, warming to her story as she drove through the foothills toward the mountains. "I planned it for months, stashing away any money I could get my hands on. When he found the birth control pills... Well, I hadn't planned on that. He was so furious. I realized he really might divorce me. I followed him into town. I knew he'd go to that girl. I wanted to have the argument at her house. I wanted people to see it. Then I drove home. I'd already torn up the kitchen, breaking everything by the time he came home from town."

He thought about how Humphrey's fingerprints hadn't been found on any of the broken dishes on the floor—a red flag that Hitch had picked up on right away. If he had torn up the kitchen, his prints would have been on at least some of the shards. He wanted to tell her that it had been one of several mistakes she'd made, including killing Birch—and now him, but he could no longer speak. All he could do was listen and pray that Hitch had gotten the messages he'd tried to pass.

"You should have seen Humphrey's face when he walked into the kitchen and saw the mess. He actually looked at me as if I'd lost my mind. He really thought it was about that waitress at the café in town." She laughed. "He was going to help me clean up the mess. But before he could pick up anything, I jabbed him with the syringe—just like I did you." She chuckled. "It's fast acting, as you know, but he still managed to take a couple of steps toward me, so I pulled the gun. He looked dumbfounded for a moment, then demanded I hand the gun over." Her smile sent ice down his spine. It was worse than her laugh. "Oh, I gave it to him, all right."

"So you shot him before you pretended to be beaten by him." His words came out so slurred, he couldn't imagine how she had made sense of them.

"Pretended to be beaten?" she demanded. "Are you serious? You saw how badly I was injured." She sounded as if for a moment she believed her own lies. "Rick got a little carried away. I told him to make it look real. He certainly did that."

But he'd forgotten to take off his ring. Rachel must have noticed at some point. That would have been when they took off Humphrey's ring and the deputy used it to hit her. He'd seen the deputy's ring only minutes ago and recognized it from the bruise photo Hitch had shown him this morning, asking if he'd seen a ring that could have made that mark.

"That was the tricky part," Rachel was saying. "I needed

someone I could trust. Rick was more than up for the job. But the fool actually thought that we would be together once I was exonerated."

Ford thought of Paul Townsend. How many other men had Rachel "interviewed" for the job before she got the deputy to help her?

She gave a slight shrug as if Birch had been dispensable, just like Humphrey. He felt his anger, once molten with rage, stir in him, cold as this woman. He knew he could kill. He had in the war. He wished he could get his hands around Rachel's neck right now. She hadn't given a thought to her best friend, Shyla.

"You probably are wondering where you came in," Rachel said to him as the foothills were behind them and he was looking out at the mountain road ahead.

HITCH SAW THE vehicle still a long way ahead of her slow and turn. She felt relief wash over her. It was Ford's pickup— just as she'd thought. Her instincts had been right. She called for backup, explaining that Deputy Birch had been shot and killed and that Rachel Collinwood appeared to have taken Ford Cardwell captive. They were now headed into the Crazy Mountains. She gave the dispatcher the name of the road they were on and disconnected as Ford's pickup disappeared into the pines as it headed up the mountainside.

She told herself that Ford was still alive. She had to believe that. Rachel hadn't killed him and wasn't only driving up into the mountains to dump the body. If she'd done that, she would have needed the deputy's help. So what was her plan?

The deeper they got in the mountains, the more worried she became. She felt helpless because no matter what she did, it might only put Ford in more danger. Rachel had already killed twice. There was nothing keeping her from killing again.

All she could assume was that Rachel planned to end it and take Ford with her. The woman couldn't possibly think that she could still get away with what she'd done, could she? Probably, Hitch realized, remembering Rachel's arrogance.

As she closed the distance between her rig and the pickup, Hitch worried that Rachel would spot her. The mountain road, bordered on each side by pines, climbed in a series of switchbacks up the steep peak.

Hitch had lost sight of the pickup as she drove up the road in the shadow of the mountain. Her heart was thundering in her chest. She could feel the clock ticking. If Ford was still alive… She sped up, realizing she couldn't be that far from the top.

RACHEL'S VOICE BECAME an annoying drone in his ears as he listened to how cleverly she'd planned to kill her husband. "So Humphrey's lying on the floor dead. Rick has finished beating me when I call you, Ford. I scream and cry and finally grab the gun and fire a shot out the open kitchen door and disconnect, tossing it into Humphrey's blood and my own on the floor. I wait until Rick is gone before I call 911."

She didn't know about the cartridge casing Hitch had found just outside the kitchen door that had fallen through the deck slats. He made a disgusted, pained sound, thinking of his once best friend and this woman who'd come between them. She'd killed Humphrey, her deputy lover, and now she was about to kill him—unless somehow she was stopped.

He tried to ask if it was worth it, but nonsense came out of his mouth. She didn't seem to be listening anyway. What galled him was that she really thought she was going to get away with all of it—and she just might.

Unless Hitch had gotten the message he'd tried to pass to her. Hopefully she'd heard enough of the phone conversation to figure it out. If anyone could, it would be her, he thought, his heart aching. He'd found her and now would lose her. But he knew that Hitch wouldn't rest until she took Rachel down for all of it.

Rachel would never see the outside again. She'd told him that she'd worried about her next meal as a child. She wouldn't have to worry about it in prison. Nor about what to wear. And she deserved everything she would get and more.

"You probably want to know if I took the foundation money," she said as she drove up the mountain road. "I had no choice. Humphrey had cut off most of my credit cards and threatened to put me on a budget. I'm sure it was his father's idea. I had already lived hand to mouth. I wasn't going to do that again." She looked at him. "I suppose you'd say I could have gotten a job." She scoffed at that. "I was Mrs. Humphrey Collinwood and I wasn't giving that up without a fight."

She was quiet for a few minutes as the road topped the mountain. Where was she taking him? He had no idea. But he knew how it would end. He could see how agitated she was. She wanted all of this behind her.

"Humphrey loved you like a brother and blamed me for you dropping out of his life," she said, shifting the pickup into four-wheel low as the road became more rocky and rough, the trees more sparse. "He saw us, Ford. At the wedding."

He had started inside, the bitter taste of regret in his mouth.

"I made sure Humphrey saw what he thought was you practically assaulting me. It worked just as I'd hoped. You couldn't stay in our life, Ford. I needed him dependent on me and no one else. If you'd been around, he would have seen through me so much sooner. He didn't want to believe it, but only the two of us knew the truth. I wasn't ever going to tell him, and you were gone from our lives."

But Humphrey had still tried to contact him several times. Had he seen through Rachel even back then? Or had he needed Ford to tell him the truth? Ford realized if he had, he might have saved the man's life.

As HITCH REACHED the top of the mountain, the pines seemed to open up, but the road still twisted and turned. She was forced to drive slowly over the rocks sticking up in the road. Each corner she came around, she feared she would suddenly come up on the pickup stopped in the road and have no time to react.

It was a relief when the trees opened up even more and she could see farther ahead. She came around the edge of a wall of rock and suddenly there was the back of the pickup. It appeared to be parked at the edge of the rocky peak. Beyond it, there was nothing but blue sky and empty air.

In that split second, she knew. Ford must have told Rachel what he'd been doing when he'd gotten her call. Hitch hit her brakes and quickly backed up so her SUV was hidden from view. She killed the engine and, grabbing her gun, jumped out. As she neared the pickup and the edge of the mountain, the wind howled, bending the branches of the pines. No wonder they hadn't heard her driving up the mountain behind them, she thought.

She moved quickly, staying at the edge of the trees as she kept her gaze on the two in the pickup. Rachel was behind the wheel—just as Hitch had suspected. Ford appeared to be half slumped in the passenger-side seat. For a moment, she feared he was dead. But Rachel seemed to be talking to him.

As Hitch drew closer, though, her heart dropped when she saw how close Rachel had parked from the edge of a cliff. The engine was still running. Hitch's stomach dropped as she realized what the woman planned to do.

Chapter Twenty-Six

Ford couldn't feel his body. His mind, though, was sharp, and there was nothing wrong with his hearing. He tried not to think about what was going to happen or why living now meant so much to him. Hitch. They'd only just started, and now...

"I didn't want it to end this way, but you have to admit, you gave me the perfect way to get rid of you." Rachel chuckled. "If you hadn't told me about how I'd saved your life with my phone call... Well, I would have found another way, but you did make this easy. I appreciate that."

He made a sound deep in his throat as he looked out at the endless sky. He couldn't see how far it was to the bottom, which was just as well, he thought.

"The thing is, I can't trust you, Ford. If I thought you'd come back for the trial and tell them how much I loved Humphrey and how much he loved me and just keep it to the phone call... But you couldn't do that, could you? You kept digging. Just like that medical examiner. Once Humphrey found my birth control pills, he wouldn't listen to reason. Maybe I wanted him to find them. Maybe I just wanted it all to be over." She sighed.

"You brought this on yourself," Rachel said, as if working herself up to what she had to do. "You should have just told the sheriff what you'd heard and gone back to Big Sky until the trial. Instead, you got involved with that...

woman." Her voice was rising. "You slept with her, didn't you. I saw the way you looked at me after that." He heard the jealousy, saw it in her blue eyes. "You betrayed me. You were the one person I thought I could trust. I trusted you with my life, Ford!" She looked at him as if she hated him. Her laugh was brittle. "She was just using you, and look where it's gotten you."

Rachel took a breath and seemed resolved. "Shyla will be driving up here soon to pick me up. Don't worry. She's coming from another road, so she won't see her husband. That marriage would have never lasted anyway. It's time to say goodbye, Ford."

He said nothing. Even if he could have spoken, he wouldn't have known what to say to someone so cold and calculating, so inherently evil.

Ford watched her as she picked up the winter scraper he kept in his truck to clean ice off the windshield in the winter. She leaned down and jammed it against the gas pedal. The pickup's engine roared. She pried the other end of the scraper against the back of the brake pedal.

This was it, Ford thought, wishing the drug she'd injected him with had knocked him out—not left him in this state where he could see and hear what was happening to him. But he figured Rachel had known what dosage to give him so he would at least mentally suffer until the end. Probably just as she had Humphrey.

As he looked at the drop-off in front of the pickup, he knew he would never have taken this way out. He would have stopped before the end of the road even if Rachel hadn't called.

What had saved his life, though, wasn't Rachel but Hitch. He was falling in love with her, which made dying now so much more painful. He desperately wanted to live to see where this relationship took the two of them. He knew she would be his last thought before the end.

Rachel looked over at him, the engine a roar, so she had to yell to be heard. "I'm sorry it had to end like this." He wondered if she'd said the same thing before she killed his best friend. She reached over and unsnapped his seat belt. Then she shoved the pickup into gear and reached for the door handle as the truck leaped forward.

KEEPING LOW, HITCH crept up the passenger side of the pickup. There had to be a reason Ford hadn't moved, hadn't tried to stop this. She thought about Humphrey. Ketamine. Rachel knew how quickly it worked—and how just as fast it left the body, leaving no trace. If she'd used it on her husband, then why not Ford?

All she knew for sure was that she would get only one chance to pull Ford from the pickup as she heard the engine rev and Rachel struggling to get the sprung driver's-side door open.

Hitch moved fast the moment she heard the engine rev up. She knew she'd have only one chance. She grabbed the passenger-side door handle and yanked it open. As she did, she saw Rachel turn in her direction as she struggled to get out of the driver's-side door.

It all happened in an instant and yet time seemed to stop in that moment, suspended as if frozen. Rachel's expression was one of surprise, then realization as Hitch reached over to unsnap Ford's seat belt and practically throw him from the moving vehicle. Rachel was still struggling to get out, her mouth a perfect O, mimicking the saucer shape of her blue eyes.

Hitch fell from the pickup with her arms wrapped around Ford. She hit the ground hard, knocking the air from her lungs but not breaking her hold on him. She felt the back tire skim past them, felt the edge of the earth so close that one of her feet dangled over the precipice. For a moment, she wasn't even sure that they wouldn't still go over the edge of the cliff after the pickup.

Over the sound of the howling wind, the roar of the pickup's engine, came Rachel's screams. They seemed to go on forever, diminishing as she fell, until the cries finally stopped just moments before the boom of an explosion. The sky below the cliff turned orange and then black with smoke as Hitch dragged herself back from the precipice to stand.

Ford lay on his back staring up at the sky overhead. For a moment, she thought he was dead. But then he blinked. She saw his fingers move. She smiled down at him, then bent and kissed his lips. She felt them move under her own. Pulling back, she brushed his hair from his face as she picked up another sound. Sirens.

Chapter Twenty-Seven

Ford drove through the gateway opening between the mountain and into the Gallatin Canyon. He felt something release inside him as if he was finally coming home. He reached over to squeeze Hitch's hand. Her fresh scent mixed with the smell of new leather. He'd thought he would miss his old pickup when he'd had to replace it. But he'd been wrong about that. He seldom gave that truck a thought.

Anyway, the new-leather smell wouldn't last long, once he went to work on the ranch hauling hay and critters. He couldn't wait.

It was one of those cloudless Montana late-summer days, the sky overhead a bottomless blue. The afternoon sun shone on the pines and the rock rims over the sparkling clear green of the Gallatin River as it wound through the narrow canyon, the mountains rising high on each side. After everything he'd been through, he felt as if he was seeing it for the first time. It was the most beautiful sight he'd ever seen.

He glanced over at Hitch. "You sure you're ready for this?" he asked, grinning. He'd been waiting what seemed like a very long time to take her home to meet his family. The investigation had taken a while to complete even with his testimony about Rachel's confession—and the evidence Hitch had accumulated.

Shyla had been shocked to hear about her husband's death—and maybe even more shocked to find out that he'd been Rachel's accomplice. She had driven up the mountain road at her friend's request with Rachel's suitcases in her trunk. It had seemed a strange request. She'd thought she was taking Rachel to the airport. Little did she know that her best friend never planned for her to leave that mountain alive.

The story all came out over the months that followed. It had been the little things that Rachel had overlooked. All together, though, they painted a picture of a woman desperate to keep her level of living and at the same time get rid of her husband.

In the end, Hitch had put together enough evidence that the investigators almost didn't need his testimony about Rachel's confession. He tried not to think about her and the lives she'd wasted—her own included.

"Meeting your family can't be that scary," Hitch said now with a laugh. "Sounds like there are a lot of them?"

"Between the Cardwells and the Savages, uh-huh. My aunt Dana will insist on throwing a party to get everyone together. It's what she does. She's the matriarch of the family. Everyone pretty much does what she tells them to— even my uncle Hud. Then there is my father and stepmother and all my uncles involved in the Texas barbecue business and my aunts and my cousins…"

"I get the picture," she said with a shake of her head. "You've told them about me? About us? About what I do for a living?"

He nodded. "There are a few cops in the family and private detectives, and of course Uncle Hud is still marshal, although he's supposed to be retiring."

"Then I should feel right at home," she said, smiling.

"I hope so." He knew they would love her as much as

he did. The woman had saved his life. If his aunt Dana had anything to do with it, they would welcome her with a brass band.

HITCH COULDN'T BELIEVE what they'd both been through together in such a short time as she looked out at the gorgeous summer day. It was hard to put it all behind her. She knew it must be even harder for Ford. She could tell coming home was the best medicine for him.

Fortunately, the drug Rachel had injected him with hadn't done any long-term damage. If the near-death experience had brought back his PTSD, it didn't show. He seemed to have come through it stronger and with fewer scars. He credited her with that, but he was strong and he was finding his footing on Cardwell Ranch. Ranching suited him. She loved seeing him happy.

But the fact that she'd almost lost him was never far from her mind. Rachel had proved to be more cold-blooded than even some of the worst male criminals Hitch had run across.

"The sad part," Ford had told her after it was all over, "is that I knew Humphrey. He wouldn't have divorced Rachel and left her penniless, no matter what the prenuptial agreement said. Even with all the lies she'd told him, he still loved her. He would have given her more money than she deserved."

"Not enough for her, though," Hitch had said. "She wanted it all."

"From what she told me, she knew that Humphrey loved her right up to the end. She seemed angry that he still did even when she shot him."

Hitch had wanted Rachel Collinwood to spend her life behind bars. She didn't even deserve a not-very-quick death. But often people didn't get what they deserved.

That thought made her smile, because a part of her thought she probably didn't deserve a man like Ford Cardwell, but she had Rachel to thank for bringing them together. Hitch had fallen in love with him, something that still surprised her, since she'd thought she'd never meet anyone like him.

"Brace yourself," he said now as he slowed the pickup after taking the turnoff to Big Sky. "I can't wait for you to meet everyone. It's just that they can be a bit overwhelming. Also, since I've never brought anyone home before, they're going to know I'm serious about you. Especially my aunt Dana. She'll spot how crazy I am about you right away. She'll be delighted and unable not to show it and get that wedding gleam in her eye. Then there is Uncle Hud—"

"The marshal." Ford drove over the bridge spanning the river. Ahead, she could see the ranch. To her surprise, she actually felt butterflies.

"Hud will be happy to have another person in law enforcement in the family. Not to mention my father. He's been worrying about what I plan to do with my life. He'll think this has happened too fast—"

"It probably has," she said.

He shook his head and smiled at her. "You know when it's right from the moment you feel it."

She nodded as he turned in front of a large two-story house. People instantly began to pour out onto the wide front porch and down the steps. Hitch laughed and couldn't help smiling.

"I wasn't kidding," Ford said. "Want to run now?"

Hitch shook her head. "Nope. You know me. I'm in it for the long haul."

"That's what I'm counting on," he said, and the two of them opened their doors and their arms to his family.

* * * * *

THE BAIT

CAROL ERICSON

Prologue

Rule number two. Don't take any undue risks for fame or attention.

He snorted, a little bit of spittle dribbling onto his chin. He swiped it off with the back of his hand. No guts, no glory. Isn't that what Coach always used to say? Or was that no pain, no gain? Whatever.

He slumped in the driver seat, the dome light spilling onto the computer tablet clutched in his hand. His finger trailed down the edge of the display as he greedily consumed the online article about a possible third serial killer copying The Player, a murderer who was active twenty years ago.

The media had dubbed the first copycat, Jordy Lee Cannon, the Copycat Player. They called the second guy, Cyrus Fisher, Copycat 2.0. Now, after the discovery of a body dumped in the foothills of the San Gabriel Mountains, the LAPD feared a third serial killer was at work, using The Player's MO.

The media had better come up with a more badass name than those stupid ones for him.

Squinting at the text once more, he continued scanning the article for information he already knew by heart. After Cannon became a suspect in the slayings of four women, the lead detective on the case, Detective Jake

McAllister shot and killed Cannon when he threatened another woman with a knife. Fisher took his own life by ingesting a cyanide tablet when cornered by Detective McAllister with evidence of his guilt in the murders of three women.

He read aloud from the article, his voice booming in the car. "'We identified and stopped the previous two killers, and I'm confident we'll put an end to this one, too,' said McAllister when questioned about this third killer. McAllister had no comment as to why these three killers decided to pick up the mantle of The Player, a serial killer who terrorized women in Los Angeles twenty years ago."

"Confident, are you?" He scrolled down the screen to the picture of McAllister, his large frame in a suit and tie, his square jaw set with determination, his eyes staring at the camera. He hated the bastard on sight.

Drilling his finger into the cop's forehead, he said, "You're not dealing with that idiot coffee dude, Jordy, or that nerd, Cyrus, this time, McAllister."

Raucous laughter erupted from across the parking lot, and he jerked his head up to witness a bunch of drunk frat boys stumbling from the club, the pink neon from the Candy Girls sign highlighting their perfect hair and chiseled features. Probably got tossed out for harassing the dancers—losers.

They couldn't do what he did tonight. He flexed his fingers and felt the bones of the woman's neck beneath his hands again. It would've been better without gloves. It would've been better with a knife. It would've been better if he could've had sex with her first.

But rules were rules—even though a few of those rules were meant to be broken. Had Coach said that, too? Probably not. Coach had been a stickler for rules.

His gaze tracked to the sign on the outside of the club,

flashing different colors of lollipops, and his mouth watered. Maybe he'd reward himself with a lap dance tonight, but only if Barbi was working. He liked her long, straight brown hair—just like Carmela's hair tonight.

When Barbi gave him a lap dance, he could scrunch up his eyes and pretend it was Jenna, just like he pretended Carmela was Jenna and Juliana before her. He'd have to remember to keep his hands to himself though. He'd gotten carried away last time and had put his hands around Barbi's neck.

The bouncer had seen him, or maybe Barbi had pressed her panic button. Either way, the beefy security guy had put a stop to the dance and never even refunded his money. He gave Barbi a tip, anyway, just to say he was sorry, and she'd smiled at him.

He started getting hard thinking about Barbi and Carmella and Juliana and even that bitch Jenna, and he dug the heels of his hands into his temples. He'd have time for that once he'd slipped into the dark confines of Candy Girls.

Taking a deep breath, he reached into his back seat for the mini cooler, which contained a couple of ice packs. He dragged the cooler onto the passenger seat and flipped it open.

He reached into the console with his fingertips and snatched up the pair of lacy panties he'd taken from Carmela's body. Pressing them to his face, he inhaled her scent. As he dropped the underwear into the cooler, he said, "One souvenir for me."

Then he picked up the plastic bag that contained Carmela's left pinky finger and placed it on top of one of the ice packs. Scowling at the bloody digit, he said, "And one souvenir for him."

Chapter One

Crouching in the dirt, Detective Jake McAllister met his partner's eyes over the dead body of a young woman, a queen of hearts between her lips, her long, brown hair placed over her shoulder, the lower half of her torso naked, her jeans tossed beside her.

With a gloved finger, Jake traced the ring of bruises around her neck. "Maybe he raped this one."

Detective Billy Crouch shook his head. "He didn't rape Juliana French, even though he removed her pants and underwear. No rape, no DNA. He's sticking to the program."

Jake shifted, crunching the leaves beneath his shoes, an uneasy feeling knotting his gut.

Raising his eyebrows, Billy said, "You know it's true, J-Mac. We can't ignore it. The three serial killers—Cannon, Fisher and now this sick SOB are all following some master plan. Our computer forensics uncovered an online link between Cannon and Fisher, and my guess is we'll see the same connection to our current killer."

"I know you're right." Jake sat back on his heels and lifted the woman's left hand, a bloody gouge in place of her pinky finger. "He's taking their panties as his trophy. They each claimed their own trophy—Cannon stole a piece of jewelry and Fisher snipped a lock of hair—but they all made sure to sever the finger."

"Pulling off their pants and underwear indicates more ambition, greater risk taking."

"I'm counting on that to trip him up." Jake lifted a lock of the woman's silky hair, letting it slide through his fingers. "This one seems to have a type. Juliana had long, dark brown hair, too."

"That's one thing he has in common with The Player when choosing victims. Cannon chose his based on young women coming to the coffeehouse. Fisher stalked women who lived alone and had poor security at their homes. This guy is using appearance to choose his victims, just like The Player did. Only The Player preferred blondes."

"I know he did." Jake swallowed, thinking about Kyra's mother, Jennifer Lake.

"Are you guys finished?" Clive Stewart, their finger-print tech, held up his black bag and indicated the waiting LAPD crime scene investigators.

"It's all yours." Jake pushed to his feet and said, "Maybe we'll get lucky again like we did with Fisher, and he'll leave a print, Clive."

Clive surveyed the body on its bed of leaves and dirt and nodded. "Could be. He's leaving a messier scene than either of the others."

Jake turned his back on the CSIs as they descended on the young woman. She didn't look like a sex worker, but sometimes you couldn't tell by appearances. Juliana French hadn't been a prostitute. She hadn't lived alone, either. She'd disappeared between a club and her car. There was some speculation on the task force that she'd hopped into a car, thinking it was an app ride.

Peeling off his gloves, Jake strode away from the dump site back to the access road that bordered the trail.

Too many cars had driven over the road to be able to make any sense of the tire tracks.

He glanced up at the trees, some leaves crisping at the edges with the coming autumn, others as green as ever with plans to stay that way through the season. LA had its own fall colors that eluded the detection of transplants from the East but made their mark on natives. He could feel and smell the changing of the seasons despite the greenery around him.

As he emerged from the foliage, the gathered press lit up, swinging their cameras and microphones in his direction.

"Detective McAllister, is this the work of another serial killer?"

"Is this the same guy who did Juliana?"

"Another copycat, Detective McAllister?"

He dropped his sunglasses from his head to the bridge of his nose and held up his hand. "No comment for now. Stay tuned for a press conference later in the week."

He ducked into his sedan. Waiting for Billy to join him, he took out his phone and tapped through the pictures he had taken of the crime scene—horrific pictures, indecent pictures. He said through gritted teeth, "What do you do with their panties, freak?"

He jumped when Billy yanked open the car door. "Talking to yourself again, brother, or singing? I saw your lips moving."

"I'm talking to this piece of scum." Jake flashed his phone at Billy.

"Did you tell him we're going to nail him, just like the other two?"

"Something like that." Jake cranked on the engine and pulled around a group of emergency vehicles, including the coroner's van. "What took you so long? You weren't giving an exclusive to your reporter girlfriend, were you?"

"I did go over for a chat, but Megan Wright isn't my girlfriend, and even if she were, she's not getting any details and she knows it."

"Is that why she's not your girlfriend?"

Billy punched Jake's arm. "Are you implying that's the only reason she's going out with me?"

"So, you *are* still going out."

"We're going out, but she's not my girlfriend. I mean, we're not exclusive…unlike you and Kyra."

"Kyra and I…" Jake shrugged. What he and Kyra had was complicated. "Did you finally meet with the PI?"

Billy knew a subject change when he heard it, and he grinned. "Yeah, we met."

"Do you like him? Do you think he's going to be able to help you find your sister?"

"She. The PI is a lady."

"Questions remain the same."

"I like Dina. I think she can help, and yes, she *is* attractive."

"Uh-oh." Jake glanced at Billy. "Is that going to be a problem for you?"

"Moi?" Billy flicked his tie in front of him. "Not at all. She happens to be involved with Jansen, Narcotics. That's how I got her name. The first guy I contacted fell through, and someone in Narcotics heard I was looking. Put me in touch with Jansen, who put me in touch with Dina."

"All joking aside, I hope she can help you find your sister."

"Me, too," Billy said, and stared out the window.

Their drive back to the station was unusually quiet, considering they'd just come from the dump site of a second body that looked like the work of a third copycat serial killer. How unusual was this? The only reason the Feds hadn't moved in yet was due to the success of the LAPD task force in identifying and stopping the first two copycat killers.

When they got back to the task force war room that had been functional for over three months now, Billy took it upon himself to start going through the files of missing women in LA to see if he could find a match to the body in the canyon.

Ever since Billy's sister, Sabrina, had gone missing, Billy had taken a special interest in the lost girls of LA. Jake left him alone with his sad obsession and trooped to Captain Carlos Castillo's office to give him an update.

The captain's door stood open and he wasn't on the phone, but Castillo favored a certain protocol so Jake tapped on the door as he hovered in the hallway.

Castillo glanced up from his computer screen and waved him into the office, his dark eyes flashing. "You don't even have to tell me. I know it's the same MO as Juliana French for our third copycat. I'm tired of this. What makes The Player so special that these sick guys are emulating him?"

Jake dropped into the chair across from Castillo. "I'm hoping our computer forensics team can tell us that. They're still looking into the online connection between Cannon and Fisher, the first two killers. It seems they both favored a certain online message board for crime."

"I'm not going to pretend I understand any of that." Castillo held up his hand as if to ward off too much technical information, not that Jake had any to give him.

"Bottom line—those message boards are a way for people to communicate without sending emails, but they usually require an email address to register. If we have email addresses, we can trace those to IP addresses and locate the person's physical address where the computer resides."

"You lost me at IP address." Castillo ran a hand through his salt-and-pepper hair. "I trust Brandon Nguyen and the others to know what they're doing. Tracing a link between Cannon and Fisher might help us ID this third killer?"

"It might." Jake rapped on the edge of the desk. "But so will solid detective work. Billy's looking at missing women now. We're running this victim's prints, and the medical examiner is doing a rape kit on the body."

"He didn't rape his first victim. These copycats haven't raped any of their victims." Castillo put his hands together as if in prayer. "They're very careful, aren't they?"

"Just like The Player was, but they always make a mistake."

"The Player didn't."

"I'm convinced he did. The detectives never discovered what it was." Jake set his jaw, feeling disloyal to Quinn, the lead detective on The Player case twenty years ago. Retired now, Quinn still felt the crushing disappointment of letting one get away.

Castillo's face screwed up as if he'd just tasted something sour. "Have you told Quinn that?"

"I don't have to tell him. He knows. He's said it himself. They missed something twenty years ago."

"Whatever they missed is long gone. We had two different cold case units go through the evidence on The Player's five victims, and they didn't have any better luck than Quinn did twenty years ago. Careful man."

"So careful he stopped killing rather than get caught." Jake hunched forward in his chair, ready to launch into his own obsession. "And I'm convinced these present-day murders are going to lead us to identifying The Player."

Resting his chin on the steeple of his fingers, Castillo closed his heavy-lidded eyes. "Are you working with Quinn to prove that?"

"No. I mean, not really. I keep him apprised, I ask him questions, but he's not as convinced as I am that the murderers are linked." Jake paused, studying the dark circles beneath Castillo's eyes. "Is that a problem?"

Castillo's lids flew open as if coming out of a trance. "Of course not. I'm the one who gave you Quinn's contact info, if I recall. I didn't realize you'd get so close to him…and Kyra."

"Is *that* a problem?" Jake's muscles tightened, and his fingers dug into the arm of the leather chair. He didn't know what he'd do if it was a problem. He and Kyra had barely scratched the surface of their relationship, one he sensed could be deeper than any he'd experienced before.

"Not a problem." Castillo waved his hand. "She doesn't report to you directly. She's in a different position than most of the people on the task force. But you've seen some of the difficulties that come along with a workplace romance. Look at Billy and his wife."

"Simone left the force when they had their first kid and still wasn't working at the time of the separation."

"What if Simone wanted to come back?" Castillo spread his hands. "Could be awkward for everyone."

"Yeah, well, divorce is often awkward for everyone." Jake's gaze tripped over Castillo's shoulder to the happy-family pictures on the wall. "You wouldn't know."

Castillo's eyebrows jumped to his hairline, and a pink tinge formed beneath his brown skin. "This is actually my second marriage. The first one ended in divorce—not pretty."

"Never is." Jake smacked a hand on the desk. "We're having a task force meeting this afternoon at four. You're invited."

"Keep up the good work, Jake. You'll nail this guy just like the other two."

"Thanks for the vote of confidence, Captain." Jake exited the office on a phone call, Castillo's tired voice following him down the hallway. The captain either needed a good night's sleep or a look into retirement.

When Jake returned to the task force war room, buzzing with activity, he automatically looked in the corner, and Kyra raised her hand with a grimace on her face.

He took a detour to her desk on the way to his and crouched beside her chair.

"You heard the news, huh? A second killing, just like the first."

"And just like the two killers before him—copying The Player." She jerked her shoulders in a shiver.

Kyra Chase had good reason to dread another Player copycat. Her mother had been one of the original's victims.

"I can hardly believe it, but that's what we've got." Jake touched her knee. "Are you okay?"

"Are you kidding? I'm getting used to it now. It's like Groundhog Day for me. I have to keep reliving these gruesome crimes with every new copycat." She clasped her hands between her knees. "But my feelings right now are nothing compared to the families'. I had a meeting with Juliana French's mother this morning, which broke my heart. She was a single mom and raised Juliana herself—just to have her cruelly ripped away like this."

Kyra's voice broke as her words ended, and Jake did everything in his power to restrain himself from taking her in his arms. Kyra was a professional all the way, and wouldn't want his desire to protect and comfort her to compromise her position on the task force as the victims' rights advocate. Castillo was correct. Things could get awkward.

"I'm sure you did everything in your power to help Juliana's mother cope." Jake cleared his throat and leaned in closer. "We're still on for Quinn's place tonight for dinner?"

"More than ever. Quinn's going to want to know all about this second murder." Kyra's gaze shifted to the side. "Have you heard anything from Brandon and the rest of the computer team about the connection Jordy Cannon and Cyrus Fisher shared online?"

"It has something to do with online message boards. They had the same message boards in their browsing history. Brandon's going to give me a report soon, and when I have a minute to breathe, I'll go through the boards to see if anything clicks."

"Wanna bet the monster who killed Juliana and the woman found today is on one of those message boards?" The lips he knew from experience to be soft and luscious formed a thin, straight line.

"I know they're all connected. I just have to prove it."

A FEW HOURS later when Jake had wrapped up the task force briefing and logged off his computer, he watched Kyra leave the war room without even a backward glance. They weren't fooling anyone with their coolness toward each other at the station, but they didn't have to feed the gossip mill by leaving together.

He wanted to stop off at his house in the Hollywood Hills first to change, anyway, and Kyra, who lived closer to Quinn, would pick up dinner for them unless Quinn's neighbor had dropped off another meal for him.

Could Quinn help him tie these copycats to the original killer and end up solving the twenty-year-old case? Consulting with the legendary detective couldn't hurt, and getting in the old man's good graces hadn't hurt Jake's chances with Kyra, either.

Detective Roger Quinn had taken a protective interest in the girl left behind by her mother's murder. While Quinn and his wife hadn't been allowed to adopt Kyra, who used to be known as Marilyn Lake, they'd taken a keen interest in her well-being—nurtured her along a horrific path through several foster families, including one where the teenage Kyra had to kill a foster father to protect a younger child in the home, and had sent her to college. Quinn's wife, Charlotte, had passed away a few years ago, but Kyra saw Quinn as the father she never had and checked up on him frequently.

Jake had passed muster with Quinn, which had elevated him in Kyra's estimation, not that he'd faked anything. Detective Roger Quinn had amazing stories to tell and solid advice to give, even though he had that one big failure on his record. Jake had no intention of following *those* footsteps.

After a quick stop at home, Jake reached the Venice Canals, a beachy Southern California replica of the real thing in Italy. The sun had just set, and the spiky palm trees reached into a sky hovering between day and night, awash in a faint orange glow. The glow had faded by the time he crossed the wooden bridge to Quinn's house and knocked on the red door. For a retired LAPD homicide detective, Quinn lived in an unlikely neighborhood, filled with movie industry people, successful artists and a few sports figures. Quinn's wife had bought the house with the proceeds from her best-selling thrillers. Quinn had lost his wife to cancer, but held on to their beach cottage and his memories.

Kyra flung open the door at his knock, the spicy smells of curry wafting behind her. She winked. "I know you like it hot, so I got some extra spicy vindaloo and tikka masala."

With Quinn looking on from the comfort of his favorite chair, Jake touched Kyra's lips with a chaste kiss and murmured, "Oh, you know I like it spicy."

"Stop whispering over there, you two. I'm starving." Quinn banged his cane on the floor for effect. Jake had seen the old man move fast enough without it.

Jake skirted around Kyra as she closed the front door. "Starving for information or food?"

"Both. Kyra didn't want to get into the second murder too much without you—just enough to let me know you have a third copycat on your hands." Quinn eyed him from beneath his bushy gray eyebrows.

"As crazy as it sounds, that's where we are." Jake crossed the room and shook hands with Quinn. "How are you doing, sir?"

"I'd be doing a lot better if these new killers would stop popping up every month to remind me of my biggest failure—and to stop murdering young women, of course. This isn't about me."

Kyra walked past them and squeezed Quinn's shoulder. "We know you care about the victims more than anything, Quinn, but your success is tied to their justice."

He patted her hand, which still rested on his shoulder. "I know you understand, Mimi."

Quinn sometimes slipped into calling Kyra by her childhood nickname, especially now that Jake knew her background.

"We can talk while we eat. I almost have everything ready." Kyra proceeded to the kitchen and Jake followed her.

"I'll set the table." Jake delved into the cupboards and drawers, grabbing plates and silverware, as Kyra finished opening the cartons of Indian food.

Quinn shuffled to the table, leaning heavily on his cane, and Jake raised his eyebrows at Kyra, who shrugged.

When they got to the table, Jake pulled out Kyra's chair before taking his own seat.

Quinn grunted as he peeled back the foil from the naan and picked up a piece of the flat bread with his gnarled fingers. "Is he always gallant like that, or is he just trying to impress me?"

Kyra choked on her beer. "Both. Jake's a perfect gentleman."

"No cop I know is a perfect anything." Quinn ripped the bread in his hands. "Now, tell me about this second victim."

The gory details of a murder might be strange dinnertime conversation for most social gatherings, but for two homicide detectives and a victims' rights advocate who happened to be a survivor herself, it made sense.

As he helped himself to rice, Jake launched into a description of the crime scene and the victim, and Quinn listened intently, the faded blue eyes in perfect focus.

Jake dropped a dollop of yogurt on his plate. "Long, brown hair just like Juliana's. I think he has a type."

"You also thought that about Copycat 2.0, Fisher, when his first two victims were African American. You were wrong."

"We were. They must've fit his other criteria—living alone, poor security habits." Finding those two young Black women murdered had sent Billy into a tailspin, reminding him of his own missing sister and prompting him to hire a PI to find her.

"I hope we don't find out if that's his type or not." Kyra had perched her fork on the edge of her plate and crossed her arms. "You need to stop him before he kills again."

"I hope we do." Jake rubbed his knuckles on her arm.

He jerked his head at the sound of his work phone, sitting on Quinn's counter. He jumped from the table. "Maybe we ID'd the second victim."

He swept the phone toward him, and his heart bumped against his chest when he saw his ex-wife's name on the display. Tess usually reserved calls to his work cell for urgent matters.

He tapped the phone to answer the call. "What is it, Tess?"

A shaky breath rattled over the line and then she said, "It's Fiona. She's missing."

Chapter Two

When Kyra heard Jake utter the name of his ex-wife, she tried to tune out his words and focus on her argument with Quinn about why he didn't need a second beer. But when Jake's voice rose, her muscles tensed, and she turned in her chair to stare at him.

He was throwing out questions to his ex in a terse, low voice that made the hair on the back of her neck quiver.

She half rose from her chair as Jake wandered toward the front door, out of earshot, but Quinn grabbed her arm and shook his head.

Finally, Jake ended the call during which time neither she nor Quinn had managed another bite of food.

When he returned to the table, the lines on his face seemed etched there permanently, and his green eyes were seared with a mixture of pain and anger.

"My daughter Fiona is missing from her mother's house in Monterey."

Kyra wrenched free from Quinn's grasp and launched herself at Jake. "How long?"

He looked at the phone still cradled in his hand as if he could find the answers there. Not seeing them, he curled his hand around the phone until his knuckles blanched.

"Sh-she's been missing since around seven thirty this morning when she left for school. She never made it.

When Tess came home from work, Fiona wasn't there. Tess texted Fiona, but the text didn't go through—her phone must be turned off."

Quinn piped up from the kitchen table. "Ping the last location."

Some of the color edged back into Jake's face. "The Monterrey PD is working on that."

Quinn pushed back from the table. "Friends? Boyfriends?"

"Boyfriends?" Jake's face took on a greenish hue.

Quinn barked. "How old is she?"

"Fourteen."

"Boyfriends." Quinn shot a look at Kyra.

Jake's nostrils flared, making him look like a horse ready to rear. "Her mother would know about that."

Kyra delivered the bad news. "Or not. I'm sure Tess has already called Fiona's friends. Hopefully, they'll start talking."

"And if they don't talk to Fiona's mother, they'll sure as hell talk to Fiona's father—the hard-nosed LAPD cop." Quinn gestured to Jake's phone. "Start the interrogations."

"You sound like you've done this before." Jake's gaze darted between Quinn and Kyra.

"Once or twice. Get going and take this one with you." He pointed a crooked finger at Kyra. "You need support at a time like this, and if anyone can tell you the thought processes of a rebellious teen, it's Kyra."

Jake took a shaky breath, and Kyra could see the tremble roll through his body. "Do you think that's all it is?"

"You and I both know the chance she's a runaway is greater than the other alternatives. Has her mother checked the hospitals?"

"The police have." Jake turned to grab his holstered

gun from the table by the front door, looking ready to use it on whomever he imagined might have his daughter.

Kyra gathered their plates from the table and deposited them in the sink. "Don't leave these overnight, Quinn."

"I know how to clean my own damn house. Go help him out. God knows, he's helped you enough."

Quinn had nailed that truth. Jake had seen her through some rough times, and now it was payback. She planted a kiss on Quinn's wrinkled forehead. "I'll call you later."

As she and Jake stepped outside, he turned to her. "You don't have to come with me. My place is out of your way."

"Quinn's right. You shouldn't be alone right now. Even if I can't help you locate Fiona, you can bounce ideas off me. I'll take my own car and follow you to your house." She nudged him in the back. "Get those numbers of Fiona's friends from Tess and start making your own calls. Quinn's right again. Her girlfriends are going to be more apt to spill the beans to an irate father than to a worried mom."

As Kyra tried to keep up with Jake, rushing home in his muscle car, gunning his engine at every stoplight, she ran through possible scenarios for Fiona. Jake had mentioned to her before that his daughter and her mother had been clashing. This might just be an attention grabber aimed at Mom. Fiona could be holing up at a friend's, maybe even a new friend her mother didn't know. She'd throw her independence in Mom's face.

While squinting at Jake's taillights as he roared onto the freeway, Kyra murmured, "You're going about it the wrong way, girl."

Kyra should know. She'd used every attention getter in the book to usually disastrous results.

Fiona could be with a boy. Kyra grimaced and stomped

on the accelerator to keep Jake's car in her sights. If that was Fiona's game, Kyra pitied the poor boy once Jake had him on his radar. Maybe Fiona's mother didn't know this boy, either. Knots twisted in Kyra's gut. There were lots of ways to meet boys these days—many of them bad news.

Kyra kept her eyes on Jake's car as it wended its way up the narrow streets in the Hollywood Hills. Every once in a while, she'd catch sight of the city lights twinkling below. Lit up like a Christmas tree and shimmering in invitation, those didn't look like the mean streets, but you should never let a pretty package fool you. She'd thought Jake was a pretty package, but he'd turned out to be the real deal.

The rumbling of Jake's engine echoed in the canyon as he idled in his driveway. She pulled up behind him and hopped out of her car.

He sat half in and half out of his vehicle, one long, denim-clad leg thrust out of the car, the dome light outlining his profile as he talked on the phone. He ended the call and slammed the car door, making her practically jump out of her heels. The call must not have procured the desired effect.

She twisted her fingers in front of her as Jake scowled at his beautiful view. "Did you learn anything new?"

"Just that my daughter had a social media presence her mother didn't know about."

Kyra's heartbeat rattled her rib cage. "Her friends fess up?"

"Sort of." He clenched his phone in his fist. "Let's go inside. You didn't have to come. I'm not going to be good company."

"That's not why I'm here." She grabbed his hand as he stalked up to his front porch.

He squeezed her hand before unlocking the door and gesturing inside. "Help yourself to something to drink. I have a few more calls to make."

She turned toward the kitchen, and Jake wandered to the massive window that took up one entire wall of the living room. He stared out at those same lights she'd been admiring on the way up the hill, but he probably didn't even see them.

Jake had bought this house from the proceeds of two screenplays he'd sold. It represented his oasis, his escape from the horrors of the job, only now those horrors had followed him home in the most personal way.

He knew as well as she did that most runaways turned up safely, but he'd take small comfort in that when the runaway was his daughter.

She got two glasses of water and brought one out to him just as he was ending a conversation with one of Fiona's friends. Quinn may have suggested Jake put pressure on the girlfriends, but Kyra knew from experience teenage girls could keep secrets like nobody's business. She would've rather traipsed over hot coals than reveal one of the other foster girls' plans to the caseworkers. That would go double for parents, although most of the girls she'd known in the system didn't have parents—at least not functioning ones.

She thrust the glass at Jake, and some of the water lapped over the lip. "Take this and sit down."

His eyebrows shot up as if he'd forgotten her presence. She didn't take it personally.

"Sit and breathe before you blast through that window."

"Thanks." He started for the couch and then jerked to a stop, causing more water to slosh over the rim of the glass. "My laptop. I need my laptop."

Placing both hands on the small of his back, she pushed his solid frame. "Take a seat. I'll get it."

She unzipped the bag he'd dropped in the foyer and pulled out the computer he toted back and forth to work. He couldn't leave it there, as these copycat murders had been occupying his time 24/7…and now he had to worry about his daughter.

Jake had taken her advice, but his ramrod posture and position on the edge of the couch defeated the purpose behind her order.

Sitting beside him, she placed the laptop on the coffee table. "What are you looking up?"

He cleared his throat and took a gulp of water. "One of Fiona's friends admitted that Fiona had a second Instagram page under a different name, a page her mother didn't know about."

"What's the name?" Kyra nudged his arm. "Enter it."

Jake's hands hovered over the keyboard, and then he let out a long breath. "Jazzy Noir."

"Sounds like a…" Kyra pressed her fingers against her lips.

Jake growled as he typed the name in the search field, the whole laptop shivering beneath his furiously pounding fingers. "Like a stripper?"

"Give the kid some credit for creativity, and Fiona didn't invent the secret social media account. Countless teens have been using them for as long as the app's been around." Still Fiona held her breath as Jake found Jazzy Noir and started scrolling through the pictures.

A couple of bikini shots had Jake clenching his jaw, but photos of crazy manicures, selfies with friends, food and even some puppies and kittens had made the cut, too.

Jake slumped. "That's not too bad, is it? I don't know why she'd need a secret account for those."

Kyra's gaze shifted to the side as she drummed her fingers on her knee. She knew a few reasons but hated blowing up Jake's world even more right now.

Whipping his head around, he grabbed her restless fingers. "What? What am I missing?"

"On… On this site, people can also send you messages—messages that don't appear on this page." She jabbed her finger at one of Jazzy's more innocuous pictures of a piece of pizza with everything on it.

Jake's green eyes narrowed, catlike, only more of a jungle cat's than the cute kitties on Jazzy's page. "Private messages from any perv who can see this page?"

"Yeah." As Jake began to click on the screen, she dug her fingernails into his arm. "What are you doing?"

"I'm going to create an account for myself and send her a message." He flexed his fingers. "Brandon Nguyen has been giving me some computer lessons. I'm gonna need them as I delve into the online worlds of copycats one and two. Might as well put them to use to find my own daughter."

"If you do that, you're going to show your hand." Her nails sank deeper into his flesh, making imprints on the tail of his tiger tattoo.

His hands froze. "I shouldn't let on that I know about this account?"

"Exactly."

"Her friend will tell her that she blabbed to me about it."

"Doubt it."

Jake tapped the edge of the computer with the side of his thumb. "I'm not sure how that will help us find her. I believe in full transparency unless that endangers someone."

"Sending Fiona a message on this account is not going

to help you find her, either, and when she does turn up, which I'm confident she will, knowing about this account will give you an edge."

"An edge? You make it sound like warfare."

Kyra cocked her head. "Fiona is fourteen, her parents are divorced, her mother is remarried to the man she cheated with and she just ran away from home. What would you call this?"

Jake opened his mouth, but the doorbell interrupted him. He sprang from the couch and stepped over the coffee table in one motion.

Closing her eyes, Kyra clasped her hands together and said a little prayer. Her lids flew open when she heard Jake utter his daughter's name in a tone of joy, relief and anger mingled together.

As father and daughter hugged at the door, Kyra reached over, exited Jazzy Noir's Instagram page and snapped the laptop shut. Then she stood up, collected the glasses and floated to the kitchen.

As Jake marched Fiona into the living room, his arm draped around her shoulders, he said, "You should've just told us you wanted to visit. We would've put you on a plane. Taking a bus all the way from Monterey into LA is not safe."

Kyra exited the kitchen and folded her arms, wedging one shoulder against the wall. Her eyes met Fiona's, which she knew from Fiona's school picture, were the same color as her father's. Any further resemblance to the smiling girl in the school photo ended there. The long, brown hair from the picture now sported bleach-blond ends, the school uniform had been replaced with a pair of ripped jeans, a black lace crop top and black motorcycle boots.

Fiona's eyes flickered, and then she threw her arms

around Jake. "I know. I'm sorry, Daddy. I wanted to surprise you. The trip took longer than I expected, and I thought I'd be here before school let out. When we drove from here to Monterey, it took about five hours."

"That's in a car." Jake patted Fiona's back. "The bus always takes longer. Why'd you turn your phone off? You could've called and told me and your mother that you were on your way down."

"I just thought…" Fiona dipped her head and peeked at her father from beneath her long, dark lashes.

"I just thought I'd surprise you…and I didn't want you guys to stop me."

"Stop you?" Jake tugged on the ends of Fiona's ombré hair. "I'm happy to see you, Fiona, but you were coming at Christmas."

"Was I?" Fiona's bottom lip jutted out, and then she glanced at Kyra and sucked it back in. "I know that, but it seemed so far away and I wanted to see you now. Don't send me back. I worked extra babysitting shifts for those Newland brat—kids to pay for the bus ticket."

"We'll discuss all the details later. Did you call your mother yet?" Jake checked the phone in his hand.

"I called her as soon as my ride turned into your driveway, Daddy."

Kyra cleared her throat. "Your phone was turned off. We thought your battery was dead."

Fiona tossed her head, flicking her hair over her shoulder in an expert move that must've taken a lot of practice in front of the mirror, and gave Kyra a hard stare. "It *was* dying. I turned it off to save the battery so I could get a ride from the bus station to my dad's."

Jake held up his phone. "How come your mom hasn't called me?"

"I asked her to give me a few minutes to talk to you."

Kyra grabbed her purse. "I'm gonna let you two figure this out."

Jake finally released the hold he had on his daughter. "I'm sorry I didn't introduce you. Kyra, this is my daughter, Fiona. Fiona, this is my…friend, Kyra Chase."

Fiona lifted a hand, waving her fingers with their black-tipped nails. "Hello."

"Nice to meet you, Fiona." Kyra hitched her bag over her shoulder. "Now I really should get going."

"Thanks for all your help, Kyra." Jake took two long strides toward her and then hesitated as he reached her.

He probably felt Fiona's eyes drilling holes into them, too. He took Kyra's hand, giving it a quick squeeze. "Quinn was right. I needed you here."

As Kyra looked past Jake's shoulder, she spotted Fiona already at the front door, yanking it open. "I'll see you out."

The girl was anxious to get rid of her.

"And I'm going to text your mother to let her know you made it inside the house."

Fiona huffed. "Where else would I go from your driveway to your front door?"

Nodding to Jake, Kyra said, "See you tomorrow."

As Jake bent his head over his phone to text Tess, Kyra walked to the open front door.

Fiona swept it wider for her and held out one slim hand for the grown-up handshake. In a bright, cheery voice, she said, "It was nice meeting you, Ms. Chase."

Kyra moved in and curled her fingers around Fiona's wrist, pulling her closer for an awkward one-armed hug. Then she whispered in the girl's ear, "You don't fool me one bit."

Chapter Three

Jake finished the text exchange with Tess, convincing her to give him some time with Fiona before Tess read their daughter the riot act over the phone. At the sound of the front door slamming, he jerked up his head.

Fiona gave him a big smile. "Ms. Chase seems nice. She's pretty, too."

"She is nice. I'm glad you like her." Jake placed his phone on top of the closed laptop. Kyra had been right about not bringing up the Jazzy business right away.

"You're glad I like her, huh?" Fiona pranced across the room to the kitchen and swung open the fridge door. "Is she your *girlfriend* or something?"

He'd been hoping for more time with Kyra to establish exactly what kind of relationship they had before introducing her to Fiona—that was supposed to be Christmas. Anger and alarm stirred in his gut when he thought about Fiona taking a bus into LA by herself, arriving at night, not telling anyone where she was, turning off her phone. He didn't buy that dying phone story any more than Kyra had.

He shoved a hand through his hair. "She's a good friend, someone I work with."

Fiona slammed down the can of soda she'd taken from the fridge onto the counter. "She's a cop?"

"She's a therapist and victims' rights advocate. She's assigned to my task force." He pointed to the soda fizzing over onto the counter. "Make sure you clean that up."

"I thought you hated shrinks." She lifted the can to her mouth and stared at him over the rim, her eyes so much like his it looked like a mirror image sometimes.

"That's a strong word. Who told you that?"

"Mom. She told me you got in trouble with the department for telling off some shrink who got one of your guys off." She slurped the soda from the top and emerged with a smile that looked too grown-up for her baby face. "Don't worry. Mom doesn't usually bad-mouth you— only when I remind her she's the one who messed things up when she hooked up with Brock."

Jake's heart stopped in his chest, and when it restarted each beat sent a shaft of pain to his head. How had Fiona found out all this information? He had a hard time believing Tess would tell her.

"It—it's true, isn't it?" Fiona's eyes widened in fear. Something in his face must've signaled that she'd gone too far.

He said quietly, "It's complicated, Fiona. Don't assume you know everything from some overheard conversation or gossip, and don't judge your mother…ever."

Fiona left the soda and scurried around the corner to throw herself in his arms. "I'm sorry, Daddy. I don't, really. I just missed you."

He hugged her hard. "I missed you, too. Now, grab some sheets from the closet upstairs and make up the bed in your bedroom and go to sleep. I'm going to call your mother and figure out a plan."

An hour later, when he'd ended the call with Tess and the water had finally stopped running in the guest bathroom, he collapsed in his own bed and stared at the ceiling. He and Tess had figured out an interim plan for Fiona that would keep her in LA for at least a few weeks, but Jake had spoken to his ex with a confidence he didn't feel.

His daughter was not the carefree, happy-go-lucky child he remembered from their years as an intact family unit. She'd turned into a full-fledged teenager…and the thought terrified him.

A FEW DAYS after Fiona's surprise arrival, with barely two minutes to catch his breath, Jake felt a guilty relief walking into the task force war room. He'd spent hours on the phone with Fiona's mother, her teachers, her LA friends' parents, and even more time grocery shopping and reeling off a set of rules to Fiona's bored face.

Catching a serial killer seemed easy in comparison.

As soon as Jake sat down, Billy scooted his chair up to Jake's desk and smacked a file folder down, next to his keyboard. "You must've been terrified."

"I was."

"Fiona's going to stay with you awhile?"

"A few weeks, at least. That frou-frou private school she attends in Carmel is going to allow her to do her lessons online. She has a friend here from elementary school she's going to visit, too."

"You're going to have a lot on your plate, brother." Billy held up his hand and ticked off each of his long fingers. "This task force, your daughter…and Kyra."

"Thanks for reminding me." Jake's gaze floated to Kyra's empty desk in the corner. He hadn't seen Kyra at all since Fiona showed up on his doorstep. She'd had an emergency session with a client, and they'd exchanged just a few short texts. He flipped open the file Billy had deposited on his desk. "What's this?"

"It's from Brandon Nguyen. He said you'd be expecting a breakdown of the chat rooms and message boards both Cannon and Fisher frequented." Billy drilled a finger into the page on top. "Let me know if you need any help with this. I can assign a few guys from my video team."

Shuffling the pages of the folder, he asked, "Any luck with cameras in the area?"

"Headlights coming from the body dump site at around midnight, but that's it—headlights. Can't get an angle on the car attached to the lights. It's almost as if he knew about the camera and swerved out of the way to avoid it."

"Something will come up." Jake twisted his head toward the door of the conference room at the sound of Kyra's voice, and he caught her eye before she sat down at her computer.

When Billy wheeled his chair back to his own desk, next to Jake's, Jake reached for his personal cell and texted Kyra: Lunch?

She replied immediately: Need to decompress?

He'd admit that: Totally.

He even sounded like Fiona now. Snorting, he pocketed his phone and delved into the file Brandon had left him. Their computer forensics team had made the discovery that both Jordy Lee Cannon, the first copycat, and Cyrus Fisher, the second killer visited some of the same chat rooms for a few TV shows and even a true-crime blog.

The two may have communicated that way or shared information. If the task force could trace their conversations, they might find a third party and be able to track him down before he killed again. Jake would put his money on the true-crime blog. They might find a certain sick ironic pleasure in posting on a site where others were trying to solve cases.

He slid the piece of paper on top toward him and ran his finger down the page until he came to the website called Websleuths. Hunching over his computer, he launched a browser and entered the URL for the site.

Inclining his head, he blinked at the rows and rows of links to murder cases, missing persons cases, cold cases. He clicked on a cold case murder in Canada and scrolled through the many messages offering tips and theories and posts with maps and sketches and articles—an entire hive of citizen detectives pouring time and effort into the case of a stranger's murder.

This site must have a thread for the current copycat case. It took him two minutes to find it and already hundreds of posts filled multiple screens. He glanced through a few, and then a breath hitched in his throat when he saw his name in one of the posts—several posts.

Did he want to read those? He didn't need a job performance review from the man on the street. He exited the thread and went to the search field. The computer geeks had given him the names that Cannon and Fisher used for this site, which they'd tracked from their computers' IP addresses. Cannon had used Rusty and Fisher was Rocketman.

Jake searched for Rusty first and sat back in his chair, crossing his arms as row after row of links filled his screen. There had to be a way to search for both Rusty and Rocketman at the same time. The user Rusty hadn't even bothered to comment on any of the copycat killer message threads.

When Billy slammed his hand against his desk, Jake jumped. He'd been lost in the message boards. He glanced at his partner, giving him a thumbs-up while he talked on the phone.

Billy ended the call and said, "We got an ID on the second victim. Her name is Carmella Lopez. Her sister wasn't sure Carmella was missing until she talked to Carmella's boyfriend who said he hadn't talked to her or seen her in days. When Carmella's sister reported finding her car abandoned, a few blocks from the club she'd gone to, with her purse and cell phone still inside, the officer requested a picture of Carmella and recognized her right away as victim number two."

Jake slumped in his chair. Identifying the victims always helped the case, even though it always came with a gut-wrenching sadness. He shot a glance at Kyra, working across the room. He'd let Billy make the announcement to the task force.

After Billy notified the room, he indicated to Jake he'd take care of the processing of Carmella's vehicle and setting up the interviews with her friends and families.

Jake went back to his message boards, the identification of the second victim distracting him. He always compared the victims to his own daughter—and with her here, it hit him even harder.

An hour later, when his phone buzzed in his pocket, Jake backed away from the screen, his eyes blurry and his neck stiff. He could understand how these online sleuths could go down the rabbit hole. He hadn't learned one thing about Rusty and Rocketman yet, but he had some of his own theories about a couple of these cold cases.

He cupped his phone in his hand and read the message from Kyra. He looked up, but she'd already slipped from the war room to hit the ladies' room and meet him at his car in the lot.

He jotted down a few notes in the message board file

and stuck it in his desk. By the time he reached Kyra waiting by his car, his brain had lost its fuzziness.

She'd be interested in his progress, but he didn't feel like going through all of it—not even for her. He unlocked the passenger door and opened it, inhaling the sweet fragrance of roses from her hair. This beat burrowing into an internet abyss any day.

They decided on a sandwich place for lunch, and when he gave her a curt answer to her question about his morning, she didn't pursue it.

They settled across from each other at a small window table. Kyra planted her elbows on the table and Jake held his breath. He wanted more than anything to put this morning's research behind him, leave it with the amateurs for a while.

"So, how's domestic life with Fiona?"

It took him a few seconds to comprehend the question, and then he dropped his tense shoulders. "It's been a lot of work the past few days just getting her settled. I actually had to stock the fridge and pantry with some nutritious foods. I worked out an online study plan for her with her teachers and even set up a few social engagements for her. I think it's going to be okay."

"Good to hear." She picked up a menu and held it in front of her face.

"She likes you."

"Really?" She pinned him with a gaze over the top of the menu, her blue eyes narrowed to slits.

"She said—" he held up one finger "—Ms. Chase seems nice and she's pretty."

"You got *like* out of that?"

He shook open his own menu. "It's better than I hoped for. Fiona's never met anyone I've dated before."

"She's a risk taker, isn't she? Bought a bus ticket from

Monterey to LA, arrived at a bus depot in downtown LA in the middle of the night and called up a car to your place in the Hollywood Hills. A lot of girls her age wouldn't have the…guts to make that trip alone."

"When I think of her riding on that bus by herself and arriving downtown…" Jake clenched his teeth and an actual shiver ran down his spine. "It scares the hell out of me."

"Yeah, she reminds me of me." She held up a hand. "And before you get all googly-eyed about that idea, let me refresh your very recent memory. I was a horrible teenager."

"You think Fiona's horrible?" Jake's mouth twisted into a smile.

"I don't know her well enough, yet." Kyra laughed. "I'm just giving you a heads-up."

Kyra must've sensed he was on overload because she didn't bring up the copycat case at all through lunch. Her mood lightened his, and he attributed her positive outlook to the fact that her stalker hadn't resurfaced with this third killer.

Someone who was familiar with Kyra's past as the daughter of one of The Player's victims had decided to torment her with that fact during the first two copycat killing sprees. She hadn't heard one word from him since they'd found the second killer, and that killer had taken his own life.

As the waiter cleared away their plates, Kyra said, "I told Quinn about your daughter. He was relieved and impressed in a weird way that she made her way from Monterey to your doorstep all by herself."

"Thanks for letting him know." He toyed with Kyra's fingers. "I think my situation reminded him of his days with you."

"Yeah, I'm not the only one who saw an echo of my behavior in Fiona's. Quinn muttered something on the phone about how you were going to have your hands full." She squeezed his hand. "But we'll be more than happy to help you out."

"Thanks, I think." Jake reluctantly disentangled his fingers from Kyra's as his work phone rang. "McAllister."

Billy's clipped tones assaulted his ear. "Another body. I'm already in the field. I'll meet you there."

Jake scribbled the address on a napkin and met Kyra's gaze as he ended the call. "Another victim. Hikers found the body near Tujunga Canyon."

"I'm coming with you." She waved her hand at the waiter for the check.

"I can't let you into the crime scene."

"Got it." She raised two fingers, Boy Scout fashion. "I'll keep my distance, Detective."

On the way to the location of the latest victim, Kyra made up for lost time over lunch by querying him about his search of the message boards.

"I confess." He released the steering wheel and held up both hands. "I got lost in the weeds for a cold case on Websleuths, a true crime discussion board, and wasted a lot of time."

"I'm assuming you checked the discussion threads for the copycat killers."

"I did a search on their usernames, which Brandon gave me, and neither of them ever commented on their own cases. Probably didn't want to seem too knowledgeable."

"That's just creepy." She rubbed her arms. "I dipped into a few of those message boards on The Player, but I had to bounce. I couldn't take it. Some of those posters knew as much about the case as I did. I always wondered if The Player was there, following along…laughing."

"Probably not a good pursuit for you, and neither is this." He pulled behind a few emergency vehicles and spotted Billy's car. The medical examiner wouldn't be here for a while.

He twisted his head in her direction. "Wait here."

"I'm not going to sit in the car." She pointed out the window. "I see my friend Megan with her cameraperson. I'll go talk to her."

Jake slid out of the car, grabbing his jacket on the way. He punched his arms into the sleeves as he trudged toward the trailhead. This third killer had copied the method of the first copycat, who had murdered his victims elsewhere and dumped their bodies in the vast canyons that ringed the LA basin. The second copycat had killed his victims in their homes and left them there. The Player had been known to do both, experimenting with the best method.

He approached the yellow tape marking the boundaries of the crime scene, and Billy met him at the edge, pinching a white envelope between his gloved fingers, creases of worry across his forehead.

Jake's heart did a backflip in his chest. "What is it? Is this not our guy?"

"Oh, it's our guy, all right—severed finger, queen of spades between the victim's lips, underwear missing— but he added something this time." Billy held out the envelope. "It's addressed to you…personally."

Jake's mouth went dry. He struggled into a pair of gloves and took the unsealed envelope from Billy. He lifted the flap and carefully pulled out a single sheet of paper, cut to fit the size of the envelope.

The corner of his eye twitched as he scanned the block printing with blue ballpoint pen.

Billy crowded him. "What's it say?"

He turned the note toward Billy and said, "'Game on.'"

Chapter Four

Kyra narrowed her eyes as both Jake and Billy emerged from the crime scene, their faces alight with some inner excitement, or maybe their gaits signaled the elation—springy, jaunty almost.

Kyra nudged Megan, her friend and a reporter for KTOP. "There's my ride. Talk to you later."

"Anything you can give me…friend." Megan held her hand to her ear, mimicking a telephone. "God knows, Billy won't tell me a thing."

With her heart fluttering, Kyra slid into the passenger seat of Jake's sedan before he reached it. They'd found something this time.

He joined her in the car and sat, clenching the steering wheel for a few seconds before cranking the engine. "He left something for me."

Kyra choked at the unexpected words. "For you, personally?"

"He left a note in an envelope with my name on it."

A feather of fear brushed the back of her neck, but she shrugged it off. Unless he lived under a rock, of course the killer would know the identity of the lead detective on his case.

Smoothing her hands against her slacks, she said, "That's good, isn't it?"

"More opportunity for clues. More room for error. I can't imagine Jordy Lee Cannon or Cyrus Fisher risking a note, can you?"

"Definitely not Fisher, way too careful. Cannon didn't have enough bravado to do that." She drummed her fingers on her knee. "This guy's a different animal."

"Emphasis on animal. He murdered a young woman—strangled her, dumped her body." Jake pulled away from his parking space a little too quickly, and the car lurched, spitting sand and gravel out behind it.

"Can you tell me what the note said?"

"I can tell you if you keep the contents to yourself."

She nodded. "Goes without saying. You already know how good I am at keeping secrets."

One side of his mouth lifted. "The note said, 'Game on.'"

"Oh, that's original." She rolled her eyes. "Not exactly a Ted Kaczynski style of manifesto that's worth releasing to the public, is it?"

"Nope."

A muscle throbbed at the corner of Jake's mouth, showing her he had more on his mind. He'd tell her when he deemed it necessary.

She asked, "Do you have the note with you?"

"Left it with the other evidence so Clive can check for prints and the lab can look for DNA transfer cells."

"Are you going to respond?" She held her breath, watching a gamut of emotions play across Jake's face.

"I'll discuss my options with Captain Castillo, but I think I almost have to. Communication with the killer can lead to more evidence, slipups on his part." He rubbed his chin. "The Player never communicated with Quinn, did he?"

"Never. Didn't communicate with the press, either.

But, so far, these copycats haven't been as particular as The Player."

"They're in his fan club, though."

Kyra clutched her seat belt with one hand as Jake took the next corner too fast. "What do you mean by that?"

"We know Cannon and Fisher are connected somehow through this true crime message board. Maybe there are a bunch of them who admire The Player. The posters to the board can hold private chats away from the main message board. They're probably communicating that way to exchange their sick ideas and gush over The Player."

"They all stamp their own personality or particular fetish onto the murder—jewelry, lock of hair, underwear. They all strangle to avoid blood evidence. Two dump the bodies to mask the crime scene. One killed in the victims' homes to avoid being in public." She'd been ticking off the killers' similarities and differences on her fingers and as she held up another digit, Jake interrupted her.

"They leave a playing card and sever a pinkie finger to pay homage to The Player."

"And you haven't brought one of them in alive, yet." She drilled a finger into the dashboard. "That's unusual. Usually these guys want the accolades and attention."

"The Player never did."

"The Player had a strong sense of self-preservation." Kyra reached for her seat belt as Jake cruised into the parking lot of the Northeast Division.

"This current guy is veering way outside the playbook there. He wants his glory, and he's determined to use me to get it."

Kyra's gaze flicked over Jake's profile, which looked carved from stone. "You're going to let him?"

"He can use me all he wants until his hubris trips him up…and I'll be right there to catch him."

KYRA SPENT THE rest of the afternoon compiling a list of the most recent victim's friends and family members. The task force had already ID'd her as Maggie Harkenridge, wedding planner who disappeared after a night on the town. She matched the physical description of the previous two victims, with her long, brown hair. This guy had a type.

After Kyra left the station, she ran her rape survivors group, and then sent Jake a quick text before heading home to change for dinner with a friend. A week ago, she'd penciled in this night for Jake, but that was before Fiona showed up on his doorstep.

She thought Jake might suggest pizza and a movie at his place so she and Fiona could get to know each other a little, but maybe Jake could read his daughter better than Kyra thought he could. Despite her smiles and happy banter, Fiona had not been happy to see a woman at Dad's house. She'd also been lying through her teeth about the dying phone and thinking the bus would reach LA before school let out.

She got it, all of it, but Jake and Tess had better stop letting Fiona call the shots or they'd wind up in a world of hurt. They could consult with Quinn on that.

As she locked up her office, Jake texted her back. He and Fiona *were* ordering pizza in—just not with her. He promised her a next time and she sent him a text back with thumbs-up and kissy-face emojis. The man had a lot to juggle right now.

Kyra spent the evening with her friend Mel, a relatively new mom, who had been anxious having her first night away from her five-month-old baby. So anxious, she'd spent half the time with Kyra FaceTiming her husband to make sure he was doing everything according to plan.

Kyra didn't mind and enjoyed Mel's stories about and pictures of the baby. Seemed everyone wanted to be with their children tonight.

When she got back to her apartment in Santa Monica, Kyra dumped her leftover chicken into a bowl outside for Spot, the stray cat she fed, and made a cup of green tea. Setting the mug on the coffee table, Kyra curled one leg beneath her on the couch. She pulled her laptop onto her thighs and logged in to her computer. Her emails held no promise of anything interesting so she launched a browser, hoping to get in a little late-night shopping.

Her fingers hovered over the keyboard, but instead of bringing up her favorite online shoe store, she did a search for Websleuths, the true crime discussion board. She clicked on the link, and threads for missing people, murder victims and ongoing investigations filled the screen.

The website boasted three different discussion boards for the three distinct copycat killers. Discussion on the first two killers had waned, but the thread on the current killer buzzed with activity.

She scrolled through the theories, links to other articles, maps of the dump sites and memorials to the three victims. Some of the members already had details about the three victims that Kyra didn't even know yet.

The posters knew about the task force and called out Jake and Billy by name in several messages. They even knew the detectives' nicknames—J-Mac and Cool Breeze. Jake and Billy had also caused some hearts to flutter among the amateur sleuths.

Kyra's mouth quirked into a smile as she slurped her tea. She could understand that, but how did they get all this information?

She clicked away from The Player copycat boards and

perused some of the other active cases. She spotted the cold case in Canada of the murdered Realtor Jake had mentioned. Apparently, DNA existed from that case, and the posters were clamoring for a genetic investigation similar to the one that had caught the Golden State Killer. If only The Player had left behind DNA. The bastard had been too careful for that, and his minions were following suit.

She stared at the usernames populating the screen—Jersey Girl, Lil Mama, Sherlock, Poppy, Mass Guy, Online Dick—Jordy Cannon and Cyrus Fisher had been posting on these boards. Did they also have innocuous usernames indicating their location or their interest in sleuthing? Although the task force knew the names, Jake hadn't revealed them to her. She'd been surprised he'd let slip the name of this message board.

Was the current copycat on here now? Was this how they all met? Had they exchanged knowledge and tips in private chats? Jake said neither Cannon nor Fisher had posted on the copycat killer threads, but they had to have been posting on other current crimes that saw a lot of action or their posts would've stood out in the wilderness if they'd been commenting on cold cases.

Kyra rolled down the page, keeping her eye on the number of posts for each board and the most recent messages to that board. A discussion on a missing college girl in Alabama showed promise.

Ugh, that sounded bad even for her.

Kyra clicked on the link to create an account with Websleuths. Staring at the blinking cursor in the username field, she reached for her tea. She should choose a name to indicate that she resided in Southern California. She started entering a name and then deleted it. She had to be a man. Her fingers tapped the keyboard, and then she backed out of that name.

She cradled her mug and studied the contents as she swirled her tea. She made a decision—one that had been swirling at the edge of her consciousness, just like this tea.

She clunked her mug back on the table, missing the coaster by a mile, and entered the only name that made sense: *Laprey*.

A surge of power coursed through her body. She owned it now—the anagram for *player*. Someone had been using it to torment her about her past. For anyone in the know, it would be a clear signal that she had an interest in that old case, in the current copycats.

She finished creating the account but couldn't post right away. The admins had to approve her account. Just like they'd approved the accounts of Cannon and Fisher? Of course, how were they supposed to know who lurked behind a keyboard and username?

Kyra shoved the computer from her lap and padded into the kitchen to make more tea. As she waited for the water to boil in the microwave, her cell phone buzzed against the counter.

She scooped it up when she saw Jake's name on the display. "Hey, you. Pizza'd out?"

"Pizza, slasher movie and I'm done…but it was good."

Jake had squeezed in that second part of the sentence to make sure Kyra didn't think he was complaining about being a dad. He didn't have to prove anything to her, but he did to himself.

"Sounds lovely. Did you happen to tell Fiona you lived slasher movies and didn't need to watch them?" Her microwave dinged and she removed her mug of water, now bubbling.

"Naw, I let her choose. Let her choose the pizza, too, and spent several minutes picking pineapple off my slices." He paused and lowered his voice. "You don't think there's anything…wrong with a girl her age interested in those kinds of movies, do you?"

"If there were, those moviemakers would go out of business. Slasher film makers cater to the bloodthirsty teen market. Why do you think so many of them feature clueless hot teens in cabins or in high school?"

"You got a point." Jake let out a sigh as if that question had been bothering him for hours. "Did you have a good dinner with your friend?"

"Good and a little early. She's a new mom and was anxious to get back to the baby. I guess she doesn't trust her husband to be a good father."

"Maybe she's right."

Kyra ripped open the foil for her tea bag and dredged it in the water. Idiot. Jake didn't need reminders of his own failures as a father, although his wife had cheated on him. He hadn't been the one to let down Fiona.

Jake cleared his throat and took a sip of something. "What did you do with the rest of your evening?"

Her gaze strayed to the laptop on the coffee table. "This and that. Answered a few emails, scheduled some appointments for my clients."

"I just wanted to touch base with you and apologize again for canceling our plans. I do want you and Fiona to get to know each other, but I feel like I need to get to know her first."

"No apology necessary." Especially since she'd just lied to him about how she was spending her evening. He wouldn't be thrilled to find out she'd been trolling Websleuths. "We can always catch up at work and maybe manage a few quickies in our cars."

He choked on his drink as he laughed. "Something to look forward to…and something to fall asleep to."

"Then I'll see you tomorrow." When she placed her phone back on the table, she dunked the tea bag into the water a few more times and carried her mug back to the couch.

She refreshed her email and clicked on the link to verify her new account with Websleuths. She launched the website and scrolled past the different threads. Current crimes made the most sense, and missing women would attract fans of The Player. Her stomach turned at the idea that the man who had murdered her mother and other young women had fans.

She dove into the discussion about the young woman in Alabama, starting at the beginning. The first post in the discussion group contained all the pertinent information about the case, and Kyra soaked in this data to get a handle on things. After reading the messages, she had her own thoughts about the crime. She'd have to take it easy and not come off like a know-it-all. The guys lurking around these boards for kicks would want to keep a low profile.

Taking a deep breath, she flexed her fingers and typed her first post as Laprey. She managed an introduction as a first-time poster, therapy student with a keen interest in this case because of attending the same college where the woman, Amanda Yates, had been abducted.

Kyra sat back and took a sip of tea. Within seconds of her post, she'd earned a few likes. Minutes later, the moderator welcomed her to the board, and a few other members asked her some questions about the campus. She scrambled around online to find some of the answers to the college questions, and she made up answers to others, such as whether or not she had felt safe there.

A hundred different girls on any campus could answer that question with their own spin.

She yawned and glanced at the time on her computer. She'd spent a good two hours on the website. It lured you in and trapped you, at least those with the same morbid sensibilities.

As she moved the cursor to the upper-right corner of the screen to log off, an alert next to her username caught her eye. She had a couple of private messages already.

Her pulse fluttered, and she clicked on the first message. She read the standard welcome message to the website, and her breathing returned to normal. Then she clicked on the second message, and her heart skipped a beat.

Some other user, Toby Dog, who hadn't been posting, had sent her a message, and it didn't look standard at all.

Her cursor hovered over the last word, as she read aloud, "You wanna play?"

Chapter Five

Jake stood outside Fiona's bedroom door and tapped again. "Fiona, are you awake?"

She mumbled and he took it as an invitation, easing open the door. His eyes adjusted to the gloom, and he figured the lump beneath the covers resembled his daughter.

"I have to leave now, but I made breakfast. Don't sleep too late. You have to do all your assignments before you can see Lyric today." He and Fiona had had a good time the night before, and he'd promised her she could go to Lyric's house in Westwood as long as she completed all the lessons her teachers had assigned.

She mumbled again and peeked from the corner of the sheet. "Half hour."

"Okay, I'll be calling you to make sure you're up." He took a breath. Should he tell her he'd be checking up on her and that she had to video chat with him so he could make sure she was really working?

Would that be too draconian? If he'd had a son instead of a daughter, he'd know what to do. A few threats of bodily harm had always worked for him and his brother.

"Close the door, Dad."

He backed up and snapped the door shut. You couldn't threaten a girl physically, but there had to be a way to come down on her. Maybe he needed another talk with

Quinn. Kyra had admitted she'd been a handful. Quinn and Charlotte must've done something right because Kyra had turned out...great and her situation had been fraught with more trauma than Fiona's.

As he grabbed his coffee cup, he eyed the bacon and scrambled eggs on the stove top. Had Tess mentioned that Fiona had recently become a vegetarian? Shrugging, he stuffed a strip of bacon in his mouth and left for the station.

When Jake got to work, he sat down immediately with the forensics team that had taken possession of the note from the killer.

Clive, their print guy sat across from Jake at the table and dangled the plastic bag from his fingers before dropping it like it was some poisonous creature. "No prints on the paper, but we didn't expect any. All of these killers have been careful with their prints."

"Except Cyrus. He inadvertently left a partial on that tape. We have to keep hoping they'll make a mistake." Jake prodded the bag, shoving it toward Geoffrey, one of the other forensic team members. "Paper? Ink?"

Geoffrey flipped through his notes. "Nothing special about either. The paper is standard printer paper that can be purchased anywhere from the local corner drugstore to a big box store. Pen is a cheap blue ballpoint, like a million others."

Jake hunched forward and positioned the note in front of Evie, their handwriting expert. "Give me some good news, Evie."

"At least it's handwritten and not made up of cutouts." She pulled her reading glasses from the top of her head and studied the note through the plastic as if looking at it for the first time, even though Jake knew she'd already analyzed every line and swirl. "Distinctive enough that if we had a handwriting sample from a suspect, I could nail him—as long as he wrote in block letters."

"If we only had a suspect." Jake shifted in his chair and took a swallow of his coffee.

"You're going to communicate with him, right?" Evie removed her glasses and twirled them around in her fingers by one tortoiseshell arm. "I mean, did Captain Castillo advise you to respond to him and keep the lines open?"

"I haven't talked to the captain yet, but I'm sure he'll suggest it."

"That won't—" Clive cleared his throat "—encourage this guy? I mean, if he has the ear of the lead detective. Won't that embolden him? Lead to more murders?"

Geoffrey snorted. "You could make the other argument. If J-Mac doesn't respond to him, it might anger him and he'll kill more."

Jake pulled the bag back into his realm and toyed with the edge of it. "Good point, both of you, but I don't think my response one way or another is going to have an effect on how much he kills. He's got an itch now, and he's gotta scratch it. But making him my pen pal might lead to more evidence for us, might lead to a mistake on his part."

He snapped up the note. "Thanks for your work. I'm sure it won't be long before we have another note to break down, but as long as this one has already been checked in as evidence I'm going to hang onto it for now."

As the forensics team left the small conference room, Jake traced over the letters of the message with his fingertip. The killer followed his own press, knew about the task force, knew the lead detective on the task force. They had to be able to use that to their advantage.

The door behind him opened and he jumped.

Kyra poked her head into the room. "Scare you?"

"Deep in thought." He pinched the corner of the bag and held it up. "Nothing on the note, but if we can keep them coming maybe he'll reveal something."

"He's already revealed a few things." She pulled out the chair Clive had just vacated and sat on the edge, folding her hands in front of her. "He's more of an attention seeker than the other two copycats. Probably means he has a lower sense of self-worth."

"Seems counterintuitive."

"A lot of psychoanalysis is. You'd know that if you were in deep therapy instead of behavior modification anger management." She scooted closer to the table and the scent of roses enveloped him. "Because he feels less worthy, small, he had to make himself into a big man, a bully. You must be very threatening to him."

He blinked and dragged his gaze away from the creamy skin of her throat. He'd once only imagined what that would feel like beneath his lips. Now he knew, and it didn't make it any easier to concentrate on her words when he'd missed her last night.

"Pay attention." She rapped her knuckles on the table in front of him, the slight curve to her full lips a sure sign that she knew what he'd been thinking. She frowned and got serious. "You're large and in charge. Physically, you're a big guy. You're a handsome guy. You have the world by the…throat. You must be very intimidating to copycat three. In fact, that's what you should call him— he'd hate it."

Jake rubbed his chin. "If he only knew I had a rebellious, runaway daughter at home and couldn't get two minutes alone with my woman, he might feel differently."

"He's not going to know that. He sees this—" she framed him with her hands "—perfect image of manhood that he can't hope to compete with, but he's going to show you because he's a killer and you can't catch him."

"Not yet." He grabbed her hand and kissed the inside of her wrist, his lips measuring each throb of her pulse. "I'm sorry about last night."

Her gaze darted to the corner of the ceiling. "No cameras in here?"

"Nope. We could lock the door, and I could ravish you on the conference table."

"You're losing it, J-Mac. I'm pretty sure that thought never occurred to you before. Now, Billy..."

"Are you maligning my partner?" He held up one hand. "I don't wanna hear it."

She slipped her hand from his. "Do you think the pizza and slasher movie helped you bond with Fiona last night?"

"I hope so. She was still sleeping when I left this morning." He checked the time on his phone. "I was supposed to call and remind her to log on to the computer for her lessons."

"One more thing before you do." Kyra tapped two of her fingernails against the table. "I didn't actually come in here to give you a profile of Copycat Three *or* to stalk your impure thoughts."

Jake narrowed his eyes at the nervous vibe emanating from Kyra. This almost sounded like confession time. "Go on."

"D-did you have any luck looking at Websleuths?"

"I only checked yesterday. I plan to dive into it some more today." He steepled his fingers and studied her flushed face over the point. "Why?"

She took a deep breath. "I did a little research myself last night when I came home from dinner. I created an account for myself on Websleuths and hopped onto a thread about that college girl missing in Alabama."

Jake swallowed. This was his fault. He never should've told her which website the previous two killers had been using to post messages, but he did feel a prick of satisfaction. The Kyra from a few months ago never would've told him about her sleuthing. He didn't want to make her regret it, either.

"I'm not sure that's a great idea, but I suppose it can't hurt for you to get an idea of what kind of people post and interact there. It might be helpful to the investigation…as long as you don't actively insert yourself into any offline chats or anything."

Kyra opened her mouth and then snapped it shut. "It's an interesting phenomenon, isn't it? All these amateur detectives. They really seem to care about these cases, these victims. Has the LAPD ever used any of the crime boards for information?"

"I haven't personally, but we've gotten a few tips from the boards. Nothing that ever checked out, as far as I know." He ran the side of his thumb along the edge of the bag with the note glaring at him from inside. "I still need to discuss my response to this note with Castillo. Any ideas?"

"Hmm." She wrinkled her nose as she tilted her head and her blond ponytail slid over her shoulder. "I do think you should call him Copycat Three. I don't think he'd like that at all, and it's good to needle someone like this. It might enrage him enough to make him slip up. Have you decided what medium you're going to use to respond? In the old days, newspapers worked, but not many people read newspapers anymore. In fact, I'm sure this guy has been reading his press online."

"What makes you think that?"

"I'm convinced he knows what you look like. I'm not sure the *Times* has ever printed your picture." She snapped her fingers. "You know that LA crime blogger, Sean Hughes, right?"

"Kind of a loudmouth who gets on the LAPD more than he should?" Jake took a sip of his lukewarm coffee, which did nothing to eliminate the bitter taste in his mouth thinking about Hughes. "Yeah, I know him."

"Him." Kyra drilled her finger into the table. "You should respond through his blog, *LA Confidential*."

"Are you crazy? I hate that guy. He recently outed one of our undercover vice guys, Trevor Jansen."

"I heard about that, but the officer was done with his assignment, anyway. The point is, Sean gets eyes, he gets attention. Anyone in this city who's a crime junkie, including all those people posting on Websleuths, is devouring Sean's blog."

"You think he'd do it? Be a conduit for me?" Jake rubbed his chin. He hated the idea that he'd be working with the enemy, but Kyra had her finger on the right pulse. Sean Hughes got people talking.

"Are you kidding? Sean would jump at the chance to post your reply to this killer. You should definitely suggest it to Castillo."

"All I have to do is tell Castillo it was your idea and he'll rubber-stamp it." Jake swept the baggie from the table and pushed back his chair.

"Really?" She followed his lead and rose from her chair. "Honestly, I don't know him that well, but Quinn does."

"There you have it. Quinn must have something on him to ensure Castillo's support of Quinn's favorite girl." He shot a smile at her just in case she didn't realize he was kidding.

She crossed to his side of the table and punched his arm. "Watch it."

He rubbed his arm, and then he opened the door, gesturing her through. "After you…because I don't trust you behind me."

As Jake walked to Castillo's office, Kyra peeled off and ducked into the task force war room. Jake tapped on the open door, and Castillo waved him in without lifting his eyes from his computer screen.

The captain tapped a few more keys with a flourish and then shoved his laptop to the side, lifting his brows at Jake. "How'd your meeting with Forensics go? Did the killer leave a print on the note or write it with some exotic rare ink?"

"If that had happened, you would've heard about it by now." Jake dropped into one of the chairs on the other side of Castillo's desk. "Still, it is a break, and I think I need to answer him. Everyone thinks that's a good idea."

"Everyone?" Castillo's eyebrows went even higher until they reached his salt-and-pepper hairline.

"Billy… Kyra. She's the psychologist on this team, right?" Jake ran a finger beneath his collar to loosen it. "The more we can get the guy to communicate, the better the odds are that he's going to trip up."

"I agree." Castillo leveled a finger at Jake. "You just need to watch out. You don't want this killer getting obsessed with you."

Jake chewed on his bottom lip. Kyra had implied that Copycat Three was already halfway to obsession and that's why he'd contacted him.

Lifting his shoulders, Jake said, "If that's what it takes."

"Have you thought about the best way to handle communication? Newspapers don't have the readership they once did. There's no guarantee this guy even picks up a paper."

"Kyra had an idea about that, too. Are you familiar with the *LA Confidential* blog?"

A flush crept beneath Castillo's brown skin. "Sean Hughes? He outed one of our undercover vice officers."

"I know that, but he has the readers we need—the number and the type. If Copycat Three is on the Websleuths site, and we think he is, he probably follows *LA Confidential*."

Castillo smirked. "Copycat Three? Sounds like a Dr. Seuss book. Our boy won't like that at all."

"Exactly." Jake winked. He didn't want to tell Castillo that was Kyra's idea, too. The captain would start wondering who was running the task force. "Can I count on your stamp of approval to reply and do it through *LA Confidential*?"

"I think that's the way to go." Castillo cocked his head and said, "And I think you should consult with Kyra about the response, but you won't have a problem with that now, will you?"

"Aren't you happy about that? She was your hire, after all."

"When we formed this task force and I brought her on, you weren't too happy about it. I think you've come to recognize her...value."

Jake smacked his hand on the desk. "I've come to recognize a lot of things about Kyra Chase. I'll get on the reply once I take care of a few other tasks—one of which is looking through Websleuths. I got caught up in the content yesterday without taking a hard look at the posters."

"Only a few people know that the first two killers were trolling on that website. I want to keep it that way.

We can't have everyone and his brother slogging through posts looking for a killer."

As Kyra could do no wrong according to Castillo, should he tell the captain that he'd let that Websleuths info slip to her?

Placing his hand on the phone, Castillo asked, "Anything else?"

"No. I'll be holding the briefing later this afternoon."

As Jake reached the door of Castillo's office, the captain's voice stopped him. "I have every confidence in you and Billy to stop this one, too, J-Mac."

"Did we really stop the other two? Cannon chose suicide by cop and Fisher offed himself with a cyanide tablet. The more I think about it, the stranger that seems to me. Most serial killers give up without a fight. They're almost relieved to get caught. Those two seemed to have… marching orders. Like they're following some kind of playbook."

Castillo shook his head. "The last thing we need is an instruction book for killers."

Jake wandered back to the task force room and stopped at Kyra's desk. "Castillo's onboard for Sean Hughes. Can you set that up, since you know him?"

Her blue eyes flashed. "I've talked to him once or twice. I don't exactly know him personally, but I will absolutely set that up. When do you want me to help you compose a response?"

He leaned in closer. "Fiona is going to visit her friend this afternoon, and she mentioned a sleepover. Would I be a bad father if I approved the sleepover to have a sleepover of my own?"

Her lips curved into a sexy smile. "You would only be a bad father if it's a sleepover you never would've allowed under other circumstances."

"Whew." He swept some imaginary sweat from his brow. "I'll keep you posted."

"You do that. I need to follow up with Carmella's family."

He left Kyra to her work and parked himself in front of his desk and opened his email. He'd barely gotten through the first one when Billy scooted his chair next to his.

"Heard the note was a bust for Forensics."

"It was, but not for other things."

"Damn right. Our boy's thirsty. He wants some attention."

"And we're gonna give it to him. I'm going to use that crime blog *LA Confidential* to respond to him." Jake tensed his muscles, waiting for the inevitable pushback.

Billy stroked his chin. "That Sean Hughes guy, huh?"

"I know he's not LAPD's biggest fan, but I think he'll do this for the publicity. It's not like he's on the side of the bad guys."

"I think it's a good idea. Megan's always talking about the blog. Her station actually gets story ideas by reading Hughes."

"Are you and Megan still seeing each other?"

Billy had an on-and-off dating relationship with Megan Wright, a reporter for a local TV station and one of Kyra's friends. Jake might believe that Megan's reason for going out with Billy was for information purposes, but Billy didn't need that lure. His partner had more women at his beck and call than he could handle—almost. That fact hadn't helped Billy's marriage.

"Megan's a…friend. Do you need her to put a word in with Hughes? I think she knows the guy."

"So does Kyra. She's going to handle it. She may have even met Hughes through Megan." Jake's personal cell phone buzzed and he felt a jolt of guilt. He'd meant to check on Fiona to make sure she was up and about, and now it was almost noon.

He snatched up the phone, and Billy wheeled back to his own desk. "So, you got up."

"Ages ago."

The yawn in Fiona's voice made him suspicious. "Did you get your schoolwork done?"

"Not yet. It's not even lunchtime." Jake heard the clink of dishes in the sink, and he could pretty much guarantee they were the breakfast dishes. "Lyric and her mother want to know if I can spend the night at their house when I go over this afternoon. I asked you before."

"You can't go at all until your schoolwork is done. Remember, it's online, and your teachers sent me a list of your assignments and the link to the portal so I can check that you've turned in everything."

Fiona heaved a sigh. "They'll be done, Dad. Can I sleep over at Lyric's?"

"Text me Lyric's mother's number, so I can check with her."

"Really?" Fiona's voice rose to an outraged squeak at the end, and he pulled the phone away from his ear.

"You know Mrs. Becker."

"It's been years since you were nine years old and playing with Lyric. Get your work done, text me the number, and when I check out everything you can have your sleepover." His gaze shifted to Kyra, hunched over her laptop. Was he giving in too easily?

"Okay, okay. I'll let you know when the work is done so you can check up on me."

Fiona ended the call without a proper goodbye.

Jake placed his personal cell on one side of his laptop and his work phone on the other and launched into Websleuths. IT had given him a history of Cannon's and

Fisher's posts to the site and he tracked back through those. They had both been regular posters almost a year ago—mostly writing messages containing theories about missing people or suspects, Cannon occasionally devolving into juvenile black humor.

What had drawn those two together? What had clued them in that they shared the same evil proclivities? After almost an hour perusing their posts, nothing jumped out at Jake. He noticed their posts dwindled to almost none in the past four to five months. They must've been communicating privately by that time, and the police didn't have access to those private messages.

Copycat Three had to be on here somewhere, or maybe he'd already moved his discourse to private messaging. The killers did have one preference in common—they confined their posts to threads on missing or murdered young women. No surprise there.

Jake scrolled through the message boards and favorited a few of those boards. He already knew Cannon and Fisher were killers. He had to find the current one.

He took a peek into a discussion about the missing college student in Alabama. That one would be prime for them. As he scrolled through the post, taking in the usernames, one grabbed him by the throat and his heart slammed against his chest.

Billy plunked a can of soda on Jake's desk. "Figured you might need this to gear up for the briefing."

"Thanks." Jake snapped the tab on the can and took a swig, ignoring the bubbles that tickled his nose while he clicked on a message posted by someone calling himself or herself *Laprey*. "I haven't been working on anything I can bring up in the briefing."

"Still looking at that true crime website, huh? Discover anything?"

Jake eyed the innocuous newbie post by Laprey and bookmarked the page. "Nothing yet. I'd turn it all over to Computer Forensics, except they'd be missing the instincts. You know what I mean?"

"I hear you, brother." Billy took a quick glance over his shoulder and lowered his voice. "Between you and me, those guys are brilliant but they're the first ones who'd get scammed by some lovely lady on an internet dating site. You know what *I* mean?"

"No street smarts. I feel you." Jake clicked off Websleuths and onto his notes for the task force briefing. "Now, you'd better brief me on what you're briefing at the briefing."

BY THE TIME Jake got home from work, Fiona had cleared out, taking her laptop with her. She'd completed her schoolwork, and he'd talked to Mrs. Becker, who assured him she'd be ordering sushi for the girls and they'd be staying in and binge watching some TV show about vampires. Not optimal, but he could live with that.

He showered, changed into jeans and ordered sushi for himself and teriyaki chicken for Kyra. By the time she arrived, he'd poured two glasses of chardonnay and had his laptop open to *LA Confidential*.

As she took the chilled wine from him, she wrinkled her nose at the bags from Mikado's. "You remembered I don't like sushi, right?"

He dug her container of teriyaki from the bag, set it on the counter and flipped it open. "Would I forget something like that? My daughter's having sushi tonight and it gave me a craving, but Mikado's has great teriyaki and I know you like that."

"I do." She touched her glass to his and the wine shimmered in her glass. "Am I allowed to kiss you in here now that Fiona has moved in?"

"Do you think she has me on security cam or something?" He took a sip of wine, and then touched his lips to hers. "I've never really dated anyone with Fiona around, but she'll get used to it. Hell, her mother is remarried and Fiona lives with her stepfather. I'm pretty sure Tess and Brock share a bedroom."

She swirled the golden liquid in her glass. "I don't want to push you, but it would be nice if I got to know her a little on this visit."

"I agree. We'll work something out." He handed her two plates. "I feel guilty about canceling last night's plans, so let's make this more like a date than a work function and eat at the table with glass and silverware, or chopsticks, instead of hunched over the computer with disposable containers and plastic."

"I concur, but you don't need to feel guilty about putting your daughter first."

"But you are a close, close second." He grabbed her and spun her into his arms. He pressed another kiss on her, this one deep and passionate, the kind of kiss that marked her as his own.

She feathered her fingertips across his face and said breathlessly, "If that's second, I'll take it."

As they ate, the conversation turned to the case, and he wondered again if he should bring up that username on Websleuths. Someone by the name of Laprey had been tormenting Kyra about her past. If this was the same person and he was involved in the current murders, Jake wanted to protect Kyra from that knowledge. He also knew Kyra would rather know all the facts—good or bad.

He'd investigate more first and tell her later. Although she was on the task force, he didn't owe her every detail of the case. Some of the officers on the task force didn't know what he and Billy knew.

"Are you thinking about your reply?"

Jake blinked. "What?"

"You're pinching that disgusting piece of sushi between your chopsticks and staring off into space. I thought you might be forming your response to Copycat Three."

He dropped the sushi onto his plate. "You still haven't heard back from Sean Hughes?"

"No, but I didn't tell him why I was calling, either. I probably should've dropped a hint. He would've gotten back to me immediately. He loves scoops and this'll be a big one for him. In the meantime—" she collected dishes from the table "—let's work out what you're going to say to a killer."

"I know what I'd like to say." He lifted her empty wineglass. "Another?"

"That depends." She scooted back her chair, carried the dishes to the sink and glanced over her shoulder with a flirtatious look. "Am I spending the night or not?"

"That's up to you. Fiona's friend doesn't have school tomorrow, so the mom is going to drop them off at the mall. Fiona won't be home until later."

"Pour the wine, baby." Kyra rinsed the dishes and stuck them in the dishwasher while Jake filled her glass and cleared the rest of the table.

She dried her hands and reached for her phone on the counter. She scrunched up her face as she stared at it. "I don't know why Sean's not calling me back. I think I need to set him straight. The sooner you get your word out, the better."

She perched on a stool at the counter and placed the

phone in front of her. She tapped the display, and the sound of Sean's ringing phone filled the kitchen.

Sean picked up after the first ring. "Hi, Kyra. I suppose I can't avoid you any longer."

Kyra shot Jake a puzzled look. "Avoid me? Why would you want to avoid me? I have a proposition for you."

"I don't work that way, Kyra. I'm sorry."

Jake lifted his brows, and Kyra shrugged as she answered Sean. "Work what way? You don't even know what I'm offering, yet."

"I'm not going to agree to kill a story in exchange for another one."

"Sean, we need to back up. I don't know what you're talking about. I called you earlier about an opportunity I know will interest you. I don't know anything about some other story."

Sean mumbled something unintelligible and then swore under his breath. "So, you don't know about the story I'm going to post about you on tomorrow's blog?"

"Me? You're posting a story about me?"

Jake had been moving toward Kyra with every one of Sean's words and now stood before her, his eyes on her pale face.

"I thought that's why you were calling, Kyra. I'm going public with your past as the daughter of one of The Player's victims…and the killer of your foster father."

Chapter Six

Kyra almost dropped the phone as the blood in her veins turned to ice water, but she didn't have to hold on to the phone as Jake snatched it from her hand.

Even though the phone was on speaker, Jake yelled into it. "Listen to me, you slimy SOB. If you publish that story about Kyra, I will personally come out there and…"

Kyra put a steadying hand on Jake's arm. He could *not* be making threats against journalists.

Sean choked and sputtered. "Who is this? Is this Detective Jake McAllister?"

Kyra held a finger to her lips. "Where'd you get that information, Sean?"

Sean cleared his throat. "I'm not going to reveal my sources, Kyra. Look, I'm sorry, but I can't pass this up, especially with you on the copycat killers task force and your…uh, relationship with the lead detective on the task force."

An ominous sound emanated from the back of Jake's throat, and Kyra squeezed his arm.

Sean continued his self-justification for exposing her very private life to the greedy masses. "I mean, it's not really going to hurt you personally. You…um, killed Buck Harmon in self-defense when you were a minor. It won't hurt you professionally. Hell, I think it might bring you more business. Anyway, I—I have to run with it. It's already written and scheduled to post tomorrow morning."

Kyra sighed. "You do what you have to do."

"Now that that's settled." Sean's tone grew crisp. "What is the opportunity you have for me?"

Jake answered him. "There's no way in hell you're getting that now, buddy."

"Actually, once Sean posts the story about me, it makes even more sense for you to work with him."

The tips of Jake's ears turned so red Kyra expected steam to start pouring out of them. "I'm not working with this guy."

"Sean, I'll call you back later."

"I'm intrigued…and I really am sorry, Kyra."

She ended the call before Jake could spew any more vitriol over the phone. Then she grabbed her glass of wine and downed half of it in one gulp.

"Don't you get it? After he posts that story about me and my connection to the case, he'll have even more readers for your response."

"At what price?" Jake placed his hands on her shoulders. "I don't want to see you hurt. You went through a lot of trouble changing your identity and moving away from your traumatic past. He has no right to bring it all crashing down on your head. I can make it stop. I can make *him* stop."

"No, you can't, but I love you for wanting to try." She cupped his strong, fierce jaw with one hand. "Maybe it's for the best. If it had all been out in the open, I never would've lied to you about my past. Once the prurient interest dies down, people will move on to another story."

"There's gonna be talk at the station." He turned his head to kiss her palm. "I don't like the thought of you being the object of…"

"What? Pity? That's not so bad. Curiosity? I can live

with that." She pressed a hand against his thudding heart. "If you're by my side, I can get through all of that."

"You can count on it, count on me, and it'll start tomorrow."

"What does that mean?"

"I'm not going to let you walk into the lion's den alone tomorrow. We'll walk into the station together. Anything anyone has to say to you can go through me first."

Smiling, she drummed her fingers against his chest. "You're going to take care of them like you threatened to take care of Sean?"

"That guy." A scowl twisted Jake's features. "I'm not gonna send my reply to Copycat Three through him."

"Yes, you are." She smoothed a hand across Jake's face. "It's perfect. He blogs about me and my past and then he segues into your response to the killer. Copycat Three is going to get what he wants…and so are you."

"Why are you comforting me when it's your life that's about to be blown to bits?" He captured her hand and kissed her fingertips.

"That's just it. The prospect of Sean outing me tomorrow doesn't fill my heart with terror as long as I'm with you. When I'm alone in my cold bed…that's another story."

Jake curled his hands around her waist and pulled her from the stool, securing her against his chest. "Tonight, you're not going to be alone in your bed, and it's certainly not going to be cold."

Once Jake started kissing and touching her, they didn't make it to his bed or even to his bedroom. Much later, sated and languid, Kyra pushed the dark hair from Jake's eyes as he studied her from beneath half-mast lids. "We should move this party to your bedroom."

"Is this still a party?" He ran a fingertip down her spine, making her shiver.

"I'll let you know after I brush my teeth and wash my face." She rolled off the couch and scooped up her discarded clothing. As she faced the wall of glass that looked out over city lights, Kyra clutched her clothes to her chest. "You're sure nobody can see in here?"

Jake joined her at the window, stark naked, and rapped one knuckle on the glass. "You see any houses facing mine?"

"What's that tall building to the right?"

"That's a mixed-use building on Sunset, some offices, some apartments. See how small those windows are? Nobody can see us from there unless they have a telescope trained on us."

Kyra hunched her shoulders as a wisp of unease tickled the back of her neck. "If you say so."

She left Jake to gather up his own clothes and cut through his bedroom to the master bath. She peeked into a basket on the vanity for the few items, including a toothbrush, she'd taken to leaving at his place.

He came up behind her and touched her hip. "I put your stuff in the second drawer."

She opened the drawer he indicated and snatched up her toothbrush.

He swept the hair off the back of her neck and pressed his lips against the nape. "I thought it was a good idea to stash your stuff there while Fiona was here. What do you think?"

She forced a smile to her face and met his eyes in the mirror. "I think that's a good idea."

Jake stuffed his clothes into the wicker hamper and grabbed his own toothbrush. "When are you calling Hughes?"

"Tomorrow morning, but we didn't even start working on your response."

Jake wiggled his eyebrows. "We had more important matters to address."

She bumped his hip with hers to gain access to the sink and rinsed out her mouth. "I suppose Sean is never going to tell me who ratted me out."

"You don't think he did the digging on his own?"

"Why would he? I barely know the guy. Why would he be looking into me?" She splashed water on her face and came up for air. "Nope. Somebody dished on me."

"Do you think it's *him*?"

"Laprey? Who else knows everything? Who else has been trying to make my life miserable for the past several months?" She dropped her toothbrush back into the drawer of shame and spun around. "I guess this is his endgame. I hope so, anyway. Maybe he'll stop after this."

"What more could he want?" Jake kissed her shoulder. "We'll face it together tomorrow."

Kyra left Jake in the bathroom and slid between his crisp sheets. When he joined her in bed, he pulled her back against his chest and draped a heavy arm over her waist. It didn't take long before Jake's breathing deepened.

Kyra lifted his arm from her body and paused as he murmured and shifted onto his back. She scooted to the edge of the bed and glanced over her shoulder at his sleeping form.

Then she grabbed one of his T-shirts, slipped it over her head and padded back into the living room with its fishbowl window on the world. Tucking her laptop beneath her arm, she curled up in one corner of the couch, inhaling Jake's scent, which still clung to the leather.

She flipped open her laptop and accessed the Web-

sleuths site. She clicked on the private message from
Toby Dog and responded.

I do wanna play. What do you have in mind?

KYRA HAD BEEN playing coy the night before by not packing an overnight bag with work clothes. Now she regretted it.

Jake had been serious about walking into the station
with her, so he'd followed her all the way to her place
in Santa Monica and hung out with Spot, the stray cat,
while she changed for work.

As she emerged from the bathroom, straightening her
skirt, she smirked at Spot circling Jake's ankles. "He's
going to get cat hair all over your pants."

"I can live with a little cat hair, but I'll keep him away
from you." He cocked his head, and his gaze raked her
from head to toe. "You look good. Fierce. Ready to take
on the world."

"I'd better be. Have you checked out *LA Confidential*, yet?" She held up her phone. She'd been perusing
the blog in the bathroom while drying her hair. "It could
be worse."

"I confess. I read it while you were in the shower and
Spot was munching his kibble. It's sensational. Hughes's
writing style is sensational, but you don't come off looking bad."

She snorted. "I come off like a shady lady from a
1940s film noir."

"Is that bad?" Jake swooped down and grabbed Spot
under his belly with one hand as the cat tried to make
a beeline for her legs. "That's the way Hughes writes. I
can see why the blog is popular."

"Megan Wright already called me, so the media have picked up on the story."

"You talked to Megan?"

"Not yet. She left me a voice mail. I can tell she's kind of hurt that I didn't give her the scoop. She assured me, she would've handled my story with a lot more sensitivity than Sean managed." Kyra raised and dropped her shoulders quickly. "Should've, could've, would've. It's out there now."

"Let's not make this worse by coming in to the station any later." Jake rotated his wrist and stared down Spot's angry gaze. "Time for you to take a hike. I gotta play wingman for the shady lady."

Kyra insisted on taking her own car and followed Jake back to the Northeast Division. On the drive over, she called Megan.

Her friend gushed over the phone. "Are you okay, Kyra? My God, I never would've guessed your background, although you always did seem interested in serial killers in general and The Player, specifically. Did Jake know?"

"Jake knew." Kyra didn't go into the details about how Jake knew, how he'd had to pull every bit of the truth from her by hook or by crook. "Now everybody knows."

"You come off kind of heroic, you know. K-killing Buck Harmon in self-defense while trying to protect a little girl. That's not a bad thing, Kyra." Megan paused. "Any way to track down the girl today?"

Kyra clamped down on the retort that rose to her lips. Megan was a journalist trying to do her job. "I think she deserves her privacy even though I've lost mine. My juvenile records are sealed, so her name won't be public—unless someone outs her like someone outed me."

"Who did out you, Kyra? Who knows your story and would spill it to Sean? Did he tell you his source?"

"I have no clue, and Sean didn't tell me. Would you?"

"I'm afraid I wouldn't, even though we're friends." Megan sucked in a breath. "We're still friends, aren't we?"

"I don't blame you for anything, Megan. Why would I? I don't even fault you for wanting more of the scoop—you're just not going to get it, at least not from me." Kyra drummed her thumbs on the steering wheel. "Unless you don't think you could be friends with someone like me."

"What are you talking about, girlfriend? You're a hero for ridding the world of a scumbag. And your mother's murder? You deserve sympathy and support for that. I suppose that's why you're so good at your job. Can you imagine what your story's going to mean to the family members of the copycat killers' victims? Now they know you can truly understand what they're going through." Megan sniffled. "I'm proud to know you, Kyra. If whoever leaked this story to Sean thought they were going to hurt you, they misjudged the public."

Megan's words made Kyra's nose tingle. She'd been keeping these secrets for so long because the truth made her feel exposed, vulnerable, but maybe she'd been wrong to hide it all.

"Thanks for your support, Megan. I'm pulling into the station right now, so we'll talk later."

When she ended the call, Kyra noticed that she'd received another call and voice mail, from Quinn this time. He must've heard the news.

She knew he wouldn't be happy about the latest development in her life. Quinn and Charlotte had been the ones who'd told her to keep her past to herself. When she wanted to change her name from Marilyn Lake to

Kyra Chase, they'd both encouraged her to do so and even helped her establish her new ID. She'd save Quinn's call for later.

She trailed Jake into the station's parking lot and parked her car with the unmarked police vehicles on the edge of the lot. She stayed in her car until she saw Jake's head bobbing above the other black sedans.

Taking a deep breath, she exited her vehicle and wended her way through the cars toward him.

He held out his hand and she took it. Squeezing her fingers, he said, "Ready?"

"As ready as I'll ever be." She disentangled her fingers from his and squared her shoulders. "Quinn left me a voice mail. He must've heard."

"Do you think he'll be upset?"

"I think I'd better see him tonight to reassure him. He never wanted me to reveal that my mother was one of The Player's victims." She tripped over a crack in the pavement and Jake caught her arm. "I don't think he wanted my name and identity revealed."

"Because he thinks The Player is still out there. But why would The Player be interested in hurting you after all these years?"

Kyra stopped and wiped her palms on her skirt. "Can we not talk about this right now? I'm about to face some curious colleagues."

"I'm sorry. I'm supposed to be supporting you, and I'm making it worse." Jake tapped the side of his head. "Can't turn off the detective."

"I know that." She tugged on the sleeve of his jacket. "Just don't go off on anyone like you did with Sean Hughes last night. People are going to be curious, and that's okay."

He touched his fingers to his forehead in a mock salute. "Got it. You haven't talked to that… I mean, you haven't talked to Hughes yet, have you?"

She clicked her tongue. "No, but we're going to work on your response today and get it to him to publish tomorrow."

Jake opened the door for her, and they walked through the lobby of the station. With her heart pounding, Kyra climbed the stairs to the second floor, which housed the conference room dedicated to the task force, or the war room, as they referred to it. Her knees wobbled, but she resisted hanging on to Jake's arm for support.

She sailed into the war room, her chin held high and her gaze sweeping the space. Was she imagining it, or did the decibel level recede for a split second? A few people looked up and then looked away quickly.

She huffed a sharp breath from her nose and nodded at Jake as she took a seat at her desk in the corner.

Two seconds later, Lieutenant Alicia Fields approached Kyra's desk. Perching on the edge, Alicia said, "Read *LA Confidential* this morning, and just wanted to let you know you rock. I always thought we were lucky to have your expertise on the task force, and that belief has increased tenfold. Keep up the good work."

Kyra blinked back tears. "Thanks, Lieutenant. Means a lot."

As soon as Lieutenant Fields walked away, a female patrol officer scooted a chair up to Kyra's desk. "Hi, Kyra, my name's Loretta, and I just wanted to let you know that I admire you so much after reading that blog. My stepfather was abusive, and he molested me and my sister. It took us a few years to get away from him. I wish we'd had someone like you to stand up for us."

Kyra flattened a hand against her chest. "I'm so sorry you went through that."

After that, a few other officers gave her thumbs-ups, and she started getting emails from some of the family members of the copycats' victims expressing their condolences for her mother and thanking her for her support.

Kyra's heart had filled to bursting when Billy came to her desk and gave her a one-armed hug. "I'm glad we have you on this task force, even though it must be incredibly hard for you to relive these crimes. We're behind you—all of us."

That was it. Kyra squeezed Billy's hand and launched out of her chair. She stumbled blindly toward the restroom, her throat choked with tears.

When she made it to the bathroom, she crashed into a stall, startling an officer washing her hands. Kyra placed her hands against the metal door, dropped her head between her arms and sobbed.

After a few minutes of release, Kyra tugged some toilet paper from the roll and mopped her face. She hadn't expected any of that. All her fears had been wiped away with a few kind words.

She peeked out of the stall, scanned the empty bathroom and walked to the vanity to inspect the damages. She splashed cold water on her face and dabbed at the streaks of mascara beneath her eyes.

She returned to the war room with greater confidence than when she'd entered it this morning, even with Jake by her side. This time, nobody shot her furtive glances and nobody abruptly stopped talking. Cops were a prosaic bunch, not given to excess sentimentality. That's why she'd always liked working with them.

She clicked through a few more supportive emails from the victims' families and then switched over to the psychological profile of Copycat Three that the FBI had provided the team.

She nodded along as she read, agreeing with the majority of the report. Jake's response needed to challenge the killer's manhood. They needed to unsettle Copycat Three and force his hand.

By the time Kyra had drafted a few responses, Jake texted her, inviting her out to a working lunch. Forty-five minutes later, they sat across from each other over sandwiches and salads, and she pushed printouts of her responses in front of him.

"This is what I have, so far."

Ignoring the papers, Jake picked up his sandwich. "Do you want to talk about what happened this morning?"

Kyra's nose twitched at the thought of the outpouring of support from her colleagues. "It was pretty awesome. Did you… Did you have anything to do with it? Did you call ahead and read them the riot act?"

"You give me way too much credit or power. What happened in there was spontaneous. You really think anyone in law enforcement is going to hold it against you that you killed someone in self-defense, or that your mother was a victim of The Player? If anything, you solidified yourself as one of us. I just wish it hadn't taken you so long to realize you had nothing to be ashamed about."

"Quinn always encouraged me to hide it, or maybe just to put it in my past." She rushed in to cover any perceived criticism of Quinn. "He wasn't wrong. I did want to put it all behind me. I didn't want to go through college being *that* girl. The freak show."

"Maybe Quinn was right. But you're mature enough to handle the fallout now, and I'm glad it's out in the open. Maybe I owe Sean Hughes an apology."

She tapped the papers on the table. "He's getting your response to a serial killer for his blog. That's enough of an apology."

"Can I eat first?"

"Since I kept you from having breakfast this morning, I'd feel even more guilty if I kept you from lunch."

When Jake emerged from demolishing half his sandwich, he asked, "Have you talked to Quinn yet?"

"No, I listened to his voice mail and he just asked me to call him." She prodded bits of veggies in her salad around her plate. "I think he just wants to make sure I'm okay."

"I think that's all he ever wants for you. I don't fault him for helping you maintain your secrets, if that's what you think."

"I don't think that at all. He had his reasons, and they were right for the time." She gave up on her salad and sucked down some iced tea. "Speaking of good parenting, did you talk to Fiona today?"

"A few times—this morning while she was having a late breakfast and just before I left for lunch as she and Lyric were getting ready to go to the mall. Even though Lyric had the day off from school, Fiona didn't, so I told her she needed to be home before dinner to get her schoolwork done."

"Have you looked any more at the alternate Instagram page?"

"Jazzy?" He dragged a napkin across the lower half of his face. "No, but I think I'd better discuss it with her. I'm learning enough from Brandon the IT guy to make me more and more uncomfortable with that page. It looks like we can't get to the private messages Cannon and Fisher wrote on Websleuths. They've all been deleted, and we haven't found a way to retrieve them yet. The internet can be a dark and dangerous place."

Kyra's hand shook a little as she set down her tea. Her own private message to Toby Dog's invitation to play had

gone unanswered so far. Did she really believe he was
some kind of serial killer recruiter?

"Maybe you should confront Fiona about it tonight.
Clue her in on the dangers of communicating with strang-
ers online and make her delete the account."

"That'll endear me to her."

"You don't want to be her dear. You want to be her father. I can tell you, there were times I hated Quinn and
Charlotte, or I thought I did."

"I know you're right. I'll have my father-daughter talk
with Fiona tonight, while you have yours with Quinn.
And now—" he shoved aside the basket with the remain-
der of his sandwich inside and stacked the printouts in
front of him "—I need to respond to a killer."

For the next hour, they hunched over the table and
crossed out words, rephrased sentences and debated psychology until they agreed on a finished statement for
Copycat Three.

"There." Kyra shoved the marked-up papers into her
purse. "I'll call Sean this afternoon and ask him to run
it tomorrow."

Jake pulled out his wallet and left a couple of bills on
the table. "Are you also going to try to convince him to
give up his source for your story?"

"I'll give it a try, but I'm sure he won't budge." Kyra
hitched her purse over her shoulder and made for the
door.

When they got back to Jake's car, he checked his work
phone and then stuck it in the holder on the dash.

Eyeing the display, Kyra asked, "Nothing new, huh?"

"Nobody's confessed, if that's what you mean." He
turned on the engine, and his phone rang. He tapped to
answer without looking at the display.

With his phone on speaker, the woman's voice flooded the car. "Jake, as long as you're seeing that…killer, I don't want her anywhere near Fiona."

Chapter Seven

Jake scrambled for the phone, dropping it on the console as he jabbed at the speaker button. When he pressed the phone against his ear, he hissed, "You've got some nerve, Tess."

Kyra relegated the rest of the one-sided conversation to background noise as she crashed from the high of the response from her colleagues on the task force to a painful low. She'd always worried her background would taint her, render her not good enough in other people's eyes. Tess had just offered confirmation of that.

Jake ended the call and slammed his phone into the cup holder. "I'm sorry, Kyra. She had no right to say those things."

"But she did have a right." Kyra pinned her hands between her bouncing knees. "Fiona is her daughter."

"Like you would somehow infect Fiona." He swore and swung out of the parking space in the strip mall. "I could've objected to her husband Brock all these years. Cheated on his own wife with Tess, breaking up two marriages and families."

"Brock didn't kill anyone, did he?"

"He wouldn't have the guts to stand up to someone like you did." Jake's jaw set into hard lines, and Kyra loved him for his ardent defense of her—but it didn't change anything.

"Tell her I'll stay away."

His head jerked to the side. "What? No. She doesn't have a right to control my dating life."

Kyra put her hand on Jake's corded forearm, the tail of his tiger tattoo exposed by his rolled-up sleeves, almost pulsing. "Just for now. Just while Fiona's with you. We can still see each other at work, and we'll figure it out when Fiona leaves. Maybe Tess will have calmed down by then."

"I have no idea how she found out. She doesn't even practice criminal law, so I don't think she'd be trolling the internet for blogs like *LA Confidential*."

"Fiona told her."

Shifting in his seat, Jake flipped up the AC. "Why would she do that?"

Kyra swallowed. She hadn't meant to blurt out those words. "Maybe the news about me scared her."

She doubted much of anything scared Fiona, but Kyra shouldn't have shown her hand that first night. She should've pretended that Fiona was pulling the wool over her eyes as much as she was over her father's.

Jake said, "I'll talk with her."

"Not about me." She squeezed Jake's solid thigh. "Don't try to talk her out of anything. She'll only dig in."

Jake grunted. "You're the therapist."

When they got back to the station, they went their separate ways and Kyra contacted Sean Hughes to talk to him about Jake's response to Copycat Three.

Sean's excitement for the story squelched any residual awkwardness over the blog he'd posted about her. After she emailed Sean the copy of Jake's communication, Kyra sat back in her seat and lowered her voice, cupping the phone against her face.

"I suppose you're not going to tell me where you learned about my past, are you?"

"Sources and all that, Kyra. I can't. I'd lose all credibility. Not even Megan, your friend, would reveal that to you."

"I know." She tapped a pen on the edge of her laptop. "Just be careful."

"Careful?"

"I've had some strange communications with someone who knows all about me. This same person seems to be connected to the current copycat slayings. If he's the same person who clued you in to my history, I'm telling you he's unstable. He may have even been responsible for the death of a homeless woman he used to reach me. When he was done with her, she died in a hit-and-run accident."

Sean caught his breath over the phone. "You have proof of this?"

"I do not. I have only my suspicions, but he's not someone you want too close to you."

"Probably not someone I want to cross, either."

She pounced on his words. "So, you're saying it's the same person?"

Sean clicked his tongue. "I'm not saying anything like that. Truth be told, my source is anonymous, but I was able to back up everything he…or she told me. That's all I'm saying."

"If you feel he or she has pertinent information about these current crimes, that's a different matter. Lives are in peril. You have a duty to come clean—just like if one of my clients threatened to do harm. I could step away from patient confidentiality and report that."

"I understand my duty, Kyra. It's nothing like that." He coughed. "How have the revelations gone for you today? I hope you've seen the comments on the blog. Most people are applauding you for taking out a dirtbag and lauding you for helping families of other murder victims. You're coming through this smelling like a rose."

"It's been fine. No hard feelings." Except it probably ruined any chance of a relationship with the man she loved.

"Good to hear it. I'm not completely heartless."

"Just run the response tomorrow and work with the police for a change."

"I'm always willing to work with the police...as long as they stay in their lane."

Kyra glanced up at Clive, standing at her desk and raising his eyebrows to his bald pate.

Smiling, she held up one finger to him. "Gotta go, Sean. This time I'm looking forward to the blog tomorrow."

Once she'd hung up, Clive said, "Hope I didn't interrupt you. Was that the *LA Confidential* blogger?"

"It was. I heard you didn't find any prints on the note."

"No luck this time." Clive shuffled his feet. "I wasn't here when you came in this morning, so I just wanted to add my support to all the rest you've been getting from the team."

"Thanks, Clive. That means a lot."

The warm glow in her belly stayed with her the rest of the afternoon, but all the support in the world wouldn't compensate for losing Jake. His daughter had to come first.

Before she wrapped up, she made the call she'd been dreading.

Quinn answered on the first ring. "Took you a while

to get back to me. I would've been worried, but I knew you'd be at the station and have Jake to look after you."

"I can look after myself, Quinn." She might have to if Jake's ex forced him out of her life. "But I'm fine. Everyone at the station has been great."

"I didn't doubt that, but...do you have plans tonight?"

"I think I do now."

"Rose sent over some stew, and I can't hope to eat it all myself. You can come over anytime."

"I have a group after I leave the station, but when that's over I'm all yours."

Kyra didn't have a chance to talk to Jake the rest of the day, and he'd be spending his evening with his daughter. Would Fiona admit to her father that she'd been the one who'd given her mom a heads-up about Kyra's lurid past? Kyra thought Fiona might welcome her relationship with her father to get him off her case while she stayed with him. She'd underestimated the girl.

Kyra finished her work at the station, conducted her group session at the office and headed home to change before visiting Quinn. He'd tried to protect her for so long, but a shifting world of quick internet searches, hacking and social media had made that impossible—even for him.

She put on a pair of jeans, a T-shirt and sneakers. On her way out the door, she grabbed a hoodie. When she reached Quinn's house in Venice, the sun had already dipped halfway into the ocean and a damp marine layer had started seeping into the canals, the moist droplets it brought clinging to her eyelashes and the loose strands of her hair.

She possessed a key, but she knocked on Quinn's door out of courtesy. As it got harder and harder for him to move around, she hated calling him to the front door. "It's me, Quinn."

"C'mon in."

She used her key and poked her head inside the house. "Smells good. I didn't bring a thing with me. I was in a rush."

"I already told you—" he waved a spoon in the air from the kitchen "—Rose provided everything the other day. She even dropped off homemade bread."

"Rose is working hard to impress you, Quinn. I hope you invited her to share the stew with you when she brought it over."

"Of course, I did. What do you take me for? You're getting the leftovers, but if Rose's trying to replace Charlotte, it's just not gonna happen." He dropped the spoon and held his arms wide. "Now, get over here."

She let her bag slip to the floor and practically skipped across the living room to the kitchen. Wrapping her arms around Quinn's waist, she rested her head against his shoulder, and he stroked her hair as he used to do when she was a kid running away from her latest disaster of a foster home.

After the support and acceptance of her colleagues at the station and the warm emails from her clients, she hadn't realized how much she needed this comfort from Quinn. He was the only one who could truly understand.

More than ten years of a carefully crafted identity shattered by a blog post.

Quinn wasn't as sturdy as he used to be, though, and he'd staggered back a bit under the enthusiasm of her greeting. She pulled away from him and kissed his weathered cheek. "Thanks for getting it."

"I know the revelations didn't hurt you professionally,

Mimi—may have even helped—but I don't like it." He turned away from her and grabbed two bowls.

"I know you don't, Quinn." She patted his back. "But even if The Player is still alive and paying attention to all this, he has no reason to come for me. He got away with murder, several murders. He's not going to risk anything now."

"You'd better believe if he's alive, he's paying attention." He picked up the spoon from the sink and shook it under her nose, sending droplets of gravy flying onto his white cabinets. "Are you kidding? He's probably following these copycats with breathless excitement."

She hated it when Quinn talked about The Player as if he were a part of their lives. He was imprisoned or dead. He meant nothing to her today.

"Be careful with that thing." Reaching around Quinn, she picked up a dish sponge from the sink and ran it under the faucet. Then she dabbed at the spots on his cabinets. "The Player might be salivating over all the death in his name, but he has nothing to do with me."

"I know. Don't pay any attention to the old man rambling in the corner about his one failure." Quinn took two steps around her with the bowls in his hands and set them down next to the stove, where a pot simmered and emitted mouthwatering aromas from its bubbling depths.

"Let me fill those. Take the bread and have a seat." She took the ladle from his hand and dipped it into the stew. When she'd filled the bowls, she brought them to the table, where they joined slices of crusty bread. "It almost feels like fall around here."

Holding up a can of beer, Quinn said, "I don't have any wine for you."

"That's okay. You'd think I'd be dying for a few drinks after getting outed by Sean Hughes, but everything went surprisingly well." She spread butter on a piece of warm bread, and it soaked in immediately.

"If it hadn't gone well for you at the station, they would've had me to answer to—Castillo knows that."

"Captain Castillo?" She bit into the bread.

Quinn reddened to the roots of his silver hair and shoved a spoonful of stew into his mouth.

Kyra brushed the crumbs from her fingers onto the bread plate. "Has Castillo known my identity all this time?"

Quinn swallowed and patted his lips with a napkin, covering the lower half of his face. "He's the only one. I didn't tell him. He just…knew."

"Makes sense." She shrugged. "He was around then. He worked on the case, didn't he?"

"He did."

"Is that why…?" She stirred the chunky contents of her bowl. "Never mind. There was one roadblock to my happiness today."

"Not Jake, he already knew. Why would he be upset?"

"His ex-wife."

Quinn clutched the handle of his spoon with a curled fist. "What did she have to say about it, and how'd she find out? She doesn't even live here, does she?"

"She lives up north, Monterey."

Quinn's spoon clinked against the bowl as he dropped it. "It was his daughter, huh?"

"I'm pretty sure she told her mother all about the woman her dad is dating." Kyra twisted her lips and took a sip of water.

"Don't worry about it." Quinn reached over and patted her hand. "As a therapist, you know it's not unusual for kids to sabotage their parents' dating lives. You never had to resort to that because Charlotte and I presented a united front at all times—even if we weren't all that united behind the scenes, sometimes, but as you never lived with us, you never saw any of that."

"It doesn't surprise me, but the ex took it to heart and called Jake to read him the riot act about me." She left off the part where Tess had referred to her as a *killer*. Quinn didn't need to hear that.

"You and Jake can cool it while his daughter's here. You were going to do that anyway, right? Then the ex will come around, and the daughter will come around, and the two of you can get married and start a family of your own."

Kyra choked on the bread in her mouth and had to wash it down with water. "Is that what you have planned for me?"

Quinn's faded blue eyes softened. "Why not? I like Jake. I trust Jake. He can take care of you when I'm gone."

That was the second time Quinn had mentioned Jake taking care of her.

She sealed her lips. Quinn wouldn't want to be reminded that she took care of him a lot more than he took care of her these days. "You're not going anywhere, and I can take care of myself. Isn't that why you taught me to use a gun?"

"Don't get your hackles up. I know you can handle yourself, but there's nothing wrong with having someone on your side while you do it. Charlotte and I took care of each other—until the end."

"I know you did." She sniffed and scooped up another spoonful of stew to blame it on the steam rising from the bowl. She and Quinn hadn't gotten so sentimental since Charlotte's passing a few years back.

"How'd that blogger get your story? Aren't the Department of Children and Family Services records confidential anymore?" Quinn ripped apart a piece of bread as if it were Sean Hughes's body.

"You know they are. It's different today, Quinn. People get access to records in all kinds of ways—some of them illegal."

He waved the bread at her and the crumbs showered the tablecloth. "Even I know about that *LA Confidential* blog. He's anti law enforcement."

"I wouldn't say that." She shoved the remaining contents of her bowl around, delaying dropping the next shoe for Quinn. "He's interested in crime. He's interested in law enforcement. He calls out injustices."

"There's no injustice in an officer like Jansen working undercover. He was with a hard-core biker gang who could've killed him."

"To give Sean credit, he didn't reveal Jansen's identity until his assignment ended."

"Don't like it."

"Then you're really not going to like this. The LAPD has decided to use Sean's blog as a channel of communication between Jake and Copycat Three."

Quinn snorted beer out of his nose and made a grab for his napkin. "Is that what they're calling him?"

"It's going to make him angry."

"Must've been your idea."

"It was."

He dragged the napkin across his nose and dropped it in his lap. "I can understand why you'd want to use the blog, but it doesn't sit right with me. Still, I'm glad Jake has a vehicle to reach out to the killer. Copycat Three has an ego, and it'll trip him up."

"The response will needle him, for sure." She placed her bowl on top of her bread plate. "Thank Rose for me.

I'll clean up, and then if you don't mind, I'll keep you company for a while. I'm in no hurry to get home."

He cocked an eyebrow at her. "Will I be seeing more of you with Jake's daughter in town?"

"Can't I just like your company?"

"I know you do, Mimi." He pushed back from the table with some difficulty, but she refrained from helping him. There was only so much assistance a man like Quinn would take. "I'll rinse and you can put the dishes in the dishwasher."

"That's a deal."

When she finished washing up the cookware, she joined Quinn in the living room where an old Hitchcock film played on the TV. She curled up in the corner of the sofa and dragged out her laptop.

Jake had texted her a couple of times during the evening and assured her he'd made some progress with his ex-wife. She just hoped he wasn't pushing things with Fiona.

She accessed *LA Confidential* and read more comments on Sean's blog about her history. He was already teasing the story for tomorrow, and despite her excitement about it a little knot had formed in her gut.

It was one thing to hunt a nameless, faceless, anonymous killer and quite another to have contact with that killer. It made the search for him that much more…personal.

She blew out a breath and took a sip of hot tea. Jake could take care of himself a lot better than she could take care of herself. If she thought Quinn's worries about her were absurd, Jake would laugh off her concerns about him.

She glanced at Quinn over the top of her laptop, and then brought up Websleuths. "Quinn, have you ever heard of these true crime message boards where people discuss missing persons and murders?"

"I've heard about them." He paused the movie. "One of them played a role in the investigation of the Golden State Killer, although more in the way of speculation than hard evidence. I suppose they're all chattering about these copycat killings."

"I suppose so. I've glanced through a few of them, and people really do want to help. It's not just ghoulish rubbernecking."

Jake had shared a lot about the case with Quinn, but he hadn't told him about the link between copycats one and two and the Websleuths site. She'd honor that—especially because she had her own interest in the site now.

Holding her breath, she clicked on her personal messages on the website. Toby Dog had responded to her, and she read his message with a hand clenched against her belly. Weird, but not serial killer recruitment level weird.

He and his special friends liked to take the action from the message boards to *real life*, as he called it. They traveled to the crime sites, they did investigative work like measuring distances and time, visited the locations where the victims were last seen.

The administrators of the website prohibited that kind of activity, and if they found out a member was conducting his or her own investigation, they'd ban that member from the website.

She had no desire to play supersleuth, but Toby Dog, which she'd figured out was the name of Sherlock Holmes's dog, piqued her curiosity about whether or not members were engaged in this activity on the copycat killer message board. What could they find out that the police couldn't?

As she clicked in the field to respond, her phone rang.

She caught her breath as she saw Sean's name pop up on the display. She hoped he wasn't having a change of heart.

As she answered, she pushed the laptop from her legs and stood up. "Hope you haven't changed your mind."

Quinn looked up from his movie, and she waved him off as she sauntered out to his front porch.

Sean's heavy breathing made him sound like a creeper or as if he'd just finished running a 5k. "I haven't changed my mind, but I need to talk to you about something—in person."

"Are you all right? You sound…out of breath."

"I am a little, but I'm okay. Can you meet me?"

"Now?" With her belly full of stew and sourdough bread, she didn't feel like hopping on the freeway to meet with a blogger about last-minute changes.

He answered in clipped tones. "Yes, now."

"Do you want me to bring Jake?"

"Just you. It's important, Kyra."

Her hands suddenly turned clammy. "Is—is this about the blog tomorrow or the blog today?"

"Both. It has to be just you. I need to meet you now, or I'm not going to be able to post the blog tomorrow."

She glanced through the window at Quinn enthralled by Grace Kelly. He'd always told her that her mother had gotten it all wrong. Instead of naming her Marilyn after Marilyn Monroe, she should've named her Grace. Marilyn or Grace, he wouldn't want her running off to meet Sean Hughes in the middle of the night.

"Kyra?"

"I—I'm still here. Where are you? At your home?" She had no idea where Sean lived, but anyone calling LA home could live a good forty-five minutes away from every other place in LA.

"I'm not at my house, but I live in Echo Park and I can meet you at the park by the lake there."

"Why there? Can't we meet at a bar or coffeehouse?"

"No!" Sean took a few steadying breaths. "We can't be seen together. This is important, Kyra. Do you want that blog to run tomorrow?"

"It has to."

"Then I'll see you when you get here. There are still people walking on the path around the lake. I'll be waiting in my black BMW in the parking lot near the little boat dock for those swan pedal boats. You know the area?"

"I know it." She checked the time on her phone. "I'm in Venice. If there's no traffic, I'll be there in about thirty minutes. This better be good."

Sean hung up without responding, and Kyra slipped inside Quinn's house.

He looked up. "Everything okay?"

"Everything's fine, but I have a work thing and I need to get going."

Quinn studied her for a few seconds, and she marched past him to grab her hoodie. She brushed a kiss against his cheek. "I'll see you next time."

Grabbing her hand, he said, "Be careful."

"I always am." She moved her hand over the gun pouch on the side of her purse.

As she drove north to Echo Park, she periodically glanced at her phone to make sure Sean hadn't texted her to call off the meeting or decide he could tell her everything over the phone. A few times, she'd reached for her cell to call Jake, but she didn't want to intrude on his father-daughter time or worry him about his response getting posted tomorrow.

Had Sean discovered something about his anonymous

source that he wanted to reveal to her? That would be the best scenario. She'd convinced herself that Sean's source was her nemesis, Laprey, the person who'd been toying with her ever since the copycat killings began with Jordy Lee Cannon.

Laprey was more than a prankster, if he were responsible for the homeless woman's death. He could've even been culpable in her foster brother's overdose. That would leave two bodies at his door.

The drive took her closer to forty minutes than thirty, and by the time she swung into the parking lot near the boat dock only two cars remained—Sean's and a white truck—both looked empty.

She parked next to Sean's car and strapped her purse across her chest as she exited her vehicle. Lights along the edge of the lot saved it from complete darkness, and the moon lit up the swan boats bumping and swaying on the water.

"Sean?" She circled his car and stopped next to the driver's side. The dome light glowed inside, and she noticed that Sean had left the door ajar. A file folder had spilled its contents onto the floor of the car.

Kyra licked her dry lips and called Sean on her cell phone. As his phone rang, a buzzing noise emanated from his car. She peeked into the window and saw a light from beneath the driver's seat. Sean had left his phone in the car.

Swallowing, Kyra stepped back from the car and called out. "Sean?"

Had he decided to take a stroll while waiting for her? Why leave his phone behind and his car door open?

Kyra eyed the truck on the other side of the small parking lot, and unzipped her gun pouch as she crept toward it. Unlike Sean, the truck's owner had locked things up.

Instinct or curiosity made her snap a picture of the truck's license plate with her phone.

Claiming a spot in the middle of the parking lot, she turned in a circle. The road wound away from the parking lot on one side, and the lake beckoned on the other. Maybe he had gone to check out the boats.

She glanced over her shoulder and made her way to the boat dock where the pedal boats floated in a corral. As they bumped together, the soft clicking noise sounded like chatter.

Her sneakers whispered against the dirt and gravel that bordered the man-made lake. She tripped to a stop as she noticed a huddled form at the edge of the water.

"Sean? Is that you?" She flicked on her phone's flashlight and rested her hand against her weapon, still zipped in her purse.

She drew closer to the man and a strangled scream clawed its way up her throat.

Sean Hughes lay curled on his side with a bullet hole in his head.

Chapter Eight

Jake's unmarked sedan squealed to a stop in the parking lot of Echo Park Lake. *She's okay. She's okay.* He repeated the mantra in his head as he threw his vehicle into Park and scrambled from the car.

His gaze darted around the scene, flooded with lights from the emergency vehicles, and landed on Kyra sitting in the back of an ambulance, her legs hanging over the end. The blood pounded against his temples as he strode toward her.

"Are you all right? Why are you in the ambulance?" He rushed to her side and put his hand against her cheek, as if that could verify her condition.

Her wide eyes sought his face. "He's dead. Sean Hughes is dead."

Jake dropped to his knees in front of her and clasped both of her hands in his. "I know that, but what are you doing here?"

"I warned him." Kyra's head twisted to the side where Sean's body lay crumpled beside the edge of the lake. "I warned him about his anonymous source."

The EMT standing next to them cleared his throat. "You're okay, Kyra, but you might want to keep warm. You're still shivering from the shock."

"Do you want to sit in my car?" Jake squeezed her hands as another tremble rolled through her body.

"Do you have to look at the body?"

"Another detective is checking it out now. I'll have a look before the coroner gets here." He leaned forward and whispered, "First, I want to know what you were doing here."

She blinked. "Do you...do you think I had something to do with Sean's death? Is that what they think? Revenge for the blog?"

"That's just dumb. Do you really believe I'd think that?" He cinched her wrists and tugged her from the back of the ambulance. "I want to hear from you what happened."

Under his guidance, she hopped to the ground. "I already told the patrol officer. I haven't spoken to Detective Villareal, yet."

"You can give a statement to me, and I'll give it to Manny Villareal." Still holding her hand, he led her to his car. When he got into the driver's seat, he buzzed down the window in case someone wanted him...or Kyra. He turned to her. "Why the hell were you with Sean Hughes in a deserted park in the middle of the night?"

"He called me." She dug into her purse and withdrew her cell phone. She tapped her display and held it out to him to prove her statement. "There's the call at 8:52."

"I believe you, Kyra." He pushed the phone back in her direction. "What did he want?"

"This." She flung her arm out to the side and hit the window with the ring she wore on her right hand. "He asked me to meet him here to discuss the blog. He basically told me if I didn't come, he couldn't guarantee your response to Copycat Three would be posted tomorrow."

"He wouldn't tell you anything else?"

"No, and I asked. He insisted that we talk in person. I even asked why we couldn't meet in a coffeehouse or bar, but he didn't want to be seen in public with me." She lifted her shoulders to her ears and held them there stiffly. "I don't know why, but I wasn't going to take a chance that he wouldn't post your response."

Jake reached over and massaged the back of her neck until she dropped her shoulders. "Did he sound...different?"

"I don't know him that well. I've spoken to him only a few times on the phone before this, but yeah, he sounded a little different."

Jake tensed. "How?"

"You heard him on speakerphone the other day. He's... he was a confident, smooth guy." She twisted her fingers in her lap. "This time...not so much. He sounded worried. His voice had an urgency. It lit a fire under me, anyway."

"Why?" Jake smacked the heel of his hand against his forehead. "Why would you agree to meet him here, of all places, in the dead of night?"

"You keep saying that—dead of night, middle of the night. It was nine o'clock. Even he told me there were people still walking around the lake." She grabbed his arm. "Did the police check out that white truck? That was the only other car in the lot besides Sean's car. I even took a picture of it, just in case."

"I'm sure they ran the plate. If it's anything or anyone connected, we'll hear about it, but I doubt a killer's going to leave his vehicle at the scene of the crime."

"Cameras?"

"They're here, and we'll find out soon enough."

"Even if the cameras don't catch the killer, the footage should at least rule me out."

He tucked an errant strand of hair behind her ear.

"Nobody's ruling you in, but why did you take a picture of the truck's license plate? Did you suspect something was off? Take it from the top. You got the call. I'll bet you didn't tell Quinn where you were going and what you were doing."

"Of course not." She took a deep, steadying breath. "After Sean's call, I told Quinn I had something to do for work—which is true. It took me about forty minutes to get here—traffic on the 110 as I went through downtown. By the time I arrived, there were no more walkers or joggers in the park. I saw Sean's car and the truck. What gave me pause was that Sean's car door was ajar and his phone was on the floor under the driver's seat. That's why I approached the truck with caution. Then I walked toward the swan boats, and I saw Sean's body. That's it. I called 911."

"Why didn't you call me?"

"You heard the EMT. I was in shock. After I found Sean, I ran back to my car and sat there with the doors locked and my gun in my hand, in case the killer came back for me."

"I didn't mean after you found the body. I meant after you got the call from Sean."

"I didn't want to interrupt you, especially after what your ex said about me today."

Jake massaged his temples. "Did you tell the police about your gun?"

"No."

"You need to do that. They're going to want to know you had a weapon." Kyra's knees started bouncing, and he put a hand on one and squeezed. "They can rule out your gun as the murder weapon. Did they check your hands for gunshot residue, yet?"

"No."

"I'm going to suggest they do that, too."

"So, you *do* think they suspect me."

"They would be bad detectives if they didn't. You found the body, you had a motive, and they're going to discover that you had the means."

"And I called 911."

"You should know by now it's not unusual for the perpetrator to call in the crime." He stroked her hair. "I'm not trying to scare you. All of those things will rule you out."

"He killed him, Jake."

He chose his words carefully. "You think Laprey is his source, and Laprey killed him?"

"Yes." She pursed her lips and her jaw formed a firm line.

"Why would he do that? Why give Sean the story, and then get rid of him?"

"Maybe he thought Sean was going to reveal his source to me and I'd finally learn Laprey's identity."

"If Sean were going to do that, why not just tell you over the phone? How would Laprey know Sean hadn't already told you?"

"I'm not sure about all that, but who else would want to kill Sean? Kill him right before he talked to me?"

"Kill him when he knew you'd find the body."

Kyra had been a bundle of action ever since dropping into the passenger seat. Now all motion ceased. Her next words came out through gritted teeth. "What do you mean?"

"Maybe this was some kind of setup for you. Lure you out here to find Sean's dead body, maybe even an attempt to implicate you in Sean's death."

"But Sean called me out here."

"Did he?"

"Of course, he did. I haven't spoken to Sean much,

but I did recognize his voice, and he called me from the number I have identified as his." She dragged a hand through her hair. "What are you suggesting, Detective?"

Jake drummed his fingers against the dashboard. "You said Sean sounded nervous on the phone, agitated. Maybe someone was forcing him to call you."

Kyra sucked in a quick breath. "You mean Sean's life was already in danger when he called me? Someone was holding a gun to his head—literally or figuratively—to get him to call me and get me out here?"

"Then he killed Sean, and left the body here for you to find."

"Why wouldn't he stick around to kill me, too? He had the perfect opportunity."

"Think about it, Kyra." He waved a hand out the open window at Manny. "When has Laprey ever wanted to harm you? Tease you? Taunt you? Terrify you? Oh, yeah. All that. But he's never once threatened you with physical danger."

"What *does* he want?"

"Better question is who is he?" He opened his door. "I'm going to talk to Manny. I suggest you come with me if you feel up to it."

"I'm fine."

He waited for her, and they walked up to Manny together. "I took her statement, Manny. I'll write it up for you and email it, but Kyra has something she wants to tell you."

Detective Villareal, who'd just made detective last month, raised his eyebrows. "What is it, Ms. Chase?"

"You can call me Kyra." She unzipped the gun pouch on her purse and pulled out her weapon. "I did want to let you know that I have a gun. You're welcome to take it."

Manny assessed the gun with an expert eye and sniffed

the barrel. "No need. We're looking for a .45, not a .22, and your gun hasn't been fired recently. Go see the guy in the blue shirt over by the crime scene tape. We have a portable sensor for gunshot residue and he can swab your hands now. Is that okay?"

"That's fine. If after reading Jake's… Detective McAllister's report, you have any questions for me, I'd be happy to talk with you. Unfortunately, I didn't see anything except the white truck."

"We know that belongs to someone who came here earlier, met his girlfriend, and the two of them took off in her car."

Jake nudged Kyra's back. "Go see Thomas to get your hands swabbed."

She nodded, correctly sensing he wanted to talk to Manny by himself.

When she'd created enough space between them, Jake turned to Manny. "Any witnesses? Anyone see Hughes here earlier?"

"We'll put out a call to the public, also ask if anyone has video or pictures on their phone from earlier this evening." Manny adjusted his tie and straightened his jacket. "The cameras are a no-go."

"They don't work?" Jake glanced up at the camera affixed to a lamppost.

Manny pointed skyward. "This one doesn't work, and the other one is at an angle that's not going to catch the action over here. Do you think the killer knew that?"

"Possibly, unless he's the one who broke the camera. Is it physically disabled?"

"No. Hasn't been working for a while. What's the point of having cameras if you don't verify they're working?"

Jake clapped Manny on the back. "Welcome to my world. And if the jacket and tie get to be too much, especially at a night scene like this, you can chuck 'em in the car."

"Good to know." Manny loosened his tie. "This is the guy who's posting your reply to the copycat killer, isn't he?"

"Interesting, huh?"

"Do you think the killer found out somehow and killed him before he could post it?"

"Good thought, but I think the killer is hoping I'll reply."

Manny's gaze shifted to Kyra, holding her hands out for Thomas as he passed the electrode over her skin. "He's also the blogger who released that stuff about Kyra's background."

"One and the same, but Kyra was cool with it. She's the one who contacted Hughes about posting my reply to the killer. He called her out here for a meeting, not the other way around. I saw a record of the phone call on her cell. Do you want her to turn it over to you?"

"She's not a suspect, but it would be too coincidental to believe Hughes's death isn't somehow related to his connection to the copycat killings."

"You'll make a good detective, Manny. Now it's up to you to figure out how it's related."

"I'm assuming the task force is going to follow my investigation closely."

"We'll be right beside you, brother."

Kyra waved and Thomas flashed them a thumbs-up.

Jake released a pent-up breath slowly through parted lips. "I guess that's it, then. Was Hughes shot point-blank or from a distance?"

"Point-blank. The killer may have forced Hughes from his car at gunpoint, led him to the water and shot him. Nobody around. Nobody heard a sound. We're hoping to round up some witnesses to find out if anyone saw Hughes here earlier. I understand when he called Kyra, he said there were people here."

"Could be. Could've been a lie to get her out here, make her feel safe."

They stopped talking as Kyra joined them. "No residue. Thomas will have it in a report."

As the coroner's van pulled into the parking lot, Jake said, "Wait for me in my car, unless Manny has any more questions for you. I'm going to take a quick look at the crime scene."

Jake strode toward the yellow tape and flashed his badge before ducking under it. One bullet to the back of the head. Maybe Hughes didn't know it was coming. Did someone force him out here? Force him to call Kyra? Did Hughes think he was setting up Kyra for her own death and not his?

Poor bastard. These laymen and amateur sleuths thought it was all fun and games—until a killer got you on his radar.

He finished examining the scene and returned to his car to find Kyra propped up against the hood. "Detective Villareal asked me a few more questions, but I don't think I'm on his short list."

"He doesn't have a list, but you wouldn't be on it, anyway." He jerked his thumb over his shoulder at Sean's body. "I'm sorry you had to see that."

"It's not my first rodeo. I've seen dead bodies before, but I'm not gonna lie. This was a shock." She crossed her arms and dug her fingers into her biceps. "Are the cameras going to help?"

"The one in position doesn't work."

Her jaw dropped. "You're kidding me? What are the odds?"

"The odds that it's a coincidence? Not good." He brushed her arm with his knuckles. "Do you want to get in the car with me and talk some more, or are you ready to call it a night?"

"I'm more than ready to call it a night. I suppose I'm going to have to tell Quinn about this and suffer his wrath." She hitched her purse onto her shoulder and pushed off the car.

Clasping his hand on the back of his neck, Jake said, "I'm worried this is Laprey continuing his escalation. If he killed that homeless woman last month and now this, we know what he's capable of."

"We just don't know why he's targeting me. I'm assuming he found out about my past from Matt, my foster brother. Maybe he's just someone Matt knew and picked up on my story to blackmail me."

Jake said, "But he's never threatened to blackmail you."

"I don't know. Maybe it's someone who gets his kicks torturing and controlling women. Matt was in prison and hung out with some bad characters. It could be someone he met there."

"I'm going to start looking into that." He grabbed the car door and yanked it open. "I'd give you a big, long kiss right here and now if we didn't have an audience."

"An audience of your co-workers." She blew him a kiss from her fingertips. "Will that suffice?"

"It'll tide me over until I get you in my arms again. You don't know how scared I was when I got the call that you were in Echo Park with a dead Sean Hughes." He squeezed his eyes closed for a second, opening them when he felt Kyra's touch on his shoulder.

"Knowing they called you and you were on your way was the only thing that kept me together." She turned to go and stopped. Without looking around, she said, "We have to find another way to get out your response to Copycat Three."

"We'll figure out something." Jake slid behind the wheel and left his door open as he watched Kyra walk to her car, her head bent over her phone.

His heart jumped when Kyra stopped suddenly and spun around, her face a white oval in the darkness. Without even thinking, he jumped from the car and made a beeline to Kyra, still frozen, her feet rooted to the asphalt.

Lunging toward her, he asked, "What's wrong?"

"I—I got a message from Sean's phone I didn't see before."

"What did he say? Is it a clue about his killer?"

"I don't think Sean sent this message." She turned the phone toward him and it said, "I did it for you."

Chapter Nine

Confusion crisscrossed Jake's face, but Kyra knew exactly what the message meant and who had sent it. She swallowed the lump in her throat. "It's him, Jake. It's Laprey. He sent this message from Sean's phone before... or after he killed him."

"The timing of it is going to be important to the investigation. Is he trying to pretend he killed Sean Hughes to avenge you when, in all probability, he's the one who leaked your story to Sean?"

She clasped the phone to her thundering heart. "It's just another way to manipulate me. What does he want? Who *is* he?"

"Let's take your phone to Manny. They're gonna see that text to you once they get into Sean's phone, anyway." Jake curled an arm around her waist and led her back to the crime scene when she'd just wanted to escape it all.

Thirty minutes later, Jake walked her back to her car. "Are you sure you're going to be okay tonight? You can stay with me and to hell with Tess."

She put her hands on his strong shoulders. "It's not just Tess. It's Fiona, too. I'll be fine. Like you pointed out earlier, he's never tried to physically harm me. In his mind he just killed for me."

"He's obsessed with you. We both know how quickly obsession can turn to violence."

She ground her back teeth to suppress the shiver creeping up her spine. "Maybe, but not tonight. I'll call you when I get to my apartment."

Jake finally let her go, worry creasing his handsome face. He followed her out of the parking lot, and his headlights stayed glued behind her until she reached her freeway where she peeled off from him.

Had Laprey been watching her in that parking lot? No, he wouldn't have stayed around for the police. Was Jake right? Had Sean's killer forced him to call her? Had he been listening to their conversation when Sean called her, to make sure Sean didn't give anything away?

This murder would make the news tomorrow, and the stories would drag her name through it all—even more reason for Tess to want to keep her far, far away from Fiona. Kyra didn't blame her.

She got home well past midnight and didn't even feel silly clutching her gun in her hand from the car to her apartment. If it got down to it, she knew she could protect herself as long as someone didn't surprise her. She had no intention of being taken by surprise.

Spot, the stray cat, didn't make an appearance to greet her, so she shut and secured her front door. Jake had mentioned cameras for her apartment, and now might be the time to act on that.

When she crawled into bed, she plugged her phone into the charger and cradled it in the palm of her hand. She studied the text message, from Sean's phone but not from Sean. Detective Villareal had discovered that the message must've been scheduled earlier and sent from a message app on the phone, as the delivery time was after the discovery of Sean's body. It had given her some comfort that she hadn't missed the message.

This was the first communication she'd had from Laprey since he sent her the email with the picture of her foster family, threatening to expose the fact that she'd stabbed her foster father to death after he'd been molesting the younger girls in the home and had attacked her for trying to protect one of the girls.

Jake had discovered the truth, anyway, and now the whole world knew about it, thanks to Sean Hughes…and his source. Laprey's harassment of her had begun during the reign of the first copycat killer, Jordy Cannon. It had continued and escalated during Cyrus Fisher's killing spree, and now had come to a head with this third killer.

Did Laprey know these killers? Was he working in coordination with them? Or had he been holding on to this information and decided to torment her with it when the killings started?

Her foster brother, Matt Dugan, had been involved with Laprey somehow. She and Jake had discovered Laprey's name among Matt's possessions when he died. In fact, several people involved with Laprey had wound up dead. Would she be next? Was that his endgame?

Sighing, she placed the phone on the nightstand and dragged her pillow beneath her head. Tomorrow, she and Jake needed to start working on another vehicle for his response to Copycat Three. She couldn't let her own problems derail her from her work with the task force, but once again she couldn't shake the feeling that the current killings involved her…and the man who had murdered her mother twenty years ago.

HER PHONE BUZZED, and Kyra opened one eye, sticky with sleep. She peered at the display before answering. "How did you manage to wake up so early after the night we had?"

Jake said, "It's not that early. I tried calling you before and got worried when you didn't answer."

Holding her phone away from her, she said, "Looks like I missed a few calls this morning. I hear background noise. Are you at the station already?"

"Yes, and I have big news for you."

She shot up, banging the back of her head against the headboard. "What is it?"

"Sean must've scheduled his blog to post today because it's out this morning, and you were right—it's creating a buzz."

"It must be creating an even bigger buzz with Sean's death." She threaded her fingers through her hair and rubbed her scalp. "Are news sources making the connection between the post and his murder last night?"

"Speculation is running rampant, and the blog is getting a lot of eyes. Copycat Three would have to be living in a cave to miss it."

"For all we know, he *might* be living in a cave. You don't have much on him." She switched Jake to speaker and hopped onto the internet, bringing up *LA Confidential*. "I'm looking at it now. I'm just sorry Sean's not around to enjoy the results."

"How are you feeling this morning?"

"Tired, but more energized now that I know all our work with Sean wasn't in vain and we don't have to start over. This is good. This is really good." She threw back the covers and planted her bare feet on the carpet. "How's everyone on the task force taking it?"

"It's like a roller coaster around here. People are shocked by Hughes's murder and excited by his blog."

"I suppose everyone knows Sean called me and that

I found the body." Holding the phone in one hand, Kyra shuffled to her bathroom and frowned at the circles under her eyes.

"Everyone knows." Jake cleared his throat. "You don't have to come into the station today."

"Of course I do. What do you take me for?" She flicked back her hair and cranked on the shower. "I'm not responsible for Sean's death. Did Villareal release the text message I got?"

"Nope. That's something we're going to keep to ourselves. I'll let you go. It sounds like you're in a wind tunnel."

"That's the shower. I'll see you when I get in." She placed the phone on the vanity and pulled her nightgown over her head. "I suppose this latest news is going to give your ex-wife even more ammunition against me."

"Don't worry about Tess. I can make her see reason."

They ended the call and Kyra stepped beneath the warm spray of the shower. She didn't want to tell Jake, but it wasn't Tess that concerned her—it was his daughter.

Later that morning, Kyra tried to slip into the task force war room as unobtrusively at possible, but she didn't have to worry because Detective Villareal came in and swooped her up for more questioning as soon as she walked through the door.

She ran through the timeline with him again and showed him her phone. He confirmed the scheduling app the killer had used to send her the message from Sean's phone. He also told her there had been several calls between Sean's phone and a burner phone.

As they wrapped things up, she asked, "Did you find any witnesses who were there earlier and might have seen Sean and his killer?"

"We have a few people coming in later who were at

the lake, but I think Sean was lying to you about people at the lake. It wasn't very crowded. We checked with the security company who monitors the footage from the cameras—when they're working—and the folks there told us traffic to the lake falls off this time of the year. The kids are back in school and the end of daylight saving time keeps people away. Sean…or someone else was trying to give you a false sense of security."

"I'll ask my friend, Megan Wright, a reporter from KTOP, where Sean might've kept information about his sources. I suppose you confiscated his computer."

"We did." Villareal's dark eyes flashed. "It's a good thing Hughes scheduled that blog before he died. Now it's getting more attention than ever. Of course, he couldn't have known at the time his murder would make the hits to his blog go through the roof."

"I wonder if the killer knew the blog was going to post anyway?" Kyra drew circles on the desk with her fingertip. "When I talked to Sean, he indicated to me the blog might not get published unless I met him at the park."

"It could've been his way to convince you to come out."

"Or he was hiding it from his killer. Maybe the guy killed Sean to stop him from posting Jake's response."

"Why would he care about that? His interest and focus were on you, not the copycats."

Kyra folded her hands to stop her restless fingers. "Detective Villareal, I'm sure you read about my past yesterday. I'm connected to the copycat killers in more ways than one."

He dropped his gaze, a habit he'd have to break if he expected to be a successful homicide detective. Victims' families didn't want a detective who was going to shy away from their pain and horror. If the cops couldn't take the heat, how were the victims' loved ones supposed to survive?

"I read about it, and I'm sorry. I guess that's how you know Quinn." He met her eyes again and curiosity had replaced uneasiness.

Better. "You know about Roger Quinn?"

"He's a legend. Who doesn't know about Quinn at the LAPD?"

"I'm sure he'll be thrilled to hear it." She didn't plan on discussing her and Quinn's relationship with Villareal. Scooting her chair back from the table, she said, "If that's all…"

"That's all for now, Kyra, and you can call me Manny."

"Thanks, Manny. Let me know if you need anything else from me."

On her way back to the task force room, Captain Castillo called out to her as she passed his office. She stuck her head into the room. "Captain?"

"Have a seat for a minute." He tapped a few keys on his laptop and then pushed it to the side. "Good work on that reply to Copycat Three. It hits all the right notes."

She sank into one of the comfy leather chairs on the other side of his desk and immediately felt like taking a nap. "I'm just glad it posted."

"I'm sorry about last night. That must've been…frightening, especially after the day you had yesterday."

"Yeah, it's been a whirlwind of emotions." She crossed one leg over the other and clasped her hands around one knee. Amid all the turmoil, she hadn't forgotten Quinn telling her last night that Castillo had known her identity all this time. "Captain Castillo, Quinn mentioned last night that you've always known about my past—that my mother, Jennifer Lake, was one of The Player's victims."

Castillo's eyes widened for a split second and Kyra

read fear in their depths. Then his chin bobbed to his chest. "Guilty."

She raised her eyebrows. Was he apologizing to her? "Nothing to confess to. I guess I should've realized it, as you worked on the case and you knew Quinn. You would've known the saga of the poor little girl left an orphan after her mother's murder."

He bowed his head again, his gaze shifting away from hers. "What else did Quinn tell you?"

"Not much. He just sort of mentioned in passing that Sean Hughes's scoop wouldn't be news to you. I guess it didn't occur to me that even someone working on the case would've known about my name change."

"My wife and Charlotte Quinn were also friends."

"I suppose that makes sense. Is that why you threw work my way and made a place for me on the copycat task force?"

Castillo jerked, and his hands fluttered like an errant bird over the various items on his desk. "You think I hired you to appease Quinn? Absolutely not."

She tilted her head, and her ponytail slid over one shoulder. "That's not what I meant, although that could be a reason. You must've thought my unenviable position as the daughter of a murder victim would give me a unique perspective, especially on these cases that mimic The Player."

"Yes, that's it." He shook a finger at her, but his playful smile didn't reach his eyes. "I don't play favorites around here, Kyra. You're an asset to the team. Everyone thinks so, even the chief."

"Good to hear it."

"Now, if you'll excuse me. I have some phone calls to make. I just wanted to offer my condolences for your shock last night and my kudos for a job well done on that response for J-Mac."

"Thank you on both counts…and thanks for keeping my secret all these years." She rose from the chair and slipped out the door, shutting it behind her.

Holding her breath and tensing her muscles, she stood at the door and pressed her ear against the wood for several seconds. All remained quiet from inside Castillo's office. He hadn't picked up the phone. He was probably too busy collecting himself.

That was the oddest conversation she'd had since… well, since the conversation she'd had with Sean last night. What had Captain Castillo been so afraid of? Had he made some deal with Quinn to watch over her here at the station? Why would he worry if she discovered that? Quinn was the one who'd have to pay the price for that one.

She'd bring it up with Jake. The thought plastered a smile on her face. When she'd first met Jake, she'd kept him in the dark about everything, just like she'd always kept everyone at arm's length. Now she shared everything with him…almost everything. She hadn't told him yet about her foray onto Websleuths.

She flipped her ponytail over her shoulder. A girl had to keep some secrets.

When she finally collapsed at her desk in front of her laptop, the sounds of lunchtime stirred around her. A quick glance at Jake's desk assured her he had delved into something engrossing and wouldn't be coming up for air for a while. He hadn't even looked up when she entered the room. Plenty of other people had, though, and she'd become an even bigger object of curiosity than she'd been before.

She'd barely gotten through an email to the mother

of Copycat Three's first victim, Juliana French, when her phone buzzed. She read the display and blew out a breath. She'd wondered how long it was going to take for Megan to call her.

Megan didn't even let her finish saying hello before she launched into an avalanche of words. "Oh my God. You were on my you-know-what list yesterday when I realized you had this bombshell story you never told me about, and then I found out you were going to use *LA Confidential* for Jake's reply to the killer instead of me, but now I'm so glad you did. Do you think Sean got killed because he revealed your true identity or because he was the go-between for J-Mac and the killer? Do the cops think Copycat Three offed Sean, or was it the source of your story or some other random person who had it in for him? And are you okay? My God, to stumble on a gruesome murder scene like that. I'm here if you need a margarita or seven."

"Take a breath." Kyra rolled her eyes. "First of all, I hadn't planned to reveal my past to anyone—bombshell or not. Secondly, Jake wanted to use a digital medium for his response. Thirdly, I'm fine and I could use several margaritas at some point, and I'll let you know when."

Megan scooped in an audible breath over the phone and Kyra braced for another onslaught, but Megan lowered her voice. "Seriously, I am so sorry Sean dragged you into whatever that was last night."

"And you're sorry about Sean."

"Live by the sword, die by the sword. The guy was always playing with fire." She coughed. "I mean, of course I'm sorry for Sean. Do you have a bone you can throw a sistah? Any details you can share that the cops aren't revealing about Sean's murder?"

Megan could take off running with the information

that Sean's killer had texted Kyra, claiming he'd killed Sean for her, but the task force was keeping that to themselves for now and she wouldn't be the one to compromise the investigation.

"I don't have anything I can give you about that, Megan, but when things settle down, I'd be happy to give you an exclusive interview if you want it."

"If I want it? Yes, yes and yes. Let me know, and let me know when you're ready for those margaritas. They are not contingent on the interview."

"I know that."

When Kyra ended the call, someone tapped her on the shoulder, and she glanced up into Jake's face. No one else she'd rather see right now.

She asked, "Are we having lunch?"

"As it seems it's the only time I get to see you, except for murder scenes, I'm counting on it. It's a late one, so can we make it a long one, too? I'm bleary-eyed from staring at the computer and Billy's knocked off early to meet with his PI, Dina."

"You must've been reading my mind. I'm thinking Mi Casa, booth in the back, a few stolen kisses."

"You must've been reading *my* mind." He jerked his thumb over his shoulder. "Just need to touch base with a few people. Meet you by my car."

Kyra logged off her computer and stashed it in her bag. If they had a long lunch, it might just turn into a work lunch. She gathered the rest of her things and walked out of the building, her gaze flicking to Captain Castillo's closed door as she passed it.

She scrolled through text messages on her phone until Jake showed up and unlocked the car with his remote. She was already seated and struggling with the seat belt when he got behind the wheel.

Cranking her head around, she asked, "When do you think we're going to hear from Copycat Three?"

"I hate to say it, but I think he'll communicate with me in the same way he did before." He backed up and pulled out of the parking lot of the Northeast Division.

"You mean, over someone's dead body." She'd finally clicked the seat belt into place and held on to the strap across her body.

"I'm afraid so."

"And you don't think he's going to kill someone just for the opportunity to taunt you again?"

"We already went through that possibility, didn't we? He's not going to stop, regardless. He already has the urge, and he's going to keep satisfying it until we put an end to his craving. He gave us an opening by leaving that note for me. I'm not going to squander that chance." Jake cranked up the AC, even though the sun had yet to make an appearance through the overcast sky. "I thought you were on board with that."

"I am." She rubbed the goose bumps on her arms. "I just can't help thinking about some woman going about her life today for maybe the last time."

"I know. Have you talked to Quinn yet about what happened last night?"

"He sent me a text asking if I was okay. He knows I'll spill everything in my own way and time." Her gaze slid to Jake's profile, still set in work mode. "I'm going to tell him about the text Sean's killer sent to me. He may have some thoughts on that, and you know he won't tell anyone."

"If you weren't going to tell him about it, I was. The more the killings relate to you and your situation, the more I want Quinn's insight."

She licked her lips. "Because you think the two are

connected by more than opportunity. You think Laprey, the person tormenting me, is somehow related to the killers."

"I think so, Kyra. Does he know who the copycats are?" He shrugged. "I don't know about that, but he's following their deeds closely. He may be on the Websleuths site, as well."

Kyra gulped down her guilt. She should tell Jake she was trolling Websleuths. She tapped the window. "Next turn if we're going to Mi Casa."

"I *wish* we were going to *mi casa*." He reached over and ran a finger down the side of her neck to her shoulder. "I miss you."

"How's Fiona holding up? Getting all her schoolwork done?" Someone had to bring them back to reality.

"She's doing fine. I'm not sure why she was so desperate to come down here. She knew I had to work and wouldn't get to spend much time with her, unlike when she visits for Christmas. I think…" He drummed his thumbs against the steering wheel.

"You think that's probably why she did hightail it out of Monterey for LA. She could escape her mother, and she knew you wouldn't be around much. Win, win for Fiona."

"Sounds like you know my daughter better than I do."

He parked the car, and they easily got their dark booth in the corner of the half-empty restaurant.

Once they'd ordered, had their basket of chips between them, two types of salsa and a couple of iced teas, Kyra brought up the subject that had been on her mind all afternoon. "I had an interesting talk with Captain Castillo this afternoon."

"I have very few interesting conversations with Castillo, but I shouldn't complain. He's not someone to force his views on a case. He's letting me and Billy run this task force with zero interference."

"Do you know that he was aware of my identity all this time?"

Jake dropped a chip back into the basket. "What? You're kidding."

"Quinn let it slip the other night. It surprised me, but I don't know why it should. He was working The Player case twenty years ago. He must've known that Quinn was the one who found me hiding in the closet in my mother's bedroom the night she was murdered. He knew of Quinn and Charlotte's interest in me. Castillo told me today that his wife and Charlotte were close, so he would've known about the Quinns' desire to adopt me and how they kept a close eye on me all those years."

"Makes sense. There's a lot that makes sense now." He scooped up a mound of salsa.

She cocked one eyebrow at him. "You mean why Castillo always seemed like my champion?"

"Yeah. Not that he doesn't think you're good at what you do. He does. Castillo may be unassuming, but he's not stupid. Just not sure he would've gone out on a limb like he did for you on several occasions if he didn't owe it to Quinn."

"You think Quinn strong-armed him into accepting me?" She tapped her chin, indicating where Jake had a spot of salsa.

He swiped a napkin across his face. "Did I say *strong-arm*? Don't get it into your head that Castillo threw you any bones. He wouldn't do that if he didn't think you were qualified—not even for Quinn."

"Castillo said the same thing to me." She twirled her straw through her tea, causing the ice to clink against the glass.

"But?"

"I don't know. His demeanor was weird."

"In what way?"

"When I brought up the subject, he seemed almost afraid."

"That makes sense." Jake cut off his explanation as the waiter delivered their food.

Kyra toyed with her tostada until the waiter finished refilling their tea and backed off. "Why does Castillo's fear make sense?"

"He was probably worried about saying the wrong thing to you and having that get back to Quinn."

She snorted and stabbed at a piece of chicken. "Quinn's not some ogre guarding me."

"Really? 'Cause I felt like I had to accomplish a bunch of daring deeds to be worthy of you in Quinn's eyes."

"You must've passed muster because Quinn has our future all planned out."

"He does, huh? I'm glad he's on my side because I kind of have our future all planned out, too."

Her cheeks burned and it wasn't the salsa. "We have to get past the objections of your ex-wife and daughter before we can do much planning."

"Tess doesn't have the right to call any shots. I didn't say a word when she decided to move up north with Brock, and take Fiona with her. I figured Fiona would be better off with a mother and a father figure who wasn't getting called out to gruesome crime scenes in the middle of the night. Tess will see reason eventually…and so will Fiona." He dragged a fork through his rice. "Fiona was actually very interested in you after finding out about your past."

"Yeah, well, I'm not sure that interest is healthy." Fiona wasn't the only one with unhealthy interests. Kyra took a deep breath and said, "You were bleary-eyed looking through Websleuths. Did you find anything?"

"Nothing from looking at the posts, not even looking at Cannon's and Fisher's posts, which are still up. We asked the site to leave them. If there's any communication going on, it must be through the private chats, and Cannon and Fisher deleted those. IT's working on it, but those messages may be gone for good." Jake sawed through a corner of his enchilada and dumped some salsa on the bite. "We may have to create a fake account and troll for comments. Can't be too obvious, though, and give it away."

"Sounds like a good plan." Kyra kept her lips sealed on the subject for the rest of the lunch and just savored Jake's company.

They hadn't been a couple for long and obstacles kept popping up in their path, but the fact that they both still seemed committed to working through those obstacles made her heart sing with hope. She hadn't let a man this far into her life...ever. She hadn't scared Jake off, yet.

When he finished his enchiladas, Jake moved his plate to the side and patted the booth seat next to him. "Slide on over here. I hope you weren't kidding about those stolen kisses—stolen spicy kisses."

And like a couple of schoolkids, they smooched their way through the rest of the lunch.

They returned to the station late, and Villareal gave Kyra the bad news that only one of the witnesses from the lake at Echo Park remembered seeing Sean's car there... but nothing else.

"We'll keep searching, though, and let me know if you get any more text messages." Villareal rapped on her desk. "I've already informed Detectives McAllister and Crouch, so the task force is up-to-date."

"Thanks, Manny. I appreciate your keeping me informed."

Kyra left without again seeing Jake, who'd been roped into reviewing footage from the last dump site. She couldn't face a third degree from Quinn, so she headed straight home for a jog on the beach bike path and leftovers for dinner.

She let Spot into her apartment to avoid the light smattering of rain that had come in from the north. Then she poured herself a glass of red wine and kicked back in her recliner with her laptop resting on her thighs.

She hadn't checked Websleuths for a while, and the site didn't disappoint. The admins had already established a new message board for the murder of Sean Hughes. Jake hadn't told her that, and he must've seen it having spent all morning on the website.

She checked back in with the case of the missing Alabama student and posted a few theories and questions of her own. A few minutes after her posts, her private message notification popped up.

Toby Dog had queried her again about joining the IRL group, which stood for in real life. This time she answered that school and work kept her too busy to get involved.

They messaged back and forth about the Alabama case, and then Toby Dog sent her a warning that made her heart pound. She took a sip of wine and read the message aloud to Spot: "Just don't want to see you get involved with some weird characters on here."

"Weird characters?" she asked.

He responded that there was a user who had sent out a

few private messages about committing murder and the
rules you had to follow to avoid capture.

Kyra stared at the blinking cursor. Rules? Both Cannon and Fisher had mentioned something about a rule
before they'd died. Her fingers flew over the keyboard
as she asked Toby Dog why she in particular should be
concerned about this member.

His answer made her take another swig of wine. Apparently, this poster had multiple usernames, and Toby
Dog thought she might be the same member under another name.

She asked him why he'd think that.

When his answer came, she rubbed her eyes and read
it through again.

Because one of the usernames he used was Laprey.

Chapter Ten

Jake finished reading the final report on the CCTV footage on the most recent dump site, just as Fiona put the last of the dishes into the dishwasher.

He snapped his laptop closed and said, "That wasn't so bad, was it? And don't pretend your mother doesn't make you do chores at home. She already filled me in."

"Was that when she was telling you to keep your new girlfriend away from me?" Fiona threw him a look that was half challenging, half fearful.

His hands clenched, and then he took a deep breath through his nose, blowing it out through barely parted lips. "Does Kyra's past really worry you? She killed a man in self-defense. She killed a man, not only to protect herself but a younger child in the home. Yeah, she's no stranger to violence, but some kids don't have it made— like you do."

Fiona had the self-awareness to look ashamed, or at least she'd dropped her bold gaze. "Actually, Mom's the one who freaked out when I told her. I think it's kind of badass."

"Language, please." Jake folded his arms. "So, you *are* the one who told your mother. I thought it unlikely that she was reading the *LA Confidential* blog up in Monterey."

"Well, you're both always telling me not to keep secrets."

Should he confront her with the Jazzy Noir page and wipe the smug smile off her face? His personal cell phone rang, saving him from making a decision. Even better, the call was from Kyra.

"What's up?"

Fiona made a show of opening the refrigerator and studying its contents.

"I made a discovery tonight." Kyra sounded breathless, which made his pulse jump.

"What kind of discovery?"

"I think Laprey has been on Websleuths, and I think he may have been in touch with the copycats."

The blood rushed to his head, and he squeezed the phone. "How do you know this?"

"Because I've been scrolling through Websleuths myself."

He should've known, but a thrumming excitement replaced any irritation he felt. "Start from the beginning. Don't leave anything out."

He scribbled notes on a pad of paper as Kyra told him about using the name Laprey to create an account on Websleuths and the private messages she'd been exchanging with people on the site.

When she finished, he asked, "What kind of rules was this person spouting off?"

"He didn't say, exactly. The whole thing spooked him, and he didn't want anything to do with that poster."

"Did he tell you some of the other names this user had?"

"LA Guy was one of them. Card Sharp was another. Get it? Card Sharp."

Jake got it. "We need to question this Toby Dog, Kyra, but don't tell him anything. I don't want to scare him off. He may not want to get involved. I'm going to have IT trace him and those usernames he mentioned. When we get in touch with Toby Dog, I want it to be a surprise."

"Jake, I'm sorry I went behind your back on Websleuths and then didn't tell you."

"I thought we were past all that. You still don't feel as if you can trust me?" His gaze shifted to Fiona, huddled over her phone, and he got up and sauntered to his window on the city.

"I absolutely trust you. You know it's my nature to be secretive. To hold back one little bit of myself." She took a drink of something. "It's a process."

If he couldn't share her with his daughter, Kyra had every right to hold back. "I get it, but I'm glad you understand the importance of sharing those secrets when it could be someone's life or death...maybe even yours."

"I may have messed things up, though. If Laprey is on Websleuths and he's had contact with the copycats, he will have seen my username. He'll understand that we must know about that site." She smacked something, and he hoped it was a table and not herself. "I could've just ruined that option for you."

"Don't worry about that now. I'm going to get Brandon working on tracing the IP address of Toby Dog tomorrow morning, so we can find out what he knows. In the meantime, stay off the site. Don't delete your account, just in case the other Laprey gets the brilliant idea of contacting you."

"I promise. I'm done with Websleuths."

"Unless Laprey messages you. Then you're going to respond to him."

"If he does that, I'll contact you first."

Jake stared into the night and traced a finger across the glass. "More and more, I'm beginning to believe Laprey is connected to the copycats. I don't know if he's egging them on or if he's also a killer. He knows about you, and that's some kind of sick side game for him."

"I don't like being someone's sick side game, but I may have destroyed any chance to nail Laprey by diving in without thinking."

"Don't keep beating yourself up. We'll get him." He ended the call and tapped his phone against his chin.

Fiona cleared her throat behind him. "Can I have the rest of this ice cream?"

"Go for it."

"Everything okay?"

He turned toward his daughter as she reached into the freezer. Did she care? She typically didn't ask him about his work, and Tess wouldn't be too happy if he answered truthfully. "All good."

"Can I stay with Lyric this weekend?" She spooned some ice cream directly from the carton into her mouth.

Jake sank down in front of his laptop again, ready to do more digging into Websleuths. "All weekend?"

Waving the spoon in the air, she said, "I'd go out there Friday after school and come back on Sunday."

"I'll call Mrs. Becker first."

"She already said it's okay."

"Then everything should check out."

"Looks like you're gonna work some more, so I'll get that last set of algebra problems done." She grabbed the laptop from the coffee table and swept upstairs.

Jake stared after her. Fiona must've been desperate to get away from her mother, or the whole thing was a ruse so she could visit Lyric. She sure hadn't come here for him.

Maybe like a high school kid with his parents out of town, he could sneak a few nights with Kyra. It wouldn't hurt to keep an eye on Kyra right now. Laprey's actions marked him as more than a merry prankster, and with every passing day he was getting closer to Kyra...and more threatening.

THE FOLLOWING DAY, Jake and Kyra crowded into Brandon Nguyen's small office on the first floor of the station, where Brandon had four different monitors running, one of them displaying the Websleuths site.

Sitting next to Brandon, Kyra jabbed her finger at the screen. "That's him—Toby Dog. He's the one who warned me about this other user."

"As I already established a rapport with the admins of this site, it shouldn't be a problem for me to get the details on Toby Dog and track him down through his IP address. If they want a warrant...?" Brandon cranked his head over his shoulder and raised his eyebrows at Jake.

"Let me know. I'll be in and out of the station, so text or call when you have something." As Jake squeezed out of the office, his phone rang and he plunged his hand in his pocket to grab it.

"J-Mac, it's LaTonya in Dispatch. Call just came in for a dead body out in Topanga Canyon." She lowered her voice. "I can tell you right now from the details I heard, it's Copycat Three."

"I appreciate the heads-up, LaTonya. I'm sure it's going to be maximum activity up at the task force." Jake pocketed the phone and told a waiting Kyra and Brandon the news. "Another body."

"Just gave me even more incentive." Brandon swiveled his chair back to one of his computers and started tapping the keyboard.

As they walked upstairs, Kyra said, "I'm going to follow you and Billy over. Can you text me the location when you get it?"

"I will."

Ten minutes later, Jake and Billy were hauling tail to the dump site in Topanga. Jake didn't bother checking the rearview mirror to see if Kyra was following them—she had as much riding on this case as anyone.

When they arrived, the LA County Sheriff's Department had cordoned off the area, and two deputies were talking to a couple with a dog prancing around their feet.

Jake nodded toward the scene. "Couple out hiking with their dog, and the dog made a gruesome discovery."

Billy had the door open before Jake even stopped the vehicle. He called back over his shoulder. "Let's see if he took the bait from *LA Confidential*."

Jake parked the car and strode up to the deputy and the couple.

Deputy Vega introduced himself and the couple. "This is Timothy Beauchamp and Skye Duncan. They were hiking and the dog found the body."

The young, bearded man slung his arm around the woman and said, "We didn't see a thing from the trail, although I guess if we were looking that way we could've. Gus, our dog, took off running. We thought he'd spotted a squirrel or something, but when he wouldn't come back to us, I went over to take a look. Sh-she had…"

Skye crossed her arms and hunched her shoulders. "We had to drag him away by the collar and snap on his leash. I—I hope Gus didn't disturb the crime scene or anything."

"Why do you say that?" Jake looked past their shoulders at Billy, who was coming out of the trees, shaking his head.

Timothy said, "He had something in his mouth when I grabbed him. Maybe it was just some trash or something."

Jake studied the ground at their feet, the dog still panting and straining against his leash. Jake scratched Gus behind the ears. "Did he drop it or eat it?"

"He must've dropped it." Timothy turned in a circle, his hiking books crunching the twigs and leaves on the ground. "I don't see it, and I don't think he'd eat anything that wasn't food."

"Don't worry about it. We'll have a look." Jake turned to the deputy. "Can you finish taking their statement? And I need you two to stick around."

Skye tugged at Gus's leash. "Can we walk away from here a little so Gus will settle down?"

"Sure." Jake patted the dog's head. "Good boy, Gus."

He tromped down the trail in his wingtips to meet Billy, stationed beneath a big maple tree, its leaves just starting to change color. "What's wrong? Not Copycat Three?"

"Oh, it's our boy, all right—queen of clubs in the mouth, severed finger and missing underwear."

"Then why the shaking head?"

"He didn't leave a communication for you. He didn't take the bait."

Jake glanced back toward Gus, who was barking as Skye led him down the trail. "Maybe he did. The dog got to the body first and took something away from the scene."

"Just great." Billy pointed up toward a ridge. "There's a road up there. I think he dumped the body from up there, climbed down and set the scene. No way he hiked in here with a body slung over his shoulder."

"Good call. We'll take a look at the road for any evidence. Strangulation?"

"Looks like it to me. I'm wondering how he's getting these women to come with him. No sign of drugging like with Jordy." Billy brushed a twig from the shoulder of his jacket with his gloved hand.

"The cars of Juliana and Carmella were found near clubs in Hollywood, unfortunately in lots with no cameras. He must be intercepting them outside the clubs. Both bodies showed high levels of alcohol. He's taking advantage of their inebriation, probably not hard for him to maneuver them into his car. Strangles them there and dumps them." Jake squeezed past Billy toward the body. "We need to get a few people at those clubs."

Jake yanked a pair of gloves from his pocket and pulled them on, flexing his fingers. He crouched beside the body of the young woman, her long brown hair neatly arranged over her shoulders. Textbook Copycat Three.

He murmured, "How'd he get you to go with him?"

"J-Mac! I got it!"

Jake looked over his shoulder to take in Billy waving something white above his head. He rose to his feet and approached his giddy partner.

Billy held out the crumpled, sticky envelope with Jake's name on it. "The dog must've had it in his mouth. There's a little drool and a little tear, but he didn't rip it open or destroy it."

Jake pinched the envelope between two gloved fingers, his breath hitching in his throat. He flipped open the unsealed envelope and slid one finger inside to retrieve the single sheet of paper with the same block letters in ballpoint pen.

He read it aloud to Billy. "'I'm more than a copycat and you're'—spelled Y-O-U-R—'going to find out how much more. I have my own rules.'"

Billy snorted. "At least we know not to look for a grammar stickler. Guess you touched a nerve naming him Copycat Three."

Jake tapped the edge of the envelope against his palm. "There's that notion of rules again. The other two killers mentioned something about rules. Cannon was frantic about breaking rule number four. They're definitely connected by something...or someone."

"I hope Copycat Three *does* start following his own rules, because the rules they've all been following so far have allowed them to kill several women—and that's gotta stop." Billy whipped a plastic bag from his pocket and held it open for Jake to drop the note inside.

That was the last minute the two partners had to themselves as hordes of CSI personnel descended on the site. Jake conferred with the techs before setting them loose on the crime scene to collect, photograph and bag the evidence.

Jake wandered back to the trail, which was clogged with more people, including lookie-loos and the press. His gaze tracked right to Kyra, her head together with Megan Wright's from KTOP, her cameraman in tow. Kyra had probably given Megan the go-ahead, but the press was going to find out, anyway. The news station had people dedicated to listening to the radio calls of law enforcement.

When Kyra saw him, he lifted his hand and pointed to his car. She gave Megan a quick word and made her way up the trail to meet him.

He leaned against his vehicle, peeling off his gloves. "LaTonya was correct. It's Copycat Three."

"No ID on the body?"

"None, but they'll fingerprint her, and Billy will go through the sad task of reviewing any missing women. It won't be long before they identify her." He shoved the gloves in his pocket. "He left me a note."

Kyra's shoulders sagged as if she'd been holding her breath. "What did he say this time? Was he mad?"

"Lashed out. Said he was more than a copycat and he'd show me." Jake scratched his chin. "Mentioned rules."

"Rules? Again?" Kyra grabbed the strap of her purse and sucked in her bottom lip. "They're all following rules from someone. They're following rules from Laprey. They must be. It's all originating from that website."

"It's crazy, but if Copycat Three is ready to go off on his own, maybe that will give us more opportunity to stop him. Think about it. Jordy Lee Cannon broke a rule by knowing his victims, and Fisher left a fingerprint on that tape. If Copycat Three wants to forge out on his own, let him."

"Forge out from whom or what? It has to be Laprey directing these guys, but why?"

"To create an army of serial killers." He touched her arm. "I'm going to talk to the couple who called in the body and touch base with the CSIs."

"I'll head back to station. Oh, and I got a text from Quinn. He wants to see us tonight. Can you make it, or do you need to be with Fiona?"

"Fiona's going to her friend's place after school, which reminds me. I need to call the mom." Jake pulled on another pair of gloves to ready himself for the crime scene. "Did Quinn text you before or after he heard about this third murder?"

"It was before, so I'm sure he's even more eager now to see us."

"So am I."

KYRA DROVE TO the station with a million questions in her head. Who was giving these killers their marching orders? Was it someone too afraid to do the killing himself? Did he get off on the power while he protected himself? There would have to be some crime the police could charge him with. You couldn't just run around and encourage people to commit murder, give them advice, egg them on.

How would this mastermind know what rules to follow unless he had committed murder himself? Had he already committed murder? If Laprey was the one behind these killers, he most likely murdered Yolanda, the homeless woman, and Sean. He *was* a killer.

When she got back to the Northeast Division, she had emails waiting for her from Juliana French's mother and more support from her former clients. If only Jake's ex-wife believed she was some kind of hero instead of some undesirable to be kept away from her daughter.

Kyra kept an eye out for the surge of activity that would indicate members of the task force had returned from the crime scene. They'd go through all the familiar steps—trying to identify the murder victim, locating her car, her home, her friends, her family. Jordy Cannon had been a fool to break that rule about knowing the victim. Usually murder victims did know their killers, and once law enforcement cast a wide enough net, they usually caught their man…or woman.

Eventually people started coming in from the field, looks of hardened determination on their faces. Billy always got the job of ID'ing the victim. He had insisted on it ever since his own sister disappeared. It had become a compulsion for him.

When Billy walked into the task force room, he didn't look left or right on his way to his desk. The task would absorb him for hours until he got a break.

Jake followed closely on Billy's heels, talking to three different people and trying to text on his phone. She knew

Jake would want to craft another response to Copycat Three, and she'd already started working on it in her head.

They'd want to challenge Copycat Three to break more rules while stoking his belief that he'd outgrown his mentor, whoever that was. They had to walk a fine line between taunting him and encouraging him to commit more murders. But, honestly, the guy didn't need encouragement. The urge had gotten in his blood.

As the day wound down, Kyra texted Jake from across the room, asking if they were still on for Quinn's.

Instead of texting her back, Jake stood up and stretched and then sauntered to her desk.

Wedging a hip on her desk, he said, "I'm good for Quinn's, but I need to go home first. I want to see Fiona before she takes off for Lyric's house and make sure she gets into a car with an actual adult driving and not a teenager. Lyric's older brother is picking her up. Then I'll head down to Venice. Who's cooking?"

"I'll pick up something. Any requests?"

"Whatever Quinn wants." He leaned in close. "We got a break today. When the coroner moved the body, there was a swizzle stick stuck to the victim's back where her shirt was pulled up."

"A swizzle stick? You mean one of those stirrers from a drink?"

"Yeah, kind of unique looking—a rainbow color. We're going to start checking the clubs, starting with Hollywood. It could just be from the victim's location before she got snatched, and if her car's in the same area, it's no mystery. But it seems odd that she'd have something like that stuck to her body from a club where she'd been drinking or dancing."

"You mean, it's more likely that it was in the car that transported her dead body to Topanga?"

"Right." He shrugged. "Unless it was on the ground already and the killer dropped her on top of it."

"That's promising. The footage of the clubs where Juliana and Carmella were before their murders hasn't shown anything yet? Nobody approaching the women? Leaving with them?"

"Nothing like that. Just shows they left alone, which is on my list of don'ts for Fiona when she's old enough to go out to clubs." Jake squeezed his eyes closed and grimaced, as if the thought of Fiona in a club caused him physical pain. "Young women should never leave a bar or club alone—or with a stranger, especially when intoxicated."

"That's the trouble with booze though, isn't it? It makes you do things you normally wouldn't."

"So does hubris." Jake winked. "And I think we have Copycat Three all ginned up on that."

Kyra left before Jake, although she didn't have any clients to see at her Santa Monica office. When she got home, she cleaned up—just in case Jake made an appearance at her apartment after dinner. Then she hopped in the shower, put on some fancy underwear—her hopes still high—and fed Spot.

She ordered and picked up Chinese food on the way to Quinn's place on the Venice Canals. He'd heard the news about the third killing today, and Kyra had told him about Copycat Three's note to Jake.

He'd seemed thoughtful and worried when she'd told him about the reference to rules again. He and Jake could analyze it tonight at dinner. She'd enjoy watching two great detectives bounce ideas off each other.

She parked outside of the walk streets that comprised

the neighborhood of Venice lining the canals. Beyond the bridges and canals where Quinn's house was located, Venice could be a rough area. Gentrification had never taken root here, despite the city's proximity to the beach.

Two gangs, Venice 13 and the Venice Shoreline Crips, still had a stranglehold on the drug trade here, but the violence and drive-by shootings that character-ized other areas of LA inhabited by gangs didn't mani-fest by the ocean. Venice still bowed down to its hippie roots, and artists had taken a firm hold of the area along the canals.

She always got a kick out of the tough, old LAPD de-tective hanging out with the artsy crowd of Venice, but all the neighbors had loved Charlotte and had accepted Quinn as part of the deal.

With the bags of food swinging from her wrists, Kyra knocked on Quinn's red door. At the same time, she called out, "It's Kyra."

His strong voice boomed from the other side of the door, "C'mon in."

Must be a good day. She used her key to let herself in and waved at Quinn coming from the rear of the house. His backyard consisted of a little square where he had installed a patio and a section where he tried to grow some vegetables.

"Don't tell me you're gardening out there." She lifted the bags. "I have everything we need right here."

"Just cleaning up some leaves."

"Don't overdo it." She placed the bags on the coun-ter and picked up a bottle of wine. "Ooh, what's this?"

"I did a little shopping and picked up a bottle for you."

She blew him a kiss. "Thanks, Dad."

Quinn stopped short and almost tripped. "You haven't called me that in a while."

"I haven't, have I?"

"You usually call me Dad when you're feeling…insecure." He narrowed his eyes. "Are you okay? Jake treating you all right?"

Was she feeling insecure? She sensed a storm brewing but couldn't put her finger on its origin. The developments in the Copycat Three case had instilled her with confidence, and they were even getting close to identifying her nemesis, Laprey. She and Jake were on shaky ground due to his ex's objection to her being around Fiona, but Jake was working on that.

"Jake's taking care of his daughter, as he should. We're fine." She pulled a container from the bag and plopped it on the counter. "So fine, in fact, he gave me a detail about the murder scene today."

"Evidence?" Quinn crowded into the kitchen next to her and washed his hands at the sink.

"A swizzle stick from a bar stuck to the victim's back. Could've been a bar she was at…or it could be from the killer or his car."

"That's good news."

Before they could say more, a knock on the door had Kyra patting Quinn on the shoulder and saying, "I'll get that. Not expecting anyone else, are you?"

"I still have a few friends, you know, even though Charlotte was the social butterfly. Ned Verona still drops by."

Captain Castillo's name came to her lips, but she shoved it aside for later as she opened the door to Jake.

He held up a six-pack of beer. "For Quinn—so don't get on his case."

"I guess everyone felt we needed alcohol tonight. Quinn even bought a bottle of wine." She stood on her tiptoes and kissed Jake's jaw. "I told Quinn about the swizzle stick. Any progress on that, yet?"

"We briefed several patrol officers, gave them a picture of the stir stick and told them to keep an eye out at the bars and clubs. No DNA or prints on it, though."

"No ID of the victim?" Quinn had been listening intently from across the room and came forward with his arm outstretched.

The two men shook hands, and Jake said, "Not yet."

Kyra moved into the kitchen and called over her shoulder, "You can get Quinn a beer, but just one."

Quinn growled. "Tyrant."

Kyra smiled to herself. Quinn loved it when she ordered him around. She'd just taken up Charlotte's mantle. "I hope nobody minds if we serve ourselves out of the cartons. I'm trying to save us some dishwashing."

"Fine by me, but don't force me to eat my food with chopsticks or we'll be here all night." Quinn took a seat at the table, cold beer in hand.

"Forks, it is." Kyra handed a stack of plates to Jake and grabbed a handful of silverware. She carried the food to the table and went back for the bottle of wine unopened on the counter. She rummaged in a drawer for a corkscrew and carried the items to the table.

"I'll do that." Jake took the wine and the corkscrew from her and peeled the foil off the top of the bottle. As he twisted the corkscrew into the cork, his phone rang. "That's work. I hope I get to finish my dinner."

He shoved the bottle toward Kyra and picked up his phone. "McAllister."

Kyra clutched the wine bottle by the neck and watched Jake's face.

Noticing her scrutiny, he gave her a thumbs-up. "That's

great news and good work, Brandon. Do you think he'll call tonight?"

Quinn took the bottle from her and poured the ruby red liquid into her glass. "Drink."

Jake said, "That works, yeah. Thanks." He ended the call and grabbed his beer for a toast. "Here's to the brains behind IT. Brandon tracked down Toby Dog from Websleuths and sent him a message, explaining the situation. The guy's name is Bret Harrison and he lives in Connecticut. He's anxious to talk to me and will be giving me a call later."

Kyra clinked her glass with the two bottles. "Perfect. I wonder if he was surprised to hear from Brandon."

"If he's a fan of Websleuths, I'm sure he's excited to be part of a real-life investigation. I just hope he's not a poser."

"Poser?" Quinn took a sip of beer and plunged a spoon into the sticky rice.

Jake answered, "Someone who's lying to get in on the action. I'm sure you dealt with plenty of phonies giving you fake information just to be involved."

"We sure did—just never from a website."

As the three of them ate, Jake filled in Quinn about the case. They'd almost finished eating when Jake's phone rang again.

He glanced at the display. "This is Bret. I'm going to put him on speaker."

Jake took a swig of beer and answered the phone. "Detective Jake McAllister, LAPD Homicide."

A voice a lot younger than Kyra expected replied. "Detective McAllister, this is Bret Harrison. I was contacted by Brandon Nguyen about some messages I received on Websleuths."

"I've been expecting your call, Bret. When did you start receiving those messages?"

Jake took Bret through several questions and had him go through all the usernames he believed belonged to the same man.

Bret was thorough, had a good memory and didn't seem to be playing Jake. Of course, he hadn't saved any of the communications so it was just his word, but with all the usernames IT should be able to track an IP address.

Jake cleared his throat. "What other rules did this guy mention?"

"Standard stuff that you'd expect anyone with any common sense to know about, but he always let stories drop about how he'd done this or that. Claimed he'd murdered a few people in different parts of the country. It was creepy."

"Could be someone bragging, but we'll look into him. Can you remember any of his stories?"

Bret huffed out a breath. "Let's see. He cautioned against taking any personal trophies. He said if you were going to take jewelry, make sure it couldn't be tied directly to the victim. He said he once took someone's unique engraved wedding ring that had a yellow diamond, and for some reason the cops never knew about that. But he panicked and tossed it, anyway."

Quinn's bottle of beer landed on its side, and Kyra pulled the napkin from her lap to soak up the fizzy spill.

Jake finished up his conversation with Bret and cupped the phone in his hand. "Interesting stuff."

Kyra glanced at Quinn's face, drained of color, the lines etched deeply in his flesh, and jumped up from her chair. "What's wrong? Are you all right?"

He shifted his blue eyes to hers, and she'd never seen

such fear reflected there, not even on the day Charlotte got her cancer diagnosis.

"Quinn?" Jake pushed back from the table.

Quinn closed his eyes and said, "He's back. The Player is back."

Chapter Eleven

Kyra swayed and gripped the back of Quinn's chair. The call had upset him. She and Jake should stop making him relive his one professional failure.

"What makes you say that, Quinn?" Jake narrowed his eyes. "What part of Bret's narration brought you to that conclusion?"

Kyra's heart slammed against her chest. Jake was taking Quinn seriously. Her greatest fear was materializing before her eyes, and Jake was asking rational questions. She felt like screaming.

Quinn opened his eyes slowly, lashes fluttering as if coming out of a trance. "It was what he said about the engraved wedding ring with the yellow diamond."

"But you said The Player never took any trophies except for the severed finger." Her high-pitched voice sounded as if it belonged to someone else, some hysterical person in a melodrama.

Jake must've heard the tone, too. He circled the table and put a hand on her back. "Sit down, Kyra. Have some wine."

With a little nudge from Jake, she plopped down in her chair and grabbed her wineglass by the stem, her grip practically snapping it off. She took a gulp, hardly tasting the wine as it ran down her throat.

Reaching over and cinching her wrist with his gnarled fingers, Quinn said, "He never did take any other trophies. That's why I was never sure about the ring."

Jake had dragged the chair at the end of the table around to Quinn and now sat next to him, elbows braced on his knees. "The engraved wedding ring?"

"That's right." Quinn released Kyra's wrist and patted her hand. "One of the victims, Delia Hopkins, had a slight indentation on her left ring finger. I naturally assumed it had been a wedding ring, although there were no tan lines and the indentation was very faint."

Jake asked, "Did her family report the ring missing?"

"That's the thing." Quinn scratched his chin. "Delia was divorced, and her ex-husband reported that she'd tossed the ring in the ocean. Nobody at her office ever reported seeing her wear a ring on that finger after her divorce."

"And the description of that wedding ring?"

Quinn locked eyes with Jake, his mouth grim. "The ex-husband described it as a yellow diamond with an engraving. Nobody—and I mean nobody—today would know about that ring. We didn't put it in the reports as missing because the family claimed she didn't have it at the time of her murder."

Blowing out a long breath, Jake glanced at Kyra. "That's it. Laprey is The Player, and The Player is the one encouraging and guiding these copycats, living vicariously through the murders he's no longer willing or able to commit."

"That means The Player, the man who murdered my mother twenty years ago knows who I am, where I live, where I work, what I drive." Kyra knotted her fingers in front of her and whispered, "What kind of game is he playing?"

Quinn covered his eyes with a slightly trembling hand. "I'm sorry. I never should've confirmed this to you, Kyra. I could still be wrong. Maybe this Laprey is related to The Player. Maybe The Player is dead, as we expected."

"You don't believe that, Quinn—not anymore." She massaged her temples. "I think in the back of my mind I always suspected he was out there watching me, responsible for these…pranks since the copycats started. Do you think he's doing the same thing with the family members of his other victims? Why would I be special among all those people? My mother wasn't even his first or his last victim."

Quinn had a ready answer. "It's because you're involved with the current cases. I kept in touch with a few of the families over the years. Some of them don't even live in LA anymore. You're right in the heart of it. You're on the task force. Anyone could find that out—and he did. Right, Jake?"

Jake nodded, and a muscle twitched at the corner of his mouth. "The Player must've been tracking Kyra before the task force, though. He may have known her as Marilyn Lake, but to know she'd changed her name to Kyra Chase he must've been looking into her life before he launched his squad of killers."

The shock Kyra had been trying to keep at bay seized her. Her leg bounced beneath the table and she clenched her teeth to keep them from chattering.

Quinn scowled at Jake. "Maybe not. *You* found out who she was."

"I'm a detective with resources at my fingertips. Look—" Jake leaned forward and gripped Quinn's shoulder "—I know you're trying to protect Kyra, but she needs to face the truth to deal with it."

Had she come across as that strong to Jake? Why in

the world did he think she could handle the knowledge that the man who'd murdered her mother had been keeping tabs on her for twenty years and was now the same person directing a cadre of killers?

She took another slug of wine and dashed at the dribble it left on her chin. "Jake's right. This is also good news for catching Copycat Three. Bring. It. On."

Jake raised an eyebrow at her and continued talking to Quinn. "The Player has been on this Websleuths site. He's shown his hand. We can find him just like we found Bret Harrison. Our IT guy, Brandon is working on it, as we speak. We're gonna nail him, Quinn. Your nightmare's over."

Quinn aimed a shaky smile at Kyra. "I just want Mimi's nightmare to be over."

Kyra left Quinn and Jake to hash through the implications of The Player being the person behind the copycat killers. She'd had enough for one night. She robotically cleaned Quinn's kitchen and put away the leftover food, wondering if she'd ever feel safe again.

As the night wound down and the two detectives got hoarse from talking, Kyra tipped another few mouthfuls of wine in her glass and sat cross-legged on the floor. "Did you figure out how you're gonna catch him, yet?"

"We're working on it." Jake pointed to her glass. "If you're planning to knock that back, you'd better call an Uber to pick you up. Can't allow you on the road, ma'am."

Meeting his gaze over the rim of the glass, she gulped down half of it. "Looks like I'm leaving my car in Venice."

Jake stood up and stretched, his hands practically touching the ceiling. "We're going to call it a night, Quinn. I'm glad you were listening when I got the call from Bret. I always had a niggling suspicion about La-prey and the connection between these killers."

"Twenty-twenty hindsight and all that." Quinn eased up from his chair. "But I was puzzled from the get-go why the killer was taking two trophies. In addition to the severed finger, Cannon took a piece of jewelry. Fisher took a lock of hair, and now Copycat Three takes their underwear."

"What do you mean?" Maybe her brain was fuzzy from the wine, and as she struggled to her feet clutching her wineglass Quinn strode over to help her to her feet.

Quinn's blue eyes sharpened. "The killers took one trophy for themselves...and the severed finger for The Player."

Ten minutes later, Kyra sat in the passenger seat of Jake's muscle car, shaking from the V-8 engine rumbling beneath her—or from the evening's revelations.

"Are you okay?" Jake ran a hand down her thigh. "I hope you know you're not spending the night alone. I saw Fiona safely off to Lyric's, so I don't have to go home tonight."

"That's tonight. What about all the other nights?" Kyra hugged herself and leaned her head against the window.

"If you're scared, you're staying with me and Fiona. That's it. Fiona's not a child. She knows her mother cheated on me with her law partner and then married him. If she can handle that, she can handle her dad having his girlfriend spend the night."

"And your ex?"

Jake swung the car onto Lincoln Boulevard and gunned it. "I can handle Tess."

"Tess has an even stronger point now, Jake, even though she doesn't know it. Danger is going to follow me like a heat-seeking missile. I don't want your daughter in my orbit. Think about it. My foster brother, Matt... Yolanda, the homeless woman I was trying to question... Sean Hughes. They're all dead."

"You're not responsible for any of that. He is."

She stroked his cheek. "I'll welcome your company at my place tonight and maybe even tomorrow, but when Fiona returns to your house, I won't be there."

"Then first thing tomorrow, I'm installing one of those camera doorbells at your place, and we can hook up a system in your carport and around the back in the alley by your bedroom window. You need security at your apartment, whether you're there or not. We can sync it all with your phone. I can spring for an alarm system, too." He poked at her purse with her gun stashed in the side pocket. "You sleep with that in your bedroom?"

"I have been, ever since he left that first playing card by the trash bin."

"That's my girl."

He found a place to park on the street and grabbed her hand as they strolled to the apartment building. When they walked inside her place, Jake did a quick check of all the windows and her sliding door to the little patio where she kept a hearty cactus and a few hanging flowerpots.

"You have good security on those windows and the door, but anyone can break a window and you might not even notice it when you first come in."

"You'll get no argument from me if you want to outfit my place like Fort Knox." She dropped her purse on the low wall that separated the short entrance hall from the kitchen. "Coffee, water, tea?"

"I'll take some water. Is Spot around?"

"You're getting fond of that mangy cat, aren't you?"

"I always had pets, mostly dogs, until my old Lab died a few years ago. I didn't get another dog because my work hours are too crazy. I'd have to hire a companion for him, and then what's the point?"

"That's why Spot is the perfect pet." She stuck a mug of water in the microwave to boil and handed Jake a glass of water. "Crazy that The Player would post that stuff on a message board."

"He probably didn't think anyone with any knowledge would be perusing those messages. Anyone can brag on there. Bret told us he thought the guy was full of it. Others have made outrageous claims just to get a reaction from people. The red flags waved for Bret when he saw your username and thought you were another iteration of the person trolling for a following."

When the microwave buzzer went off, Jake held up his hand. "Sit down. I'll get your tea. Is that wine gonna give you a headache? Do you want an aspirin?"

"I ate enough Chinese food before Quinn's bombshell to counter the effects of the alcohol. I'll be fine, but I have to admit the wine helped." She sank on the couch and pulled a pillow into her lap. "In the back of my mind, I always knew he was out there, but having Quinn confirm it socked me in the gut."

"Nothing changes." Jake carried a steaming mug to her, the end of the tea bag fluttering off to the side. He placed the cup on the coffee table and took the cushion next to her. "He was always out there, and now you just had it confirmed."

"He wasn't so careful this time, and you'll get him." She turned toward him and grabbed his hands. "Won't you?"

"I promise you that." He slid a hand through her hair and brought her in for a kiss, the taste of beer and Szechwan chicken still on his lips. "Is my toothbrush still here?"

"As the only one I have here who could possibly object to your presence is Spot, and he's out on the prowl, your toothbrush is in the holder right next to mine."

"As it should be." He planted another kiss on her mouth. "Drink your tea. I'm going to brush my teeth and warm up your bed."

Folding her hands around the mug, she watched Jake lope off toward her bedroom. How had she gotten so lucky? Bad luck had been dogging her most of her life, and then she'd caught a break with Jake...and Quinn. He and Charlotte had been her guardian angels and Jake had joined their ranks.

She drank half her tea and then put the cup in the sink. She double-checked the locks, retrieved her gun from her purse and shut out the lights. Jake had left ajar the bathroom door that led to the bedroom, and the TV glowed from the room next door.

She poked her head in the room to find Jake installed in her bed, the sheets at his waist exposing his bare chest. He had his phone in his hand and her pulse ticked up.

"Everything okay?"

"I'm texting with Fiona." He held up the phone. "Lyric had a few other girls over for the night, and they just came in from the Jacuzzi."

"Must be nice. Wish I had a Jacuzzi."

"If you hurry up, I'll give you a nice, warm massage." He quirked his eyebrows up and down.

With a thrill tingling through all the right parts of her body, she brushed her teeth quickly and shed her clothing on her way from the bathroom to the bed. When she crawled in beside Jake, he pulled her flush against his body with one arm and pressed a kiss against the side of her head.

She clung to him, running her hand down his bare

chest and flattening it against his belly. "It's going to be all right, isn't it?"

He rolled toward her and scooped her close, every line of his torso meeting hers. He smoothed his hands over her derriere and touched his warm lips to her ear. "As long as you're with me, I'll make it all right."

And as he made love to her, his hard body firm against hers, his lips whispering all the words she ever wanted to hear...she believed him.

THE FOLLOWING MORNING, Jake dropped off Kyra at her car, parked in a public lot across from the canals in Venice. He continued on his way to his own place in the Hollywood Hills to shower and change for work. He'd called an emergency meeting of the task force on a Saturday to break the news that they now had evidence The Player was directing the copycats. They planned to keep the press in the dark...for now.

He dialed up Fiona on the way, his call going straight to voice mail. Nine o'clock must be too early for a teenage girl on a Saturday morning after a sleepover.

By the time he got to the station, half the task force had arrived. He'd told Kyra to stay put and start calling around to find out who carried the security systems he'd listed for her before he left.

When he dropped the bombshell at the meeting, the buzz in the room reached epic proportions. He hadn't given Captain Castillo a heads-up first, and Carlos's face across the room had taken on an ashen appearance. It was similar to the way Quinn had looked last night— disbelief, horror and...something else, known only to the people who'd worked that case.

After the meeting, Jake touched base with Brandon,

whose job of identifying the creepy poster on Websleuths had taken on a whole new aspect.

The young man smacked his forehead with the heel of his hand. "I can't believe it. Just that one little bit of information about the ring, which he never even mentioned to me, and we've got The Player."

"Not yet." Jake clapped him on the back. "But we're counting on you. Go, do your magic."

"I wish it was magic. One of my guys and I are going to be here this afternoon working on those addresses. I'll let you know when we have something."

Jake approached Captain Castillo, still stationed in the corner at the back of the room wearing a crumpled suit that looked like he'd dragged it out of yesterday's dirty clothes. "Sorry I didn't have time to touch base with you, Captain."

Castillo rubbed his unshaven chin. "Quinn told you about that ring, huh?"

"You knew about it?"

"I knew about Quinn's hunch. I never saw that victim's body. Quinn's partner at the time wasn't convinced the line was from a ring and when the ex and the family told us Delia Hopkins never wore a ring on that finger after the divorce, we gave it up."

Jake braced a hand on the wall next to Castillo. "Delia must've lied to her ex. She'd obviously kept the ring, probably wore it around the house. Maybe she was planning to sell it and didn't want to split the proceeds with the ex, so she pretended she threw it out. The description rings true to you?"

"I didn't remember, but I looked it up this morning before your briefing." Castillo rubbed his eyes. "I'm going to get out of here. My wife wants me to get some decorations down for Halloween."

"Thanks for coming in, sir." As Jake turned, he almost bumped into Trevor Jansen, a detective in Vice, the same detective who'd been outed by Sean Hughes's blog a few months ago. He barely recognized the guy out of his undercover disguise. Jake nodded. "Jansen."

"McAllister, I have some information I think you'll wanna hear."

Jake crooked his finger in the air. "Let's get out of this crush."

He led Jansen to the conference room that housed the task force war room, now devoid of its typical chaos. Jake sat at his desk and kicked out Billy's chair in Jansen's direction.

The detective straddled it and folded his arms on the back. "I saw the swizzle stick that was stuck to the most recent victim's back."

"Yeah?" Jake got a burst of adrenaline that made his head throb.

"I have a pretty good idea where it came from. You know of a strip joint on Hollywood Boulevard called Candy Girls?"

"Neon out front, high-end place as far as strip clubs go?"

Jansen's lips twisted up at one corner. "The owner would call it a *gentlemen's club*."

"Of course. Aren't they all?" Jake snorted. "You're sure about it?"

"Not saying other clubs can't use the same stir sticks, but I recognize that rainbow design from Candy Girls."

Jake raised his eyebrows. "Frequent visitor?"

"My alter ego TJ Jones was a big fan."

"That's right." Jake snapped his fingers. "Some drug sting went down there. How are they still open?"

"Manager wasn't involved." Jansen lifted a shoulder. "Didn't know anything about it."

"Thanks, Jansen. We'll check it out and get the video footage." As Jansen rose, Jake stopped him. "How's your…friend getting along with Cool Breeze's case?"

"I think she can help Billy find out what happened to his sister. Dina's tenacious." Jansen touched his fingers to his forehead and left the room.

When Jake walked out of the station for his house to change before meeting Kyra, he called Fiona again, and this time she answered. "Did you girls have fun last night?"

"Yeah, it was fun. We're gonna see a movie in Westwood Village today and go shopping. I'll text you later."

Jake sent a quick text to Fiona's mother with the update and headed home. Almost ninety minutes later, metal toolbox in hand, he pulled up to Kyra's apartment building.

She met him at the door and aimed a toe at a box in her hallway. "Ring camera and two more systems for the carport and the alley."

"Great. I hope your management company doesn't have any objections."

"I doubt they will." She grabbed his sweatshirt and pulled him in for a kiss. "How'd the briefing go?"

"As you'd expect—shock, surprise, excitement. Captain Castillo took it hard, like Quinn."

"This is their chance to nail him, though." She sawed her bottom lip. "There's definitely something going on between those two, some secret they share."

"Maybe it's just the shared misery of a serial killer cold case." Jake dropped the toolbox and nudged it. "I brought these because I figured you wouldn't have the right kinds of tools to install this stuff.

She raised her hand. "Guilty, unless a hammer, rusty screwdriver and a broken pair of pliers will do the trick."

Jake pulled the boxes from the bags, and they borrowed a ladder from one of her neighbors. A few hours later, they sat hunched over Kyra's phone, bringing up all the views from her cameras.

"This is awesome. I can check out my place before I even drive up."

He rubbed a circle on her back. "Does it make you feel safer?"

"Of course."

"Don't get overconfident." He pulled her into his lap, wanting to keep her there forever. "You still have to watch your back. Do you need to go to the gun range? I can get you into the range at Elysian Park." He squeezed her bicep. "Get some practice in."

"I was recently recertified. I think I'm good." She twined her arms around his neck. "Do we get another night together, or is your daughter coming home tonight?"

"Another night." He tugged on a lock of her hair. "How do you feel about strip clubs?"

She widened her blue eyes. "As a patron or a performer?"

"I wish." He tightened his arms around her. "When I was at the station, Jansen stopped me and said Candy Girls in Hollywood uses those rainbow swizzle sticks. I'm going to get eyes on their CCTV, but in the meantime we can check it out on a Saturday night and ask a few questions."

"Wouldn't surprise me one bit if Copycat Three frequented a place like that. Probably thinks he's *the man*," she said, using air quotes. "Don't forget, Jordy visited sex workers after his murders."

"Does that mean you're in?" He held out his fist for a bump and she obliged.

"Hell, I haven't had a good night out at a strip club in forever."

JAKE'S MOUTH WENT dry when Kyra sashayed out of her bedroom in a pair of skintight black leather pants, a flowy white silk blouse and sky-high spiky heels. "That's what you're wearing?"

"Exactly. So, you'd better up your game because this—" she smoothed her hands down the thighs of her pants "—is not going to be seen with jeans and a T-shirt."

"Yes, ma'am. Take some clothes for the morning. We'll drive to my place so I can change, and then later you can spend the night." He wiggled his eyebrows up and down.

"Okay, but one condition. I'll drive my own car to your house."

"Let's dump these boxes in the trash, arm your security system and head out."

Later at his house, Jake shook out a black jacket and slung it over his arm before jogging downstairs. When he hit the bottom step, Kyra turned and shimmied her shoulders.

"That's what I'm talking about. You look hot." She tilted her head to one side, her blond hair fanning out across her shoulder. "Did Billy help you choose that?"

"Give me a little credit for having some taste." He straightened his cuffs. "Doesn't hurt having a partner who's a fashion plate, though."

They drove down the hill and into Hollywood. The pink neon of the Candy Girls sign flashed a welcome, and Jake parked his car in a lot down the street. The club attracted all sorts of people, but the better dressed you were the better chance you had of getting inside.

The bouncer ushered in Kyra and Jake, and before the pumped-up watchdog could feel the gun on his hip beneath his jacket, Jake flashed his badge.

The man's eye twitched. "Official business?"

Jake tucked away his wallet. "Not exactly, and the club's not in any trouble. We're more interested in your patrons."

"I'm Greg. Just let me know if I can help in any way. Buddy, the owner, had a scare recently, and he put out the word that we're supposed to cooperate with you guys at all times."

"We appreciate that, Greg. I'm not here to cause Buddy any trouble. Is he here tonight? I would like to talk to him about getting a look at some of your surveillance tapes."

"He's not, but the manager, Pepper, can help with that. I'll send her over." Greg jerked a stubby thumb over his shoulder. "Would you and the lady like a seat up front?"

Kyra jabbed him in the side with a sharp elbow.

"I think a place in the back will work."

"You got it."

Jake insisted on paying the cover charge although Greg was more than happy to let them in, gratis. Then a scantily clad hostess led them to a table in a dark corner, away from the hootin' and hollerin'.

His gaze wandered to the stage where a woman in a cowboy hat and not much more was slithering around a pole. He tipped his head toward the dancer and whispered to Kyra, "Do you think you could do something like that?"

She slid her hand up his thigh, and his muscles coiled. "Are you planning to install a pole in your bedroom?"

He swallowed. "That could be arranged."

She laughed, a low, throaty sound that made him hard.

"Actually, that's becoming quite the exercise trend among suburban housewives."

"Birth rate going up in the suburbs?"

A waitress came to their table. Jake ordered a beer, and Kyra ordered a fruity cocktail.

"That's a first for you. Thought you were a beer and wine girl with the occasional margarita thrown in there for girls' night out."

She tapped his arm. "I'm not likely to get a swizzle stick with beer or wine, am I? Or did you already forget the purpose of this little foray to the dark side?"

"Quick thinking, but you need to give this boy a break. My senses have been overwhelmed from the minute you paraded out of your bedroom in that outfit." He leaned in close, inhaling her sweet scent. "I've had one thing on my mind ever since."

Before their drinks arrived, another woman visited their table. Dressed in black slacks and a white oxford shirt, she straddled a chair and snapped a card in front of Jake. "I'm Pepper, the manager. Greg told me who you were. You want our video footage?"

Jake slid his own card across the table. "Depends on your swizzle sticks."

"Excuse me?"

Their waitress returned, and as she set their drinks in front of them, she said, "Can I get you something, Pepper?"

"No, thanks, Anna." Pepper flicked a finger toward Kyra's drink, indicating the rainbow-colored swizzle stick sporting a cherry and a chunk of pineapple. "Does that meet your approval?"

Kyra dislodged the fruit from the stick and held it up. "This is the one."

Jake asked, "Do you know of any other clubs or bars in the area that use these particular sticks?"

"Couldn't tell you, but they're kind of unique. We order them special from a place in Albuquerque." She waved her hand with its black-tipped nails in the air. "They fit our decor."

"Then, I think we'll want that footage."

"You got it. Can I ask you why?"

"I'm sure you get a lot of regulars here, huh?" Jake's gaze swept the room, and his gut knotted at the thought of some psycho getting his kicks here after killing women.

"Oh, yeah." Pepper ran a hand through her short, red hair. "All kinds."

Kyra stirred her frothy drink. "Anyone get handsy with the women?"

"Oh, yeah."

"We wouldn't mind talking to a few of those women and hearing about their experiences." Jake tapped the side of his beer bottle. "Doesn't have to be tonight. We're here doing a little reconnaissance. We can set up formal interviews later, and I'll send someone over on Monday with dates and times for the footage."

"Hope we have it all for you." Pepper stood up and pocketed Jake's card. "We do tape over."

"Hold off on that for now."

"Will do." Pepper rapped her knuckles on the table. "Drinks on the house?"

"Sorry, can't accept that, but we appreciate the offer… and your cooperation."

When Pepper left the table, Kyra puckered her lips around the straw and took a sip of her drink. "Shouldn't get our hopes up. That stick could've been on the ground when Copycat Three dumped the body. The victim could've had it in her back pocket."

"I realize that, but from hanging around Quinn you must know about a detective's gut feelings."

She patted his belly. "You have it about this?"

"I've had it ever since the coroner placed that swizzle stick in my hand. Felt it even more when Jansen cornered me."

"I trust your instincts." She pointed her straw at the stage. "You don't seem that interested in the entertainment."

He grabbed her hands. "I've got all the woman I need right in front of me."

A dancer sidled up to their table and dipped beside it, her long brown hair swinging over her shoulder. "I'm Barbi. Pepper told me you were a cop interested in our clientele."

Jake asked, "You have a story?"

"A regular. He's a weird dude. Kinda scary."

"Scary how?" Jake kicked out the chair. "Can you sit down for a minute?"

She glanced over her shoulder and perched on the edge of the chair. "When he comes in, he usually requests a lap dance from me. Even in the private rooms, the men aren't supposed to touch us, unless we allow it, but this guy…"

"What does he do, Barbi?" Kyra hunched forward, putting on her therapist's voice, inviting all kinds of confidences.

"He—he likes to put his hands around my throat."

Jake clenched his fists under the table. "Does he hurt you?"

"I have a panic button, and I had to push it once. Security came in and kicked him out."

"That must've been terrifying." Kyra patted the other woman's hand. "He should be banned."

"There's something else. Both times he did it, he called me a different name."

Jake froze for a second. "Was it Juliana or Carmela?"

All the color drained from Barbi's face. "It was actually Jenna, but is that what this is about? Copycat Three?"

A pulse throbbed in Jake's throat. "You're familiar with the killer?"

Barbi placed a hand over her heart. "Not only am I familiar with his crimes, the guy I'm talking about came in here late all hyped up on the same nights as the murders."

Chapter Twelve

Jake almost pounded the table but didn't want to startle an already nervous Barbi. "He was here two nights ago?"

Barbi nodded. "He was here tonight."

Jake gripped the edge of the table. "Is he still here?"

"No, he left about an hour ago."

Jake exchanged a look with Kyra. They'd arrived just about an hour ago. Had he spotted them? "Barbi, can you get away from here and talk to us? I can let Pepper know, if you like."

"I'm sure she'll be cool with it. There's a diner across the street that's open all night. I can meet you over there once I change."

Jake paid the tab, added to the bill to cover the two-drink minimum and left a large tip. After alerting Pepper that they'd need the security footage from tonight ASAP, he steered Kyra out of the club and they crossed the street to the diner.

They nabbed a booth in the back and ordered coffee.

As Jake curled a hand around his cup, he said, "If he was there, he saw us. He already knows what I look like."

"He may not come back to Candy Girls, but surely they know his identity, have his credit card receipts." Kyra poured cream in her decaf coffee. "Still, for all we know, Barbi's weirdo might just be some creep who gets off on threatening women. He wouldn't be the first or the last."

"And a swizzle stick from the club he frequents ends up at a dump site for one of the victims? I can't wait to ID this guy and check his alibis, his phone records, his computer."

Kyra put her hand up and wiggled her fingers. "Barbi just walked in."

The woman who approached their table in jeans, sneakers and a hoodie looked like a college student. She adjusted her glasses and slid into the booth next to Kyra.

Jake said, "Thanks for meeting with us. Coffee?"

"Lottie knows what I like."

Barbi waved to the waitress behind the counter, and she called back. "You want the regular, hon?"

Barbi nodded and gave her a thumbs-up. When she turned her attention back to Jake, she said, "I'm glad you came in. I never called the police because I thought I was overreacting. I didn't want to be laughed at."

"We never laugh at possible tips. We get thousands. It's our job to figure out what's viable. Not yours. How and why did you make the connection between your customer and the murders?"

"I've been following all of the copycat cases. In my line of work, you need to watch your back. For Copycat Three, I noticed his victims all had long, brown hair." She flipped her own long, chocolate-brown locks over her shoulder. "I also know he strangles his victims. This guy, Mike is his name, is strange. He always comments on my hair. When I give him lap dances, he wants my hair over my shoulders, and then he put his hands around my neck twice."

Jake tapped a fingernail against his cup. "So, you checked his appearances against the dates of the three murders?"

"I didn't have to dig that much. I keep a notebook of

my lap dances for tax purposes." Barbi shoved aside the silverware as the waitress brought her a vanilla milkshake. "When the third woman was murdered the other day, I noticed the coincidence and it gave me a chill."

"Do you know Mike's last name?" Jake had pulled out his phone to take notes.

"Afraid not. I don't even know if Mike's his real name." She held up a perfectly manicured finger. "And before you ask, he always pays cash. You won't find any bar receipts for him."

"But we will see him on camera."

"For sure. I can identify him for you." She stirred her milkshake with a straw. "How did you tie him to Candy Girls?"

When Kyra opened her mouth, Jake nudged her foot under the table. They'd already told Pepper. They didn't have to announce it to everyone. "We'd rather not say right now."

He questioned Barbi for another half hour. She had her stuff together and would make a great witness if they got that far. After the interview, Jake and Kyra walked Barbi to her car, and then returned to his.

Back behind the wheel, Jake said, "This evening turned out even better than I expected when I saw you in your leather pants."

"The night is still young." She trailed her fingernails along his forearm, and he shivered at the promise.

He started the car and pulled out of the lot. "I am going to have to hit the station again tomorrow. I need to get all this info out and send someone over to collect the video from Candy Girls. Barbi said she's available to view it."

Kyra fluttered her lashes better than any one of those Candy Girls. "I promise not to keep you up too late."

THE FOLLOWING MORNING, Jake left Kyra asleep in his bed as he got on the phone and ruined a few weekends. He didn't know how he was going to let Kyra go back to her own place. Now that they knew The Player was still alive and had his sights set on Kyra, Jake wanted to keep her by his side always.

He put a call in to Fiona and almost dropped the phone when she answered after two rings. "I wasn't sure you'd be up this early."

"Who said we ever went to bed?" He heard giggling in the background.

"Man, you just ruined it. How long are you staying at Lyric's today? Is all your schoolwork done for tomorrow? You have one more week to hit it hard online before I put you on a plane back to your mother's and back to regular school."

"Until I come back for Christmas?"

"Yeah, you're still coming for Christmas. I think you handled yourself well this week. I—I'm proud of you."

"Aw, thanks Dad, and yeah, I'm done with homework until my teachers pile on more tomorrow. I even got some help from Lyric's brother on my algebra this weekend."

Was she piling it on too thick? His hinky meter twanged. "Really?"

"Lyric had some math homework to finish before her mom let the other girls come over, so we worked with Ocean."

"You worked with what?"

"Ocean, he's Lyric's brother."

"Figures." Jake glanced up as Kyra came down the staircase in one of his T-shirts. "I can pick you up this afternoon."

"That's okay. Ocean can give me a ride back. He likes driving down Sunset."

What young man didn't? "All right. Keep me posted. I have some work to do today, but I'm available at any time to pick you up if you change your mind—or if Ocean does."

"Okay. Gotta go. Love you."

The back of his eyes prickled. He didn't hear that from her too often.

"I love—" She'd already hung up and cut off his words. God, he needed to say that more often, too.

Kyra climbed onto the counter stool next to him and yawned. "Is Fiona okay?"

"She's going to hang out with Lyric until this afternoon."

"Lyric? That's a pretty name."

"You don't even wanna know what her brother's name is." He pushed away from the counter and moved toward the stove. "I made eggs, I've got coffee going and I can make some toast."

"Sounds good." She tapped his notes on the counter. "Working hard already?"

"The task force is excited about these new developments." He pounded his chest. "I can feel it in here. We're close."

He didn't tell her about the other feelings he had— the sense of dread that had been hanging over him since they'd found out Laprey was The Player.

Someone had suggested that maybe The Player had given the information about the yellow diamond wedding ring to someone in prison, and that person was the one trolling message boards. Jake didn't believe that. The Player had never told anyone about his crimes before this.

"I hope so." Kyra held her hair back with one hand as

she took the plate of eggs from him. "I don't know how long I can stay on high alert."

"Have you checked your security system yet this morning?"

"I've barely opened my eyes. Haven't even looked at my phone, yet." She speared a clump of eggs and waved the fork toward her purse on the floor next to the couch. "I didn't charge my phone last night."

"Hope it's not dead." Jake carried his coffee mug into the living room and retrieved her purse. "You also left your gun in your purse."

She dropped her lids halfway over her eyes and said, "I had other things on my mind last night…and other forms of protection."

"Don't remind me about those other things, or we'll never make it out the door this morning." He swung her purse onto the counter, and she pulled out her phone.

"Still juiced." As she cupped her phone in her hand and scrolled through messages, Jake's work phone rang, the jangling sound that always got his heart pumping when he was in the middle of an investigation.

He glanced at the display before he answered, tapping the speaker function at the same time. "Tell me you nailed the SOB, Billy."

"Not yet, but we ID'd the third victim. Her name is Sydney Walsh. Found her car blocks away from a bar downtown, purse and dead cell phone in the car. He must've snatched her there, like the other two."

"Getting the security footage from the bar and the street?"

"On it. The lot where she parked her car doesn't have any cameras, but there's a bank across the street. We're going to be looking at their ATM camera. Maybe we can catch something from that."

"Family here?" Jake shifted his gaze to Kyra, who'd dropped her fork.

"I don't think so. Roommate reported her missing. Tell Kyra I'll send her the family contact when I get it. Good work, last night, by the way. Hopefully, Sydney will be Copycat Three's last victim."

"I sent Vickers and Moreno out there to retrieve the video. They'll review it with Barbi this afternoon. I was going to have them grab the footage tomorrow, but once Barbi told us Mike had been there last night I expedited the request."

Billy asked, "What are the chances his name is really Mike?"

"Most likely slim and none, but you never know. He probably didn't think we'd be tracking him back to Candy Girls."

Billy lowered his voice. "How was Candy Girls, anyway? I heard the girls there are first-class hot all the way."

Kyra cleared her throat. "Hi, Billy. It's Kyra."

"Damn, J-Mac. Can't you warn a brother?" He coughed. "Hi, Kyra. I meant to say, I heard there were some fine young women working there."

"There are. One of them just might help you catch a killer."

Jake finished some business with Billy and ended the call.

"Now I have an excuse to go into the station today." Kyra ate the last of her scrambled eggs. "I'm going to start working on resources for Sydney's family and friends. Is that okay with you? I have to be near the action, Jake."

"I know you do, and it's fine with me. You *are* part of the task force."

"Aren't you glad I brought my own car? Now you can

head off to work anytime you like, and nobody will be the wiser."

Jake threw back the rest of his coffee. "Don't kid yourself. Everyone already knows we're sleeping together."

As he turned, Kyra put her hand on his arm. "Is it more than that?"

He pulled her off the stool and whispered against her lips, "It is for me."

An hour later when he arrived at the station without Kyra, Brandon pulled him aside. "Amid all the good news today, I gotta be the one to spoil the party."

Jake tensed. "What is it?"

"Those IP addresses for Laprey and his aliases? All fake."

Jake shook his head. "Fake how?"

"All housed with servers in other countries. He patched and spliced through. Probably why he used so many different usernames and accounts. He moved from server to server."

"That means you can't track him."

"Not through the accounts he used on Websleuths."

"Damn." Jake slammed his fist on his desk. "Can you keep trying to recover his private communications?"

"I will. I'll get as much data as I can on this guy—who else he messaged on that board, what he communicated. It's not nothing, Detective."

"I know that, Brandon. It allowed us to connect him to the copycat killings and identify him as The Player—the original." Jake studied Brandon as he adjusted his glasses and looked away. "What? What's wrong?"

"I mean, is he really The Player? I heard that's based on some flimsy proof from Roger Quinn, the detective who couldn't solve the case. Some people are saying Quinn is just piggybacking on this to clear his own cold case."

"Is that what they're saying?" Jake squinted and Brandon took a few steps back. "They can believe what they want, but as long as I'm head of this task force, that's the party line. Believe it or not…at your own risk."

"Yes, sir. I mean, I'm not saying I don't. I'm just saying…" Brandon trailed off and swallowed.

"Glad you told me." Jake aimed a finger at Brandon's chest. "Now you're treating him as if he is The Player, right?"

"Absolutely, sir." Brandon retreated from the desk.

Jake rubbed his chin. Did the rest of the task force think he was too tied to Quinn and the old cases? Kyra's mother's case? Hell, what did it matter? They'd stopped the first two copycats and with the information from Barbi, they'd stop the third. And if his instincts proved right, they'd catch The Player, too, and he could hand him on a silver platter to Quinn…and Kyra.

A hushed whisper rippled through the room, and several of the guys crowded at the window.

He looked at Morgan Reppucci, the lone woman in the room "What's going on?"

Morgan rolled her eyes. "They just heard that the dancer from Candy Girls is in the parking lot."

Jake clapped his hands. "What're you guys? Thirteen?"

Morgan said, "That's what I'm saying."

Morgan's partner peeled away from the window and shoved her shoulder. "Don't give me that. When we saw The Rock in that restaurant, you had to wipe the drool from your face."

Jake laughed along with the guys, and Morgan reddened. "That's different."

One of the officers peering outside said, "Never mind. She looks more like a Barbara than a Barbi, anyway."

Luckily for Barbi, she was not headed for the task force war room. Brandon had set up a computer, queuing last night's Candy Girl surveillance video in one of the small conference rooms. Billy was meeting her downstairs and taking her up to the viewing room.

Barbi had requested that Kyra be in the room with them, and Jake approved of that. Kyra had been in the club last night, too. Maybe she'd remember the guy.

Jake tried to keep things in perspective. All they had right now was a swizzle stick on the body from a gentlemen's club where Mike liked to place his hands around the neck of a lap dancer. So far they only had Barbi's word that Mike had been there on the same nights as the murders. But once they had a suspect, they could start looking into him.

Kyra walked into the war room, nodded in his direction and stashed her purse in the bottom drawer of her desk. She pointed at the door and exited again.

He followed her out. He'd have to give her the bad news about The Player's IP addresses, but that could wait. When he caught up to her, he asked, "Everything okay at your place?"

"Everything's fine. I reviewed my security cam, and nobody even came close to my apartment last night or this morning."

"Good. Did you feed Spot?"

"I swear, if you're so worried about that flea-bitten critter, you should take him in at your house."

"That would give Fiona even more reason to come back." They arrived at the conference room where Barbi, her face devoid of makeup, her hair in a braid, sat in front of the computer.

Still a pretty woman, but not what the guys in the other room had expected. "Hi, Barbi. Thanks for coming to the station."

From behind her glasses, her eyes sought Kyra's face, and Kyra smiled and took the seat next to Barbi. "Are you doing okay?"

"Yeah, just want to get this over with. I am so creeped out right now."

Billy reached for the mouse. "It'll be easy."

Jake hovered over Billy's shoulder as Billy clicked the mouse and said, "This is the club's opening last night. Pepper gave us everything."

Jake held out his hand. "Before we start, to be clear, Barbi, you're saying Mike came to the club twice this week, right? The night before we found that body in Topanga Canyon and last night."

"That's right. The first time, he was all excited and pumped-up, last night not so much. He has mood swings like that. When he's down, he usually doesn't request a lap dance."

"Okay, hit it, Detective Crouch."

Billy started the footage, and Barbi hunched forward to peer at the customers coming through the door. Thirty minutes in, she jabbed her finger at the screen. "That's Mike."

They all seemed to expel the same breath, as Billy stopped the video and snapped a picture of the frame showing a big guy with sloping shoulders in a jacket with a motorcycle on the back.

That was the only distinctive thing about him. He'd turned his face away from the camera—as if he knew it was there—and his hair, an indeterminate shade of brown, obscured his profile.

Starting up the video again, Billy said, "Maybe we'll get a better look at him when he reaches his table."

The camera at the entrance didn't include the club itself, and they lost sight of Mike after he paid—with cash—and slipped through the black doors.

Billy noted the time on a piece of paper, clicked on another folder on the computer's desktop and sped through the video of the area surrounding the stage to a few seconds after Mike walked through the doors.

They got a good look at some of the patrons as they took their seats, ordered drinks and waved at the stage, but none of the footage included Mike.

"I don't see him. He doesn't usually sit at those tables. He's off to this side." She jerked her thumb to the right.

Billy held up his finger. "All is not lost. There's one more view Pepper gave us from over the bar. Maybe he got caught in that."

Jake murmured, "Or maybe he knows where the cameras are stationed and keeps clear."

Billy launched the third camera view and zeroed in on a table Barbi picked out.

"That's his leg. That's all I can tell you." She slumped in her seat. "I'm sorry I couldn't be more helpful."

"You're not done yet." Jake put his hand on Billy's shoulder. "Detective Crouch is going to take you to see our sketch artist. We called her in today. We'll get a composite out there. That'll be a huge help."

Barbi scooted her chair back. "I can definitely do that."

"And if Pepper can get us footage from the night earlier this week, maybe we'll have better luck finding a full view of Mike." Jake leaned in toward Billy as he rose. "Can you find Jansen from Vice and send him in here?

I saw him earlier. He used to hang out at Candy Girls when he was undercover."

Billy nodded. "Some guys have it rough."

When they left, Jake said to Kyra, "It's a start."

His personal phone buzzed, and he fished it from his pocket. "Hi, Tess."

"Where's Fiona?"

"She's still at Lyric's house. Lyric's brother is giving her a ride home this afternoon, but I told Fiona to give me a call if she wanted me to pick her up—and I can."

"Jake, it *is* the afternoon. I just texted her and the message didn't show as delivered, so I called her and it rolled right over to voice mail."

Jake's belly fluttered for a second when he glanced at the time on his phone. He hadn't realized they'd spent so much time with Barbi. "Did you call Lyric?"

"I don't have Lyric's phone number, do you?"

"I don't." Jake licked his dry lips. "But I have Mrs. Becker's number. Do you want me to call her?"

"I guess not yet. I'll call and text Fiona a few more times, and you can do the same…when you have time. If we don't get any response by four o'clock, then call Mrs. Becker."

"Okay, I'll text her right now." Jake ended the call and typed a message to Fiona. He tapped the display to send it and watched the little blue text balloon sit there. He twisted his head toward Kyra, busy on her own phone. "I'm going to text you as a test."

"Go right ahead." She held her phone in front of her face. "Everything okay with Fiona?"

"I'm sure it is." He sent the text to Kyra, heard a zipping sound from his phone and watched the Delivered message appear beneath the text. It hadn't done that with the text he'd sent to Fiona.

"Got it." She held up her phone.

"Yeah, I know you did because it says *delivered* beneath it." He switched to Fiona's text and leaned over to show Kyra. "Your text said it was delivered. Hers doesn't. That was what happened the night she traveled from Monterey to LA and turned off her phone."

"Turned off or dead."

"And calls go straight to voice mail."

"Yes."

He hadn't waited for Kyra's answer, tapping Fiona's name on the display. His gut tightened when he heard Fiona's voice. "Not here. *T-T-Y-L*."

"What does *T-T-Y-L* mean again?"

"It means *talk to you later*." Her eyebrows knitted over her nose. "Straight to voice mail?"

"Yeah. I'm sure she's okay. She was going to hang out with Lyric this afternoon. If something had happened to the girls, Mrs. Becker would've called by now."

Jansen stuck his head in the room. "Cool Breeze said you wanted to see me."

"We might have a suspect in the Copycat Three case who frequented Candy Girls."

"Got a hit on the stir stick, huh?"

"Thanks to you." Jake gestured with his hand. "Can you have a look at this guy in the video and tell me if you recognize him? It's not very good, but it's all we got. Our witness is with the sketch artist now."

"Sure." Jansen nodded to Kyra.

Jake rubbed his eyes, his gut still knotted. "I'm sorry. Kyra Chase, this is Detective Trevor Jansen, with Vice."

Jansen took Barbi's chair and ran through the portion

of the video where Mike entered the club a few times. "Can't help you, but that jacket he's wearing is for posers."

"Huh?" Jake tried to focus.

"He has a jacket with a motorcycle on the back. No hard-core biker is going to wear that. You can cross the bikers off your list of suspects."

"Thanks for your time, Jansen. I'll send you a copy of the sketch when it's ready."

As soon as Jansen stepped out of the room, Jake called Lyric's mother. Her phone went to voice mail, too, but not immediately. "Mrs. Becker, this is Jake McAllister, Fiona's father. Again, thanks for having her over this weekend. Her mother and I are trying to reach her and it seems her phone is turned off. Could you please have her call me? Thanks."

Jake captured his phone between his hands. "If she's pulled another stunt like she did last week, she is going to be in big trouble."

"I'm sure her phone just died—for real this time." Kyra squeezed his biceps. "Maybe you should go home. Everything's under control here. Everyone's doing what they should be doing."

"Go home?" He paced a few steps, dragging his hand through his hair. "You're right. I can't concentrate. I'll check in on the sketch session."

Jake peeked into the room where the sketch artist, Jessica Finch, was working with Barbi.

Jessica gave him a thumbs-up. "We're almost done. She's doing great."

"Great. I have to run so I'm going to hand you off to Detective Crouch. Thanks, Barbi."

Jake practically plowed into Billy in the hallway outside Castillo's office. "Billy, can you handle the sketch when Jessica's done? Make sure Jansen gets a copy. I—I have to get home."

Billy's nostrils flared. "Everything okay with Fiona?"

He must look as panicked as he felt. "She's with a friend, but we can't reach her phone. It's turned off."

"Or the battery died." Kyra pressed a hand against his back.

"Go, go, go. I'm sure she's okay, but you need to be home." He snapped his fingers in the air. "Don't worry about anything. I can handle the sketch and anything else that comes up. It's Sunday. Most of the team will be out of here soon, anyway."

On the way out of the station, with Kyra by his side, Jake tried to text and call Fiona again, with the same results.

Kyra walked with him to his car. "I'm following you home, and I don't even care if Fiona's already there and sees me."

"Do you think she's there?" Jake had a new hope to cling to.

"She might be. Maybe Lyric's brother dropped her off and she fell asleep. She's probably tired after the weekend she had."

"Maybe you're right."

Jake watched both of his phones on the drive back to his place, jumping every time a text came through. By the time he got home and through the front door, it was four o'clock. He expected a call from Tess at any minute, and he hoped like hell he could tell her their daughter was asleep in her room.

He left the front door open for Kyra and bounded up the stairs, two at a time. He burst into Fiona's room and nearly dropped to his knees when he saw her empty bed.

When his personal phone buzzed, he snatched it from

his pocket with an unsteady hand. He took a deep breath before answering. "Mrs. Becker, is Fiona with you? Put her on, please."

"I'm sorry, Mr. McAllister, Fiona isn't with us. She said you were picking her up at The Grove. That was almost two hours ago."

Chapter Thirteen

By the time Kyra reached the bedroom upstairs, Jake was on the phone, pacing, his hand by his side, clenching and unclenching. His gaze wandered past her, unseeing.

"Wait, what are you talking about? I'm here, at home. I didn't pick her up. That wasn't our arrangement, and she never called me."

Kyra balled a fist against her belly. Then she tugged at his sleeve to slow him down.

Jake seemed suddenly aware of her presence and put the phone on speaker just in time for her to hear Mrs. Becker's voice come over the line.

"I'm sorry, Mr. McAllister. That's what Lyric told me."

"Call me Jake. Is Lyric there now? Can I speak to her?"

"She's not home. Sh-she went out to eat with her father."

"Lyric's been home? You've seen her? Talked to her?"

"Yes, yes. Her brother drove her home from The Grove. She was here for about an hour, and then her father picked her up."

"When do you expect her back? I need to talk to your daughter, Mrs. Becker. Fiona turned off her phone. She hasn't answered our texts or phone calls."

"Oh, my God. I'll get on the phone to her father right

now and have him bring her home. You can come right over...and call me Ellie. I'm so sorry, Jake. I didn't know. I shouldn't have allowed the girls to change the plan."

Jake closed his eyes, his nostrils flaring. "It's all right, Ellie. It's not your fault. I'm coming over right now."

"You are a police officer, right? Is there some process you can expedite to find her?"

"I'm going to track down the location of her phone before it went dead...or was turned off."

"Lyric will tell you whatever you need to know... I promise you that."

"Thanks, I'm leaving now."

Jake ended the call and threw his phone at the bed where it bounced once and landed on the floor. "Dammit. Fiona did it again. She lied. But she wouldn't lie this time to get back to her mother's. Then, why?"

"Don't break your phone. You're going to need it." Kyra circled the bed and picked up the phone from the floor. As she pressed it back into Jake's hand, she said, "You're going to have to call Tess."

He grabbed the back of his neck. "I wish I didn't have to tell her anything until I know more."

"Let me drive. You need to get on the phone and start making calls. How fast can the phone company ping Fiona's cell, and do you need a warrant for that?"

He jogged downstairs and she followed, her hand on the rail so she wouldn't tumble down and plow into him.

"I pay the bill on the phone. I don't need a warrant. I'll have Billy contact the provider, and they'll at least be able to tell me where the phone was when it...went off."

"She must know you're looking for her by now. She may realize what trouble she's in and call you, like last time." Kyra hitched her purse over her shoulder and scrambled for her keys.

As Jake veered toward his car, she took his hand. "My car, remember? Where am I going?"

When they got in the car, Jake reeled off the Beckers' address as he snapped on his seat belt. Then he immediately got on the phone.

Kyra said a silent prayer for Fiona's safety as she half listened to Jake's phone calls. He was calling out all the stops for his daughter.

By the time they reached the Becker residence in Westwood, Jake had spoken to Tess, too, trying to calm and reassure her. Kyra hadn't been listening, but she couldn't block out the frantic voice of Fiona's mother blasting Jake's ear. Parents blamed each other.

Kyra parked on the street in front of a lush green lawn that must've used a lot of water to reach that shade of emerald green in the dry weather they'd been having. A Lexus occupied one side of the driveway, right next to the Tesla.

Jake had the passenger door open before she stopped the car. He strode up to the front door, which swung wide when he hit the first step.

A woman in capris and flip-flops stepped out, her arm extended as if to drag Jake inside. "I'm Ellie Becker. We're having an interesting conversation with Lyric right now."

Kyra joined Jake and stuck out her hand. "I'm Kyra Chase, Jake's friend."

"Come in, both of you. My husband had to leave."

She gestured toward a girl seated cross-legged on a white damask couch that wouldn't survive two minutes under an onslaught from Spot.

The girl sniffled and looked up through a thick fringe of curly hair, her eye makeup creating black rivulets down her face. "I—I'm sorry, but she's okay. She's with Nico."

Jake's body tensed beside hers, and Kyra touched his fingers to ground him. He had a frightened teenager in front of him, not a suspect.

He worked his jaw for a few seconds and managed to form some words in a reasonable tone. "Who's Nico, Lyric?"

"He's Fiona's boyfriend."

Jake twitched, and Kyra tugged at his hand. "Let's sit down and figure this out."

When he sat down stiffly, his shoulder bumping Kyra's, Jake asked, "How does Fiona have a boyfriend down here when she lives in Monterey?"

"She met him online." Lyric's dark brown eyes popped open, as if everyone had online boyfriends. "He's super cute. He's a surfer and lives in Malibu and he's a junior at Crossroads in Santa Monica."

Sounded too good to be true. Jake must've thought so, too, as the news hadn't relaxed him one bit. His body was so tightly strung it was vibrating.

He barely moved his lips as he asked the next question. "Did you happen to meet this paragon of surfing when he picked up Fiona at The Grove? Were you even at The Grove?"

Nodding vigorously, Lyric said, "Yes, we were at The Grove, but I never got to meet Nico. Ocean, my brother, picked me up before Nico got Fiona."

"You've seen pictures of Nico?" Kyra placed a hand on Jake's forearm, which seemed made of marble...or granite.

"Yes, of course. Fiona wouldn't just meet any random guy that she hadn't seen before." Lyric pushed her curls out of her face and squared her shoulders, as if talking to a couple of fools.

Jake took a deep breath, his chest expanding, giving him a bigger presence that dwarfed the dainty love seat.

Lyric flinched.

"Do you know where Fiona and *Nico* went after The Grove? Do you know what kind of car he drives? Do you know when and where he was going to drop her off? Where online did they meet? Dating site? Gaming? Social media? Message boards?"

That last suggestion gave Kyra a chill, and the rapid-fire questions only confused Lyric. She cast puppy-dog eyes at her mother, but Ellie crossed her arms.

"Answer him, Lyric. How was Fiona communicating with this boy? How many times have I told you not to chat with anyone online that you don't know in person?"

Lyric's mouth dropped open, her ruby-red lipstick smeared across her cheek. "How are you supposed to meet anyone?"

"Answer his questions." Ellie aimed a finger at her daughter that promised hell on earth.

"I don't know any of that other stuff. Wait, he said he had a VW van."

Jake murmured, "Of course, he did. What else do you know?"

"He was supposed to drop her back off at The Grove, but I don't know where they were going. And she met him through Instagram, where else?" She shrugged.

Ellie groaned from across the room.

Kyra asked, "Private messages?"

"Uh-huh." Lyric's pretty face was set in mulish lines. "Direct messaging. Everyone does it."

"Everyone but you, as of now." Ellie retreated to

the vast kitchen where she banged around some pots and pans.

Jake's phone buzzed and he answered right away. He paused for a few seconds and then said, "Got it. Yeah, that makes sense. Thanks, we'll start there, pulling footage." He listened. "I'll let you know."

He reported to the rest of them. "Fiona's phone last pinged at The Grove, so no surprise there. It's been off ever since. We can start looking at video as soon as Lyric tells us where Fiona was meeting this guy."

"Oh… Oh, I know that." Lyric wriggled in her seat. "He was supposed to pick her up in front of the movie theaters there, where Ocean got me, but when Ocean and I were driving away I saw her walking on Fairfax and I yelled out the window at her. She said Nico was picking her up at Uncommon Grounds, the coffee place around the corner from The Grove."

Ellie slammed something down in the kitchen. "Are you telling me your brother knew about this scheme?"

"No, I told him it was Fiona's dad picking her up." Lyric started gnawing on a fingernail. "Sorry."

"One more thing, Lyric." Jake managed a smile. "What was Fiona wearing when you last saw her?"

"Oh, I know that, too." Lyric sat up straight and flicked back her hair. "She was wearing a denim skirt with a frayed hem, distressed on one side, a gray T-shirt with red sleeves and the word *honey* on it and white Vans. So cute."

"You were a big help, Lyric." Jake stood up and towered over the girl on the couch. "But you should know that anybody you talk to online can be anyone, tell lies. I hope you're right about Nico being a cute surfer boy, but he could just as well be a thirty-five-year-old predator and Fiona walked right into his trap."

JAKE SLUMPED IN the passenger seat of Kyra's car and dug his thumbs into his temples. "How'd I do in there? I didn't want to scare Lyric or blame her or Ellie."

"You did amazing under the circumstances." Kyra brushed the back of her hand along his cheek, her touch cool and soothing against his flaming skin. He'd been alternating between ice-cold fear and hot rage during that entire interview. How could Fiona be so naive? She should've spent more time in his nitty-gritty world and less in the bubble of Monterey.

"I'm going to have Billy request the footage from Uncommon Grounds. Damn, is that place a magnet for weirdos or what? The first copycat worked and found his victims there, and now some scammer has snatched my daughter from the same place."

"Don't think that way. It's not the same place, anyway. Jordy Cannon's Uncommon Grounds was in West Hollywood. This is a new one at The Grove."

"That makes me feel not one bit better, but thanks for trying. Do you think the Instagram account where she met this guy is the secret one?"

"The Finsta."

"The what?"

"That's what the kids call the second, secret Instagram account. It's a combination of fake and insta. I did a little research the night Fiona showed up on your doorstep."

"I feel so…old." He pulled out his work phone and put in another call to Billy, who was almost as upset about Fiona's disappearance as he was. He instructed him to request the footage for around two o'clock from Uncommon Grounds.

Then he called Tess, who answered on the first ring. She seemed encouraged by the news that Fiona was meeting a boy, and Jake didn't have the heart to set her straight. He wished he could believe Fiona was giggling and stealing kisses with a slightly older high school boy, but his gut and experience had him on a precipice of a black hole of terror.

Kyra tapped the steering wheel to get his attention. "I'm driving straight to Uncommon Grounds at The Grove, right?"

"Yeah, we should get there before Billy, but he'll call ahead so they can be ready for us." He smacked his fist into his other palm. "I should've called her on that secret account. I should've made her show me her private messages."

"Before you go blaming yourself, I'm the one who told you to play dumb on that account. Who knows if you would've discovered anything that way? Seems as if she's been keeping this secret for a while." Kyra sucked in her bottom lip. "You know, it's probably why she came down here, don't you?"

"You mean to meet Nico instead of see me?" Jake clenched his jaw. "Yeah, I know."

When Kyra drove up to the coffeehouse, Jake directed her to park in the small lot next to the building even though cars already filled every slot. "Go ahead and squeeze into that space on the end. I guarantee you will not have to pay any ticket."

She parked and they strode into the coffeehouse, Jake two paces ahead of Kyra. He took a deep breath and slowed his gait. She'd put her life on hold to support him…and he needed her.

Getting his badge ready, Jake approached the counter. "I'm here to see the manager, Melissa Cho."

"One second, please." The young woman at the counter spun around and disappeared into a room off the kitchen. She returned with a woman only slightly older than herself, sporting purple streaks through her straight, black hair.

"I'm Mel Cho. You must be the detective from the LAPD. Can I see some ID?"

Jake flipped his wallet open to expose his badge, and Mel studied it through a pair of chunky-rimmed glasses. "Come around the side. I'll let you into the office. Since your partner called, I've been queuing up the security cam footage from about one forty-five. Do you want me to run it for you?"

"That would be great, thanks." He tipped his head toward Kyra. "My associate will be joining us."

"It'll be a tight squeeze, but we should all fit." She swung open the bottom half of a Dutch door, and Jake waved Kyra through first.

She hadn't been kidding about the size of the office, which boasted one built-in desk, two chairs and a filing cabinet. Jake pulled out the chairs in front of the computer, which had a picture of the front of the shop frozen on the screen. "You two sit down. Mel, you can drive, and I'll hang over your shoulder, if that's okay."

"That's fine by me. I have two camera views up—one for the front of the store and one facing the counter."

Jake said, "Let's go with the one out front first. I doubt they were here for a coffee."

Mel clicked the mouse on the frame, and the figures started moving across the screen. Several minutes had passed by when a girl's bare legs came into view. She had white Vans on her feet.

Jake pointed to the image. "That's her. Can you capture that frame?"

"Just let me know which ones you want, and I'll save them and print them out for you."

"Thanks, Mel. Keep going."

Fiona walked a few more feet, and Jake got a look at the skirt and the red sleeves of her T-shirt from behind. "Save it. Just save every frame with her in it. It looks like she's waiting. She's not going inside."

Kyra tapped her fingers on her knee. "I hope he doesn't just pick her up at the curb. We might see the car, but unless it takes off at just the right angle, we won't get a license plate."

"I don't think anyone can stop on Fairfax on a Sunday afternoon." Mel flicked her fingers at the monitor. "She might walk around back to meet a ride."

Fiona tripped to a stop and turned. Her arms came up and she crossed them over her chest. Her eyes widened and Jake's heart lurched. Even from the grainy footage, he could see fear there, or at least uncertainty.

Kyra must've sensed the same thing, as she shifted in her seat and drew in a breath. "What does she see?"

Jake said grimly, "She probably sees a guy who looks nothing like the cute surfer, Nico."

A larger figure came into the frame, a man with dark hair and a jacket. The hat pulled low on his forehead hid his face. He moved close to Fiona, and Jake clenched his fists.

"Is he touching her? Grabbing her?"

Kyra hunched forward. "I can't see, but he's very close to her."

Mel whistled. "Is he forcing her to go with him? That's what it looks like to me."

"She's going with him." Jake's jaw ached from clenching as he watched this strange man—too big and bulky to be a teen—lead his daughter away.

Mel froze the tape and captured the frame as the couple began to move out of the frame. "We'll get this, and one more as they walk away."

When they turned and Mel stopped the video, a roaring sound rushed through Jake's head and he gripped the back of Mel's chair so he wouldn't fall over. "Zoom in. Zoom in on the back of the guy's jacket."

He didn't need Kyra's cry to confirm the horror before his eyes. The man escorting his daughter away from Uncommon Grounds had a motorcycle on the back of his jacket—just like Copycat Three.

Chapter Fourteen

Kyra covered her mouth with both hands. It couldn't be. Why? How? What did Copycat Three want with Jake's daughter?

Mel twisted her head around to look at Jake. "What's wrong?"

Jake cleared his throat. "That jacket belongs to a very dangerous man. That girl is in big trouble."

The steadiness of his voice amazed Kyra…and worried her a little. "Mel, print all those out. Are there any other cameras that point to your parking lot? Bank nearby? Convenience store?"

"Th-there are a few." Mel clicked the keys on the keyboard, and the printer on the corner of the desk woke up and started spitting out pages.

Jake gathered the printouts and thanked Mel. He walked out of the shop without saying a word to Kyra, who was trying to keep up with him. When he hit the sidewalk, he staggered and placed a hand on the corner of the building. "He has her. Copycat Three has Fiona."

She put her hand over his. "We'll find her. We'll get her back. You're onto him, and he doesn't even know it. He's gone too far, Jake."

"What does he want with her? Is he using her to get back at me? Does he want ransom or clear sailing out of here?" He pulled Kyra next to him and buried his face in her hair. "I'll give him anything, Kyra. Then I'll kill him."

"Let's get back to the station. Call Billy and tell him. Get the task force on it. You can't do this alone, Jake. Maybe Copycat Three knows you have him in your sights, and this is his way to negotiate an escape plan." She cupped his chin in her palm. "Fiona is not his type. We know that. She's not going to satisfy his urge."

A tremble rolled through Jake's large frame. "It'll satisfy his urge to gut me. He's been planning this for a while. That's what he meant in his note."

When they got back to her car, Jake resumed his phone calls—the first to his partner, Billy.

One thought swam in her head. The Player, the person directing Mike—Copycat Three—wouldn't like this latest development. Mike had gone rogue. The other two serial killers taking orders from The Player had ended their own lives rather than give up their mentor and his secrets. Mike would have to be reminded that The Player would never condone engaging with the police like this—it put him at risk.

When Jake ended one call and before he punched in the next, Kyra touched his arm. "How far did Brandon get with the IP addresses of The Player's aliases on Websleuths?"

He blinked at her for a few seconds. "I'm sorry, Kyra. I never had the chance to tell you that The Player has been using masked IP addresses located all over the world. There's no tracing those back to someone's computer sitting on a desk somewhere."

The news socked her in the gut, but Jake had his own problems right now. "That's bad news, but you'll get

him too now that Mike has outed himself in a spectac-
ular way."

"We'll deal with The Player later. If I have an opportunity, and I'm hoping for one, I'll kill Mike without a
second thought to nabbing The Player. He just needs to
give me one excuse."

"I understand that. Do you think we can communicate
with Mike through Fiona's Instagram account? Brandon
can probably get us in. It might give Mike pause when
he realizes we know about that account."

"That's a good idea. In the meantime, Billy has officers talking to every employee at Candy Girls about
Mike—what he drinks, how he pays, who he talks to,
what he drives, if they've seen it. I just know it's not a
VW van." He slammed his fists against her dashboard.
"I can't get over Fiona's face when she saw Mike instead
of her teenage dreamboat. She must've been scared. She
must've realized she'd made a mistake."

"Fiona is a resourceful girl. Although she showed incredibly poor judgment, she's no dummy. She's going to
be fine." Kyra gripped the steering wheel so Jake couldn't
see her trembling hands.

When they walked into the station, the task force war
room was buzzing with activity. Billy had called in the
troops, and they were here on a Sunday night to support
their leader.

She touched Jake on the shoulder before letting him
get sucked into the waiting masses. "I'm going to find
Brandon."

Jake held up his phone. "Don't bother. I've got a call
from an unknown number coming in now."

He put the phone on speaker for the entire room to
hear, and the voice proved Jake correct.

"Hey, *J-Mac*, it's the Hollywood Strangler because

that's the name I prefer, and I'm calling the shots now. I have something you want."

"Where's my daughter and what do you want?"

Copycat Three choked. He hadn't been expecting Jake to know he'd been the one who'd snatched Fiona.

He recovered quickly. "I'll let you know when I have my list of demands. My *own* rules."

"You mean instead of The Player's rules. We know you've been taking orders from him. You all have. He's not going to like this new development, is he? What rule did you break by kidnapping the daughter of the lead detective on your case? That must be rule numbers five, six, seven and eight."

"Shut up. I'm my own man. He just gave us some tips. I'm my own boss. I don't answer to no one."

"What are your new rules, Mike? What do you want? We can work with you."

"Mike." He snorted. "Who gave you that name? That bitch Barbi? You'd better tell that whore to watch her back. I'll give you my rules when I'm good and ready."

Jake's jaw formed a hard line. "How do I know you haven't harmed her already?"

A rustling noise came over the line and then Fiona's voice. "Daddy? Daddy, I'm so sorry. I'm—"

She didn't get to finish her sentence. Mike returned. "There. She's okay...for now."

Mike ended the call, and it was as if the people in the room who'd been holding their breaths, hanging on to every word, were released from a spell. Talking, movement, phone calls, keyboards—everything came to life at once.

Including Kyra.

She bolted from the room and jogged downstairs to Brandon's small cube. He sat in command over the four computers on his desk, scooting his chair between the keyboards and monitors.

"Brandon, did you hear?"

"I heard." His fingers raced across one keyboard, bringing lines of characters up on one screen. "I just wish I knew who Mike was on Websleuths. Jordy Cannon and Cyrus Fisher never bothered to mask their IP addresses. I doubt Mike did, either."

"There's something else I want you to look at." She wheeled a chair next to his. "Can you get into someone's Instagram and their direct messages if I give you the address?"

"Compared to this?" Brandon spread his hands, encompassing his computers cranking away and spewing out data. "Child's play."

"The account is for a user called Jazzy Noir." She held her breath as Brandon cleared one of his computers and launched Instagram.

He brought up Fiona's secret account, and Kyra scanned it for any new activity. Fiona had posted a few new pictures from LA, nothing too explicit or disturbing—she'd saved that for her private messages.

"Is this it?"

"Yes, can you get into the direct messages?"

"I can if I'm logged in as Jazzy." Brandon's fingers froze. "Wait, is this J-Mac's daughter?"

"It is." She put a finger to her lips. "He's working on something else upstairs. Mike called him on a burner phone, and they're working on tracking down the serial number of the phone and where it was purchased. I told Jake I was going to check Fiona's Finsta. She thinks it's a secret, but Jake has known about it for a while."

"Yeah, I remember those days. I used to have a secret

Facebook account that my parents didn't know about."
Brandon flushed under her side-eye and got to work.

Lines of numbers and characters raced down the monitor until the display stopped. Brandon crowed, "Got it,
baby."

He accessed the application again, bringing up the
log-in page. He entered a username and password, and
Jazzy Noir's account opened in user mode.

"Oh, my God. You are *the man*. I'm not even going to
tell your mother about your secret accounts." She pulled
the keyboard toward her. "May I?"

"It's your party. I'll go back to what I was doing before
you came in. Let me know if you need any help. I can't
believe this guy has J-Mac's daughter. She's just a kid."

Kyra leaned in close to the monitor and clicked the
message icon in the upper-right corner of the screen. A
list of messages tumbled down the page, the little circles
with profile pictures lining up with the names.

She caught her breath when she saw most of the messages from an account featuring a suntanned blond in
board shorts with the name of Surfernico. She'd hit the
mother lode.

Her heart pounded as she scanned through the messages. Nico/Mike had been filling Fiona's head with everything a girl would want to hear and had roped her in
easily. Kyra got to the last message exchanged where
they discussed meeting up in LA, but there was nothing
about meeting at The Grove. How had they communicated? Hopefully, when Jake got Fiona's phone records,
he would be able to see those texts or calls.

Kyra flexed her fingers and took a deep breath. She
entered her first message.

Mike, this is Kyra Chase. If you want to make The Player happy, you'll exchange Fiona for me.

She knew enough about this platform to know Mike should be getting an email with a notification that he had a new direct message. She watched the cursor, biting her lip so hard she drew blood. When her phone buzzed, she jumped.

She swept the blood from her lip with her tongue before she answered Jake's call. "Any news?"

"Not yet, but we're doing everything we can. We have a lot of people talking to us about Mike, telling us who he hung out with at the club, maybe even a description of his car."

"Have you gotten Fiona's phone records, yet?"

"Working on it. Where are you?"

"Getting some information from Brandon."

"Anything on Fiona's fake Instagram account, yet?"

Kyra shifted her gaze to Brandon and said, "Not yet. Let me know if you need me, okay? I love you."

Jake paused, taken aback.

Not wanting to put him on the spot, she ended the call. She whispered to the screen. "C'mon, c'mon."

Ten minutes later, she got her wish. A reply came through on Fiona's direct message. "Who are you?"

She typed back furiously, telling him to check with The Player. Telling Mike that The Player wouldn't be happy that he took a cop's daughter, but he'd be very happy if Mike had Kyra Chase. She made a play for his emotions, suggesting that Fiona wasn't even his type. He wouldn't be punishing the woman he wanted to punish if he killed someone like Fiona.

She held her breath. Had she gone too far?

He made her wait almost twenty minutes, but the wait was worth it. A pulse danced in her throat as she read his message: I'll take you.

JAKE HAD TWENTY things going on at once, but it helped him keep the panic at bay. They were drawing the net tighter around Mike, but he still hadn't called Jake with any demands. Maybe Mike would wait on those demands until he felt he didn't have a choice. The police still hadn't come knocking on his door, so he had time.

He checked the time. Copycat Three had kidnapped Fiona over six hours ago. What was he doing to his little girl? Jake squeezed his eyes closed and ground his back teeth together. He wanted just ten minutes alone with the guy.

"Jake, Fiona's phone records." Billy shoved a sheaf of papers at him and clapped him on the shoulder. "It's going to be okay, brother. We got you."

Nodding, Jake greedily snatched the papers from Billy's hand and slammed them onto his desk. He pulled up his chair and ran a finger down the last of Fiona's calls and texts. They included calls to Tess and him, Lyric and several texts that looked like they were to friends. He didn't see anything out of the ordinary. How had she been communicating with him?

Must be that fake Instagram account, but if Kyra had found something she would've let him know by now. He grabbed his phone and checked the time. He hadn't heard from Kyra in almost two hours.

Jake stuck Fiona's phone records on Billy's desk. "I'm going to check in on Brandon downstairs. I can't see anything on here from Fiona's phone that points to our guy, but maybe it needs some fresh eyes."

Billy said, "I've got it covered."

Jake jogged downstairs to the IT department and squeezed into Brandon's cubicle. "Where's Kyra?"

"She's, um—" Brandon shoved his glasses up the bridge of his nose "—not sure. She was on the computer for a while, said she had to take a phone call, stepped into the hallway for several minutes and then popped back in here to grab her purse and take off. I thought she was going back upstairs to see you and tell you about Fiona's account."

"Fiona's account?" Jake drew his eyebrows over his nose. "You got in?"

"Yeah, it was easy. I nailed the username and password pretty quickly and handed them off to Kyra."

"Why the hell didn't she tell me that?" Jake pulled out the chair next to Brandon and sat on the edge. "Can you get me into that account?"

"Absolutely." Brandon pulled the keyboard into his lap and accessed the application. Leaning over, he checked another computer monitor and then typed in the log-in information for Fiona's Jazzy Noir account. "There you go."

When he placed the keyboard back on the desk in front of him, Jake started scrolling through the page, his eye twitching at the corner. "Brandon, how do I see direct messages on here?"

"It's that little airplane icon in the upper-right corner."

Jake moved the cursor over the icon, but before he could click on it, his personal phone rang. He glanced at the unknown caller and answered, "McAllister."

"Daddy? Daddy, I'm so sorry. Please come and get me."

Jake jumped up so fast the chair shot out from beneath him and hit the wall. "Where are you, Fiona?"

"I—I'm not sure. I'm in an alley. He dumped me off in an alley, but he had me blindfolded."

"Are you…all right?"

"I'm okay." She sniffled. "He tied me up. He hit me, but I'm all right, Daddy. He's gone now."

Rage throbbed against his temples. "Are you borrowing someone's phone? Ask them where you are."

"Wait, I see two street signs. I'm at a corner, a busy corner."

"What are the street signs?" She couldn't just ask the owner of the phone?

"It's Selma. Selma and Wilcox."

Relief swept through his body, and he took the first deep breath he'd had in hours. "Sweetie, you're in Hollywood. You're near Sunset. I'm going to send a squad car and an ambulance out to you right now, but I'm on my way. Where is he? Where's… Nico?"

Fiona sobbed. "His name wasn't Nico, Daddy. He was an old man."

"I know that, sweetie. He took you to get back at me. Why'd he let you go?"

"I—I thought you sent her."

A feather of fear brushed the back of his neck. "Sent who?"

"Kyra. Kyra Chase. He let me go…and took her."

Chapter Fifteen

Kyra strained against the zip ties binding her wrists behind her. "She's safe? You left her someplace safe?"

The man in front of her, on the other side of the battered kitchen table, ran a hand through his messy brown hair and crossed his arms over his belly, which hung over the waistband of his jeans. "I dropped her off in an alley with her purse. I left her tied up, but not too tight. Just to give us some time to get away. When she gets loose, she can get to a phone. Glad to get rid of her. She was annoying."

Kyra flattened the smile from her lips. She could only imagine. Fiona had gotten from Monterey to LA by herself; she could figure out how to contact her father or hail down a cop car.

"Who is she, Mike?"

He scowled, his heavy brow hanging over his eyes. "What do you mean? Who is she?"

"The woman with the long, brown hair you keep killing over and over."

He snorted. "You psychologists think you're so smart. Not one of you could ever figure me out. Not one at that third-rate college I went to ever knew what I was capable of. Nobody did."

"Except The Player."

His head shot up, and fear raced through his dark eyes. He tilted his head from side to side, cracking his neck. "Not even he knew. Be careful, he said. Don't engage law enforcement, he said. Don't communicate, he said. I didn't follow that stupid rule, and look where it got me? It got me you."

Kyra locked her jaw for a second to stop the chattering of her teeth. "You told The Player you had me?"

"I did." Mike slammed a fist against the table. "He was worried about that, even after I told him our deal."

Their deal consisted of Kyra staying on video call with him so he could see her leaving the station alone. Nobody would be able to track the phone to her location now because she'd tossed it, along with her purse and weapon, out the car window on the way to their meeting place.

Mike had picked her up on a deserted street corner in Hollywood with Fiona in the car, and Kyra got a quick look at the girl, her face white beneath her blindfold, before he'd shoved Kyra into the car with her and blindfolded and zip-tied her, too. She'd been able to assure Fiona that everything was going to be okay.

Mike had driven around for a while before parking and leading a sobbing Fiona away. Kyra had kept her ears tuned to any sounds of gunfire or violence, but hadn't heard anything ominous.

Fiona'd had no idea where Mike had taken and held her. Mike had turned off Fiona's phone and dumped it. There was no way Jake could trace her back to this small house. The best she could hope for was that the police would locate her car, and maybe Mike's car would show up on CCTV in the area.

"Is he coming here? The Player?" She'd managed to utter his name through parched lips.

"We haven't figured it out yet." Mike stared off into space, and a smile touched his lips. "Her name was Jenna."

"What was she to you?" Kyra straightened in her chair. The more she found out about Mike, the better chance she had of getting away alive.

"College girlfriend, at least I wanted her to be. I played football in college, Division 3 school. I thought that would be enough to score points with her, but she always went for the pretty boys."

Kyra lowered her voice. "Did you hurt Jenna?"

"She had to pay." He rolled his big shoulders.

"You killed her?"

"No." His eyes flashed. "She screamed and some guys from a frat house stopped me. Three on one, that's the only way they could handle me. Kicked my ass and then got me kicked off the football team and out of the school."

"And you've been making her pay ever since." Kyra swallowed. "What do you do with the…panties?"

"I hide them here at home." He puffed out his chest, which consisted of more flab than muscle. "That's how far I got with Jenna. I got her panties off. Kept 'em, too. I shoved them into my pocket when those frat boys attacked me. Got away with them."

"What do you do with the severed fingers?"

The corner of Mike's mouth curled. "Those are for him."

A shaft of pain pierced her head. "What other rules does The Player have you follow?"

Mike flattened his hands on the table and hunched forward. "What do you know about the rules?"

"The police know more than you think, more than they let on."

He tucked a clump of hair behind his ear and fell back into a chair. "Just the regular stuff. He's not that brilliant. No fingerprints. No DNA—that's why we don't rape them. And then this stupid rule about not taunting law enforcement. What's the point if you can't lord it over them? Lord it over *him*."

"Jake McAllister?"

"Yeah, him. I bet he played quarterback on his football team. Didn't he?"

"I don't think Jake played football. He played water polo. He was a goalie because of his height."

"Water polo?" Mike giggled, an uncomfortable sound coming from a big man. "That's not a man's sport."

"So, maybe McAllister isn't as perfect as you think."

Mike hit the table with his fist, and she jumped. "I don't think he's perfect."

"Did you kill Sean Hughes?"

"Me?" His eyes rounded. "I didn't kill him, but I know who did."

"The Player." Kyra used her legs to scoot her chair forward. "Who is he, Mike?"

Mike bared his teeth when he smiled, which, when coupled with his shaggy hair, gave him a feral appearance. "I guess you're gonna find that out real soon."

ON HIS WAY to meet Fiona, Jake tried Kyra's phone over and over. Just like Fiona's phone before, Kyra's was dead. He'd put in an order to ping Kyra's phone so they could at least get her last location.

How could Kyra have done something so stupid? Why would she trade herself for Fiona? He could've met Mike's demands to get Fiona back, but The Player would have no demands for Kyra's safe return. Jake knew that was the only possible reason Mike would give up Fiona for Kyra—to placate The Player. Kyra had known it, too.

With his heart pounding, Jake pulled up behind the

ambulance and jumped out of the car. Fiona hopped off the back of the vehicle and ran into his arms, the silver blanket from the EMTs crunching around her. She sobbed against his chest, and he crushed her like he never wanted to let her go.

"I'm so sorry, Daddy. I didn't know. I never meant for this to happen."

He patted her back. "I know. It's okay. I'm just so happy to have you back and safe. I already called your mother from the car to let her know you were okay. You are, aren't you?"

She pulled away and touched her swollen jaw. "I'm okay. He didn't, you know, do anything to me, but he hit me a few times because I told him what an idiot he was and how he was so much uglier than the picture he used."

Jake's mouth twitched. "Not a great idea to goad a serial killer. D-did you see Kyra?"

"I didn't see her, but I heard her." She covered her eyes with one hand. "Dad, she was so brave. She got into Mike's car, and she told me that everything was going to be okay. That you were all looking for me, and I would be safe now. But, what about her, Dad?"

"We'll find her." He choked. "We'll get her back."

The EMT approached them and said, "She's fine, sir. A little shaken up. We put some ice on her jaw and gave her some ibuprofen for the swelling and pain."

"Thanks. Do you need the thermal blanket back?"

"She can keep that."

A patrol officer approached. "Detective? We're canvassing the area for cameras. We have a description of his car from the club and we'll try to find it on the footage."

"Perfect."

Before he got another word out of his mouth, a second officer approached him. "Sir, we found Ms. Chase's car."

He sucked in a sharp breath. "Anything?"

"Nothing—no purse, no phone, no ID...no blood."

Jake massaged the back of his neck. "Okay, I'll be over in a minute." He turned back to Fiona.

"I'm not sending you back to my place alone. I think it might be best if I had someone take you to the station. You can wait for me there until I'm done with this scene. I'm so glad to have you back." He pulled her into a hug. "You never told me whose phone you used to call me. Can you point them out? I'd like to thank him or her, personally."

"I didn't use someone else's phone." Fiona looked down at the ground and kicked at a rock with the toe of her shoe.

"I know he didn't give you your phone back. You called me from a number I didn't recognize."

She held up one finger and then dug into her purse. She pulled out a flip phone. "I called you from this phone. I'm sorry. I bought a second phone that you and Mom didn't know about."

A surge of adrenaline flooded his body. "Did Mike know you had this phone?"

Shrugging, she said, "I don't think so. I had my other phone in my hand when he...picked me up. I turned it off myself, but he made me throw it out the window. This other phone was at the bottom of my purse. He didn't ask, and I never told him."

Jake's mouth dropped open. "You had this phone with you the whole time and it was turned on?"

"Well, yeah. Nobody ever uses it to call me—except Nico, who isn't really Nico."

Jake grabbed her shoulders and kissed her on the forehead. "I'd forgive you ten burner phones right now."

KYRA CLEARED HER THROAT. "When is he coming?"

Mike glanced up from his phone, a shock of hair hanging in his eyes. "I'm not sure. We'll figure it out. I turn you over to him, and I can go on with my plans."

"Are you sure about that?"

"What do you mean?" He wiped the back of his hand across his mouth, smearing the grease left over from the fast-food tacos.

She lifted a stiff shoulder. "Maybe he won't let you continue. You've broken the rules. You've jeopardized yourself and him."

"He doesn't have a say in whether or not I continue. I'm good at this. I haven't gotten caught yet, have I?"

"Haven't you? Once you snatched Detective McAllister's daughter, you entered a whole other realm of being public enemy number one. Do you understand how many people are working to find you now? The Player isn't going to like that."

He bit into his taco and answered with his mouth full of food. "Who cares?"

"I think you should care. Look at what happened to Jordy Cannon. Look at what happened to Cyrus Fisher." She tapped her temple. "Do you have one of those cyanide tablets, too?"

"What if I do?" He dropped the taco, which fell to pieces on his plate right next to a .45. "If you don't shut your mouth, I'll make you take it."

"Where is he?" Kyra caught sight of a light blinking outside behind Mike. Her breath hitched in her throat. Was that The Player now? Would she finally get a look at the man who had murdered her mother?

"He does things in his own way." Mike cranked his head over his shoulder, but the blinking light had stopped.

He returned to his taco, picking up chunks of meat and cheese with his fingers and stuffing them into his mouth. "He was happy I brought you in. You were right about that."

As soon as Mike turned back around, she saw the light flash again. Then a red beam lasered into the window. Would Mike see it against the wall behind her? Where had it stopped? Was it aimed at her forehead?

She tentatively rocked her chair to the side while Mike scooped up the rest of the contents of his taco. As his face dipped to his plate, she rocked harder until the chair tipped on its legs. She threw all her weight toward the floor.

On her way down, she saw Mike jump up and grab his gun.

She crashed to the floor, her cheekbone hitting one of the table legs. At the same time, the front door of the house burst open.

"Drop your weapon!"

From her vantage point, she saw Mike's feet pivot toward the other room. He screamed out at the cops, "Did he send you?"

He must've raised his gun because, in an instant, a hail of gunfire erupted in the room and Mike toppled against the blood-spattered wall.

One second later, before Kyra had time to process what had happened, Jake was crouched beside her, snipping the zip ties away and pulling her into his arms. "Are you all right? Did he hurt you?"

She looked into his face, her fingertips lightly resting on his chin. "How'd you know where I was?"

Capturing her hand, he kissed her raw wrists. "We owe it all to my sneaky, rebellious daughter."

Epilogue

"I don't know why he's your favorite person. He doesn't even feed you." She shuffled her feet against Spot to move him away from the door.

"It's male bonding." Jake scratched the cat under his chin to lessen his ire at being denied entry into Kyra's apartment.

Jake placed his hand on the small of her back as they walked to his car, parked on the street. Ever since he'd rescued her from Mike's house, he'd been hovering over her like a mother hen—a hot mother hen.

Mike turned out to be Mitchell Reed, a twenty-six-year-old security guard and former college football player. His story about Jenna had proved to be true. He'd been using his security guard credentials to lure slightly tipsy women into his car as they stumbled out of bars and clubs by themselves.

Whether or not The Player ever had any intention of collecting her from Mitchell's house, they couldn't know for sure. They traced Mitchell's IP address to an account on Websleuths. Like the others, all private messages between him and The Player had been erased. Brandon was never able to track any of The Player's IP addresses to one location.

As Jake opened the passenger door for her, he said,

"Are we picking up food for Quinn tonight or did Rose cook something for him?"

"Neither. I'm ordering delivery." When Jake came around and slid behind the steering wheel, she squeezed his forearm. "Fiona get off okay?"

"She did."

"It's a good thing she had that burner phone. She even tricked Mitchell."

"I don't think she was trying to. He tossed her real phone, and she sort of forgot about the other phone at the bottom of her purse. She was accustomed to hiding it in the lining of her bag." Jake shook his head. "How did she get to that point?"

"Don't start blaming yourself. Even Brandon Nguyen told me he had fake social media accounts to trick his parents."

"Brandon?" Jake grinned. "I gotta give him a hard time about that."

"Are you still allowing Fiona back here for Christmas?"

"Are you kidding? She's *demanding* it now because she wants to hang out with you."

Kyra's nose tingled. "The feeling is mutual. Maybe this taught her a lesson, and she'll be better behaved from here on out."

They looked at each other at the same time and said, "Nah."

"She's going to suffer her mother's wrath for a while. Tess is beating herself up for not monitoring her social media access better." Jake brushed her cheek with his fingertip. "You have a new fan there, too. Tess is so grateful to you for trading yourself for Fiona."

"I knew Mitchell would go for it. These guys have an almost slavish devotion to The Player. Cannon and Fisher literally died for him. Mitchell definitely went rogue in that respect. I don't think he was willing to lose his life for The Player."

"Quinn is so rattled by the idea that The Player is still alive."

"That's why I didn't tell him anything about your abduction until it was all over." Jake drummed his thumbs on the steering wheel. "There are still people on the task force who don't believe this guy is The Player, even if he does have information known only to him."

"Are they aware of the information about Delia's ring?"

"Only Brandon. We're keeping that close to the vest, so maybe that's why."

They rode in silence for several seconds, each lost in their own thoughts until Jake broke it.

"The last time we talked on the phone, you already knew you were going to traipse off to meet Mitchell, didn't you?"

"I didn't know for sure it would work out, but that was my plan. Why?"

He traced his finger around the curve of her ear and she shivered. "You told me you loved me. Did you say that because you thought it might be the last time we talked?"

"I said it because it's true." She closed her eyes. "The circumstances made it easier to say. Before, I didn't feel as if I had a right to declare my feelings while Fiona hated me and your ex didn't trust me."

"Neither of those things is the case anymore." He kissed his thumb and dragged it down the side of her throat. "I love you, too. When I thought I had lost you to Copycat Three, I felt dead inside."

Her throat closed and tears pricked the back of her eyes. "You've killed twice now to save me. You don't even have to tell me you love me. I'll take actions, any day."

"And I'll do it again, if necessary, but there are easier ways to show my love for you."

Several minutes later, they pulled into the public parking lot across from the Venice Canals and the walk streets that meandered through them. As they walked over the bridge to Quinn's house, clasped hands swinging, Kyra said, "Let's not talk too much about The Player tonight. Fill him in on the case, because he'll demand it, and then let's go easy. He's really upset at the thought of The Player still among the living."

"That's a deal. I'm burned out, myself."

They reached Quinn's red door, and Kyra knocked and called out at the same time, "We're here."

She cocked her head, listening for Quinn's response or footfall. On his better days, he answered the door himself. On other days, he invited her in and she used her key. Only silence answered this time.

"Quinn?" She dragged her keys from her purse and shoved the one to his house in the lock. She clicked open the door and hit it with her hip. "Quinn?"

She stepped inside with Jake close on her heels. Then she saw an arm splayed on the floor and a shock of silver hair. She charged forward and dropped to her knees beside Quinn's body.

"Quinn? Quinn?" She put her fingers at his throat, avoiding his blue eyes that had lost all their spark.

As Jake crouched beside her, she grabbed his arm. "He's dead, Jake. Quinn's dead."

* * * * *

COMING SOON!

We really hope you enjoyed reading this book.
If you're looking for more romance, be sure to
head to the shops when new books are
available on

Thursday 10th June

LET'S TALK
Romance

For exclusive extracts, competitions
and special offers, find us online:

 facebook.com/millsandboon

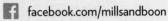 @MillsandBoon

@MillsandBoonUK

Get in touch on 01413 063232

MILLS & BOON

THE HEART OF ROMANCE

A ROMANCE FOR EVERY READER

ODERN

Prepare to be swept off your feet by sophisticated, sexy and seductive heroes, in some of the world's most glamourous and romantic locations, where power and passion collide.

STORICAL

Escape with historical heroes from time gone by. Whether your passion is for wicked Regency Rakes, muscled Vikings or rugged Highlanders, awaken the romance of the past.

EDICAL

Set your pulse racing with dedicated, delectable doctors in the high-pressure world of medicine, where emotions run high and passion, comfort and love are the best medicine.

True Love

Celebrate true love with tender stories of heartfelt romance, from the rush of falling in love to the joy a new baby can bring, and a focus on the emotional heart of a relationship.

Desire

Indulge in secrets and scandal, intense drama and plenty of sizzling hot action with powerful and passionate heroes who have it all: wealth, status, good looks…everything but the right woman.

EROES

Experience all the excitement of a gripping thriller, with an intense romance at its heart. Resourceful, true-to-life women and strong, fearless men face danger and desire - a killer combination!

To see which titles are coming soon, please visit

millsandboon.co.uk/nextmonth

JOIN US ON SOCIAL MEDIA!

Stay up to date with our latest releases, author news and gossip, special offers and discounts, and all the behind-the-scenes action from Mills & Boon...

 millsandboon

 millsandboonuk

 millsandboon

It might just be true love...

MILLS & BOON
True Love
Romance from the Heart

Celebrate true love with tender stories of
heartfelt romance, from the rush of falling
in love to the joy a new baby can bring,
and a focus on the emotional
heart of a relationship.

MILLS & BOON
MEDICAL
Pulse-Racing Passion

Set your pulse racing with dedicated,
delectable doctors in the high-pressure
world of medicine, where emotions run
high and passion, comfort and love are the
best medicine.